Cover Story

Cover Story

Robert Cullen

All the characters and events portrayed in this work are fictitious.

COVER STORY

A Felony & Mayhem mystery

PRINTING HISTORY
First U.S. hardcover edition (Atheneum): 1994
First U.S. paperback edition (Ivy/Ballantine): 1995
Felony & Mayhem edition: 2007

ISBN-10: 1-933397-71-3
ISBN:-13: 978-1933397-71-9

Manufactured in the United States of America

This one is for Peter

The icon above says you're holding a copy of a book in the Felony & Mayhem "Espionage" category, which features spies and conspiracies from World War I to the present. If you enjoy this book, you may well like other "Espionage" titles from Felony & Mayhem Press, including:

The Spy's Wife, by Reginald Hill
Who Guards a Prince, by Reginald Hill
The Cambridge Theorem, by Tony Cape
The Labyrinth Makers, by Anthony Price
The Romeo Flag, by Carolyn Hougan
Shooting in the Dark, by Carolyn Hougan
Soviet Sources, by Robert Cullen
Disorderly Elements, by Bob Cook
A Gathering of Saints, by Christopher Hyde

For more about these books, and other Felony & Mayhem titles, or to place an order, please visit our website at:

www.FelonyAndMayhem.com

or contact us at:

Felony and Mayhem Press
156 Waverly Place
New York, NY 10014

Cover Story

CHAPTER ONE

IN THE SHADOW OF THE KREMLIN WALL, it was growing cold. A wind blowing in from the north kicked up stinging bits of dust. Burke turned up the collar of his overcoat. He noticed a dull pain in his calves. He had only been standing there, waiting, for two hours.

Next to him Elliott Lantz of ABC News shivered and stamped his feet on the gray cobblestones. The tassels on his loafers flapped up and down.

"Damn! It's freezing, and it's only September," Lantz grumbled. He turned to Burke. "How can you stand it?"

Burke looked down at his own feet, shod in scuffed brown thick-soled boots he had bought from an Arctic trekkers' outfitter in Helsinki. The Kremlin and Red Square were the only places he knew in the world where cold rose. It seeped up through the cobblestones and into the feet of people like television correspondents, who had to pay attention to how their clothes looked.

1

"I'm insensitive," Burke said. "It has its advantages."

Lantz looked puzzled for a second, then scowled. "Very funny," he said, hunching his shoulders and folding his arms.

He turned and faced a patch of grass and flowers fifty meters to the south, set back from the Kremlin walls and still sunlit. It was a small park where a statue of a pensive Lenin once had stood. Lantz separated himself from the loose pack of reporters in their pen of iron fencing and approached one of the soldiers outside the enclosure.

"How about if we wait over there where it's warmer?"

The soldier had a wispy mustache and a major acne problem. He looked at Lantz and grinned, showing two steel incisors, shrugged, and said nothing.

"I said, How about..." Lantz began, then stopped. He tried hand signals, pointing to the soldier, then to the reporters' enclosure, miming the removal of a section of fence, and pointing to the sunlit patch of grass. He got no response. Exasperated, he put his hands on his hips and turned around. His gaze fell on Burke.

"Translate for this bozo, will you?"

"*On khochet stoyat tam, na trave, gdye tyepleye,*" Burke said to the soldier, gesturing toward the patch of grass. "*Tonkaya krov u nyevo.*"

The soldier looked at Lantz, then at Burke. "*Nyet,*" he said, shaking his head and smirking. "*Nelzya.*"

"What'd you say to him?" Lantz demanded. Among Lantz's virtues, the abilities to speak Russian and to laugh at himself were both conspicuously absent.

An extremely tall, thin, sallow Russian journalist standing next to the soldier smiled shyly and answered Lantz's question in English. His Adam's apple bobbed as he talked. He looked like Ichabod Crane in a rabbit-fur *shapka.*

"He tried to obtain for you the medical excuse," the Russian said. "He told him you have the thin blood."

"Thanks a bunch," Lantz said to Burke.

"Maybe I should have told him you're a personal friend of Barbara Walters," Burke replied.

"Would do no good," the Russian journalist said quickly, glancing at the soldier. "He has the orders."

Lantz peered over his horn-rimmed glasses at Burke, his lips set. "If we don't wind up standing here all night, I'm going to clean your clock at poker, Colin," he said.

"Revenge is the best revenge," Burke said equably.

The sound of a door opening in the ocher building that housed the presidium of the Russian Supreme Soviet halted the conversation before Lantz could reply.

The pack of journalists, led by the television cameramen, surged toward the doorway until they had pinned themselves against the wall of their pen. Vasily Grishin stepped out and stood like a man bemused by the antics of small children, waiting for the reporters to achieve a semblance of order.

Grishin was a Moscow survivor, as adaptable as a cockroach. He had thrived under the old system, working as the London correspondent for *Pravda.* He had thrived under *glasnost* as the foreign ministry's spokesman. And he had thrived in the Russian Republic, which found his talent for the telegenic quip in English, French, or German equally valuable.

"Ladies and gentlemen," Grishin said. "I have a brief announcement. Former presidents Gorbachev and Carter will hold a briefing on the progress of their

Middle East mediation effort at the Foreign Press Center tomorrow morning at ten o'clock."

"Did they reach an agreement?" a CNN producer screeched as the pack started to disintegrate and surge backward toward Red Square and their cars. The soldiers picked up one of the fence segments and pushed it aside.

Grishin smiled benevolently. "I used the word 'progress,' but you'll have to get details from Mr. Carter or Mr. Gorbachev," he said.

Burke cast a glance at the reporters moving toward the gate, then sidled quickly in the opposite direction. He turned the corner of the presidium building and began striding rapidly along the perimeter of a parking lot that flanked the building, toward a cluster of black Volga sedans parked at the far end. He heard footsteps behind him and looked over his shoulder.

Ichabod Crane was striding behind him. Burke kept walking.

"Are you a cop?' he said over his shoulder in Russian.

The man's reply, in his awkward English, sounded hurt. "No. I am journalist like you, Mr. Burke. Pavel Plotnikov, *Nyezavisimaya Gazeta*." It was the best of the new post-Soviet, independent Russian newspapers.

The Russian lengthened his stride and pulled abreast of Burke. Burke kept his eyes on the cars ahead.

"Why are you following me?"

"Because you work for the *America Weekly*."

"What?"

"I wish to see how you perform your job."

Burke looked at the man. His brown raincoat showed a few deftly stitched repairs, and his pants were shiny at the knees. Plainclothes police, in Burke's experience, usually dressed better. But these days, who knew? Even the police were poor.

"I generally do it alone," Burke said, walking faster. The Russian kept pace. If he understood Burke's message, he gave no sign. "Why?" he asked. "To get the exclusives?"

Burke snorted. "Uh-uh. I'm just misanthropic."

"Oh, yes," the Russian said, nodding. "Misanthropic," he repeated, nodding again. "I am just beginning as the journalist, you see."

Burke looked at him. Plotnikov's face showed the wrinkles and broken capillaries of a lot of Russian winters. The lank tendrils of hair protruding from his *shapka* were gray.

"Aren't you a little old to be starting out?" he said.

The Russian looked sad. "Yes," he said simply.

Ahead Burke saw a small cluster of men moving toward the parked cars. He recognized the Arab delegation. Exhaust smoke began to billow from their tailpipes. He started to trot. The tightness in his legs dissolved.

All but one of the men in the group had entered the cars by the time Burke pulled within earshot. The straggler was a short, rotund Egyptian with thin strands of graying hair pulled over a shining bald pate. He looked grim as he turned toward the sound of Burke's and Plotnikov's footsteps.

"Dr. El-Moualem," Burke called out. The man stood impassively behind the open door of the black sedan.

"Dr. El-Moualem," Burke continued in a more conversational tone as he pulled to a stop. Two security men moved warily toward him, and he made sure they saw the notebook in his hand.

"Yes, Mr. Burke?" The Arab looked mournful more than grim, Burke decided.

"How did the talks go?"

"I can say nothing," El-Moualem replied. "You will have a briefing, I believe."

Burke tried again from a slightly oblique angle. "Has your position on Jerusalem changed?"

El-Moualem hesitated. Then he replied. "No. It cannot."

"And has the Israelis'?"

El-Moualem hesitated again, a second longer. Burke prompted him.

"It's still their unified capital, now and forever?"

A faint flicker of a smile ran across El-Moualem's face.

"So they say."

"And have the talks broken down on that issue?"

El-Moualem nodded. "But you did not hear it from me, understood?"

Burke nodded. "Understood. What are the chances of getting started again?"

El-Moualem frowned. "I don't know. I have the sense that something is going to happen—that unusual forces are at work. But I am not privy to who they are or what they are doing." The Arab's face brightened. "You are supposed to be a good journalist, Mr. Burke. Perhaps you can find out. I'll be reading your magazine closely."

Without waiting for a reply, El-Moualem's face disappeared into the car.

Burke stood for a moment with the Russian, watching the Arab delegation pull away toward the Kremlin gate. Probably, Burke thought, they would be in the air and out of the country within an hour.

He turned to the Russian, whose rheumy eyes had popped open. His face looked a little flushed.

"We have a scoop!" Plotnikov said.

"Don't count on it," Burke replied. "Your next issue isn't until Monday. So's mine. Even if Carter and Gorbachev manage to bullshit their way around it, on Sunday morning the Israeli cabinet meets; and by Sunday noon, Israeli radio'll be playing a transcript of whatever happened today. It'll be all over the world on Sunday afternoon."

Plotnikov's face fell like a basset hound's.

"You're right," he said. "And besides, Carter and Gorbachev will tell all what happened anyway."

Burke snorted. "Yeah. And then tomorrow Lenin will jump out of his coffin and apologize. If they wanted us to know what happened, they wouldn't be hustling the Arabs out the side door and out of town before they hold their briefing."

They turned and began to retrace their steps.

"Do you think the negotiations can really fail?" Plotnikov asked Burke. "They have made so much progress. The treaties are almost all written."

"It's the last step that's the hardest. The commitment step," Burke said. "They've jumped into bed together, but now it's morning and do they really want to get married?"

Burke stopped, uncomfortable in the awareness of the conclusions a psychiatrist might draw about the roots of that analogy. He changed the subject.

"What did you do before you became a reporter?" he asked the Russian.

"I was the mathematician," Plotnikov said.

Burke laughed. "Really?'

Plotnikov's eyes and jowls dropped again, wounded. "You think a mathematician cannot become a journalist." He sounded as if he had heard the same doubt expressed before.

The evident pain in Plotnikov's face embarrassed Burke. "Well, I don't know," he said, trying to be encouraging. "You're the first one I've ever met who's tried. The only math I know is padding expense accounts."

Plotnikov smiled wanly. "Well, I always wanted to be reporter. But I could not. I refused to join Party, you see. So I stayed with the mathematics. Party could not corrupt the mathematics, you understand?"

Burke nodded. "Then, after *glasnost*, you switched."

"Not right away," Plotnikov said. "I have wife. Son. I didn't want to give up my job. But then wife told me I would die unhappy unless I tried it. I had the chance to work as journalist in free press! So I started looking for job, and *Nyezavisimaya Gazeta* finally hired me as editor. Now I am having tryout as reporter. Now I will try to write the truth."

Burke smiled, trying not altogether successfully to keep the smile from looking bitter.

"I think maybe you should've stuck with mathematics. There's a lot more truth in numbers than in newspapers."

Plotnikov looked perplexed, but he nodded. They turned left by the little park where Lenin's statue had been. The Spassky Tower gate came into view.

"I have one more favor to ask of you," Plotnikov said.

"Sure."

"You mentioned you play poker tonight."

"Yeah, it looks like we'll have time for the game."

"I may play?"

The question startled Burke.

Plotnikov read rejection in Burke's face.

"Well, if you do not allow Russians..." Plotnikov began.

Burke recovered. "No, that's not a problem. But it's hard currency only. No rubles."

Plotnikov brightened. "I have some dollars. For years I saved expense money I got to go to scientific conferences."

For an instant, Burke was suspicious. He always was when Russians introduced themselves and suggested meetings. But that, he reminded himself, was a hangover from earlier, less friendly times in Moscow.

Still, he hated to fleece an innocent, especially in a country where a stash of a hundred dollars could see a family safely through the winter.

"You don't want to risk your hard currency playing poker," he said.

"You forget," Plotnikov said, with a smile that showed two steel teeth. "I am the mathematician. I have studied probabilities in poker."

Burke shrugged. "Okay. I'll call Ethan Worthington. He's hosting tonight. Meet me outside the American Embassy compound at nine-thirty."

Plotnikov beamed. "Who is Ethan Worthington?"

"The embassy science officer. Nice guy."

Plotnikov nodded vigorously.

Burke started to turn and walk to his car. But a pang of guilt made him spin on his toe and turn back to the Russian. "One condition," he said.

"What?"

"If you see me scratch my left ear, fold."

❀ ❀ ❀

If Ethan Worthington felt uncomfortable at the prospect of taking a Russian's dollars, he was too professional to show it when he strode into the guardhouse to admit Burke and Plotnikov. The American Embassy compound presented roughly the same image to Moscow that Fort Apache had presented to the Indians. Visitors had to wait in the guardhouse for someone on the staff to come and vouch for them before they could pass through the high brick wall and go inside. But Worthington had a knack for hospitality; and by the time he finished smiling and shaking hands, the embassy seemed friendly and welcoming.

"Plotnikov," he said in a musing tone as he walked them through the courtyard toward his townhouse. "Didn't I see your name on an article about topology recently? In *Zhurnal Akademii Nauk?*"

Even in the pale light coming from the windows of the townhouses, Burke could see Plotnikov flush proudly.

"Yes," he said. "My last scientific article."

Worthington opened a black wooden door with a polished brass knocker, and they stepped inside onto a soft pile carpet. Either Worthington or his wife, Burke had decided long ago, came from some old New England money, because their government-issue quarters were furnished well, with a combination of good Danish furniture and old portraits that looked as though they came from a mellow brick house on Beacon Hill.

They stopped by the kitchen, and Elizabeth Worthington offered Burke a perfumed cheek to kiss and a silver platter of toasted triangles spread with black caviar, the kind with the tiny eggs and the gray sheen.

"You guys are in luck tonight," she said. 'We had a reception for the head of the National Science Foundation yesterday. You get the leftovers."

Burke passed on the caviar but poured himself, not without a twinge of conscience, a glass of Stolichnaya. He had promised himself to stick to Diet Coke this evening, If he stuck to Diet Coke every time he promised himself, he thought, Coca-Cola stock would split three for one.

Plotnikov took a healthy slug of the Worthingtons' Scotch, and Worthington picked a couple of beers from the refrigerator. He looked at Burke's glass.

"You know you've been in Russia too long when you start chugging that stuff," he said. It came off as friendly concern, but Burke blushed.

They walked through the living room toward the study, where Worthington set up the poker table.

"What're you working on these days?" Worthington asked from behind Burke's shoulder.

"Middle East talks," Burke said.

"What do you hear?"

"Grishin says they're going well."

Worthington laughed. "That's what he said about *perestroika.*"

The third card slid across the table. King of clubs. Burke picked up his hole cards, fanned them, and took a peek. King of spades. King of diamonds.

"King bets," Rudiger Goff announced.

"Check," Burke replied.

"A buck," Worthington said, slouching a little and showing the queen of hearts. He tossed a white chip into the pot.

"Raise a buck," said Catherine Morrison, peering over the oversized lenses of her glasses at the three of diamonds. With a flip of a slender hand, she tossed a red chip into the middle of the table. Twin gold bracelets on her wrist clicked quietly.

Pavel Plotnikov, showing a ten, inspected his hole cards and a modest pile of winnings. Burke scratched his left ear. Plotnikov folded.

Everyone else at the table called. It looked like at least two low hands would be betting in a game where the high and low hands split the pot. Burke tried not to squirm in his seat.

Goff doled out nine more cards. Burke picked up a deuce. Morrison got an ace. Worthington picked up a jack to go with his queen. Goff dealt himself a nine, grimaced, and turned his cards over before the betting could start.

"Can't get *scheiss*," he growled. "So what do you hear about the Middle East?" he asked, addressing Burke.

"Cut the crap and run the game, Rudy," Elliott Lantz growled back.

"Sony," Goff said, "But you know, we Germans don't have great sources in that area." Goff worked in the political section of the German Embassy.

"Don't the Syrians tell you anything?" Worthington asked innocently. "When you're selling 'em all that stuff?"

"No," Goff said, smiling. "We only sell to them on the condition they not tell us what they intend to do with it."

He peered at the up cards. "Still your bet," he said to Burke.

Burke checked again.

"Five bucks," Morrison said, and tossed in a blue chip. She turned and looked expectantly at Neil Fenno, whose face was shrouded by a graying beard and a wreath of cigar smoke. Fenno was showing a three and a four. He grinned, almost sneering at her.

"Bump five," he said. He tossed in two blues.

Worthington squinted at Burke's king-deuce and called. Sitting to his left, Darrel Stedgren folded. So did Winn Gregory and Grant Stephens, the next in line.

Burke took an extra moment to decide, feigning an inclination to fold and trying not to be too theatrical about it. "Call," he said.

Goff dealt out four more cards.

Burke watched as impassively as he could as a second deuce slid across the table to him. Morrison got an ace and Fenno a six. Worthington pulled a ten.

'Pair o' ducks," Goff said, nodding to Burke. Burke looked carefully at Worthington's hand, praying that he had at least the makings of a straight. He could afford to string him along for one more round and hope that he picked up the straight, preferably with the deck's last king.

"Check," Burke said.

Elliott Lantz looked at his watch. "Time out," he said. "I believe it's CNN time." He looked at the big, nerdy digital watch on his wrist and pressed a button on the case. "Two o'clock here, six o'clock on the East Coast."

Stedgren, out of the hand already, got up and switched on the television, which was connected to the rooftop dish that picked up CNN and all the other American networks for the embassy staff. They watched for a moment as a gray-haired woman touted the latest advance in diapers for the elderly.

"CNN's demographics must be going to hell," Gregory observed, not without satisfaction. Gregory worked for CBS.

Burke stifled the urge to protest the interruption of the game. It would sound too eager. Then Morrison did it for him.

Her scowl scratched lines into her pink gamine face. "Are we here to play poker or watch the tube?" she demanded of Lantz.

Lantz shrugged. "Sorry, Cath. Maybe the *Post* doesn't care, but my ass is grass if I get a call and don't know what's been on CNN." He arched his eyebrows. "You must have a good hand."

She shook her head in disgust and turned to Burke. "Is it true that in the old days, the KGB didn't allow CNN?"

Burke nodded. "And they used to take down the international phone circuits for repairs that lasted years. You couldn't call out. You couldn't get called."

"Then bring back the KGB, I say," Fenno growled. The cigar jumped up and down in his mouth as he talked. "Ever since they bought me that damned cellular phone with the satellite hookup I haven't been able to sleep at night. If they're not calling at five in the morning, I'm lying awake thinking they might."

"Quiet, okay?" Stedgren hissed.

On the screen, one of CNN's rotating, anonymous anchors appeared and started reading the news.

"We begin with an exclusive report from our chief

Washington correspondent, Susan Blackstone," the announcer intoned. Blackstone slid into view.

Fenno grinned maliciously. "Roone is going to love this, Elliott." Susan Blackstone had worked with Lantz at ABC until Ted Turner hired her away. Roone Arledge consequently hated getting beaten by Susan Blackstone almost as much as he hated the people who put Murphy Brown on opposite Monday Night Football.

Lantz groaned.

"Shut up!" Stedgren squealed.

On the screen, Susan Blackstone was sitting in front of a bookcase in what appeared to be her office at CNN. She wore a tight black sweater.

"If you weren't here, Catherine, I'd make a crude, politically incorrect remark about the size of her breasts," Fenno said.

"If I had her plastic surgeon, you could make crude remarks about mine," Morrison replied.

Stedgren turned around. "Do you mind?" he scolded them. He scrambled toward the television set and turned up the volume.

"After a lengthy investigation, CNN can now report, based on intelligence sources, that Syria has used Russian sources to assemble all the parts and equipment necessary to construct at least five atomic weapons," Blackstone said, her chin jutting toward the camera.

"Oh, great," Lantz moaned.

"I hope they drop one on you, Susan," Gregory said to the television set.

"The equipment, including krytrons and a sophisticated extraction system for making explosive material from spent reactor fuel, has been bought by Syrian agents over the past two years from a variety of sources in the former Soviet military-industrial complex," Blackstone went on. "Since the breakup of the Soviet Union and the introduction of a market economy in Russia, those military technology factories have been told to make money or go out of business. Many of them have apparently found that Arab oil money is the easiest way to turn a profit. Russia has an export control system that is supposed to prevent leaks of nuclear weapons material. But that system, CNN's sources say, doesn't work. Apparently, the Arab money has bought the silence of some ranking officials in Moscow.

"American officials are frankly worried that the Syrians have bought this technology as insurance against the failure of the Middle East peace process, still stalled on the brink of success."

There was more, but neither Lantz nor Worthington wanted to hear it.

"I fold," Lantz said, getting up from his chair. "Gotta get to the office."

"Me, too," Worthington said. American diplomats had to respond to CNN as much as reporters. He looked at Burke. "Had four to a straight, too, Colin."

"Good for you," Burke said, smiling faintly.

"Might not've been good enough, though," Worthington finished.

"Right," said Fenno, throwing in his cards sadly. "I'm out. Potentially a nice hand, too."

Gregory and Stedgren got ready to leave.

"Times like this I envy you working for a magazine, Colin," Fenno said. He worked for *The Guardian*. "You don't have to chase every fire bell."

Burke scowled. "Yeah. I'm lucky as hell. Split it, Catherine?"

Morrison nodded and started to divide the chips. Burke tossed his cards in and stood up. His legs had stiffened up again, and he winced.

Plotnikov sidled over to Burke as the players hastily started cashing in.

"How'd you do?"

The Russian could barely contain the satisfaction he was feeling. "I made twenty dollars," he said, as casually as he could. It was a week's salary for, say, a Russian bus driver. Or a reporter.

"I cannot thank you—" he began.

Burke waved his hand. "Don't bother," he said. He was about to add that he was a sucker for a Russian with a sad story. But he didn't know the Russian word for sucker, so he swallowed the thought.

"And how did you do?"

"Broke even, I guess," Burke said.

Plotnikov looked genuinely sad that Burke had not won. "Next time your luck will change," he said.

"Story of my life," Burke said.

They got their coats and stepped out into the courtyard. Worthington sidled up next to Burke.

"Next time I see you scratch your ear," he whispered, "I'll remember to fold."

A cold rain started to fall as Burke drove home. He studied the drops on his windshield for a moment in the glow of a streetlamp. They splattered heavily on the windshield and sat there until the wiper blade swept them away. Autumn in Moscow brought so many days of brooding grays skies and rain verging on sleet that by the time temperatures dropped and snow fell, people welcomed winter.

The rain drove away what little street life there might have been at that hour. Burke saw only *militsioneri,* massive and stolid, standing watch in the middle of the Garden Ring Road. When he reached the segment of the road called Sadovaya Samotyochnaya, he found a parking space and jogged the remaining two blocks to his building.

Sadovaya Samotyochnaya 12/24, known to its residents as Sad Sam, was a grimy, brown brick box that looked somehow tired, as if its corners slumped. Burke nodded to the *militsioner* at the entrance to the courtyard, who nodded back and made a note on a list, checking Burke back into his place like a shepherd counting sheep at the end of the day. Still at a jog, Burke picked his way through a cluster of Volvos, Saabs, and Audis to the door to his stairwell. The paint on the door had long since chipped and peeled away. The board that had been used to replace a cracked window in the door for the past six months had come loose from its nails and hung askew, letting the cold rain form a puddle inside the threshold.

America Weekly maintained two apartments at Sad Sam, one set up as a bureau on the third floor and the second, on the fifth floor, for its correspondent to live in. Burke walked up to the bureau, shook the rain off his coat, and noticed that a button had come off. Maybe, he hoped, Olga Semyonova, his translator, would see it in the morning.

A dozen magazine covers, glued to wooden plaques and covered with varnish, glinted in the light of the anteroom. They were the trophies amassed by Burke and his predecessors, the evidence that their work had led the magazine. A visitor could see a brief pictorial history of the decline and fall of the Soviet Union on the walls of the bureau. It began with a cover that depicted Brezhnev in his dotage, as a wax effigy melting down, proceeded through numerous Gorbachev portraits, and ended with the three consecutive covers about the failed putsch of August 1991. There was room on the wall for more covers, but it had been nearly a year since Burke had gotten one. He had heard from one of the writers in New York that Christopher Canfield, the foreign editor, was telling people that Russia had become "like Canada—only bankrupt."

A few drops of rain dripped from his scalp as he sat down and turned on the computer. The incoming file was empty, and he grunted softly with satisfaction. Canfield had not left a CALL ME ASAP message. Burke might get the first word. He began to write, throwing thoughts onto the screen, hoping they would not strike the top editors in New York as the maunderings of a reporter resorting to hype to push a weak story.

Nothing he wrote, he knew, was likely to impress Canfield. Nothing had in the six months since Canfield had arrived, fair-haired, at *America Weekly* from *Newsweek*.

Burke had learned several things about Christopher Canfield since that time. He had a wealthy wife with a summer home in the Hamptons, where he played in socially correct softball games. He was thirty-three years old and the first younger man Burke had ever worked for. He chewed paper clips and wore suspenders from Paul Stuart. He had fired two correspondents in his first six months and replaced them with people who also chewed paper clips and wore suspenders from Paul Stuart.

When the phone rang at a few minutes before three, Burke scowled and thought about letting it ring. Then he swiveled in his chair, propped his legs on the windowsill behind him, and picked up the phone. He could hear the nimble of predawn delivery trucks rolling past on Sadovaya Samotyochnaya.

"Burke," he said.

"Hello, dear, it's Gen. How are you?" asked a woman with British vowels. The voice was faint. He could only guess at the number of agencies that listened in on international calls to his office, but he assumed that each of them diminished the sound, like farmers diverting river water to their fields until only a trickle was left.

"Hi, Gen. Fine. You?'

Genevieve Owen, a soothing influence on the *America Weekly* news desk for twenty years, kept track of the magazine's correspondents for the foreign editor. In her Rolodex she had the telephone and telex numbers of hundreds of hotels, dozens of bars, a half-dozen psychiatrists, and a few jails. She did her job extremely well.

"Not so well here," she said quietly. "Jim Venneman's just quit in Beijing."

"Quit?" Burke asked.

"Officially," Gen said. "Unofficially, Chris Canfield is saying that Venneman lost a couple of feet off his heater. What does that mean?"

"Baseball talk," Burke explained. "Can't throw the fastball as hard as he used to. Means he's getting old. Canfield says it that way to make sure people know he's a regular guy."

"I'll never understand the American language, I'm afraid," Gen said.

"Read the *Daily News* sports section, Gen," Burke

suggested. "You'll pick it up. So how're people taking it?" he asked, referring to Venneman's dismissal.

"Shock," she said.

"Well, working for this magazine has always been like working for the Jacobins in 1793," Burke said. "Not a lot of long-term security."

"Thanks for switching metaphors," Gen said. He could hear a smile in her voice. "But surely you don't have to worry. Your heater is still hard."

Burke laughed. "So was Danton's. Anyway, I've never had a heater. I've always gotten by on good control and the occasional spitball."

"What?"

"Too long to explain, Gen," Burke said. "So to what do I owe the pleasure of this call?"

"You-know-who wants to talk to you," she said. "Good luck."

Burke felt a tickle of nerves as she put him on hold and transferred the call. Nothing happened. He looked at his watch and wondered if Canfield was sitting in his office, letting him sweat.

Just as Burke started to think the connection had been broken, Canfield came on. "Ah, Colin," he said. "What're you up to these days?"

"You got the file on the Middle East talks—" he began carefully.

"We're cutting it and we'll fold a paragraph into this bomb story," Canfield interrupted. "Have you been watching CNN?"

Canfield sounded almost feline in his enjoyment of the question.

"Yeah," Burke replied. "You mean Blackstone's piece."

"You read my mind. Got a matcher for us?"

Sure, Chris, he wanted to say. I called the CIA on my car phone coming over here and got the whole story.

Briefly, Burke considered arguing over the newsworthiness of his own Middle East story. He had a sense that this time the talks had reached a dead end, that there was not much more Carter, Gorbachev, and their team of language manipulators could do to write compromises unless one side or the other had a change of heart. He had a sense that the failure of the talks would leave the Arabs and Jews, despite all the progress they had made, closer to war than they had been since 1973. Saying so, of course, would only make Canfield want the nuclear components story more. He and every correspondent in the Moscow press corps had chased nuclear leak stories. No one had ever turned up anything solid. Now, in Washington, Susan Blackstone had sources who said they had. He would like to see their evidence. But saying that would only sound to Canfield like a loser's whining.

"Not a matcher," Burke finally said. "We'd just look like we're chasing. And besides, it comes out of Washington." Let the Washington bureau take some of the heat, he thought.

"I've thought of that. Washington says they might be able to gin something up by tomorrow morning."

"Rather than try to match it, let's try to get ahead of the curve," Burke suggested. He sounded to himself like some kid out of Columbia mouthing the newsroom jargon, and he hated hearing it. But that was the way the people in New York talked.

"You know the Syrians. They buy airplanes or tanks—they also have to buy someone to drive them and someone to fix them," Burke started. "If this weapons components story is accurate, there've got to be some scientists involved. I mean, Assad could get a crate of bomb parts tomorrow and he'd wind up with plutonium ashtrays unless someone helped him put it together."

"Um," Canfield said. He sounded slightly interested, but skeptical.

"Well, why not see if we can find any evidence that Assad has bought himself some scientists. Whatever we find out, it gives us a way to come at the components from an oblique angle."

"But if you don't find anything, it means we're a week late or we have no story at all."

Burke swallowed. "If I don't find anything, we say that."

Canfield paused for a moment to let his skepticism show. The image of a shark swimming lazily in the water flitted through Burke's mind.

Then Canfield stuck a needle in and twisted it. "And what if, perchance, two days later Blackstone comes on with film from Syria of some Russian Dr. Oppenheimer who's giving Assad the bomb?'

"Then I guess it's my neck," Burke said.

"Both our necks," Canfield replied. "But yours first. Quite so."

There was nothing Burke cared to add.

"One more thing, Colin. Sorry to dump this on you, but this comes from Schofield." Peter Schofield owned, *America Weekly* along with several television stations and a dozen acres of midtown Manhattan.

"What is it?"

"He's heard something about the revival of the

Jewish community in Moscow. I don't know who's been talking to him, but he absolutely wants a piece on it. I don't like to keep him waiting. Can you handle it next week on top of all this?"

"Sure," Burke said. Why not? He had only one neck.

CHAPTER TWO

BURKE LAY IN BED FEELING sorry for himself. Twenty-four hours ago, he had planned to spend this morning on a long, slow jog through the Lenin Hills and a long, slow slog through the dishes piled up in his kitchen. Instead, he would spend it chasing after Russian bomb parts and scientists and attending the Gorbachev-Carter briefing, which was doubtless intended to divert everyone as far as possible from the actual state of the Middle East negotiations.

Mornings in Moscow depressed him anyway. He had lived there, off and on, for the better part of nine years, working first for the *Washington Tribune* and then for *America Weekly*. He sometimes wondered why he had stayed so long. The quick answer, and a true answer, was that he had never found a beat that engaged his mind like the Moscow beat, from the days of Brezhnev, through *perestroika*, and into the present slouching chaos. He was a man of intense curiosity and a low threshold of boredom; and the challenge of Moscow, with its unending sequence of riddles and puzzles, suited him.

Occasionally, usually when he was hung over and in a mood to excoriate himself silently, he would let slip the thought that Moscow's distance from America also suited him, that it relieved him of the need to confront, very often, the consequences of a failed marriage and a sour divorce. He would usually manage to bury those thoughts by spending extra hours at the office.

But there were still mornings like this when he awakened a little surprised and a little disappointed that no one delivered *The New York Times* or *The Washington Post*, that he was eight thousand miles from what remained of his family, and that even though he probably had the names and phone numbers of a thousand Russians in the address files of his computer, he remained a stranger.

Burke got up and went to the window. A bank of gray, heavy clouds hung over the skyline, matching his mood. He stood for a long time under the shower, then went into the kitchen, wedged the kettle between the spigot and the pile of dishes in the sink, and filled it with enough water to make a cup of instant coffee. He looked in the refrigerator. There was still a half grapefruit, a bit dry and brown at the edges, the remnant of his last visit to the Irish joint venture grocery store on the boulevard that he still called Kalinin Prospekt, even though it had a new, noncommunist name. He tried to remember how long the grapefruit had been in there, but could not.

He picked through his closet, searching for some clothes that would not make him look as if he'd spent the night on a park bench in the rain. But he hadn't found time to get to the cleaners in a month. Finally, in a corner of the closet, he found some khaki slacks and an old brown tweed coat that he'd forgotten he owned, and he put them on. He noticed that the pants seemed loose. He had not been trying to lose weight.

His keys were not where he usually left them, on the night table next to the bed, and he cursed under his breath as he looked for them. The wife of his predecessor as bureau chief had furnished the apartment, and he had added only his books and his clothes. He would have furnished it with a table in the entrance hall to serve as a receptacle for keys, umbrellas, and odd papers, but she had envisioned a spare, Scandinavian sort of place, and that was what he had. He found the keys, finally, on a shelf in the bookcase of the living room, next to the copy of *The Brothers Karamazov* he was trying to read in Russian to improve his vocabulary. He had managed, he recalled, about two paragraphs last night before sleep blurred his brain.

It began to rain again as soon as he stepped outside. In the Volvo, he turned on the wipers and turned onto the Garden Ring Road. Although it was Saturday, trucks clogged the road just as they did on weekdays. They were pale blue Soviet copies of trucks the United States had sent over a half a century ago during World War II. They belched a noxious cloud of black exhaust, and driving among them was like driving back into the Great Depression in America. He pulled over into the left lane, cutting off a truck whose driver flipped a big, black-haired forearm out the window at him. Once he was in the left lane, he accelerated, pushing the car up to fifty until he crossed the Moscow River near Gorky Park and arrived at the Foreign Press Center. He pulled his car onto the sidewalk and left it there in a cluster of foreign makes that all had yellow license tags beginning with the letter "K," which stood for *korrespondent*. The special license plate made reporters easy for the police to spot and track. But, as with most things in Russia, there was an under-the-table trade-off. It also gave them an informal immunity from parking rules.

Inside the auditorium, he took a seat toward the back. He was reading *Izvestiya* when a shadow fell across the page. He looked up to see the stooped, gawky body of Pavel Plotnikov looming over him like a crane.

Plotnikov was smiling, and Burke noticed that one of his front teeth was set at an oblique angle to the other. He wore a brown plaid shirt, a maroon-and-white striped tie, and some odd fragments of old suits; gray pin-striped polyester pants and a bluish plaid jacket. His socks drooped toward his ankles.

That was another reason, Burke thought, why Moscow suited him. It was the only town in the world where the natives made him look dapper.

"Free?" Plotnikov said, pointing to the chair next to Burke.

Burke nodded and moved his knees to the right so the Russian could sit down. Plotnikov folded his long, spidery legs into the narrow space between the empty seat and the row in front. His knees protruded above the back of the seat in front of him.

"Thank you again for your assistance yesterday," he said.

Burke nodded.

"I enjoyed the poker."

Burke nodded again and pulled the left half of his mouth upward in a half-hearted attempt at a smile.

"You were—" Plotnikov paused, searching for the right word, "upset by story on CNN."

Burke looked sharply at him. He had always distrusted Russians who introduced themselves and seemed eager to get friendly. But all he could see in Plotnikov's face were honest age lines. Burke told himself that his suspicions were just a hangover from the old days.

"Not by that. By the game ending. You should have seen what I had," he said, gently.

"Ah, yes," Plotnikov smiled conspiratorially. He scratched at his ear. "I got signal."

There was a silence, and Burke felt his eyes pulled back toward the newspaper in his lap. But Plotnikov still looked at him, making him feel awkward.

"Beyond poker, though—was not good news for you, right?" Plotnikov finally pressed him. "I could see in your face."

Hearing that his feelings could be read on his face annoyed Burke. He liked to keep his feelings to himself.

"You're confusing that with bloodshot eyes," Burke said. A shadow of doubt passed over the Russian's face as he considered whether Burke was being deliberately rude. He changed the subject.

"So why did you become journalist?" Plotnikov asked him.

Burke paused, reflecting. "Somewhere back there, I thought maybe I could write the truth about things and people would react by changing for the better," he said. He smiled slightly. "But that was a long time ago."

Plotnikov nodded solemnly. "You have been journalist for long time?"

"Too damn long," Burke said. Plotnikov looked surprised and a little dismayed, so Burke tried to offer him an explanation.

"It's a tough business to get old in," he said.

At that moment, Carter, Gorbachev, Grishin, and Vittorio de la Rossini, the UN representative, walked out onto the stage in single file and sat down behind a long, low table. They put earphones on their heads.

The job of special Middle East mediator for the United Nations seemed to agree with Gorbachev more than Carter. Gorbachev looked tanned, slightly slimmer, and more vibrant than Burke had seen him since he resigned the Soviet presidency. Carter's face, though, had grown half a dozen new wrinkles since he joined the negotiations; and the last traces of color had disappeared from his hair, leaving it a yellowish white in the television lights.

Grishin leaned toward his microphone. "Good morning. Mikhail Sergeyevich will have a statement on the negotiations, and then there will be time for perhaps two or three questions. President Carter has a plane to catch."

Gorbachev removed the earphone and took a breath. In the rows in front of Burke, correspondents rolled their eyes. Gorbachev was notorious for turning opening statements into forty-five-minute lectures.

"The twenty-seventh round of negotiations on peace in the Middle East has just concluded under the sponsorship of the United States, the Russian Republic, and the United Nations," Gorbachev began. "I would say the talks were frank and useful. The sides further narrowed their differences over security arrangements for Israel after the autonomy period ends and authority passes to a Palestinian government in the West Bank and Gaza. That issue, I think, can be considered settled. So can the issue of rights to water from the Jordan River. I look forward to more progress in the next round. I would like to thank the representatives of Israel, the Palestine Liberation Organization, and the participating Arab states for their cooperation."

Gorbachev stopped abruptly. He seemed surprised, himself, that he had nothing more to say. After a moment of silence he turned to Carter. "President Carter, do you have anything to add?"

Carter flashed his grin; it seemed to stretch from one side of the hall to the other. "No, I think my friend President Gorbachev has summed it up well."

Plotnikov poked Burke in the elbow. "They lie!" he hissed.

"Not really," Burke whispered back.

"Why not?"

"In diplomatic terms, 'frank' means the two sides just about punched each other out."

Plotnikov raised his eyebrows and nodded.

Grishin called on an *Izvestiya* correspondent for a question.

"Can you tell us what areas of disagreement remain?"

Carter fielded the question by ducking it. "I don't think it would be helpful to rehash the remaining differences," he said. "We're hopeful that they can be resolved, given the enormous progress so far."

The Al-Aram correspondent got the floor. "In Damascus today, the government said that it will advocate that the Arab parties withdraw from the talks unless Israel agrees to negotiate about Jerusalem," he said, with the clipped consonants of an Egyptian trained in an English school. "Do you have any comment about that?"

Gorbachev had put his headphone on again. "We haven't seen the statement from Damascus, so it would be premature to comment," he replied.

Grishin pointed to Sam Jorgensen from CNN. "Last question," he warned.

"Are you concerned that the failure of these talks to conclude a comprehensive peace will lead to a new, possibly nuclear, phase of the arms race in the Middle East? And what can you tell us about reports that Syria has obtained nuclear weapons components from Russian sources?"

Carter and Gorbachev looked at each other.

"Mikhail Sergeyevich," Carter said with a slight bow of his head.

Gorbachev bowed back. "As you know, neither of us has access to intelligence data any longer," Gorbachev said to Jorgensen. "We cannot comment on those reports. I would not characterize the talks as a failure. But if a settlement is not reached, then the danger you point out very definitely exists."

Grishin interrupted. "As a spokesman for the Russian government, I can tell you that we know of no evidence to support that report. We will, however, be asking the appropriate people in Washington whether they do."

"If I can follow up," Jorgensen said, his voice rising. "Do you deny that this has happened?"

Grishin's eyebrows made little arcs over his blue eyes. "The last time I checked, Mr. Jorgensen, it was impossible to prove the negative."

Burke sat upright. Prior to today, Grishin had always maintained that the Russian export control system could keep track of all the old Soviet nuclear weapons and components. Why had he stopped saying so?

He started to raise his hand. Before he could get it past waist height, Plotnikov had leaped to his feet.

"Are you saying it's possible this could happen?" he demanded in Russian.

Grishin shrugged. "I'm saying that we have no evidence that it did."

Plotnikov sat down.

"Good question," Burke leaned over and whispered to him.

Burke had only one decent source in the Russian Defense Ministry. After Grishin's briefmg, he called him from a pay phone in the Park Kulturi Metro station, across the Ring Road from the press center. In his early days in Moscow he had made almost all his calls from pay phones. That was when there was still a KGB. Now the KGB was split into two parts, a foreign intelligence agency and the Russian Ministry of Security; and Burke made most of his calls from his office phone. He assumed someone bugged that phone, but it seemed atavistic to care. As he dialed, Burke wondered why he felt a sudden desire to be stealthy. He decided that Grishin's briefing had surprised him, and he didn't like being surprised.

He dialed, waited, and heard someone pick up the phone on the other end. He dropped his twenty-five rubles into the coin slot.

"General Stankevich?" he asked.

"*Nyet,*" a woman's voice answered. "There's no Stankevich here. You've got the wrong number."

Burke cursed silently, jammed his right hand into his pocket, and pulled out his change. He had one more twenty-five-ruble coin.

He checked the number in the little address book he carried with him and dialed again. Someone picked up the phone. He dropped the coin.

"General Stankevich," he began.

The voice on the other end, which sounded like Stankevich's, if Stankevich were talking from the bottom of a swimming pool, said, "Allo? Allo?"

"General Stankevich!" Burke yelled.

"*Allo? Allo?*" Then click.

He leaned his head against the cold gray metal of the telephone in tired resignation for a moment before he began looking for change.

Behind him, an old crone in a threadbare black overcoat was selling flowers.

"How much?" he asked.

"Ten thousand rubles."

He pulled out a fifty-thousand-ruble note.

"Can you give me some coins with the change?' The woman looked at the coins in a small saucer in front of her and shook her head. Coins of any kind were hard to find. Rumor had it that people were melting them down and sellng the metal, worth more as scrap than in the debased Russian currency. Twenty-five-ruble coins, the kind the pay phones accepted, were especially rare.

"I'll give you thirty thousand rubles for the flowers if you can give me a couple of coins."

The woman smiled; put a wrinkled hand with cracked, blackened fingernails in her pocket; and pulled out some coins. One of them was for twenty-five rubles, and she held it out so he could see it.

"Fifty thousand rubles," she said.

Scowling, Burke stuffed the fifty-thousand note into her hands, taking the flowers and the coin. He turned around and tried a different phone.

"*Allo?*" Stankevich growled.

Burke dropped his coin into the slot "General, it's Colin Burke from *America Weekly.*" He waited to learn whether Stankevich was in fact on the line this time and whether he could hear him.

"Burke! Was that you before?'

"Yes—"

"Then you should learn how to use the telephone. You're interrupting my work here."

"Okay, General," Burke went along. "I'd like to talk to you."

"I can't see you Monday. Busy all day. Call Shura in my office and tell her to set it up Tuesday."

"Well, I was hoping we could do it today."

"Today? It's important?"

"I think so."

Burke waited while Stankevich thought it over. Russian officials, like the Soviet officials they had replaced, generally loathed meeting reporters at home. Either their flats were small and dingy, which embarrassed them, or they were too large and furnished with too many treasures from the West that they would find hard to explain.

But Burke had interviewed Stankevich at home before. Then he had been a frustrated officer, squeezed into retirement late in the communist era because he had protested that the General Staff systematically exaggerated the threat from the West. Burke had heard rumors about Stankevich, found him, and persuaded him to speak openly about his complaints. The publicity had reversed Stankevich's fortunes. He had become a hero to Russians who believed that the military-industrial complex and its institutionalized paranoia were strangling the country. His neighbors elected him to the Russian parliament. And after the revolution of 1991, he had become, in an irony lost on no one, deputy minister of defense in charge of purging the General Staff that had once purged him.

All of that history, Burke assumed, was going through Stankevich's mind.

"All right," the general said. "The entry code is one–three–five–eight–six."

Burke headed southwest on what used to be Komsomolsky Prospekt, named for the Young Communist League. It had a new name now, the name of some tsarist aristocrat's country estate. But he could never remember it. He crossed the river into a barren region of white Brezhnev-era apartment blocks that stretched as far as he could see. He waited until he saw a hotel called "Sport" and turned right. As he traveled, he thought of all the Russian bureaucrats he knew who had eagerly moved into the apartments and dachas vacated unwillingly by the old Soviet bureaucrats. He found it mildly reassuring that Stankevich still had his old address.

The coded lock on the building's entrance failed to

work. Burke pushed at the brown wood door, and it scraped open. The elevator wasn't working either. His nostrils filled with the odor of stale cabbage and old tears as he walked up to the fifth floor. He was puffing slightly, and he regretted missing his chance to jog.

A short, slender woman, her gray hair pulled taut from her forehead, answered the buzzer. She wiped her wet hands on a white linen apron before taking his coat and the flowers; if the flowers surprised her, she did not show it. She gestured silently toward a pair of slippers on the floor. Burke slipped out of his shoes but declined the slippers. That was a Russian custom he had decided not to adopt.

He entered a room lined with heavy bookcases finished in cheap, dark veneer. Stankevich was standing at the opposite end, next to a desk filled with papers. A teacup sat to one side. He wore gray slacks, a plain white shirt, and a drooping gray cardigan. Burke had never seen him out of uniform. He looked smaller, even grandfatherly, except for his stern, ferretlike brown eyes. He had been, Burke had heard, a martinet in his field command days. He shook Burke's hand and smiled; but Burke could sense, as he usually did, a tense reserve in the man. Stankevich had spent the bulk of his life under strict orders not to talk to foreigners. He accepted the fact that times had changed, but he had not quite gotten used to it.

He wasted no time on small talk after motioning Burke toward a seat.

"So," he said. "What can't wait until Tuesday?'

Burke told him about Grishin's hastily arranged briefing. As Stankevich listened, he began to glower and his forehead reddened. He jotted some notes.

"Bastards," Stankevich muttered as Burke lapsed into silence.

"Who?" Burke asked.

"The Ministry of Foreign Affairs!" Stankevich glowered at Burke now, as if the answer to the question had been obvious to all but cretins.

He hesitated to ask another stupid question, so he tried to lead the general.

"Because they—what's the word?" he said, feigning an inferior Russian vocabulary.

"They lie."

Stankevich, Burke reminded himself, tended to accuse anyone who disagreed with him of lying.

"How, specifically?"

"We have control of our components and our nuclear weapons," Stankevich shrugged, as if this, too, was only an assertion of an obvious fact. "If Armageddon comes to the Middle East, it will not be Russia's doing."

Burke tried to be tactful, but there was no way to put the next question delicately.

"How are you sure?"

Stankevich reddened again. "That's classified."

"I don't have to quote you on it," Burke offered. "We could talk on background. I'd just say 'government sources' gave me the information."

It was the wrong ploy to take, and he knew it as soon as he saw Stankevich's face freeze. The man was not conversant with the American concept that an honorable man could say things off the record and not take responsibility for them.

"Anything I have to say I will say publicly," Stanlcevich said, coldly.

"Well, of course I'm not interested—" Burke began to reply. But he could see from the way Stankevich's brow began to furrow that the old man wouldn't buy a line.

"—well, actually, I would be interested in classified information; but I know you can't give it to me," he resumed, amending himself. Stankevich's face softened slightly.

"But maybe there is some useful information you can give me that's not classified."

"I doubt it," Stankevich said.

"Let's see," Burke essayed. "In the old days, I've heard, the Ministry of Medium Machine-Building made the nuclear weapons under the supervision of the Ministry of Defense."

Stankevich said nothing, neither confirming nor denying. "That ministry's been succeeded by the Russian Ministry of Medium Machine-Building."

Again, Stankevich said nothing. He folded his arms in front of himself. Burke noticed knobby, veined fingers.

"The old ministry had about one hundred thirty enterprises, with about eighty percent of them in Russia and the rest in Ukraine and Byelorussia. Ukraine and Byelorussia supplied some components, but they couldn't produce bombs themselves. They say they've closed those plants down and transferred their functions to Russia."

He looked at Stankevich, who nodded grudgingly.

"So that means the potential sources are all concentrated exclusively, or almost exclusively, in Russia."

Stankevich nodded again.

"And there're still Russian officers at every plant to monitor what goes in and comes out."

Another nod.

"And representatives of other 'organs' to check on the officers?"

He had hoped Stankevich would smile at his reference to the Ministry of Security. He didn't.

"If you know all this, why bother asking me questions?" Stankevich said, testily.

"Well," Burke said, "I'm hoping you might be able to tell me if I've got something wrong."

Stankevich frowned, but he did not stop the conversation. "And there's a nonproliferation council within the Russian government that coordinates all this and sends inspectors to verify the reports from the military officers and the other intelligence sources in the factories."

Stankevich looked mildly startled. "How did you know that?'

"Western sources," Burke said. In fact, a junior political officer from the British Embassy had speculated at lunch recently that there might be such a council. It made sense. Now Burke knew it was true.

He decided to goad Stankevich a bit.

"And it's supposed to keep track of every krytron and every gram of uranium," he went on. Stankevich said nothing.

"But does it?"

Stankevich smiled thinly, unamused, to let Burke know that he understood the ploy. Nevertheless, he rose to it.

"I can tell you, Mr. Burke, that we Russians are not quite as inept as you seem to believe we are. This is not Uzbek cotton we're talking about. When it comes to our own security, what we are supposed to do, we generally do. And besides, as you probably already know, we're not the only ones."

"Not the only ones? Who else?"

Stankevich's mouth congealed into a thin line across his pale face. He said nothing.

The general's wife, at that moment, glided silently into the room, bearing a tray with a chipped cup full of tea and a small plate of cookies. Burke thanked her, wondering whether the break would make Stankevich more recalcitrant. He took a token sip of the tea and resumed.

"But does the council receive reports often enough for you to know that nothing's gone astray in, say, the last six months?"

Stankevich glowered again. "What would be the point if it did not?"

"How do you know that some of the people involved have not been—" He almost said "bribed," but caught himself. "—have not been compromised?"

Stankevich looked saddened for a moment. "I can't speak for the Chekists. But I know my fellow officers. I know the kind of men picked for this assignment. They are *poryadochniye.*"

Poryadochniye was a Russian word that Burke had never been able to translate satisfactorily. It literally meant "orderly." But he had learned that when men like Stankevich used it, it carried connotations of decency and honor. Burke nodded.

"Well—" he began, but Stankevich cut him off.

"No more questions," he said abruptly. "I told you this whole area is classified."

Burke tried one more time.

"Okay," he said. "But then why would Grishin say what he did?"

Stankevich scowled. "You'd have to ask him."

"Thanks," Burke said.

Driving back to the office, Burke pondered what he had heard from Grishin and Stankevich. He knew Grishin had lied in the past and would lie again when his superiors told him to do so. Everything Stankevich had ever told him, on the other hand, had proven true. But why would Grishin lie about this? And how could Stankevich be so certain that Grishin was wrong and that the officers guarding Russian nuclear components were *poryadochniye*? And why had he said they weren't the only ones?

He thought back to his first encounter with Stankevich, when the general had been a retired officer in official disgrace. A marshal named Sergei Akhromeyev had forced Stankevich out of the army. Akhromeyev, too, had a reputation for being *poryadochny*. He had it until the failed coup of 1991, when he hanged himself from the chandelier in his Kremlin office rather than face prosecution for conspiring to overthrow the government.

Inside the office, everything was dark and it seemed cold. His coat still hung on the coatrack, buttonless. It occurred to Burke that he had come to like the office much more when Olga was there. That was strange. There had been times in the old days when he had barely been able to tolerate her presence.

Olga Semyonova worked in the room immediately ahead of him, a narrow space jammed with wooden shelves containing back issues of Soviet newspapers and magazines. She was officially his secretary-translator, which meant in practice that she read the newspapers, clipped the articles she thought would interest him, filed the ones he wanted to save, answered the phones, and typed when he wanted to send a letter in

Russian. In the old days, she reported on his activities to the department in the KGB that monitored correspondents. At first it had bothered him. But over time he began to hope she did it reluctantly. Even if she hadn't, he found he preferred a spy he knew to one he didn't know. Especially one that brought a little calm and warmth to the office.

She had worked for him for four years, since his days with the *Washington Tribune*. She worried about how much coffee he drank, and she coaxed him to switch to tea. And when he changed jobs, she had, she told him later, worried for days that he would not ask her to change jobs with him. She had an alcoholic ex-husband somewhere and a ten-year-old daughter whom he had never met. She was not a friend, exactly, but she was the closest thing to a permanent presence in his life. It would have been nice, he thought, to walk in and find her sitting in her chair, having divined somehow that he would be working.

He walked into the closet-sized room that housed the teletype and wire service tickers. He pulled the Associated Press file off its machine and scanned it.

The situation in the Middle East was deteriorating rapidly. One of the die-hard Israeli settlers in the Golan Heights had shot a small Arab boy picking apples in an Israeli orchard. Apparently in retaliation, Hezbollah guerrillas had fired Katyusha rockets into a kibbutz in northern Israel, killing three people. A story from Jerusalem said Israel was holding Syria responsible for any violence emanating from southern Lebanon. The piece speculated about Israeli air strikes on Syrian positions in the Bekaa Valley. The Middle East, so close to peace, was at the same time closer to war than it had been at any time since the Israeli-P.L.O. breakthrough.

A story with a dateline from a town somewhere in the 'Alawite country of Syria quoted Assad as defiantly rattling his sabers at the Israelis and at the same time denying that Syria had a bomb. That was predictable, as was the fact that no one would believe him.

Or, more precisely, no one would believe that if he had a bomb, he'd say anything about it until he used it.

CHAPTER THREE

HE FORCED HIMSELF TO WORK the phone until the sun was a streak of silver glinting behind the clouds in the west. He managed only to confirm that nearly all of his sources had taken Saturday off. They were, he imagined, picking mushrooms in the woods, or lying around their dachas and drinking, or whatever else amused them on their weekends; and they would be slightly puzzled if they could see what he was doing now, dialing their numbers and listening to the phones ring in their empty offices. Burke had always operated on the theory that the more calls he made, the more people he would talk to; and the more people he talked to, the better his chances of picking up some useful information. But now he was beginning to seem, even to himself, a little compulsive, a little desperate, a little pathetic.

Silently, he cursed Canfield. The thought of Canfield and the sight of the low light in the western sky outside his window made him think about his second assignment. The Sabbath was ending, and maybe the smart thing to do would be to complete the story about Moscow Jewry before Monday and resume work on the nuclear story then. He dialed the number Canfield had passed along.

A male voice answered; and Burke, in Russian, identified himself and said he would like to speak to Rabbi Mirshinsky.

"This is Yakov Mirshinsky," the voice replied in English. "And look, I'll make a deal with you, okay? Don't inflict your Russian on me, and I won't make you listen to mine."

"Okay," Burke said. "Where are you from?"

"Borough Park, Brooklyn. Isn't it obvious? You?"

"California. Originally. Washington as much as anyplace else now."

"My mother always said, 'Watch out for people from California and Washington.'"

"Your mother was right."

"So what makes a big magazine like *America Weekly* interested in my humble synagogue?"

For a moment, Burke thought about telling him the truth. Then he thought better of it. If Mirshinsky didn't already know that Schofield wanted a story, so much the better. He'd try harder to make the interview interesting.

"We heard that you've got interesting things going on over there."

"You heard right. When do you want to come over?"

"How about tonight?"

"What, a surprise inspection?" The rabbi tried to sound aghast and failed to pull it off.

"You don't want to be like one of those old collective farm managers, do you?" Burke asked him.

"What do you mean?"

"Well, they always want to know way in advance when a reporter's coming. So they can spiff things up. Dig new outhouses, that sort of thing."

Mirshinsky laughed. "Well, if you don't mind an old outhouse, come on down. I'll show you around."

The synagogue was in one of Moscow's transitional neighborhoods. Dzerzhinsky Square was called Lyubyanka now, and Dzerzhinsky's statue was gone. Peddlers hawking children's clothing packed the sidewalk across the square from the building that used to be the KGB headquarters. Down the road, the anthill complex of office buildings that used to house the Communist Party Central Committee apparatus belonged to the ever-growing Russian bureaucracy.

Burke walked down a steep, narrow street named for an artist called Arkhipov. He paused outside the synagogue.

Burke noticed buildings. He thought that unlike most of the people he met, buildings told their stories plainly and honestly. In Russia he had found coal mine headquarters that looked like Roman temples, built in the days when Stalin wanted miners to think of their pits as places of proletarian worship. He had seen new apartment buildings falling down before people ever moved into them, testifying eloquently to the slovenly apathy of the last communist years.

The synagogue looked Greek, with a triangular

pediment and six heavy, classical columns. He thought about the nineteenth-century Jewish merchants of Moscow who had commissioned and paid for it, and he wondered about the message they were trying to convey to the Russians with its design. Had they wanted to say that they were learned people? Or to remind the Russians of the western tradition of tolerance? He shook his head. Whatever the message, it had rarely gotten through.

Years earlier, he had come to the synagogue to report on the *otkazniki*, the Jews the Soviet Union refused to let go. The *otkazniki* story had played itself out. Nobody had trouble any more getting permission to leave. The Jews' less newsworthy current problem was getting permission to arrive somewhere. The United States would take only fifty thousand a year. The western Europeans would barely take any. Israel wanted all the Russian Jews; but it offered few jobs and no security, and it found each year a dwindling number of takers. He had not heard the word *otkaznik* in years. It seemed almost quaintly anachronistic, a verbal relic of another time, like GOSPLAN and *komissar* and KGB.

The front door was open, and he went in. Straight ahead he saw the entrance to the sanctuary with the six-pointed star mounted in glass over the door. He went inside.

A couple of dozen men, wearing yarmulkahs, with *tefillin* strapped to their foreheads, stood praying. Some rocked back and forth. Burke watched them as his eyes grew used to the dim light cast by crystal chandeliers that seemed short of bulbs.

He felt a tug on his sleeve and looked down into the face of a gnomish boy with a slight body, a harelip, and a nest of greasy brown curls under his yarmulkah. He might have been fifteen, Burke estimated.

"I can help you," the boy said in guttural English.

"I wish," Burke replied.

The boy shook his head vigorously. "No! No! I can!"

"Can you tell me where Rabbi Mirshinsky is?"

The boy appeared to be thinking for a moment or two. Then he shook his head. "Rabbi Mirshinsky is busy now. You like to see our synagogue?"

He would need to describe it. "Sure," he said.

The sanctuary had a vaulted ceiling, square pillars covered with pale green tiles, and gilded arcades along the side balconies where the women once had sat.

"When was it built?" he asked.

"Before the revolution," the boy replied. "By merchants. It wasn't the main synagogue of Moscow. This is just the only one the communists didn't tear down."

They walked down the center aisle. The place reminded him of a second-hand suit worn for years by someone poor but proud. It was clean, cared for, and threadbare. They came to a table in the rear that testified to the economic situation of the current Moscow Jewish community. It had a padlocked box with a slot in the top and a sign that said "Only for the feeding of children."

The boy smiled, showing wattled teeth. "Would you like to help us feed the children?"

Burke nodded. He took out his wallet and winced when he saw that he had run out of rubles. There were only greenbacks, the smallest a fifty.

He stuffed one in the box and the boy's eyes widened; it was a couple of month's wages for many Russians. Burke wondered how he could write the money off on his expense account. Then he tried to banish the thought as unworthy.

"Th—Thank you," the boy managed.

"The least I could do," Burke grumbled.

The boy nodded gravely, uncomprehending.

"You have a nutrition program here?"

"We have lots of programs," the boy said proudly.

"I didn't know that," Burke said. "Last time I was here, I don't think I heard of any."

"Everything has changed since Rabbi Mirshinsky came."

"How?"

"Before that, we had a rabbi who—well, who didn't do much."

"What happened to him?"

"He went to Israel."

"How did you get Rabbi Mirshinsky?"

The boy shrugged. "I don't know."

"Why is he better?"

"He's not afraid to do things. And he's got lots of friends in Israel and America. You'll see when you meet him."

"And where will that be?"

The boy pointed to a balcony in the rear of the hall. "His office is up there."

❀ ❀ ❀

Burke had not seen the inside of a clergyman's study since his marriage; the one that he remembered had been paneled in cherry wood, carpeted to match, and lined with appropriate books. He had not expected cherry paneling in Moscow, but he had thought there might be a rug or some bookshelves and a gray-haired man hunched over his Talmud.

The rabbi's office, though, was decorated in Soviet Squalor. He had a desk that appeared to have been fashioned from an old door and a pair of sawhorses. Laminated plastic wainscoting rose halfway up the walls, topped by a faded, water-stained pink paper that looked like the underside of an old mattress. Books, newspapers, and odd lots of board were strewn across the rough planks of the floor. Only two things shone: the telephone and the fax machine on the desk, both clearly new and imported.

The rabbi sat behind the desk, writing. Except for the gold-colored frames of his eyeglasses, he displayed no color: a black yarmulkah over black hair; full black beard; black suit with tailcoat, white shirt, and a black vest with the fringes of a prayer shawl slipping out from the bottom. Only when he looked up and his pink, unlined face caught the light did Burke realize that he was still in his twenties. He looked like a boy masquerading as a rabbi.

Mirshinsky stood up and offered Burke a pale hand. His grip was strong. He motioned toward a frail-looking chair of battered wood. Burke sat down carefully.

Mirshinsky picked up a pen again and doodled something on a scrap of yellow paper. "California, eh? So what do you want to know?" he asked.

"Well, let's start with you. Seems odd to find someone from Brooklyn running a synagogue in Moscow. What's your background?"

"Like I told you. Born in Brooklyn. Studied at a yeshiva there. Rabbinical training in Israel. Got married there and had a kid. Came here a few months ago."

"How'd that happen?"

Mirshinsky grinned behind the black beard. "You're right. My wife had the kid. Can't put anything over on you, can I?"

Burke grinned back.

"I meant, how did it happen that you came here?"

"Oh, that. Well, the old rabbi here emigrated. The congregation was looking for a new rabbi. They contacted my school in Israel. It happens that I speak Russian and I've worked with Russian emigrés. So it was arranged."

"How do you like it?"

"It's okay, but I was just thinking. You know what I miss?"

"What?"

"Football."

"Football?" If Mirshinsky had said playing polo, Burke would have been only slightly more surprised.

"Yeah, football. I was a big New York Giants fan. Lawrence Taylor. Phil Simms. I miss being able to watch them play. Season's underway soon."

Butte grinned again and made a note, shaking his head slightly. Mirshinsky caught the motion.

"What? A rabbi can't like football?"

"No. But if that's all you ever miss here, you'll be a fortunate man."

Mirshinsky shrugged.

"So what are you up to here?"

'Well, it's just like being the rabbi at any Jewish congregation that's emerging from seventy years under a totalitarian police state."

"What does that mean, specifically?"

"People know they're Jewish, but they don't know what being Jewish means. We have to teach them."

"Religious instruction?"

"Not just that. Judaism is the first holistic lifestyle, you know. We teach them about food. We teach them about living conditions. About their history. We have evening schools for adults, day schools for children. We have a man who's trained to slaughter beef properly, and another in Israel now getting training in slaughtering poultry. We have a meals on wheels program for the elderly and a hot lunch program for children. And, of course, we're working on renovating the building here."

"How are the city authorities treating you?"

"They're bureaucrats, but they're friendly bureaucrats. Basically, they've given us what we need. Two school buildings—"

"You have Moscow city schools?"

The rabbi nodded. "Number 283 and Number 175. That's 283 for boys and 175 for girls. You passed Number 175 on your way in here. It's across the street."

"And they let you turn them into Jewish schools?"

"No, they're part of the Moscow system. We provide the religious and Hebrew teachers for classes in the morning. They provide the teachers for the normal subjects during the afternoon."

"Where'd you get teachers?"

"Volunteers. Mostly from the States and from Israel."

"And the state lets you divide them up by sex, then teach them religion in its facilities?"

Mirshinsky nodded.

Burke shook his head. Sometimes the new Russia seemed like another country.

"May I see one of these schools?"

"Sure. The one across the street."

"Anyone in it now?"

"Our evening Hebrew classes."

"Great," Burke said. "Let's take a look."

Mirshinsky put on a black hat and overcoat, and they walked across Arkhipova Street to a four-story building of dingy red brick.

"Welcome to P.S. 175," he said.

He opened the door, and Burke smelled the sawdust and paint. Mirshinsky stepped around a pile of lumber immediately inside. "Pardon the mess," he said. "We're renovating."

They walked up a central staircase of stone with the grooves of millions of footsteps worn into it. Upstairs the smells were the same. Mirshinsky opened the door to an empty classroom. "Our new chem lab," he said proudly. The room was full of half-built lab benches. New stainless steel sinks lay against the far wall, awaiting installation.

"Where's the money come from?"

"Some from the city," Mirshinsky said. "But, of course, a lot of it from abroad."

Before Burke could ask about the donors, he and the rabbi walked into a classroom. About twenty girls who ranged in age from fourteen to seventeen jumped from their seats as they saw Mirshinsky. He said something to them in Hebrew, and they sat down.

"This is our elementary Hebrew class for teenagers," he said to Burke. "And this is the teacher, Shoshana Levine."

The teacher was a young, plump woman, very pale, with her hair tied up behind her head and covered by a scarf. Her formless blouse and skirt covered everything but her face and hands.

"Shoshana comes from Baltimore," Mirshinsky said. "Her husband teaches in our boys' school."

Burke stepped forward and extended his hand. After an awkward second, the woman took it limply.

"How long have you been in Moscow?" Burke asked her.

"Six months," she said.

"How do you like it?"

She looked at Mirshinsky, not at Burke. The rabbi nodded. "It's very good," she replied.

"Want to ask any of the girls questions?" Mirshinsky invited him.

Burke walked up to a girl in the first row. "How do you like not having boys in your class?' he asked her.

The girl blushed, and the girls around her giggled. Finally, she managed to get a word out.

"Easier," she said.

"For the boys or for the girls?" Burke asked. The girls tittered.

"For both," the girl smiled.

Burke turned to Mirshinsky. "Obviously," he said, "they're already well trained."

Mirshinsky's eyebrows flickered under his hat. "I'll take that as a compliment," he said. They walked out.

In the hall he waited for Burke to pull abreast and said quietly: "Don't try to shake hands with an observant woman."

"Sorry," Burke said.

"Don't be. You didn't know," the rabbi said soothingly.

"No wonder she didn't talk much."

"Well, you may get a little more dialogue with the

next group. They're adults, and the teacher is a little different."

He could hear droning voices as they entered the room; the class was repeating something in Hebrew. Burke stopped trying to comprehend it as soon as he caught sight of the teacher. She was lithe, darkly tanned, and brown-eyed. She wore her gleaming black hair up, with tendrils straying down over a long, taut neck. She was dressed in jeans and a denim shirt with two buttons open, and a simple gold chain set off the tanned skin above the shirt. She turned to him and gave him a quick, appraising look. It seemed to him that she embodied a sensual self-assurance he had seen before when he had reported in Israel, a self-assurance verging on arrogance that he thought came from knowing how to handle a gun as well as how to handle a man. She could have been any age from twenty-five to thirty-five. Her body said she was in her mid-twenties, but she looked as though she knew too much to be that young.

He realized, an instant too late, how attracted he was; and he forced his demeanor into a neutral position. But as he did he saw something in her eyes that told him she realized how she affected him.

The Hebrew class, which comprised about a dozen women, including a few wizened grandmothers, rose as the rabbi stepped into the room.

"*Molodtsi,*" the teacher complimented them, smiling broadly and speaking for the first time in Russian. Obviously, they had gotten something in their lesson right.

Mirshinsky again made the introduction. "Ronit Evron," he said. "This is Colin Burke from *America Weekly.*"

"A correspondent?" she said, in English.

She had a throaty voice, and she roiled the "r"s in "correspondent" the way Israelis did.

Burke nodded. "And you're from Israel," he said. She nodded.

"Been here long?"

"Two weeks."

"You speak English and Russian."

"I was born here. I emigrated when I was twelve. And I spent a year at Brandeis in graduate school." She had, he thought, a very direct, forthright face.

"Like teaching here?"

"Very much."

"Mind if I speak to some students?"

"Of course not."

Burke managed to turn toward the class and picked out one of the *babushki,* a woman with pale, soft skin furrowed everywhere by enough wrinkles to start a raisin factory. He asked her name.

She answered very formally: "Kuznetsova, Tatiana Vladimirovna."

"And how old are you?"

She picked up her chin and looked at him with a glint of humor in her blue eyes.

"Old enough."

Burke smiled, some of the students giggled, and the old woman smiled back. She had three golden teeth.

"And when did you start studying Hebrew?"

The old woman's face turned mischievous, and suddenly Burke could tell what she had looked like when she was a girl.

"Right after I heard they served supper before class."

More giggles. Tatiana Vladimirovna glanced quickly

over Burke's shoulder to check the reactions of Rabbi Mirshinsky and Ronit Evron. Apparently she saw nothing to worry about. She grinned again.

"And are you planning to emigrate to Israel?"

"I don't know," Tatiana Vladimirovna said. "How's the food there?"

"It's very good," the rabbi interjected. "Everything is healthy in Israel. The food, the climate, the sun." He paused for an artful instant. "Look at Miss Evron. Did you know she's seventy-three years old?" He watched the reactions flit across the old woman's face. First her eyes widened, and then she realized Mirshinsky was teasing her. She smiled at the rabbi, almost coquettishly.

Burke turned to look at the teacher, who was smiling broadly, showing off teeth that looked very white against her burnished skin and high cheekbones.

"I ought to move there myself," he said in Russian. "I just look seventy-three."

Then he added, in English, "Thanks for your time, Miss Evron." He stepped toward the door and the rabbi moved with him.

Evron walked with them into the hall and offered her hand again.

"Thank you for taking an interest in us, Mr. Burke," she said, as he shook it. "Do you have a card?"

Her request surprised him a little, but he reached into his wallet, fumbled around amid a small stack of old credit-card receipts, and produced one. He had the sense that she was observing him as he looked for it.

She took it and slipped it into a pocket on her hip.

"I may call you with a business matter," she said.

"Sure," Burke replied. He hoped she did not notice the surprise he felt.

Burke set aside his curiosity, pulled out his notebook, and began jotting down notes to help him remember what the old woman had said. He and Mirshinsky, who had stood silently during the exchange with Evron, started walking slowly down the hallway toward the next classroom. Burke heard a semi-scream from down the hall, and his head jerked up.

"Rabbi! Rabbi! Come quick!"

It was the boy from the synagogue. His sallow face was reddened with a fear that caused his mouth and eyes to widen. He sprinted up to Mirshinsky, jerked at his sleeve, and began pulling the rabbi toward the stairs.

Mirshinsky lurched forward. 'What is it, Volodya?" he demanded.

"Fascists are coming!" the boy wailed.

"Oh, God," Mirshinsky muttered, and began to run.

Burke stuffed his notebook into his pocket and bolted past Mirshinsky and the boy, down the steps, and out into the small yard in front of the school.

In the darkness, he could see flickering torches first. As his eyes adjusted, he could make out people and banners. There were, he estimated, three hundred people massed in front of the synagogue and more coming down Arkhipova Street.

"Bastards!" The word exploded into the air over Burke's shoulder as Rabbi Mirshinsky saw and evaluated what was happening. Mirshinsky moved quickly past Burke toward the street, the tails of his long, black coat flapping behind him. He put a pale white hand atop his fedora to keep it from blowing off as he ran.

Burke heard the sound of glass breaking.

"Dear God, it's a pogrom!" the rabbi moaned.

Three torches marking the leading edge of the crowd had reached the granite stairs in front of the synagogue when Burke made his way across the street.

In the flickering light, he could make out some of their signs and banners.

FOOD FOR THE PEOPLE! one said in hand lettering. Another person carried a red banner with a portrait of Lenin on it that seemed to have been salvaged from some old Party closet. Someone else had a gold banner with the Orthodox cross embossed on it.

As they massed at the entrance, someone at the front shouted, "Food for the people, not just the Jews!"

Others in the crowd took it up and turned it into a low, menacing chant.

Mirshinsky took off his hat and tried to make himself heard.

"Please! Please!" he yelled. His voice sounded high and scratchy. "We give away much of the food we get! I'd be glad to arrange—"

He stopped and wiped his face. Burke saw moisture. Someone had spat on him.

"Where are the police?" a voice hissed behind him. He turned and saw Ronit Evron. Her face had paled under her tan, and her eyes narrowed in rage.

He heard the sound of shattering glass and turned back toward the crowd. Three men with clubs had begun systematically to smash the windows they could reach from the sidewalk. The sound of glass shattering took on a harsh rhythm. Burke's knees suddenly trembled and his stomach turned.

"Yids back to Israel! Liberate the food!" someone shouted. Then Burke saw a club flash in the firelight against Mirshinsky's forehead. It sounded like a baseball bat smacking a grapefruit. The rabbi went limp and crumpled in quick stages, first his legs, then his arms, and finally his head, tilted at a curious angle, hitting the street.

"No!" Ronit Evron screamed. She dove into the front of the crowd and crouched over Mirshinsky, picking his head off the pavement and cradling it in her right arm. His eyes opened and rolled back. Blood trickled from his temple.

"Let's get it!" someone yelled. The crowd started to surge forward. Someone kicked Evron. She held her free arm up to her head and waited to be trampled.

Burke lurched forward, mounted the synagogue steps an instant ahead of the torchbearers and wheeled around to face them.

"Stop!" he yelled. For an instant, the leaders froze.

Burke reached into his coat pocket and took out his notebook and a pen, hoping desperately that the people in front of him would deem this gesture slightly less foolish than he did. He picked out a stubby, barrel-chested man with a shaven head at the front of the pack and made eye contact.

"I'm Colin Burke from *America Weekly,*" he said, as calmly as he could. "Happened to be here, and I want to get your names and your organization for this on a story…"

He stopped, looked for the right word in Russian. He realized that his nerves were messing up his syntax.

"Get out of the way, asshole!" the stubby man shouted. He looked like the kind of man Burke could easily hate.

"Not yet," Burke said, wondering what he could say to delay the man further and wondering when the damn police would show up.

"You foreign correspondents all lie anyway. Just call us Russian patriots!" the stubby man yelled. He started to move forward.

Burke stood in the way, unable to move. Someone spat at him and the hot, wet saliva landed on his check. He saw a fist come out of the crowd and felt it glance off the side of his head. Burke fell back and tripped against the step behind him. His spine thudded against the granite steps, and pain shot through to his brain. For a second the stubby man stood still, watching him, flanked by two men with torches. Behind him Burke could see dozens of other faces, glowing and ugly in the light of the torches. He saw a couple of two-by-fours in their hands.

Then he heard sirens. Out of the corner of his eye he could see flashing lights.

The stubby man turned to look.

"Shit," he cursed. "Cops!"

For a moment, the stubby man hesitated. Then he picked up his foot and brought it down viciously, heel first, against Burke's ribs. Burke felt the pain explode under his liver. It gasped and writhed away.

The stubby man turned and took off down the steps. After a second, the torchbearers followed. In a few seconds Burke could see Moscow *militsioneri* in blue helmets and riot shields coming toward him. He looked down and saw Ronit Evron and Rabbi Mirshinsky, still intact on the sidewalk below him.

He tried to get up; but his whole body was trembling, and his legs, curiously, had turned to water beneath him. His stomach twisted itself like a wet rag. Spasms coursed through his body, and he vomited.

CHAPTER FOUR

THE PHONE RANG FOR A LONG TIME before he answered it; when he reached out to lift the receiver, he felt a stab of pain in his ribs. He pulled his arm closer to his body and waited until the pain subsided.

"Burke," he finally grunted.

"How are you?" a woman's voice said in English, and he knew immediately that it was Ronit Evron. She had just the right tinge of feminine solicitude in her voice. By not identifying herself, she created the impression that they were continuing an intimate conversation that had begun the night before. These things dimly registered in Burke's awareness as he struggled against the pain in his ribs.

"Okay, I think. Nothing broken."

"You disappeared last night before I could thank you for helping us," she said.

"Shucks, ma'am. Nothing that any red-blooded

American *goy* wouldn't've done," Burke said. He wondered if she would get the pun.

She laughed.

"How is the rabbi?" he asked.

"The doctors say he has a concussion but no fracture. I want him to go back to Israel to have it looked at, but he says he won't. He should be all right."

"It was a nasty business," Burke said. "He's lucky you were around."

That seemed to exhaust the topic of mutual congratulations.

"Well, look," she said, "I want to thank you personally, and I still have a business matter I want to discuss with you. Can we get together?"

Burke felt a tickle of unease rise in his belly. This was happening a little too quickly.

"Well," he said, "maybe we could have lunch next week."

"I won't be free then. I have to teach. Could we do dinner tonight?'

The tickle of unease in his stomach blossomed into a gnawing sensation. Either this was a beautiful and attractive woman who had quickly and inexplicably developed a yen for his company, or she wanted something. Experience suggested that he not discount the latter alternative. But he saw no reason to refuse.

"Okay. Where?'

"Please, you choose."

"Well, there's a place called Moosh. It's on Oktyabrskaya Street. Can you eat Armenian food?"

"I don't see why not."

'Well, um, it's not kosher, I don't think."

She laughed again. He liked the sound of it. It was a throaty, earthy laugh.

"Colin, not all Israelis keep kosher, you know. I don't."

"Okay, fine," he said, embarrassed. "You know where it is?"

"No," she said. "I've only just arrived in Moscow."

Obviously, she wanted him to pick her up at her apartment. She wanted him to think of this dinner as a date, not a business meeting. Again the doubt gnawed at him, and again he set it aside.

"All right," he said. "I'll pick you up."

She gave him her address, and he told her when to be ready.

He spent the day on several more hours of fruitless phone calls and on writing his file about the synagogue. When it was time to get ready for dinner, he stood for a while in front of the closet, searching unsuccessfully for something that needed no pressing. Finally he gave up and put on a pair of wrinkled gray slacks and a baggy, wheat-colored corduroy jacket

She lived in a crumbling white high-rise off Krasnopresnyenskaya Street that came equipped with a flock of curious *babushki* who sat on benches in front of the door and eyed him thoroughly as he approached. To reach the door, he had to negotiate a narrow wooden plank that stretched over a muddy ditch littered with twisted pipes.

"Careful," one of the old crones said as he stepped carefully onto the plank. "You'll fall into the ditch and get mud all over those nice clothes." Her comrades cackled gleefully.

Burke smiled quickly at them as he realized the old woman had meant to be complimentary.

"The Israeli girl's on the fifth floor," another of the *babushki* piped up, setting off another burst of cackles. Blushing, Burke went inside.

"It's the hero of Arkhipova Street," Ronit Evron said brightly as she opened the door. She had, he thought, a smile that was pure sunshine, bright and white against her tan. She looked up directly into his bloodshot eyes.

"All heroes are inspired by beautiful women," he said, and he waited to see her reaction. She dropped her eyes demurely and blinked. When she looked back up, the big smile had been replaced by a warm, slightly amused bend in her lips.

She was wearing jeans again, but with a white silk blouse. His eyes followed the curve of her neck past a broad necklace of beaten silver to the point where the shirt came together over her breasts. She inhaled and he could see the outline of her nipples against the fabric. He looked up, and he knew that she had noticed him doing it.

She picked up her coat and paused just long enough to give him a chance to help her put it on. But he didn't move, and she slipped it over her shoulders herself.

In the car, she disposed of all the formalities their conversation would necessarily entail. The rabbi, she informed him, had gotten up and left the hospital, insisting he was all right. He looked, she said, quite dashing with the white bandage under his black homburg. The police had thus far, predictably, failed to arrest anyone. In Burke's opinion, which she elicited, there was about a one-in-three chance that the authorities had inspired the demonstration.

"In the old days," he said, "they would have had to. Now, I don't know. I can't immediately see what they'd have to gain by it. And there are a lot of free-lance crack-pots running around these days."

"Are you going to try to find them?" she said.

"I don't think I'll have time," he replied. "I've got too much else to do."

He waited to see whether she would follow up. She did. "Oh? What are you working on?" It sounded quite casual.

He decided to tell her. "Russian nuclear scientists going to Syria, for one," he said. "Same as everyone else."

He shifted gears and looked down. In the darkness, he could make out her hand against the thigh of her jeans. It was clenched in a fist.

He asked for a table as far away as possible from the musicians—a pianist and a guitar player. The waiter nodded and gave them a table in a corner under a por-trait of a glowering Armenian in a floppy sheepskin hat, with two bandoliers crossed over his chest. Next to the picture hung two old rifles crossed to form an X, and a red, blue, and orange tricolor: the Armenian flag. There were more mounted guns and soldiers' pictures and a relief map of Armenia. At the next table a group of eight men, all with black hair and eyes, sat polishing off the remains of a feast. Empty vodka bottles and empty plates littered their table.

He asked her if she liked shashlik; and when she smiled, he ordered it for her, along with some appetiz-ers, bread, and red wine. The bread came first. It was fresh and chewy and smelled of wheat and a warm oven.

He swallowed some wine and left the bread alone and

decided to see how much she would tell him about herself "So what's a nice, nonkosher Jewish girl doing in a place like Moscow?" he asked.

She rewarded him with a quick smile. "At school, I did my master's in Russian history. Then I worked for a few years in a program to settle new emigrants. When I heard that they were recruiting teachers for the Jewish school here, I thought it would be interesting to come back and see how much things have changed."

"And have they?'

"Until last night I thought so."

"And how did last night make you feel?"

She shrugged. "I was in the army, of course. I live in Jerusalem, not far from the old Green Line, so I have seen the *intifada*." She paused. "I have seen worse things."

"But how did it make you feel?"

She looked at him for a moment before she answered, and he had the impression that she was appraising him and his curiosity. The gnawing sense of unease returned to his stomach.

"I was frightened," she said, carefully and neutrally. "And angry. Mostly frightened."

He nodded. He doubted that a few Russians with clubs would frighten this woman; but it was the kind of lie men were expected to believe, so he pretended to do so and tried to draw her out some more.

"So do you think you'll stay on?" he asked.

"Of course. I did not leave Jerusalem because of some rock throwers. I won't leave here because of some fascists with two-by-fours."

Her voice hardened as she spoke, and he sensed that she had revealed a small part of herself to him for the first time.

"And you? Were you frightened?" she asked him.

"Scared shitless," he grinned. It was the closest thing to a real smile he had shown her.

"Then why did you jump in front of that mob?"

He shook his head. "Damned if I know. Temporary insanity?"

Her look remonstrated him for false modesty.

"I don't think so. I think you were quite brave. And I don't think you're being honest with me."

He grinned again, but the grin was lopsided. "Honesty has never been part of my job description," he said, telling her the truth. He paused and decided to tell her a little more. "I guess I don't like bullies. Ever since I was a kid, I've hated them, in fact. I hated being picked on; I hated having to fight them."

She nodded sympathetically. "It's hard to believe someone your size was picked on."

He shrugged. "I grew late. And then I was thin. Awkward."

"But you fought them?"

He arched his eyebrows and sipped some wine. "What else is there to do?"

"An Israeli can sympathize with that."

He decided to bait her a little and see how she would react. "Of course," he said, "that phase of my life ended when I was about twelve."

She did not rise to it. She bit off some more bread, and her eyes remained opaque.

The waiter brought the shashlik, big, steaming chunks of juicy roast lamb and beef dressed with onions and green peppers. Burke cut a chunk in half and tasted it, and the meat seemed almost to dissolve in his mouth. It tasted of wood fires and blood.

Ronit tasted hers. When she did, some real warmth came into her eyes. "It reminds me of camping trips in the hills of Judea and Samaria," she said.

He looked at her and he could have sworn that she was telling him the truth and that she was just an Israeli woman, new in town, glad to be having dinner with an American she found interesting and attractive, and not someone fencing carefully and professionally with him for reasons he could only speculate about.

"So do you live here by yourself?"

His wineglass stopped halfway between the table-cloth and his lips.

"Most of the time," he said, guarded.

She dropped her eyes and let her lips turn up. "I'm sorry," she said, peering up from under her half-lowered eyelids. "Subtlety is not an Israeli virtue."

"I'm divorced," he told her. "I have been for ten years. I have a son who goes to Berkeley and periodically writes to fill me in on the latest increase in the cost of living. I have a widowed mother who lives in Los Altos, California, and takes frequent trips to Lake Tahoe and Reno, where she loses at craps. I have an ex-wife named Barbara who lives outside San Francisco with a hot tub, a Volvo, and a second husband named Stephen, who I'm told is a very sensitive guy."

"And you're not?"

"The hell I'm not. I cry whenever I see *Our Town.* I'm definitely a nineties kind of guy."

He leaned back, rested his chin on his hand and gazed at her, sardonic to the core, for a moment not really caring what she was up to.

"So why did you get divorced?"

"Back then, I was an eighties kind of guy."

She said nothing, waiting to see if he would embellish it. He did.

"No—well, to tell the truth, I was tough to live with. Well, so was she. We lived together in college and afterward. I worked for an underground newspaper that doesn't exist anymore. *The Berkeley Barb*. She taught school. She got pregnant and she wanted to keep the baby, so we got married. Then I decided if I had a family I had to support it, you know, so I went to work for the *Oakland Tribune*, and I had to work nights. She decided she had to have a 'non-traditional career,' so she went to law school. After a while, we didn't see each other much anymore. A while after that, we didn't want to."

She nodded.

"And did I mention I was tough to live with?" She nodded again and smiled.

"So why did you become a journalist?"

He finished his wine, topped her glass off, and filled his again. He drained about half of it before he answered. That was his third glass, he noted. He should stop, but he didn't want to.

"Reporter," he corrected her. "Guys who call themselves journalists usually wish they went to law school."

"Okay, so how'd you become a reporter?"

He swallowed some more wine. "You really want to know?"

She knitted her fingers together under her chin and nodded solemnly. "I really want to know."

He laughed. "At first, I thought I'd be part of the revolution, change the world, all that."

He tried to look embarrassed by the memory. Answering her questions was harmless, he decided, and it would make her think he was too absorbed in himself to pay attention to whatever she was up to.

"What happened?"

"Well, my first big pieces after I got out of school were for a series we did during Ronald Reagan's reelection campaign for governor. We did a piece about how Reagan's welfare cuts were contributing to poverty and drugs. We did a piece about how his education budget was gutting the schools. We did a piece about how his environmental policy was letting a few guys get rich but ruining the Bay. The pieces got picked up by other papers all across the state. We really thought we were hurting him. Of course, he won. After the election I ran into the other guy's campaign manager. 'You know,' he said, 'every time you ran one of those pieces, Reagan moved up two points in the polls.'"

She laughed, and so did he. "So why did you stay with it?"

"It kept me from being bored."

She laughed again, that good nongiggle that he found so attractive. He tried to look charmed by it, and then he changed the subject.

"So," he said, "what is this business you want to talk about?"

Before she could reply, a cheer from the next table startled them and they turned to look. One of the dark-eyed men had stood up with the bill in front of him. To the cheers of his companions, he was tossing thousand-ruble notes into the air and watching them flutter to the floor in the middle of the room. He counted twenty bills and then gave up trying to calculate how many thousands of rubles were lying on the floor.

Grimly, the waitress who had presented the check got down on her hands and knees and started picking up the money. She was blonde, and she looked Russian.

Burke sighed heavily and turned back toward Evron. Her bewilderment was evident on her face.

Burke shrugged and explained. "Armenians, like everyone else, don't think very much of the value of Russian money. So they let the waitress know it. They probably added enough to what they owed that they knew she wouldn't complain. And besides, the owners are Armenian."

"Where do they get such money?"

"Who knows? They bring something up here and sell it. You know that French cognac that's for sale all over town for ten thousand rubles a bottle?"

"No, but what of it?"

"It's Armenian, with fake labels. Used to sell for ten rubles a bottle before the Soviet Union fell apart."

She nodded.

The waitress finished picking up the money, thrusting the stack of bills into a pocket in her apron. But the man with the money wasn't quite through. He turned a couple of vodka bottles upside down until he found one with something in it and poured himself a shot for the road.

Weaving slightly, the Armenian walked over to the piano player. The musician stopped playing. The Armenian stood in front of the microphone until the conversations at the other tables stopped.

"I wanna propose a toast," he said.

The men at his table raised their glasses.

"I see we have foreigners in the room," the man went on. He looked at Burke and Evron. "That's great. I wanna drink to their health. An', you know, I'm a lucky man. God has given me good businesses. I have three homes—one here, one in Sochi, and one in Yerevan. I have three cars." He grinned slyly, conspiratorially. "I have three women, but don't say anything about it because they all think I got one!"

The men at his table laughed and cheered. So did the people at the other tables. Burke smiled thinly, but he did not look amused.

"So I wanna drink," the man resumed, "to the health and happiness of all God's children! Except, of course, for the fuckin' Azerbaijani Turks. Turks can rot in hell!" He lifted his glass high, tilted his head, opened his mouth, and poured the vodka down. His comrades cheered and did the same.

Evron looked at Burke. His glass was on the table, and he had turned his back on the Armenian. This surprised her. Why should an American reporter care about an insult to Turks? Carefully, she set her own glass back on the table, untouched, near his.

The Armenian wobbled over to their table, his face contorted in a frown.

"'Smatter? You like Turks?"

Burke turned and looked squarely at the man. "Not particularly," he said. He turned his back again.

"Then why don't you wanna drink my toast?" the Armenian demanded.

"I'm sorry," Burke said to the man. "I'm a teetotaler." He turned to Evron. "I think I'll pass on dessert," he said. "Shall we go?"

She nodded. He threw fifty thousand rubles on the table, and they got up and walked out.

"Go eat with the fuckin' Turks!" the Armenian

shouted after them. As they put on their coats, the piano-guitar duo started playing something; and the customers in the dining room began boozily to sing.

"The dulcet sounds of the Armenian national anthem," Burke said to her. "Sorry for what happened. I've eaten here several times and never had a problem."

They were out on the street.

"You did the right thing," she said sincerely.

"Thanks," he said. "Amazing, isn't it, how one nation can feud so irrationally with another?"

The words came out before he could consider their effect on her, and he wanted to take them back. But she showed no reaction. They got in the car and he began to drive.

"Can't think of a place where we could just drop in for coffee this late on Sunday night," he said. "The Russians close early unless you make reservations ahead of time."

"It's all right," she said. "I had enough to eat. But we haven't finished our conversation."

'Well," he said. "I'll let you make me a cup of coffee at your place."

"No," she said. She paused long enough to sound uncomfortable. "It's not that I wouldn't like to. It's just that, um, another Israeli teacher from the school lives on the same floor; and I wouldn't want her to know that I was entertaining a, um..."

"Man," he finished for her.

"Yes." She smiled warmly and gratefully. He took his eyes off the road and took her smile in. The *babushki* at the door to her building had indicated that only one Israeli lived there. He had to assume now that her every word, every laugh, and every smile were calculated. Then he smiled back.

He saw no reason to confront her immediately. As a reporter, he had found that there were times when he learned more by playing dumb. He told himself that this was one of those times and that he was not going along because part of his mind refused to let go of the possibility that he was really charming this beautiful and intelligent woman.

"All right," he said. "How about my place?"

"Well, I wouldn't want to put you to any trouble," she said. "We can talk another time."

"No trouble. My pleasure," he said.

"Well all right," she said. "Thanks."

❀ ❀ ❀

He had cleaned the apartment, though it would have embarrassed him to acknowledge it was on the chance that she would see it. Her eyes quickly took in the furniture, the photographs on the walls, and the titles in the bookcase. As he went to find her some wine, a photo in a silver frame caught her eye. It was Burke with a young man who had his blue eyes and his chin. They were standing in Red Square, with the domes of St. Basil's in the background, looking quite solemn.

"Your son?" she asked when he came back in and found her there, in front of the picture.

"My son," he nodded. "He visited in June. I told you I didn't always live alone."

"A good-looking boy," she said. "Takes after his father." Burke smiled. "Thanks," he said. He wondered briefly if she were closer to his age or his son's.

She looked expectantly at the sofa, and he invited her to sit down. He took a chair across the room.

"So what's your business proposal?" he asked abruptly.

She decided to answer directly. "I want to work for you," she said.

He tried to look surprised, but he had half expected her to say this.

It made him angry, he realized. Someone, a presumed professional, had decided that an agent could be planted in the *America Weekly* bureau just by sending in someone beautiful to seduce the correspondent. It was an insult, but it was frightening as well. It made him see himself as someone else had seen him, someone who had deemed him to be gullible.

"Really?" His tone was too cool.

"Yes," she said, leaning forward earnestly, hands cupping her wine glass in front of her. He let his eyes go to the opening in her blouse. She smiled.

"You see," she went on, "journalism is my ambition. I studied it as a minor at Hebrew University and at Brandeis. I want to be a foreign correspondent. But the Israeli newspapers can't afford to hire very many. I want to break into the American media. One of the reasons I came to Moscow was because I heard a lot of the correspondents here have part-time assistants."

Suddenly, he wanted to see how far she would go to get this job. "Well," he replied. "I do have a part-time opening." This was true. Burke's last assistant had been the wife of a UPI reporter. She and her husband had left Moscow two months ago, one step ahead of UPI's bankruptcy. He realized that Evron and the Israelis no doubt already knew that.

"So you could use help," she said. "My Russian is fluent, of course. I could translate for you, make phone calls…"

"I don't get it," Burke said. He sensed she would be suspicious if he rolled over too easily. "I thought you were a teacher."

"I am," she said. "But that's only in the mornings and at lunchtime. My afternoons are free." She paused. "So are most evenings. Teaching happened to be the only way I could find to get to Moscow and be paid for it."

"Well, to be honest, I was thinking of taking on a Russian," he said. This was true.

She got up and moved across the room to his chair until he could smell her.

"Please," she said. "No Russian will work harder for you."

"I'm sure you would…"

"Someone gave you a chance. That's all I want. Just try me for a week, If it doesn't work out, you can fire me."

He smiled. "Well, I'd have to check with New York before I hired anyone."

"But you will check?"

He nodded.

"Thank you!" she said. She hung there for a second, her face in front of his. He made no move.

"How is your bruise?" she said. She reached out and ran her hand gently, slowly, over the cotton of his shirt, past his ribs and up under his arm. "I hope nothing's permanently damaged," she said.

"Everything is working," he replied, smiling.

She waited expectantly, but he only stood there. He was damned if he was going to give her the satisfaction of being too easy.

But he would, he decided, let her seduce him if that was what she had come here to do. His motives were too muddied to sort out in the seconds that she stood in front of him, waiting, but they had to do with lust and curiosity and anger in about equal proportions. Despite everything he suspected, he still wanted her. If getting him into bed was part of some plan, he had to go along with it to be able to watch the further steps in that plan unfold. And he was angry enough, he realized, to want to fuck her and then watch her face when the time came to tell her that he had known all along what she wanted—and wouldn't get from him. "Don't make me beg you," she said.

Finally, then, he kissed her. She nibbled at his ear and her breathing rose smoothly up the scale from deep, slow inhalations to quick, urgent pants.

She unbuttoned his shirt and kissed the dark brown bruise on his ribs. Her hands, he noticed, were actually trembling.

Burke responded with a hand outside her shirt and then, after unfastening a couple of buttons, inside, running his finger lightly over her hardening nipples.

She pressed gently against his groin. He was ready.

"Can we go to the bedroom?" she asked.

His eyes half-lidded with lust, he nodded. He took her hand and led her to the bedroom, leaving the light off.

To his own mild surprise he turned out to be unhurried, gentle, and thorough with her. When he finally mounted her, she responded immediately with a rapid, harsh rhythm. The headboard banged against the wall.

He spent himself, propped up on his hands, his

head a foot or two above hers. She let her own movements slowly subside. He rolled off and lay on his back, still breathing heavily.

A thumping came from the ceiling. She started, "What's that?"

He turned slightly toward her, and she noticed that their bodies were barely touching

"My upstairs neighbor. A German correspondent" She caught a pattern in the thumping and listened intently. She began to laugh.

"What's funny?"

"It's Morse code," she giggled.

"What's he saying?"

She suppressed her laughter. "N-G-R-A-T-U-L-A-S-H-O-N-S," she translated.

Burke snorted. "His sense of humor is as good as his spelling."

She turned toward him and ran a hand down his chest. "Well," she said flirtatiously, "you did have me going rather loudly there."

"I guess I should call him," Burke said. He started to turn toward the phone.

"No," she said, and caught him by the shoulder, pulling him down until he was on his back. "Let's annoy him again."

She kissed his nipples, one after the other, and then moved her mouth down toward his groin, letting her hair and breasts trail behind her mouth on his chest. He stiffened immediately.

When Burke finished the second time, he gave her a few pro forma kisses and a few pro forma nuzzles, said a pro forma good night, sighed, and rolled away from her. Within a minute, he was breathing deeply and evenly.

After ten minutes, she got up, naked, and went silently out toward the living room. In the darkness, Burke scowled. He told himself that he should be pleased with himself for sizing her up correctly, but he found that scant comfort. More than anything else, he realized, he would have liked to have been wrong.

CHAPTER FIVE

BURKE WAITED IN BED, straining to hear what she was doing. He heard a few quiet creaks as she padded barefoot around the apartment. Then he heard nothing. It was time, he decided, to stop playing possum.

He got up as quietly as he could, pulled his robe from the hook on the back of the door, and walked rapidly into the living room, flipping on the light as he entered.

Naked, she was bent over the telephone. The harsh light of the overhead lamp bounced off the drying fluids on the insides of her thighs. She whirled around, making no effort to cover her body. Instead, she stuffed something into the purse on the table beside her. Underneath her tan, her face paled and for a moment her mouth hung open. She had, he saw, removed the plastic cover from the telephone to work on the insides.

"I—I thought you were asleep," she stammered.

"Obviously," he said.

She said nothing, and he yielded to the temptation to say something vengeful.

"You shouldn't confuse being horny with being stupid," he told her. "In your business it could be dangerous."

"It's not what you think," she snapped.

He watched an angry flush spread from her neck down to her breasts.

"Stop assuming you know what I think," he said.

She scowled and said nothing.

"Don't be angry," he said. "I'm not. The folks who usually bug phones in this town aren't as good-looking, they don't work in the nude, and they only screw you metaphorically. You're an improvement."

"I want to leave," she said through tight lips.

"Come into the bedroom," he said.

She stood still. Her hands flitted up and down the sides of her thighs. The sinews on her neck stood out like cords.

"Come into the bedroom," he repeated.

"I'm leaving," she said. Her tone had changed rapidly from embarrassed to defiant. He could feel her anger, like radiant heat. Involuntarily, he took a half step backwards.

He sighed heavily. "You just used me for my body. Okay. But you might want to go into the bedroom first. You left your clothes there."

She picked up her bag and walked past him, turning her shoulder as she did so that her breasts and belly were hidden. He followed.

"Don't follow me," she said.

"Afraid I have to," Burke replied.

She turned and confronted him as she reached the bedroom door. Her brown eyes glittered, and her breathing was ragged.

"Stay out or I'll hurt you," she said levelly.

"I'm sure you could," Burke said. For a second he felt frightened. She could probably kill him with her hands if she had to. But he sensed that her rage was directed almost entirely at herself for being caught.

"I need to get my clothes, too," he said.

Without a word, she turned and walked into the bedroom. In the faint light coming from the living room, he saw her bend gracefully to pick up her clothes. Quickly, she stuck her legs into her panties. She snagged a toe and cursed. She tried again and this time pulled them up. He scooped up his own clothes, went out into the hall, and closed the door behind him. Then he dressed, not bothering with socks.

In a minute she emerged, her hair still tangled, wearing her jeans and the silk shirt. The second button, he saw, was fastened this time. She had mastered whatever anger she had felt, and her face was blank. He opened the door for her, and she went outside.

"Okay," he said. "Let's talk."

"About what?"

"About who might want to know what happened here."

"Not here," she replied. "On the street."

Wordlessly, they got into the elevator and faced the front, not meeting each other's eyes. A stranger, Burke thought, would think they were just two people who found, after sex, that they couldn't stand each other. He almost blurted the thought out, but he checked it. He didn't want to push her sense of humor.

Outside, she looked at the building and the *milit-sioner* in his little brown hut.

"Across the street," she said.

They strode across the broad boulevard, setting a pace that avoided the few cars and trucks going past at that hour. It was chilly now. Burke had forgotten to grab a coat.

They hit the curb in front of the puppet theater, under a relief sculpture of clowns and animals. The sculpture cast a long, oblique shadow on the granite façade of the theater.

"Okay, far enough," Burke said. "People in worse trouble than you have had conversations here."

It was true. In the old days, dissidents like Shcharansky had often rendezvoused with correspondents from Sad Sam on the sidewalk in front of the puppet theater. Burke decided she might not appreciate this bit of Moscow lore.

"What makes you say I'm in trouble?" she asked, glaring at him.

"Your cover is blown," he said.

"You don't know anything. You can't prove anything," she said, her voice low.

"Don't have to," Burke said, trying to sound more confident than he felt. "All I have to do is call the good folks at the Ministry of Security and let them know what I think I saw. I'm sure they'd be happy to have the information."

"You wouldn't do that."

She was right. But he knew she couldn't be certain of it. "I would think you'd have stopped assuming things about me," he said gently.

"Are you blackmailing me? It won't work," she spat.

He detected a hint of vulnerability in her voice for the first time. He imagined that if she thought he had blown her cover, she would have to go back to Israel, where it would not be easy to explain her mistake.

"No," he said, trying to sound friendly. "I'm just reminding you of the realities of the situation."

A drunk wobbled down the sidewalk toward them. She watched him pass, pensive now more than angry. When he was gone, she turned to him again.

"Which are?" she asked.

"You got sent in here to help keep track of bomb makers and bomb parts going to Arab countries. The best cover you could get was as a teacher in the school," he said. He was winging it, but it seemed logical.

"You heard, no doubt before CNN did, that the Syrians are collecting bomb parts and maybe have enough. You decide you have to accelerate matters. You need a cover that will allow you to do some direct research, to ask questions, and so on. An American magazine is perfect, particularly after you find out I'm working on the same thing. It's better than a newspaper because it has only one deadline a week—and you wouldn't want to waste a lot of time actually writing stories."

He paused. "Stop me when I'm wrong," he said. But before she could say anything, he pushed on. "So you figure the quickest way is to find a magazine with a single male correspondent and jump into bed with him. You have some friend or agent in New York plant the story suggestion with my publisher. And when I show up at the synagogue, you take it from there. Once you're in my apartment, and you think I'm asleep, you put a bug on my phone just to make sure you're able to monitor everything I learn."

When she replied, it was in a low, carefully modulated and reasonable voice.

"You don't have your facts straight," she said.

"Which ones were wrong?" he challenged her.

She shook her head. "I'm not going to get into that. But let's assume for the sake of argument that just one part of what you said is true. That I don't want Syria to have nuclear weapons. Is that wrong? Do you want Syria to have them?"

"All I know," he said, "is you wanted to use my office as a cover. Whether Syria gets the bomb or not is something I have no control over."

He paused. He generally tried not to argue with the people from whom he wanted to extract information But he still wanted to lash out at this woman.

"Anyway," he went on, "I'm not going to debate with you. I have a story to get, and I think you probably know some things that will be useful to me. And I think you're going to tell me what they are."

Her posture changed. She tilted her head slightly to the left. He sensed he was going to have to bargain. He hated bargaining. He never felt devious enough.

"Such as?"

"Such as whether, how, and where Assad is trying to recruit nuclear scientists. Who they are."

"I may know a few things about that," she said. "But I want something in return."

"What's that?"

"I want that job."

She looked serious.

"Sorry," he said. "It's out of the question."

She crossed her tanned arms in front of her blouse. "Why?"

He shook his head. "Well, because a reporter just doesn't put an int—someone like you on his staff. We don't let ourselves get used for cover."

"You still don't even know who I am," she said. "You only have a suspicion."

"What—you were calling out for postcoital pizza? Come on."

"You don't *know*."

"What do you mean? That I'd have deniability?"

She shrugged. "Call it what you want."

Burke scratched his head. For a woman whose IQ was probably twice as high as his, she could be very dense.

"Let me try to explain," he replied. "I don't want deniability. I want credibility. Maybe it doesn't work this way in Israel, but an American reporter doesn't want to be used by intelligence agencies. We have to be independent. We have to have people know we're independent. It's just..." He searched for a word that wouldn't sound pompous, but couldn't find one. "Ethics," he completed the sentence.

"Ethics!" she snorted. "Ethics! You accept no responsibility for preventing a maniac from getting nuclear weapons. You try to blackmail me. You want me to give you information, and you want to give nothing in return. And you call that a code of ethics?"

Suddenly, the situation seemed laughable, and Burke laughed. "Well," he said, "I also pick up my own checks. I protect my sources. That's about all the ethics I can afford."

"I'm sorry," she said, shaking her head. "I don't think we can do business. You can tell the authorities what you want." She sniffed. "Assuming you would consider that 'ethical.'"

She turned her back and walked away.

Burke watched and wanted to let her go; he realized he couldn't afford to.

"Wait," he called softly.

She stopped and waited. He walked up to her.

"Look," he said. "I'll tell you what. You tell me what you know. I check it out. I can't help you directly. But what I find out goes into the magazine. For two bucks you can buy it and read it."

She said nothing. Her arms were folded.

"And I don't tell anyone what happened in my apartment tonight," he said, trying to reestablish who had the best hole card in this game.

"I still get nothing out of it," she said.

He shrugged. "Maybe. Maybe not. Maybe if you tell me what you know, I'll find out something you wouldn't have been able to. When you read it, you're ahead of the game."

"All right," she said, nodding slightly. "We'll try it."

He looked up and down the street. Even the drunks had apparently gone home. He saw no one.

"Okay," he said. "Who's recruiting, who's being recruited, and how?"

"We don't know yet," she said. "But have you heard of a company called Switsico?"

"Switsico'?"

"An acronym," she said, "For the Switzerland-Siberia Oil Company."

"No," he admitted. "Never heard of it."

"It's a joint venture. Founded two years ago by a group of Swiss oil brokers and the Tyumen oblast. The chartered purpose was to invest about $50 million in new drilling equipment to capture oil left behind in the fields by the Soviet equipment, then export it and split the profits fifty-fifty."

"And have they done that?"

"No. Ostensibly because the government's export tax is so high that it's not feasible."

"Lots of oil companies say the same thing."

She nodded. "I'm not saying it's not true. But about three months ago the Swiss side sent in a new partner in charge of the office here. His name is Rafit Kassim. We heard about him just the other day."

"An Arab?"

She nodded. "He has a Swiss passport. But he was born in Saudi Arabia."

"What else do you know about him?"

"Not much. He hasn't come to our attention before."

"How'd he get a Swiss passport?"

"They're available to Saudis with the right connections."

"And what makes you think he's involved with Assad?"

"Since he came here, he's started to make contact with nuclear energy enterprises, military plants—says he wants to expand the company's operations in case the oil business doesn't work out."

"So? What else do you have?"

"Nothing else," she replied. She said it ruefully enough to make him believe it was true.

"Why not?"

She shrugged. "There are only so many resources."

"But you're pretty sure this is the guy?"

She nodded. "One of them, anyway."

He wondered how much the lead was worth. Presumably, she was calculating that a reporter might

learn something about Switsico faster than she or one of
her colleagues. And if he started poking into Switsico
and learned nothing, it might still spook Kassim and
hinder Syria's effort.

What's more, it was the only live lead he had.

"Where's he located?"

"In an office building behind Gorky Street, not far
from Pushkin Square. Number Six Maly Gneznikovsky
Pereulok."

"I'll find him," Burke said.

She nodded.

"One other thing."

She waited.

"Do you know who else, besides the Ministry of
Defense and the State Security people, monitors what
goes on in nuclear facilities here?"

She reacted blankly. After a long moment, she
shook her head.

"No," she said simply. "Does someone?"

Burke had the feeling she was lying, but he let it
slide.

"I don't know," he answered.

"I'll be in touch," she said. She turned without
another word and walked off toward the Novoslobod-
skaya Metro station.

Burke watched until she faded into the darkness
two blocks away. He told himself that he was the one
doing the manipulating. He told himself to be satisfied
with the evening's exchange. He couldn't make himself
believe it. He went home, took a long shower, and
found, to his relief, that he still had a half bottle of
vodka.

CHAPTER SIX

THE SECRETARY WHO ANSWERED the phone at Switsico had one of those feminine alto Russian voices that sound sweetly melodic in their native tongue but slightly stupid in a foreign language. This one was speaking French.

"*Bonjour*, Switsico," she said.

"Colin Burke from *America Weekly*. Mr. Kassim, please," Burke said in Russian.

"He is not here right now," the secretary replied, sounding smarter in her native language, but guarded.

"When do you expect him?"

"I don't know."

"Is he in Moscow?"

"I don't know."

"Could I leave a message for him?"

The woman hesitated, presumably wondering if even this would be somehow indiscreet.

"Well, all right," she finally said.

Burke gave her the details slowly enough so that she could write them down. He doubted she would bother. He would wait a couple of hours, then try more active measures.

In the meantime, he had other people to talk to, beginning with Ethan Worthington. Burke called him, and Worthington cheerily suggested an early lunch. He gave Burke the address of a new hole-in-the-wall near Mayakovsky Square.

Worthington was waiting inside when Burke found the place, a little room that called itself *Russkaya Kukhniya*, "The Russian Kitchen." The room had windowless concrete walls, freshly painted a bilious green, and a concrete floor. Burke could faintly smell leather and polish under the odor of onions, and he thought he remembered a shoemaker's shop once occupying the space. The restaurant had a collection of six tables that looked as if they had been scavenged from the carcasses of failed state restaurants. Of the motley assortment of chairs, several had stuffing leaking out of the backrests. He hung up his coat, noting that Olga had indeed sewn his button back on. He would have to buy her a present.

Russkaya Kukhniya was the kind of place Ethan Worthington loved to discover. Most American diplomats spent as much time as possible within the walls of the embassy compound; it had been designed, by bureaucrats obsessed with security, to help them avoid rubbing up against the country they were supposed to be watching. They ate, for the most part, in an embassy snack bar that looked like a McDonald's in a southern California suburb.

But Worthington believed in mixing with the natives. He prowled around the city, looking for new shops and bakeries and restaurants. Occasionally he would come to the poker game and recommend one. Burke found that half of them went out of business before he got around to trying them. But he respected Worthington for searching them out. It was what he would do, he thought, if he were a diplomat.

Worthington should have looked out of place in his precisely creased gray trousers, yellow button-down shirt, and a muted but rich Harris tweed sport coat. With his thick chestnut hair slightly tousled, he looked as if he belonged in a J. Press catalog. But he had a gift for looking at ease in any situation, which was another reason Burke liked him.

Burke entered and peered around the room, letting his eyes adjust to the dim light. They shook hands. Worthington had a bottle of mineral water on the table, and he poured Burke a glass.

Burke didn't know whether Worthington's sense of honor was offended by his signal to Plotnikov at the poker game. He decided he ought to clear the air.

"Look, I'm sorry about that bit with my ear the other night," he said. "The guy wanted to play, but I figured he was putting up every dollar he had. I didn't want to be the one to take it from him."

Worthington waved his hand. "It's okay. I just wish you were always so charitable." He smiled mischievously.

"If I were any more charitable," Burke said, "I'd have to join the Little Sisters of the Poor."

A grim waiter in an old checked shirt walked up to the table and silently handed them each a greasy piece of paper with a menu typed on it. Burke ordered "House Salad." From experience he knew it could be anything from a few bits of green leaf with a rotten tomato to a moist, delicious concoction of diced meat, crumbled hard-boiled egg, carrots, onions, and mayonnaise. He would let them surprise him. Worthington ordered borscht.

"By the way, great piece on the con men at the train station," Worthington said. "You managed to make them seem rapacious and, I don't know—kind of innocent at the same time."

Burke had written an article the previous week about a team of hustlers fleecing travelers with a Russian variant of three-card monte. The piece had run only in the international editions of *America Weekly*, which carried more news from abroad. Canfield hadn't used it in the United States edition.

"Yeah. The domestic edition editor liked it so much he decided to hold on to it for a while," Burke said.

Worthington raised his eyebrows. "Even with that good-looking woman in the picture? She seemed quite captivating."

"Didn't impress him," Burke said.

"Your editor must be a tough guy. I heard what happened to Jim Venneman."

Burke's brows rose. "How'd you hear that?"

"Friend of mine is the press attaché in Beijing. We both knew Venneman when he was in Berlin. I thought he was a good man."

Burke nodded slowly. "He was. Is."

Worthington said nothing, and Burke had the sense he was waiting, as a friend, in case Burke wanted to bend someone's ear about his own status at the magazine. But that was not the kind of thing Burke talked to people about.

"So what's on your mind?" Worthington finally asked. He took a sip of his mineral water.

"Russian nuclear scientists," Burke replied.

The waiter padded up and placed two plates on the table. Burke's salad was the rich kind, and he noticed that Worthington's borscht was the real, Russian village variety, topped with sour cream called *smetana*, the kind he saw only when he visited Russians at home. The restaurant obviously had a genuine *babushka* laboring in the kitchen.

Worthington ladled a bit out of the bowl, spooned it into his mouth, and let it sit there for a minute, the way some people tasted a new wine. Then he swallowed and nodded approvingly.

"How are we talking?"

"Background?"

Worthington shook his head. "Sorry, pal. None of that 'Western diplomats said,' I'm afraid. Everyone knows that comes from us. It will have to be deep background. No attribution."

Burke nodded. He had no problem with hiding sources except in cases where they wanted to smear someone else. Then they had to be on the record.

Worthington took another spoonful of borscht and swallowed quickly.

"Well," he said, "it's a real problem."

"Even with the talks so close to a final settlement?"

Worthington looked at him.

"You know they're stalled. And in this case, I think missing by an inch is the same as missing by a mile. If they fail, everyone in the region assumes it's back to square one. Or maybe worse. There are recriminations. Maybe the hawks come back to power in Israel. Maybe the Palestinian radicals take over. It's a more dangerous situation than we had before."

"So Assad has reasons to want the bomb."

Worthington nodded.

"So he looks for scientists. What's the universe of people we're talking about? How many might Assad really want?"

"It depends," Worthington said. "If he just wants to build a bomb and set it off in the desert, he might not need any. Or he can get them from Pakistan. Just building a bomb isn't too tricky if you've got the right equipment and materials."

"And does he?"

Worthington shrugged. "Not my department. That sort of thing's monitored by the intelligence folks on the other end. Then it goes to Washington. You heard what CNN said."

"Why's the equipment monitored that way?"

Worthington shook his head. "Can't tell you, Colin. Goes to sources and methods. Besides, I don't know much. Knowing how badly penetrated this place is, they'd be stupid to tell me."

"So you don't know about Blackstone's report?"

Worthington smiled. "I can tell you I haven't seen anything from Washington knocking it down. Do I detect a hint of competitive jealousy here, Colin?"

Burke rolled his eyes. "Could be."

Worthington had a little more borscht and wiped his mouth. Burke picked at his salad. It was delicious, and he tried to look interested in eating it.

"So," Burke said, "do you know who besides the KGB—I mean the Ministry of Security and the Ministry of Defense—-would monitor what goes on in the nuclear weapons plants?"

Worthington's eyebrows went up. "Is there some-one?'

"I think so."

Worthington shook his head. "News to me. Haven't heard of anyone."

"All right," Burke said. "Let's get back to scientists. What do you mean it depends on the kind of bomb Assad wants? And if even Pakistanis can build bombs, why should Assad be interested in Russians?"

"Okay, look," said Worthington. "If you're Syria, and you get a bomb, and you actually want to use it against the Israelis, how do you do it?"

"I don't know," Burke said. "Airplane?"

Worthington shook his head. "No chance. The Israelis'd blow it out of the sky before it got out of Syrian airspace."

"Okay, how?"

"Essentially, there are two ways. One is a missile. The other is a suitcase."

"Okay. What about the missile?"

"There, he's got two options. One is to buy a war-head designed for that missile, mount it, and launch it."

"Like a SCUD warhead?"

Worthington nodded. "Yep. But our arms control agreements let us keep very close tabs on the old Soviet missile warheads. I can tell you for sure that none have gotten out."

"So he'd have to build one?"

"Right. And building one small enough, light enough, and reliable enough to sit on a missile and blow up when you want it to is something several orders of magnitude more complicated than what the Pakistanis or the North Koreans are trying to do."

"I see."

"And even then, with missiles you have problems. They're vulnerable before they're launched—the Israelis would take 'em out if they thought the Syrians might use them, If you do launch one, the Israelis have a chance to knock it down with the Arrow. And they can tell where it came from. If you go with a missile, you better take out all of the Israelis' nuclear weapons and air force, because they're gonna come after you with whatever they have left."

"Whereas, with a suitcase bomb, they might not know where it came from?" Burke said.

"They might, they might not."

"So you think that's what Assad would do?"

Worthington spooned some meat out of the bottom of his soup. "Makes sense," he nodded. "Build a dozen of them, and start trying to get them into Israel— through Jordan, through Gaza, lots of different routes. Eventually, a few will get through. Then you set them off when it suits you."

Burke put down his fork, salad still untouched. It was remarkable, he thought, how casually they could sit at a table and discuss an event that would be indescribably horrible. Then he dismissed the thought and sought more information.

"A suitcase bomb, I take it, would be even harder to build?"

Worthington nodded. "Very much harder."

"How many people could build one?"

He shrugged. "We have about a dozen. The Russians have about a dozen."

"That's all?"

Worthington grinned briefly. His teeth were perfectly white and even. "How many did you expect? This isn't something they teach undergraduates at M.I.T. You have to be both a physics person and a design person to get started in it. Very talented. A bit of a sculptor, really. And you have to have access to some very classified stuff."

"Stuff?"

"Knowledge. Equipment."

"So how well do you keep track of Russia's dozen?"

"Pretty well."

"How many have gone to the States in that exchange program?"

Worthington paused, "Exact number is classified."

"Nearly all? More than half? Just a few?"

Worthington smiled at Burke's persistence. "The latter," he said.

"And how many are working here for dollar salaries?"

"About the same," Worthlngton said.

"So there are maybe half a dozen who are paid in rubles?"

"I see what you're driving at. But remember two things. First of all, no one can pay a salary big enough that Assad can't top it if he wants to. If someone wants to work for the highest bidder, it's hard to prevent—"

"But a guy making a good living would be harder to tempt than a guy scraping along on a few thousand rubles a month," Burke interjected.

"True," Worthington nodded. 'The second thing to remember is that when I say about a dozen, it can't be an exact figure. Who knows what some junior guy in a lab can do until he gets the chance? There might be another half dozen or a dozen guys out there with capabilities that we don't know about."

"Okay. But how do you keep track of the ones you do know about?"

Worthington shook his head. "Can't say," he answered firmly.

"I mean, do you physically keep an eye on them? Or do you just check in with their offices once in a while to make sure they're still there?"

Worthington just shook his head. "Sources and methods," was all he said.

Burke tried another question. "Do you have any evidence that Assad's been trying to recruit them?"

"Well, you know, it's not like the Syrian embassy has a guy that goes around asking people if they'd like to move to Damascus and make bombs," Worthington said.

"What might the approach be like?"

"Oh, maybe a joint venture with scientific interests. Looking for general scientific talent. That sort of thing," Worthington said.

"Like Switsico?"

Worthington stopped chewing. For the first time in the conversation, he looked surprised.

"Where'd you hear that?"

"Sources and methods," Burke said.

Worthington smiled and put his right index finger to his lips. Then he scratched an imaginary mark in the air. "Score one for the press. Okay."

"So you've heard of Switsico?"

"Well," Worthington said judiciously, "they're in the phone book."

"But you've heard of them in this context."

Worthington shrugged very eloquently.

"C'mon, Ethan."

"Strictly off the record?"

Burke nodded. It meant he could not print what Worthington would say at all, unless he could find it from other sources.

"I would say that it might be worth your while to have a look at Switsico," Worthington said quietly.

"Thanks," Burke said. "That'll make a great cover line."

"Cover line?" Worthington looked surprised for the second time.

Burke laughed. "On the cover of the magazine. What kind of cover were you thinking about?"

Now Worthington looked slightly offended. He picked up his napkin, dabbed at a smudge of sour cream on his mouth, and put the napkin on the table next to his plate.

Burke immediately regretted his wise remark, just as he had been regretting similar remarks to similarly edgy sources for twenty years. Someday he would master the art of keeping people comfortable during an interview. It was on his self-improvement list, right after giving up drinking, finishing *The Brothers Karamazov*, and keeping a daily journal.

"Sorry," he said.

Worthington shook his head and waved his hand again. "Don't worry about it," he said. "It's just that you still never know in this town who might be listening. And if people get the misapprehension that a diplomat is working for the Agency—well, you understand, he's..."

Burke nodded. "Compromised."

Worthington shrugged and nodded back. "Yeah."

"One more question," Burke said.

Worthington nodded carefully.

"Could you possibly suggest the names of a couple of the people Assad's recruiting?"

Worthington shook his head firmly. "No way."

"Why not?"

Now Worthington looked truly exasperated. "Colin, don't make me repeat the obvious."

"All right," Burke said, smiling.

"I mean, why advertise who these scientists are?" Worthington went on.

Burke only shrugged.

Worthington still seemed edgy about the turn the conversation had taken. He stood up and balled his napkin on the table.

"Sorry, but I've got a meeting to run to. Thanks for lunch," he said.

"My pleasure," Burke replied, and picked up the check.

Outside, the clouds had parted, and the air felt warm and dry in the sun. He stood by the car door and opened it, then thought again. He could walk to the Switsico office in ten minutes. He could use the exercise.

He strode up the side street where he had parked, which was called Accountants' Lane, down toward Tversky Boulevard. As he did, he noticed two men get quickly out of a white Zhiguli parked on the side street near his own Volvo. They, too, started walking toward Tversky.

He walked slowly until he reached a grocery store with a long line of people outside the door, waiting to buy vodka. He stopped. He saw one of the men, wearing a blue windbreaker and a brown cap, suddenly turn and begin to gaze into a nearly empty clothing store display window. He did not see the second man.

No one had followed him, as far as he knew, since well before the botched coup of 1991. He wondered who might be doing it now. Or was he just getting paranoid?

He set off briskly down Tversky. But instead of continuing on foot to Pushkin Square and Kassim's office, he turned left and ducked past a row of flower and lottery kiosks into the Mayakovskaya Metro station. He took the train one stop to Pushkin Square and got out. He looked back at the station platform. He saw no one familiar—no blue windbreaker, no tweed cap.

He shook his head and walked up to the street. The clouds had regained control of the sky, and the air had turned chilly.

CHAPTER SEVEN

BURKE FOUND A PAY PHONE and dialed Switsico's number.

"*Da.*" A man's voice.

"Is this Switsico?"

In reply he heard a click. He cursed and dug into his pocket. He found one more twenty-five-ruble coin. He dialed again.

"*Bonjour,* Switsico."

"Hi, this is William Mays from the carbide drill tip division of Candlestick Oil International," Burke drawled. "Is Mr. Kassim there, darlin'?"

"One moment please. I'll check," the woman said in English.

Burke waited for about ten seconds. A man came on the line.

"This is Kassim," he said.

Burke hung up.

He walked a block down Tversky and turned right through a gateway onto Maly Gneznikovsky Pereulok. He did not have to search for No. 6. One building on the block of faded old Moscow tenements stood out like a blooming tulip in a field of wheat. Fresh, lime green stucco graced its façade. In a discreet bow to post-modernism, it had a circular window mounted in the third, and highest, story. A Mercedes and a BMW stood at the curb in front, and the door was of polished glass and brass. It was patently a building that had been gutted and refurbished for western businessmen.

Burke walked inside onto a soft gray carpet, consulted a directory mounted on the wall, and climbed the stairs to the second floor. The third door down the corridor was of dark, polished wood. A polished brass sign said "Switsico."

He opened it without knocking and went inside. The carpet got deeper, and the walls changed from painted plaster to a seriously expensive mahogany paneling. Two women sat at secretaries' desks.

"May I help you?" said the one on his right. She was the secretary he had heard on the phone. Her tone was polite, but cold.

"Colin Burke from *America Weekly*. I need to see Mr. Kassim," he said.

"He's not in," the woman said instantly.

"Oh, come on," Burke said. "I just talked to him on the phone. Now are you going to get him, or shall I go looking for him?"

The woman looked momentarily uncertain. Burke looked over her shoulder down a short internal hallway. He saw three doors, all closed. None had a sign. He thought about opening the first one he could reach. But he had a vision of barging into an empty conference room, and he decided against it.

"Tell him I'm going to write about him anyway, and it won't look good if I say he evades questions," he told her.

The woman picked up the phone and punched a button. Burke listened carefully as she spoke, but all he could tell was that she spoke in French. He wondered if she was calling a security guard.

But a moment later, one of the inner doors opened and a man emerged. He had a dark, smooth-skinned face, cocoa brown; curly black hair; and a minor belly. He wore sharply creased gray pin-striped trousers, a monogrammed pink silk shirt with French cuffs, blue suspenders, and the kind of flimsy Italian loafers that would wear out if he ever had to walk to a bus stop. Burke caught the dull glint of raw, unpolished gold in his cufflinks as he extended his hand.

"Mr. Burke," he said. "Rafit Kassim. Sorry about the confusion. If you had identified yourself as William McCovey instead of William Mays, I would have received you instantly."

Burke tried not to look startled as he shook the extended hand. "How nice to run into a Giants fan," he said.

"Just a fan of excellence," Kassim smiled. His teeth were perfect white squares.

Burke nodded.

"So to what do I owe the honor of a visit from *America Weekly*?"

'Well, I'm working on a story—" Burke began.

"—And you got a tip that I'm buying krytrons or recruiting nuclear scientists," Kassim finished the sentence. His smile was gone, and he looked suddenly stern.

Trying once again not to look surprised, Burke smiled. "For Hafez el-Assad, as a matter of fact."

Kassim angrily shook his head. "Some people cannot accept the idea of a legitimate businessman who happens to be Arab."

"Well," Burke said, "I can't account for some people."

"But you immediately accepted the idea that an Arab would logically be involved," Kassim said. He seemed less angry than resigned.

"You've got it wrong," Burke said. "I'm an equal opportunity cynic."

Kassim smiled faintly and waved a hand. "It's not important," he said. 'Well, I suppose I should talk to you and make sure the record is straight."

"Thanks," Burke said. "Can we use your office?"

Kassim shook his head. "Not this afternoon. I have an appointment in a few minutes." They both looked at their watches. It was ten minutes until two. "We'll have to try to schedule something next week."

"I think we'd better do it sooner. By next week, this story will be in the magazine."

Kassim scowled. "This week is already impossible."

"In the evening perhaps? I'll take you to dinner."

Kassim smiled. "All right. In the evening. But not dinner. Do you know the Olympic Club?"

"No."

Kassim pulled a fountain pen out of his shirt pocket and scratched some words on a scrap of paper from the receptionist's desk. "Here's the address. Eight o'clock tonight."

Burke looked. The address was somewhere on Volokholamskoye Shosse. He nodded. "Eight o'clock."

❀ ❀ ❀

He was almost at the gate leading to Sad Sam when he heard his name called with a Russian accent: "Kaw-lin!"

Burke turned. Pavel Plotnikov, waving a newspaper, was half running, half skipping down the sidewalk. He wore a blue plaid shirt, brown pin-striped trousers, and the brown open-toed sandals that the old Soviet shoe industry had turned out for summer wear. One of his socks had a small hole near the little toe.

"Colin!" Plotnikov shouted again. As he approached, Burke could see he was grinning broadly and carrying a dozen red carnations in his left hand.

He rushed up to them, lurched to a stop, and thrust the flowers under Burke's nose. They smelled like the cellophane they were wrapped in.

"For you, my friend. With thanks."

Startled, Burke took the flowers. "You're welcome, but what for?"

"For this!" Ploinikov thrust the newspaper into his face. It was *Nyezavisimaya Gazeta*. In the off-lead position, over the fold on the front page, he saw a headline: GORBACHEV, CARTER CAN'T DISGUISE TALKS BREAKDOWN. The by-line was Pavel Plotnikov.

Burke smiled. He looked up at Plotnikov, who had pulled himself nearly erect and thrown his shoulders nearly back.

"Congratulations," he said. "I see the Israelis didn't spoil the story."

"Well, they did," Plotnikov said. "But editors decided to place on front page anyway. My first front-page name-line!"

Burke smiled. 'That's a big event."

"Do you remember your first time?"

"I'm not sure..."

He had a sudden vision of the old *Daily Californian* office, the piles of copy paper and the old gunmetal gray Remington typewriters; he remembered a story about Governor Reagan cutting the budget for the university system. Was that the first? Or was it something else? And how could he have forgotten?

"But it was a big event," he repeated. "I'm happy for you."

"So, let us go get drunk," Plotnikov offered. "In honor of the occasion."

"Sorry," Burke said. "Gotta do some work. I could use a by-line myself. On the cover."

Plotnikov looked disappointed. "I thought you were a good drinking man, like myself," he said sadly.

"You're too close to right," Burke replied.

"If you get a cover by-line, you'll drink with me?" Plotnikov asked.

Burke snorted. "It's more likely I'll be drinking with you if I don't get a by-line on the cover," he said.

As darkness fell, he drove out the St. Petersburg Highway and found the fork where Volokholamskoye Shosse diverged toward, he assumed, a village called Volokholamsk. He entered a neighborhood of massive 1940s apartment blocks, grimy and black. A few pedestrians, their shoulders slumped, shuffled along the sidewalks past the empty windows of the shops. Half the streetlights seemed to have burned out; and Burke drove slowly, trying to spot the number 56 on the side of one of the buildings. Behind him a tram rattled up and blew a piercing whistle. He started so hard that his head hit the ceiling of the car, and he cursed.

He found the number finally, next to a sign that said PRODOVOLSTVENNY, for the grocery store that occupied the ground floor; the "D" and the "V" had fallen halfway to the street and dangled below the rest of the letters. The store was closed and dark. He had expected another well-lit, renovated foreigners' building; and he walked cautiously around toward the rear, looking for an entrance. In the alley he stepped over a twisted length of rusting pipe and saw the silhouette of a male figure, facing the alley wall. He stopped, then heard a hissing sound and caught the smell of urine. Just a drunk.

He turned the corner and entered a courtyard. Toward the rear he could see the outlines of a tiny wooden cottage and a swing—a playground. A naked spotlight, mounted atop a telephone pole, cast a cone of illumination that picked up the gleaming black metal of a Mercedes and a doorway. He had seen the car that afternoon on Maly Gneznikovsky Pereulok. As he walked past it, he peered inside. A driver snoozed behind the wheel. Apparently he had found the right place.

Inside the door, the darkness was nearly complete. His nostrils caught the usual scents of a Moscow hallway—a mixture of old cabbage, old sweat, and stale gasoline fumes. He thought he could detect pulverized concrete and fresh paint in the mix. Somewhere ahead, there was a faint light. He reached out until he found the wall with his right hand and shuffled forward. His feet found the first step, and he walked up to a second-floor landing, then up to a third floor. A bulb burned in a ceiling fixture, showing him an oaken door with a tiny glass peephole and a small sign: OLYMPIC SPORT AND HEALTH CLUB. He could see smooth, fresh plaster around the lintel. He knocked on the door and heard footsteps on the other side. He sensed someone inspecting him through the peephole.

A woman in a white uniform opened the door. She was tall and blonde and beautiful, with hair falling in gentle waves down her back. She looked as if she came from St. Petersburg, where women sometimes combine the tall earthiness of central Russia with the fine cheekbones and fair skin of Scandinavia. Her black eyebrows and pink lips were precisely drawn. Under her blouse he could see the outline of her breasts.

"You are?"

"Colin Burke."

The pink lips parted slightly in a smile. She nodded and opened the door all the way. As he went in he caught the smell of her perfume.

After a long moment, he managed to take his eyes off her and noticed the setting. The walls behind her were paneled in light birch, like a good Helsinki sauna. The floor under his feet was of a dull marble, and marble stairs behind her led down to the building's second floor.

"Mr Kassim is downstairs," the woman said. "Follow me."

He did. She had long legs, tanned and taut.

At the bottom of the staircase, they entered a large room paneled in the same light wood, filled with modular, pastel-colored furniture. It was a lounge of some kind. An empty fireplace, the freestanding kind made of black metal, filled one corner. A couple of large abstract paintings that looked like Morris Louis copies hung on the walls. The lights were soft and recessed. At one end of the room he saw a heavy, reinforced door with a small window, the kind that lead into saunas. Or cells, he thought. There were a few other doors, all shut. At the other end was a bar; and behind it stood a second woman, this one a redhead, in the same short-skirted white uniform. Rafit Kassim, dressed in a white towel, sat in the middle of the room, a glass in one hand and a cigar that looked big enough to hit fungoes in the other. He was watching CNN on a Japanese television set.

With a smile, Kassim got to his feet. He was a trifle bowlegged, Burke saw; but the arms and chest and little belly looked much firmer than he had expected. The man was in shape.

"Mr. Burke," he said, extending his hand. "I'm so glad you could join me."

"Thanks for inviting me," Burke said.

"What will you have to drink?"

"Diet Coke," Burke said, with an effort.

"Are you sure you wouldn't like something stronger?"

"All right. Regular Coke."

Kassim laughed. "Galya, a Coca-Cola please," he said in the direction of the bar. The woman behind it got busy and walked out from behind the bar holding a glass of Coke filled with crushed ice. Burke took it. Except for the hair, she looked as though she had come from the same mold that had produced the blonde.

"Interesting place," he said to Kassim.

"Thank you."

"Kind of hard to spot from the street."

Kassim laughed. "No need to advertise."

"Who owns it?"

Kassim hesitated. "There is a corporation."

"You have stock?"

Kassim laughed again and shook his head. "You're one of those blunt Americans. May I offer you a cigar?"

He pulled a small wooden box from the television table and opened it. The cigars lay in a neat row. Davidoffs. A clipper and a gold lighter lay in a separate compartment.

"Thank you," Burke said. He clipped the end off the cigar, lit it, and puffed. The smoke tasted smooth, fragrant, and a little damp.

"So you own stock?" he repeated.

Kassim's eyebrows described a neat arch. "I am a small investor in the club."

"And the only member?"

"No. But the premises belong to a different member each night. Tonight is my night. It is a useful place to unwind. I find the sauna among the few pleasant northern customs. And it is a useful place to entertain. There are not many such places in Moscow now that the Party has gone out of business."

Kassim smiled again, clenching the cigar in his teeth.

"Whom do you entertain?"

Kassim waved the cigar. "A variety of people. Even journalists. I will be glad to tell you about it. But let's do it in the sauna."

"Hard to tape you in there," Burke said.

He spread his palms. "Mr. Burke, I assure you, you will find nothing worth quoting."

"All right," Burke said. "The sauna. You'll just have to trust me to quote you right."

Kassim opened one of the closed doors; and Burke

stepped into a small, carpeted room with the same recessed lighting and paneling as the lounge. A massage table stood in the middle of the floor, and there was a closet for his clothes. He stripped, found a towel like Kassim's, and wrapped it around his waist. He looked at himself briefly. He needed to do more pushups, but he hated pushups.

When he emerged, Kassim was looking intently at the television set. He beckoned Burke over. "The president is having a news conference," he said.

Burke stood behind Kassim and watched. In Washington it was a warm, sunny afternoon; and the president, looking grim, was taking questions in the Rose Garden.

"Mr. President, what's your reaction to the Israeli air raid in the Bekaa and to the reports that dozens of women and children were killed?" Helen Thomas of UPI asked.

Thomas, who had the face of an aging bulldog on her good days, was looking especially incensed. Her roots were in Lebanon.

"We deplore the resumption of a dangerous cycle of violence in the region," the president replied, obviously delivering remarks that were carefully scripted and balanced. "I have telephoned responsible officials in both the Israeli and Syrian governments, urging them to be restrained. The peace process has come too far to falter now."

"When did the raid happen?" Burke asked Kassim.

"A couple of hours ago," Kassim replied. "It was horrible. The worst since 1982."

"Follow-up, Mr. President!" Thomas yelled on screen.

The president nodded.

"When are the talks going to resume? Or has the whole process broken down?"

The president adopted a calm and authoritative demeanor. "The process has not broken down. We're working on setting a date for the next round of talks now, and I'm confident that Mr. Gorbachev and Mr. Carter will have an announcement shortly. I said when Prime Minister Rabin and Chairman Arafat first shook hands here that the United States was not going to let the process fail. I stand by that commitment." The president paused to let his words sink in.

"Yes, Vickie," he said, pointing at another of the reporters sitting in neat rows in front of him, dressed in their church clothes. The words "Victoria Swensen, CBS News," crawled across the screen.

"Mr. President, President Assad has denied the reports quoting American intelligence to the effect that Syria has bought the parts and equipment needed to manufacture a nuclear bomb. Can you tell us what you know?"

The president shook his head. "I can, but I won't. You know it's our practice not to comment on intelligence matters."

"Follow-up, Mr. President!" Swensen called out. "Without commenting on intelligence matters, can you tell us whether you perceive a nuclear threat from Syria?"

"Well, that leads pretty close to intelligence matters. I think I'll leave it where it is."

"Mr. President!"

"Yes, Carl."

A graying reporter in a tweed jacket stood up. "Carl Reinsdorf, Houston *Chronicle*," the screen said.

"Would you take preemptive action if Assad did get the bomb? Would you sanction Israeli preemption?"

"Well, we don't answer hypotheticals. But, as you know, I'm not a believer in unilateral preemptive action..."

"Since when?" Burke said to the screen.

"There is a battery of international organizations concerned, and properly so, with such matters."

"Follow-up, Mr. President," Reinsdorf said.

"No, Carl, have to give someone else a chance. Only got another minute or so," the president said. He pointed toward the back. "Sarah."

"Sarah McClendon, McClendon News Service," crawled across the screen.

"Mr. President! Are you aware that with the connivance of some members of your White House staff, the Veterans Administration has chosen to cut off medical services to the children of men who died in combat in Vietnam, Korea, and World War II? Is that the way you want to treat people whose fathers made the ultimate sacrifice?"

"No, I wasn't aware of it, Sarah," the president said, gravely. "I'll look into it. Well, Dave is waving at me. I have another appointment."

Helen Thomas took the cue. "Thank you, Mr. President."

Kassim and Burke watched the president smile, wave, and disappear behind the white pillars at the end of the Rose Garden.

"'International organizations!' That'll help the Israelis sleep at night," Burke said.

Kassim dipped his head and looked skeptically at the reporter.

"You're joking," he said, hesitantly.

"Of course," Burke replied. "I meant the opposite."

Kassim smiled. "Yes, I imagine that's so." He paused. "But on the other hand, I would think the Israelis would already have trouble sleeping at night."

Burke said nothing. Few things in life, he had learned, wasted time more efficiently than arguing about the Arab-Israeli conflict.

Kassim waited for a moment, then realized Burke was not going to offer an opinion on whether and why Israelis might toss and turn. He smiled with a polished hospitality. "Well, are you ready?"

Burke nodded.

The wood paneling in the sauna lacked the gloss of the birch in the lounge; it looked like cedar. Burke tried to calculate how much it must have cost Kassim and his fellow investors—if there were other investors—to build it. And whose palms had they greased to take over at least two floors of a Moscow apartment building?

They settled on benches. Kassim took a ladle full of water from a wooden bucket and poured it onto the hot rocks over the heating element in the corner. The water evaporated instantly, adding a little humidity to the dry sauna air. The thermometer read 75 degrees. Burke tried to translate that into a Fahrenheit temperature. Maybe 150 degrees. He felt the sweat break out on his body and decided not to worry about it. Kassim, he noticed, still looked dry. Just another desert morning to his genes.

Without much confidence that it would work, he decided to try to get Kassim answering innocuous questions before he switched to the hard ones.

"So did you see Willie McCovey while you were at Stanford?"

"Once. In my second year at Stanford, I was drinking beer in a bar in the city with some friends. Someone told me that to understand America, I had to see a baseball game. So we all went to the stadium and saw the Giants play the Chicago, um, Bears?"

"Cubs."

"Yes, Cubs," Kassirn said, smiling again. "Something like that."

"So how did a good Arab boy wind up in a San Francisco beer bar?"

Kassim stroked his chin with his right hand.

"When I first got to Stanford, in the autumn of 1974, you understand, I was the darkest person in my dormitory. I roomed by myself, although everyone else had a roommate. I ate my meals by myself. I went to class, and sometimes I would ask questions to which I knew the answers just for the pleasure of speaking to another human being. You understand?"

Burke nodded. "America isn't the most cosmopolitan place in the world. Even Stanford."

"They didn't know what to make of me," Kassim said. "I wasn't Negro, I wasn't Mexican, but I certainly wasn't white. So they couldn't figure out how to treat me."

"So what'd you do?"

"After about a month, I was ready to go home. Then I heard the two boys next door talking about going to a bar in the city that was famous because it never asked for identification. Anybody could drink there. So they went. And I followed them.

"I got there, and they were sitting around a big table playing a drinking game called Thumper. Do you know it?"

Burke smiled. "No, but I suspect I've played something similar."

He looked at the thermometer. It had edged close to 80, Celsius. What was that in Fahrenheit? Maybe 180. He slumped down on his end of the bench, hoping the air would be cooler toward the floor. If it was, it was only a degree or two.

"So with all of my courage I walked up to the table and asked to play. Understand, I had never touched alcohol. I came from a good Muslim home. They were silent for a moment. Then one of them said, 'Let's give him a shot.'

"I sat down. And the next thing I remember, I woke up in my bed, fully dressed, stinking of beer and vomit. But when I walked out into the corridor, someone said, 'Hey, Rafi, how's it goin'?' " Kassim's imitation of American student speech sounded like another language entirely. "And from then on, I was accepted. So beer is responsible for my American education."

Burke smiled. It was a good story. He suspected that the first half, at least, was true.

"Stay in touch with any Stanford friends?"

Kassim shook his head. "No. You know how it goes. After a few years, you drift apart."

"When'd you finish there?"

"Class of '77."

Judging only by appearance, Burke would have guessed about five years later.

"What'd you take there?"

The smile diminished slightly. "Engineering."

"What kind?"

Kassim rolled his eyes. "You are going to misinterpret this; but it is something your magazine could check very easily, so I might as well tell you. Nuclear engineering."

Burke leaned back. "And how should I interpret that?"

Sweat started to run down Kassim's forehead. It was dripping down Burke's face and chest, and he could taste it on his lips.

"Well, the truth is that I was supposed to become one of the first submarine officers in the Royal Saudi Navy. His Majesty, King Khalid at that time, arranged for me to enter the naval ROTC program at Stanford. But then, in the summer before my senior year, I discovered I was prone to two maladies that required me to change my plans."

"They were?"

"Claustrophobia. And seasickness. So I never became a naval officer. But by that time, I had so many engineering credits that I decided to complete the degree."

Burke didn't believe it. Maybe parts of it would check out. "And then you went into business?" he asked.

Kassim nodded. "I got my MBA in Switzerland at the University of Zurich. And I went into business."

"As what?"

"My family has investments in Switzerland. I look after them."

"Including Switsico?"

"Naturally. What better place for an Arab than the oil business?"

"And do you—"

"Mr. Burke," Kassim interrupted. "You are, if you'll forgive me for saying so, beginning to look like a lobster. I suggest we get out, have a shower and a massage, and continue our conversation over dinner."

Relieved, Burke stood up. The heat at the top of the sauna felt capable of singeing his hair.

The two young women were waiting, each stationed by a door, in their white uniforms.

"Do you have a preference?" Kassim asked. He might have been asking Burke to choose between cognacs.

"No," Burke said.

"Well, I prefer Galya. Katya will take good care of you," Kassim said. He opened one of the closed doors, and the redhead disappeared behind him.

Wordlessly, Katya opened the door to Burke's changing room. He followed her, and she handed him two thick white towels. They felt as if no one had ever used them. She opened an inner door into a small bathroom.

"The shower," she said.

He nodded his thanks and stepped into the tub. He could have been in a German hotel. The faucets were of gleaming chrome; and the temperature controls, when he adjusted them, worked precisely. He took the towel off, got the water tepid, and stood under it, facing the wall, until his body started to cool down.

Katya got into the tub so quietly that he did not sense her presence until he felt a soapy washcloth on his back.

Startled, he turned. She was standing a foot away from him, her hair pinned back. She had spent much of the summer on a beach somewhere. The skin of her breasts and her hips was pale white against the soft pink of her nipples and the brown, downy triangle between her thighs. It flashed through his mind that, judging from the way her breasts jutted firmly from her chest, she must have been no older than twenty.

Washcloth in hand, she reached out to his groin and began soaping it gently.

Burke let her do it for a moment, then put his hands on her shoulders and gently pushed her away. "Sorry," he said, "but I'm afraid you wouldn't respect me in the morning."

Katya either failed to understand or decided to ignore it. She continued gently rubbing soap, now working on his testicles.

He let it go on a long moment, until he could no longer ignore the voice in his brain reminding him that Kassim would have hidden cameras all over the room.

He pushed her away again, more firmly.

"Sorry," he said again. "Much as I'd like to get really clean, I can't."

"Why not?" she asked. Her eyebrows rose over her blue eyes and her head tilted quizzically. She let her eyes fall deliberately to his erection. "I think you like it."

For an instant, he thought about explaining that an ethical reporter, even one whose ethics were as frayed as his, drew a line at sleeping with someone involved in a story. Then he thought of Ronit. She'd been the subject of a story. Well, a minor story. And at first he'd thought—well, anyway, a reporter didn't let someone he was investigating for a story pimp for him. That was clear. But how to explain that to Katya?

"I belong to a monastic order of journalists," he said, edging toward the side of the tub. "We take vows of chastity and poverty."

She looked at him dubiously. "I've not heard of it."

"Well, most reporters take only vows of poverty." She smiled, then frowned, but got out of the tub. He rinsed off, waited until his erection subsided slightly, and stepped out.

She was standing, still naked, holding a fresh towel,

her expression uncertain. "Would you like me to dry you off?" she said.

"No, thanks," he answered, trying without complete success to look at her face instead of her breasts. "I'd like you to get dressed."

Katya's lower lip came out and she pouted like a little girl. She handed him the towel, then very slowly reached toward the hook where her panties hung, making sure he saw the way her breasts rose on her chest. She turned her back and bent over to put them on, presenting him with the cheeks of her rear end and the crevice between them as she twitched and put the left leg, and then the right, into the panties. Then she took the white uniform, turned to him, and lifted it up over her head. She let it slowly fall over her shoulders, breasts, and hips. She looked vengefully at him as her head emerged, and he realized he had been mechanically drying the same spot on his stomach throughout her performance.

"Thank you," he said.

"You are a difficult one," she replied.

"Why difficult?" He continued to dry that portion of his body that allowed him to keep the towel in front of his groin.

"Because my job is to please the members and their guests," she said. "If I don't, I lose the job."

"Too bad," he said.

She frowned. "Can I at least give you a massage? I'm very good at it."

Her offer tempted him. But he remembered how he had snickered at the senator who insisted that Miss Virginia gave him only a massage. He shook his head.

She left him, and he dressed alone in the changing room, trying to avoid looking at the massage table.

When he came out to the lounge, she was seated, watching the television. He went to the bar, and this time he did not deny himself a vodka.

Silently, he waited. Ten minutes went by, and he drummed his fingers on the bar, wondering how long Kassim might take with Galya.

"So how long've you been working here?" he asked Katya.

She did not turn from CNN. "A few months," she replied.

"What'd you do before that?"

She shrugged, her back still toward him. "A student."

"What kind of friends do you entertain for Mr. Kassim?"

She shook her head. "That's his business, not yours."

He gave up and watched the tube with her for another five minutes before Kassim, wearing a white terry-cloth robe and an expression of benign satisfaction, emerged from his changing room. Galya followed, pushing the hem of her dress down as she stepped through the door.

"Ah, Mr. Burke," Kassim smiled. "I trust you enjoyed your massage?"

"It was a rousing experience," Burke said.

"Shall we eat, then?"

"Whatever you like," Burke replied.

He followed Kassim upstairs through the entrance foyer to a dining room he had not noticed when he had followed Katya in the first time.

The table was laid with two places and enough food to begin a banquet for twelve. A silver dish piled high with caviar—the good kind—sat in the center.

"Would you like some blini?" Kassim asked.

Without waiting for Burke's reply, he turned to Katya, who had followed them up. She removed the cover from another dish and revealed a stack of the thin pancakes Russians eat at Easter season. She spread each with a little butter, a thick layer of caviar, and some sour cream, then rolled it up into a crepe.

Burke tasted his. The caviar eggs exploded individually, with a tang of salt, on his tongue.

"So where were we?" Kassim asked.

"We were talking about Switsico."

"Ah, yes. What would you like to know?"

"Why do you visit nuclear power facilities and labs if you're interested in oil?"

Kassim smiled serenely. "And how do you know I do?"

Burke shrugged. "Sources."

The serenity remained on Kassim's face. "And what do these sources tell you I am doing?"

"Recruiting engineers for Syria's nuclear program."

Kassim shook his head sadly, as if dismayed by the discovery of disinformation in the world.

"Your sources are wrong, Mr. Burke. I visit these places—and many others, your sources should have told you—because I am seeking Russian technology that might be worth something on the world market. The Soviets had a very good scientific establishment, you know? They just couldn't bring their science into their industry. But there are valuable ideas and technologies out there. That's clear from the success of their space program. I'm just trying to find them and be the middleman."

"But you're supposed to be in the oil business."

"My friend," Kassim said smugly, "any oil man in

Moscow will tell you that no one is drilling oil right now because of the export tax. When the government sees fit to remove it, the oil business will be attractive again. Meanwhile, we have this investment in staff and office space and contacts. Why let it sit idle?"

"It makes a perfect cover," Burke persisted.

Kassim shrugged amiably. "I cannot help what people perceive due to their own prejudices."

Burke hesitated, wondering how much more he could get out of Kassim. If nothing else, he needed denials for the pro forma paragraph in which Kassim would deny whatever Burke wrote about him.

"And you don't recruit engineers?"

Kassim laughed. His self-assurance was beginning to irritate Burke. On the other hand, if, by chance, he was telling the truth, Burke's questions would be irritating him.

"Heavens, no. I assure you I am not a personnel agency."

"And you don't work for Syria?"

"Never been there."

Obviously, Burke thought, he would have to find more sources. Kassim clearly thought his cover story was solid. Otherwise, he would not have given Burke an interview in the first place.

Burke wiped the caviar and sour cream from his lips with a linen napkin and stood up.

"Okay," he said, smiling at Kassim. "You've convinced me. Thanks for the hospitality, and good luck with the business."

Kassim did not try to detain him. He stood up and offered his hand. 'Thank you, Mr. Burke. But there is one thing I wanted to mention. I have very good attorneys in London and New York. Be careful what you write about me."

Burke's stomach twisted gently. He tried to look smug in return. "I always am," he replied.

Kassim nodded, coldly this time. "Katya will show you out."

She walked with him into the foyer and opened the door. As he started to move past her, she suddenly threw her arms around him, ran them down his back and over his hips and kissed him. Over her shoulder, Burke could see Kassim, seated, watching. He kissed her cheek and tried to look satisfied. He saw no point in jeopardizing her job.

At home, he switched on his computer and checked for electronic mail. There was a message from Canfield: "How goes it?"

"Slow," Burke typed out in reply. "Will advise further tomorrow."

He sent a message to Gen Owen, asking her to have a researcher check out Rafit Kassim's records at Stanford.

Then he undressed for bed. He found a slip of paper in his right hip pocket.

Katya, it said. *239-81-53.*

CHAPTER EIGHT

ANOTHER COLD, DAMP WIND had blown in from the north during the hour he had spent in his apartment. Or so it seemed to Burke as he stepped out into the courtyard at Sad Sam, dressed in just the slacks and jacket he had worn earlier in the evening. He stuck his hands in his pockets and hunched his shoulders against the penetrating chill. He walked past the *militsioner* in his little brown hut and wondered if the man would make a note of his second departure of the night. He looked at his watch. It was half-past eleven. Not late enough, he hoped, to be remarkable.

He went to the Metro station that used to be named for Sergei Kirov and now bore the incongruous title of Clean Ponds. He knew of only one pond in the area, and no one would confuse it with clean. He picked the third in the rank of gunmetal gray pay phones along the white tile wall of the station and dialed.

The phone rang half a dozen times. He was about to conclude that he had not given her enough time to get back from Kassim's health club when he heard a click. He dropped his twenty-five rubles through the slot.

"*Da*?" A female voice, a little breathier than he remembered.

"Katya?"

"Yes, I know," she said, not giving him a chance to talk. "I am late. But I forgot where you told me to meet you. Where was it?"

Burke groped for an answer. Did she think he was someone else? Not likely. She probably wanted to prevent him from identifying himself on the phone. He would have to sound like a client. The only image that flashed into his mind was the Mezhdunarodnaya Hotel. It catered only to foreigners with hard currency, and it had the most expensive hookers in Moscow.

"On the embankment outside the Mezh," he said.

"Oh, yes," she said, less breathy. "I remember. In twenty minutes?"

"Fine," he said, and hung up. He looked at his watch. If he jogged to his car, he could just make it.

He jogged, feet sliding inside his loafers as they pounded the concrete, much to the amusement of the drunks still on the street as midnight approached.

He spotted her before she spotted him. She was walking slowly along the embankment, silhouetted against the reflected light glittering on the turgid black water of the river. He made a U-turn and pulled up to the curb. She came up to the car and stood there.

Her hair was up again, and she wore a denim jacket over a black cotton turtleneck, black tights, and black pumps. She had scrubbed the makeup off her face; she looked very young, despite the black clothing, and very nervous.

When he realized she was not getting in, Burke got out. She waited until he was close to her, and said, quietly, "I don't want to talk in the car."

"All right, let's walk," he said. She nodded. But her nerves were contagious, and he decided he did not want to remain where they had agreed to meet.

"Get in, be quiet, and we'll go someplace," he said. He waited to see how she would respond. Had she refused, he would have left her there. But she opened the door and sat in the passenger seat.

He drove over the Kutuzov Bridge, turned right by the Ukraina Hotel, and headed west on the embankment road, out to the foot of the Lenin Hills. A light rain misted on the windshield, and he turned the wipers on. He parked in the same spot he used when he jogged along the river, out of sight of the road. He saw no one.

The rain started to fall a little harder as they got out and began walking. Across the river, the diffuse lights of the city pushed a faint glow into the misty sky and glinted weakly off the angular, golden domes of Novodevichy Convent. The asphalt walkway in front of them started to gleam with the moisture.

"You surprised me," he said. She did not reply.

"When you slipped me your phone number," he explained lamely, knowing that she knew that. How did one start this kind of interview?

"I want you to know," he said, "that I respect confidences. No matter what you tell me, no one will ever know that you told me. Except me. I guarantee it."

She folded her hands in front of her chest. "How can you guarantee it?"

He pulled his pants pockets inside out. "I have no notebook, no tape recorder. I told no one I was coming to meet you."

"They could make you tell," she said.

"If I could resist you in the shower," he said, "I could resist about anything."

She smiled, but the smile vanished instantly.

He decided to be realistic. "All right," he said. "I can't guarantee it. All I can say is no one has ever made me reveal a source before this." He grinned, trying to look a little cocky. "I'd make it damn hard for them."

She did not return the grin, but continued to walk, head down, arms folded in front of her.

"What Kassim told you is a lie," she finally said.

He tried to remain matter of fact.

"I know."

"He does recruit people to make bombs."

"So I understand," Burke said, with as much boredom in his voice as he could muster. "How did you find out?"

"He brings them to the club. I entertain them. I hear what they say."

"Whom does he recruit for?"

"I don't know. An Arab country, I think. With lots of money. Kassim tells them that they will have all the money they could want. And houses, and cars."

He looked at her carefully. She kept her face pointed straight ahead, looking at the ground. Her tone was flat, strained, and believable.

"How many have you, um, been around when he's been recruiting them?"

"Two."

"Have they gone to work for him?"

She shook her head. "I don't know about one. Kassim saw him only once. The other, though, is just about to do it."

He stopped and waited until she looked at him. "Do you know his name?"

"Yes," she said. "Nekronov, Sergei Vladimirovich."

Suddenly it all seemed too easy.

"Why are you telling me this?"

Her lower lip protruded again, but not so demonstratively as it had in the shower a few hours earlier.

"I have good reasons."

"Tell me one."

She looked contemptuously at him. "What do you want me to say? That I care about nuclear weapons? That I care about whether the Arabs get them?"

His eyes asked the question. Did she?

"All right," she snapped. "I care. Of course I care. I'm a human being."

"But that's not why you're doing this."

She shrugged.

"What is it?"

"It's Kassim," she said, spitting the name. Then she said something in a coarse Russian that he could not follow. He picked out three words that he recognized: Galya, I, and asshole.

"I'm not sure I understand," he said.

"When he doesn't have guests around to impress, he's an—" and she used another Russian word Burke didn't know. It did not sound complimentary. The

anger and disgust in her eyes gave him a rough translation.

"How much does he pay you?"

"Three hundred dollars a week."

It was, Burke knew, as much money as a Siberian
miner, stooped over and digging coal in a dark, frigid
tunnel, made in two months. It was more than a lot of
Russians made in a year.

He did not want to let the conversation be diverted
from the engineer.

"When did you meet Nekronov?"

"About a month ago."

"At the club?"

She nodded.

"Same situation as tonight?"

Another nod.

"And you helped serve the meal?"

A third nod.

"What did they talk about?"

"Kassirn was, um, telling him what good working
conditions he would have—a lab of his own, all the
equipment he needed, all the assistants. He said he
thought he could win the Nobel Prize someday."

"And what did Nekronov say?"

"He was worried about getting in and out of the
country. He said he was afraid the security would be too
tight."

"Did he say which country?"

"No."

"And what did Kassim say about the security?"

"He said that he would have to have security, there
was no sense lying about it. To protect him from the
Israelis. But at the second dinner, Kassim said the gov-

ernment had places in France and Italy that he had arranged for Nekronov to use for vacations. And that after his five-year contract was over, he would have enough money to retire and live anywhere in the world."

"Did Kassim say how much money he would be paid?'

"Not while I was listening. But on the second visit, Nekronov told me it would be five hundred thousand dollars a year."

"Not bad."

"No." She nodded gravely. "Not bad."

"Why did he tell you about it?"

"Because I asked him," she replied. She had a sardonic look in her eyes.

"And he told you just because you asked?"

"He likes me," she said, shrugging her shoulders. "He asked me if he left his wife and child behind, would I go with him."

"And what did you say?"

"I told him I would think about it."

"And would you?"

"No."

"Why not? It's a lot of money."

"He's not my type."

"What's he like?"

"He's short, strong. Curly hair. He's about thirty. He has blackheads on his nose. To talk to him, you would never guess that he's a genius."

"But he is?"

"I think so. Why else would Kassim want him?"

"I don't know."

They reached a point opposite the great black hulk of Lenin Stadium on the opposite side of the river.

"Let's turn around," he said.

"No," she shook her head. "I am going that way, toward Gorky Park." She pointed vaguely in the direction of the Ferris wheel, visible above the tree line.

"On foot?"

"Why not?"

"Okay. Um, what else can you tell me about this Nekronov? Where does he live? What's his phone number?"

She pulled a Russian postal envelope from the small leather purse she wore slung over one shoulder.

He saw her name and address on one side of the envelope and a return address, on Kondratieva Street in the city of Tula, underneath it, in the Russian style.

"He wrote you a letter?"

"Yes," she said, a note of pride and a counterpoint of contempt in her voice. "He is obsessed."

"Can I keep this?"

She shook her head firmly. No.

He pulled a scrap of paper from his wallet and wrote down Nekronov's return address. Quickly, he scribbled hers beside it. He handed the envelope back to her.

"What else can you tell me about him?"

She almost giggled. "He's ticklish."

Burke smiled. "Okay. Anything else?"

"No."

"Well, then, thanks. Don't worry about being named."

She nodded gravely.

His store of questions exhausted, Burke suddenly wished that he could do something to help this girl, to make up for the father she probably had never had, or wished she hadn't had, to make up for the economy that offered her no other way to make three hundred dollars a week, to make up for all the men who had abused her. But what he did was tell her good-bye.

He took her hand. "I wish we could have met under, urn, other circumstances," he said. "You're a beautiful woman. Good luck to you."

She leaned forward and lithely kissed him on the cheek. "If your monastic order ever permits it, you know where to reach me." He thought he saw a little mockery in her eyes.

He watched her walk away for a second, then called to her.

"Katya?"

She turned and looked at him, expectantly.

"How old are you?"

Irritation passed over her face. "Twenty-two," she said, grudgingly.

"No, really," he persisted. "How old?"

Her demeanor crumpled for just an instant, and she said, "Nineteen."

He didn't believe that either, but he let it go. "Thanks," he said. "Take care of yourself."

"And you, too," she said.

He turned and walked back to his car, listening to her footfalls going in the opposite direction until the night muffled them.

Ronit Evron called him early the next morning, still pretending to be trying to start a career in journalism.

"What news do you have from New York?" she

asked. Burke assumed she was doing this for the benefit of whoever listened to his telephone conversations.
He felt a strong urge to tell her to stop playing cloak-
and-dagger games. He swallowed the words before they
came out. He had, he realized, a stake in disguising their
relationship. Not as big a stake as hers, but a stake. It
would do him no good if the Ministry of Security determined that he was receiving information from an Israeli
agent.

"Nothing," he said, anxious to end the conversation

"Well," she persisted, "I have some writing samples
that I'd like you to see. I think they're quite good. May I
drop them off in an hour, say?"

He looked at his watch. He had nothing on his
schedule besides going to Tula.

"Yeah, sure," he said. "In an hour."

"Great! See you then," she replied, sounding eager
and perky.

Even not knowing what he knew, he thought, he
wouldn't hire her. He could tolerate a lot, but perky was
more than he could stand in the morning. On the other
hand, he suspected she did perky just as she did seduc-
tive. It was an attitude she assumed when it suited her
purposes. He wondered for a moment what she was
really like.

He picked up the phone and started to dial the
number for his travel agent, hesitated, and put it down
again. No one, except for Katya, suspected he intended
to go to Tula. Perhaps no one should. For years, Tula
had been closed to foreigners because it contained military industries. Now, in theory, it was an open city; but
the Foreign Ministry still required that he register his
travel plans before he went there.

He could decide later whether he wanted to register or make the trip without permission. Ordering a ticket through the hard currency desk at the travel agency, as he normally would, would generate pieces of paper that would land on the desks of people in charge of monitoring correspondents. It would foreclose the possibility of going without permission.

He walked downstairs, got in the car, and swung around the Ring Road two miles, parking at the end of a taxi rank in front of the station.

The usual crowd of travelers, taxi drivers, baggage porters, and hustlers was milling around the grimy, gray stone steps at the entrance. Burke pushed inside, wishing he had taken the time to change into appropriately shabby clothes. With his corduroy jacket and knit tie on, he stood out. But not so much, he hoped, that the ticket clerk would call anyone about him.

He found the display board with the train schedule. A local left for Kursk at 1 P.M., stopping in Tula at five o'clock. Five hours was a long time to cover a distance he estimated at 150 miles, but the timing ought to work well.

He got in line behind a dozen people with muddy shoes and tired shoulders. He was, he noticed, the only one in the line without a parcel or satchel wrapped in newspapers and tied up with string.

Up ahead, a hunchbacked old woman argued shrilly with a ticket clerk who didn't want to accept the ticket she was proffering in return for the one she wanted. The old woman's voice rose to a keening wail, like an alley cat in mourning, until the hairs on the back of Burke's neck stood up and the muscles in his jaw ground behind his cheeks. But the clerk folded her arms and waited the old woman out. After a while she trudged away, a tear trickling down her wrinkled face, her lips trembling silently over her toothless gums.

Like the rest of the people in line, Burke kept his eyes on the shoulders of the person in front of him until he reached the ticket window.

"Tula," he said, and thrust five thousand rubles at the clerk. The second-class ticket and a few wilted hundred-ruble notes came back. He looked at his watch. He was late. He wondered how Olga was getting along with Ronit Evron.

She was sitting by Olga's desk, drinking tea and chatting like an old friend, when he got back to Sad Sam.

After Evron got up and walked into his office, Olga caught him by the elbow.

"I think you should hire her," she whispered. "She's a nice girl. And bright!"

Burke rolled his eyes. Though they were both veterans of failed marriages, Olga had an unshakable faith in the proposition that a nice girl would make Burke's life happy.

He invited Evron into his office and shut the door. She was wearing a short black skirt, black tights, and a bulky white Irish fisherman's sweater that made her look slender and a little frail inside it. And perky.

"Here are the writing samples I told you about," she said.

She handed Burke a red plastic portfolio. He opened it. Inside was a sheet of plain white paper. At the top were the words "Switsico," "Bank of Zurich," an account number, and a heading, "Transaction Summary."

Switsico, with Rafit Kassim signing the paperwork, had opened the account twelve months previously. A month later, the account received five million dollars from a bank in Geneva. The transmitting account number was given, along with the identity of the account holder, a company called Mediterranean Holdings, Ltd. "Mediterranean Holdings," the report stated, "is reliably believed to be a Syrian government front, financed with money from Gulf states."

"Impressive," Burke said, closing the folder and mindful that the office was bugged. "Thank you for bringing it by. May I walk you out?"

Impassively, Evron nodded. They walked, in silence, down the stairs and out to the courtyard.

"How do I know this isn't disinformation?" he asked her, stopping about five yards away from the *militsioner*'s hut and gesturing with his eyes to the portfolio. He wanted to believe the piece of paper. He was inclined to believe it. But her track record turned his normal skepticism into suspicion.

Evron remained impassive. "Why do you think we would do that?"

"To smear an Arab," Burke replied, knowing that he was baiting her. He realized dimly that he was still angry at her for the way she had tried to use him.

She frowned. "Look," she said. "I know I started off wrong with you. I didn't want to. And I know you're hurt and angry. But don't let your feelings affect your judgment."

He tried to hide the anger but couldn't.

"Don't tell me what I feel," he snapped.

A little wave of uncertainty washed over her face, and she seemed off balance. They resumed walking.

"I know you have no reason to trust me," she said quietly. "But we don't smear Arabs for the sake of smearing Arabs. So please believe me. I believe this to be true, or I wouldn't have given it to you."

He said nothing.

"I'm giving this to you," she said, "because I want something in exchange. Is that reasonable enough to you?"

"Maybe. What do you want?"

"Did you see Kassim last night, and what did he tell you?"

His first thought was to tell her again to subscribe to the magazine. His second thought was to see what else she might offer him before he refused to answer her question.

"Why should I tell you something I know in return for something you've typed on a piece of paper?" he demanded.

"It's reliable," she said. "Check it out."

"Sure," he replied. "We'll just send someone into the Bank of Zurich and demand to see the records."

"I'm sure you have some sources there," she argued. "*America Weekly* is a powerful, resourceful publication. Why else would I have wanted to work…"

Her voice trailed off. Burke looked at her. Her face froze in an expression of shock. "Dear God," she whispered.

He followed her eyes to the sidewalk. A thin, dark-eyed woman, her black hair streaked with gray, was standing there, tears streaming down her face.

Convulsively, the woman opened her arms and staggered toward Evron. Burke heard her say "Aleksandra" before she embraced Evron silently, almost desperately.

She clutched Evron for nearly a minute, then put her hands on the younger woman's shoulders and pushed herself a foot or so away. She looked greedily into Evron's face. Evron, Burke noticed, had tightened her face into a steel mask; and muscles were quivering in her neck with the effort to retain control.

They began speaking to one another in a Russian so rapid and fragmented that Burke could hardly follow. He thought he heard Evron say "Mama." Then he heard it again.

"Excuse me," he interrupted. He addressed Evron. The two women, one crying and both talking, either did not hear him or ignored him. He let them go on and watched them.

He could see a resemblance. They had the same bone structure in their faces.

"Excuse me," he said again, louder. His curiosity and fear overwhelmed his sense of intruding on a private moment. He caught their attention, and they both turned to him. As they did, their eyes seemed to merge into a single set of four matching pieces, erasing any doubt of their relation.

"This is your mother?" he asked Evron.

The question seemed to calm the older woman; and she stopped crying, nodding her head. Evron made a simple introduction.

"Nadezhda Nishanova," she said, gesturing toward the woman. Her voice quavered a little, but otherwise she seemed under control. "Colin Burke."

Out of habit, Burke thrust his hand forward, and the woman in front of him took it.

"You're her mother," he said in Russian. The woman nodded, still unable to speak.

"It's a long story," Evron broke in, speaking in English. "When my father and I decided to emigrate, my mother did not want to go. They divorced—"

"And you haven't been in touch since then?"

Evron shook her head. "There was bitterness. A lot of bitterness. And apparently, mail did not reach me. She just told me she'd always written, but I never got the letters."

Burke had a dozen additional questions buzzing through his mind, but one seemed more urgent than any other.

"And you didn't tell her you were in Moscow?"

Evron shook her head.

"Then how did she know where to find you?"

CHAPTER NINE

FEET PROPPED ON THE WINDOWSILL, Burke gazed dully at the raindrops dribbling down his office window, trying to force himself to pick out and analyze two or three of the facts and images ricocheting around his brain.

His attention kept stopping on the memory of the two women's faces as they saw each other for the first time in nearly twenty years: the pain and exaltation in Nadezhda Nishanova's face and the fierce struggle for self-control in Ronit Evron's.

Ronit Evron, he had learned, was a name she had taken on with Israeli citizenship. She had been born Aleksandra Nishanova; her mother was Russian, a pediatrician in a Moscow polyclinic.

They had gone off together, a little stiffly. Before they did, he had gotten the answer to his first question.

Nadezhda Nishanova had received a telephone call from a man who identified himself as a translator for

America Weekly, inviting her to come and see her daughter, and giving her the address and the time. The man had hung up without giving her his name.

That was all right. It would have been phony, anyway.

The call, Burke reasoned, had to have been placed by someone who tapped his phone or Evron's. That meant, most likely, the Russian Ministry of Security.

But why?

They must have wanted to send a message: We know who Evron is and who her relatives are, and we are watching her.

But who was the message for?

Was it for Evron? Was it just a coincidence that she got it outside Burke's office?

Or was it for him? To let him know that he was getting involved in things correspondents shouldn't be involved in?

He didn't know.

He wheeled in his chair and turned his gaze from the cold, wet glass and the trucks rumbling past on Sadovaya Samotyochnaya to the flimsy piece of white paper on the desk:

TO: Burke, Moscow
FROM: Canfield, New York

As of Monday story conference, your proposed package on Russian nuclear scientists is the lead segment in a cover story on the deteriorating situation in the Middle East. Alternative cover is yet another date-rape piece, but it involves a good-looking woman, so your piece will have to deliver. Need advisory soonest on sidebar possibilities. Call art department soonest to confer on photos.

Regards.

Burke ground his teeth together and tossed the paper on the desk. It was the nature of the news-magazine business to decide early in the week what the cover would be, then tell the reporters to go out and find the facts to match the editors' expectations. He didn't like it. It made him think fondly of his newspaper days, when the editors waited for the news to come in, then decided what deserved to be on the front page. But that was why *America Weekly* paid its reporters more than newspaper wages—to make the editors' Monday decisions look good on Friday. And that was what Canfield would expect of him.

He sighed.

Then he turned to his computer screen, where he had written a message to be faxed to Grishin's office at the Foreign Ministry:

> I will be traveling to Tula to interview Sergei Nekronov via the 1:00 P.M. train today. Return late tonight via last train.
> Burke
> *America Weekly*

He imagined what would happen if he sent the message. Someone in Grishin's office would read it. Most likely, that person would stick the paper at the bottom of a pile and resume working on his crossword puzzle. But maybe that person would ask who Nekronov was and why Burke wanted to go to Tula. Maybe they would call down to Tula and the local security *apparatchiki* would start their own inquiries. And maybe Nekronov would be gone when Burke got there.

On the other hand, if he failed to send it, someone in Grishin's office would read the story in the next issue of *America Weekly*. Maybe he would ignore it. But maybe he would ask why Burke went to Tula without registering his travel plans and getting permission. And maybe they would throw him out of the country or lift his accreditation or stop inviting him to the Kremlin for cocktails on August 19, the anniversary of the failed coup.

He weighed the possibilities and decided that the chance of being punished for going to Tula was slim, as long as the Russians depended on the IMF and the World Bank, and as long as the United States had the decisive voice in them. The Russians wouldn't want to roil the relationship by cracking down on an errant reporter.

Canfield, on the other hand, had already demonstrated how he could crack down. Burke tapped the abort command into the computer and erased the message.

He went to his apartment and found an old, wrinkled pair of pants from a blue suit and an equally old and wrinkled jacket from a gray suit. He put them on over a brown plaid shirt and added an old rabbit's fur *shapka* he had picked up once for a trip to Siberia. He used one heel to scuff up the tops of his brown Finnish boots. He looked, he decided, as inconspicuous as he would ever be.

Then he packed his Nikon and his Sony microcassette recorder into a carrying bag and stuffed some spare batteries, cassettes, and film in along with them. He dropped his copy of *The Brothers Karamazov* into the canvas bag with the camera and tape recorder, then inserted the bag into a big plastic shopping sack and took the Metro to the train station.

The Tula train was electric, with hard wooden seats and no compartments. He took a seat by himself next to a window and, with the sleeve of his jacket, rubbed a hole into the crust of brown crud caked on the glass. That made the window semitransparent. There was not much he could do with the dirt on the outside of the pane. Two men and a woman, the men already wearing their winter *shapkas,* took the seats facing and next to him. Their stubby, blackened fingers clutched bags like his. Noticing this, he relaxed a little.

The woman in the facing seat looked old enough to remember the tsars, and her clothes dated from about that period. She had a brown woolen shawl with a fringe pulled up over her iron-gray hair, and her face had more wrinkles than a prune. She reached into the bag between her muddy black rubber boots and pulled out four apples, mottled green and red. She handed one to each of the two men and then proffered one to Burke.

"No, thanks," he grunted, slurring the words as best he could. He turned his eyes outward, through the window, toward the rusted debris sitting in the rain along the tracks.

The old woman rubbed the apple against her shawl and proffered it again.

"Eat," she said.

He smiled with his lips, nodded his thanks, and took the apple. It tasted sour and mealy on his tongue.

"So what country are you from?" the old woman asked abruptly.

So much, Burke thought, for traveling inconspicuously.

❀ ❀ ❀

The rain started falling harder in Tula as darkness fell. Every drop added to Burke's frustration.

He was standing on the edge of what he took to be the central square of Tula. A dark bronze statue of Lenin, his left arm outstretched to the workers of the world, stood in the center of the square, impervious to all storms, meteorological and political. Hulking gray granite buildings that housed the provincial and city bureaucracies formed a rectangle around him. Yellow buses and red trams clattered along the streets.

He stopped a pedestrian, a kid of about sixteen who looked reasonably alert.

"Can you tell me where Kondratieva Street is?"

The boy looked blankly at Burke, shrugged his shoulders, and hurried on his way.

Burke turned to a middle-aged man, scurrying along under an umbrella, an ancient, scuffed leather briefcase bulging under one arm.

"Kondratieva Street?" he asked.

The man stopped, scratched his head, and thought for a moment. "Kondratieva Street?" He shook his head. "Never heard of it. Not in Tula."

Burke glowered at the sky and the rain and the passersby.

"Idiots," he muttered.

He had hoped to make his way to Nekronov's by bus or on foot. But with the cold rain trickling down under his collar, he pulled a rain slicker from his bag and put it on, knowing that a rain slicker would scream "foreigner" to everyone who saw it. There was no helping it, though. If he was going to get to Nekronov's, he would have to use dollars anyway. He turned back toward the train station and the rank of three taxis in front of it.

A long line of dour, stolid people stood waiting for a chance to negotiate with a cab driver. At its head, a woman with three shopping bags in her hands, apparently just back from Moscow, was arguing with the lead driver.

"I'll pay three times the meter!" she said. 'That's more than enough for you, comrade!"

The driver, dry and warm inside the car, shook his head.

Burke poked his head over the woman's shoulder.

"I've got ten dollars," he said to the driver.

The driver jerked to attention, leaned over, and pulled the lock up. Burke opened the door and squeezed in.

"Dollars!" the woman with the shopping bag said, making it sound like a curse. "Dollars!"

"Let's go," Burke said.

The driver pulled away from the curb, stopped at the exit from the station drive, and looked expectantly at Burke. "Where to?"

"Kondratieva Street," Burke said, not very hopeful.

"Where?"

"Kon-dra-tye-va," he said, very slowly.

The driver, a man with red sideburns under an old cloth cap, shook his head. "No such street in Tula," he said, confidently.

Burke fished the paper from his pocket. Trying to be casual about it, he folded it over so only Nekronov's address showed, not Katya's, and thrust it toward the driver's side of the car.

The driver peered at it, shook his head, and threw the car into reverse. He pulled up to the rear of the cab line, which had grown to four cars. The same woman, Burke saw, was glowering at the front of the queue.

The driver snatched the paper from Burke's fingers, walked up to one of the waiting taxis, and got in. Soon, by some form of osmotic communication, the other drivers got out of their cars and joined him. Burke could see them passing the piece of paper around, gesturing, and talking.

Burke's driver emerged from the conference cab and climbed back into his own.

"The index isn't in Tula," he explained.

"Index?"

"Postal index," the driver said.

Burke nodded. "So where is it?"

"Probably in Nauchny Gorodok."

"Nauchny Gorodok?" The Russian words meant "Scientific Village."

The driver grinned. "Outside of town, maybe twenty kilometers. A secret."

"Well, let's go, okay?"

The driver shook his head. In crude English, he said, "More dollars."

Burke sighed in resignation.

"How much?"

"A hundred."

"In your dreams."

Russian cab drivers were true Reaganites. They thought free enterprise meant freedom to gouge. Even though it was *America Weekly*'s money, Burke could not bring himself to give a cab driver as much as a factory worker earned in a year just to take him twenty kilometers out of town. They both knew that if the cabbie thought the Russian government was still capable of protecting secrets like Nauchny Gorodok, no amount of dollars would have been enough to persuade him to go there.

"A hundred dollars," the driver repeated.

"Forty," Burke said.

They settled on seventy-five.

Grumpily, Burke watched the scenery change as the car rattled along. One provincial town, he had found, looked much like the other, beginning with the Lenin statue in the central square, passing through the smokestacks and rusty factories, and ending where the five-story, drab apartment houses gave way to one-story, sagging cottages at the edge of the countryside.

They passed a collective farm called Friendship of the Peoples. He could see dim lights inside its long, low barns. Abruptly, and without a sign to announce its presence, a small city jumped out of the sodden wheatfields. Burke tried to remember the maps he had seen of the Tula oblast; they showed, as best he could recall, nothing but empty spaces here. He shook his head.

"Nauchny Gorodok," the driver announced.

Two police outposts flanked the road, bearing the initials of the traffic division of the Interior Ministry. But the *militsioneri* on duty had chosen to stay inside and dry. The cab rolled past the checkpoint, unstopped. In the back seat, Burke shook his head. Carelessness offended him, even when he benefited from it.

The town was compact and vertical. Cubic buildings faced with slabs of dull Russian marble surrounded a green central square. Beyond them he could see half a dozen apartment buildings, each about ten stories high.

It was a sign of affluence. In a standard Soviet town, the apartments were no more than five stories high, which meant they didn't have to have elevators. The scientific toilers of Nauchny Gorodok had the privilege of not walking upstairs at the end of the day.

A quarter of a mile from the central square, he could see electric lights outlining the perimeter of a massive cubic building set off by itself. Most likely, he thought, it was a reactor, set cozily close to the town.

Abruptly, the driver stopped. "Kondratieva Street," he announced.

There were only three buildings on the block. Burke counted the seventy-five dollars out and handed them to the cabbie.

"Do you want me to stay?" the cabbie asked.

He had only another twenty-five dollars. He had seen a bus heading toward Tula. He sent the driver on.

The address on the second building matched the one he had copied from Katya's letter. He groaned as he approached the building. It had a numerical code box outside the door. He looked around, hoping to see someone, maybe someone walking a dog, coming up the walk and about to enter the building. There was no one, only a children's playground with a few rusty wooden swings and a carved wooden bear, ghostly in the dim light from the streetlamps.

He gave the door a push and it opened with a sound of metal grating against metal. The coded lock was broken.

So, he soon found, was the elevator. He trudged up the darkened staircase, checking at each landing for Apartment 32. He found it on the sixth floor. A small card on the door said NEKRONOV.

Burke took a moment to stop puffing, then pressed the button near the door, which was padded in black leather. He heard the bell ring behind the door, and after a moment he heard footsteps shuffling toward him.

The woman who opened No. 32 had a puffy, florid face and little pink eyes, framed by badly dyed blonde hair. She wore a housedress and slippers. She looked at him dully.

"Hello," he said. "I'm Colin Burke. I'm a reporter with *America Weekly*. Is Sergei Nekronov home?"

Behind the woman, a sallow-faced little girl, about six years old, her feet bare, wearing a thin cotton dress, padded silently into the hallway and silently took a look at the stranger at the door.

After a moment, the woman shook her head and began to close the door. He got his foot and a knee into it before she could shut it completely.

"You have the wrong apartment," she said.

"Your name is on the door," he reminded her.

"He's not here," the woman said.

"Mind if I wait for him?'

The woman sighed demonstratively and opened the door. She gestured for Burke to enter.

"Please, hang up your coat."

Burke draped the sodden slicker over a red cloth overcoat that hung from a peg in the wall of the little foyer. He slipped off his shoes.

The woman opened a door at the end of the hail. "Seryozha," she said. "A visitor. A journalist. American."

There was a surprised yelp from inside the room.

"Why'd you let him in?" he heard a male ask. The voice sounded a little scratchy.

The woman shrugged. "He wouldn't go away."

The woman seemed less than alarmed by the appearance of a journalist at her door, and Burke wondered how much she knew, or suspected, about Kassim.

He patted the little girl on the head and pushed past the woman into the room at the end of the hall.

Burke walked into a long, narrow room that seemed no wider than a shoebox because of the bookshelves lining three of its four walls. Burke caught a glimpse of books stacked in front of books, of magazines and journals, their bindings frayed, lined up in long rows. He saw the usual Soviet black-and-white vignette photographs of serious, unsmiling parents. A massive, awkward television set jutted out over one shelf.

At the end of the room, at a desk placed before the window, sat a thick-bodied man Burke guessed to be about thirty years old. He wore an open-necked, shapeless beige sport shirt, gray slacks, and black leather slippers. His black hair rose luxuriantly in waves from his forehead and crested a couple of inches above his scalp in a natural pompadour. His hands, clasped in front of him, moved nervously back and forth, gripping and letting go of one another. Burke noticed the sinews in the forearms. The man may have been a scientist, but he had peasant ancestors. As Katya had said, he suffered from blackheads on his face. She had understated it. They looked like manhole covers.

His grip, when he shook Burke's hand, was firm but wet. Burke handed him a business card. He put on thick, wire-rimmed eyeglasses to read it. He did not offer a card in return, nor a place to sit.

Burke sat anyway, on a lumpy red daybed that ran along one of the room's long walls in front of the bookshelf. It was, he guessed, the parents' bed when

Nekronov wasn't working. The little girl probably had the second room.

"Why did you come?" Nekronov said abruptly.

"I'd like to talk to you about a story I'm writing," Burke replied. He tried to make his voice calm, quiet, gentle. Nekronov did not look like a man who wanted to unburden himself. He seemed to be having difficulty looking Burke in the eye. His gaze flitted like a water bug from the window to the business card in front of him, to various spots on the bookshelves.

When he replied, Nekronov sounded like a man with gravel in his throat. "Why—" He stopped and coughed. "—come to me? What story?"

"It's a story about nuclear scientists," Burke said. "You are one?"

"I can't talk about that," Nekronov said. "It's all classified. Against the law." He smiled with his lips—nervously, it seemed to Burke. "I can't talk about my work," he repeated. "I'm afraid you've wasted your time."

Burke frowned. He had anticipated Nekronov's response. He disliked doing what he was about to do. But he pushed the tickle of guilt out of his mind, leaned forward, and lowered his voice.

"Dr. Nekronov," he said, trying to create the impression that what he was about to say was just between the two of them, "I've already talked to someone with whom you've discussed your work."

Nekronov reacted just as Burke had hoped. He swallowed visibly and his face stiffened. "That's a lie," he said. His voice sounded flat and mechanical.

"His name is Rafit Kassim," Burke went on. "I had a long talk with him. According to him, you did discuss your work. And how you could continue it in Syria."

"That's a lie," Nekronov repeated, but feebly.

"Then tell me the truth," Burke said quietly. "I wouldn't want to print a lie, but if you don't talk to me, it might turn out that way."

Nekronov said nothing.

"Look," Burke said, "I saw that health club Kassim runs. I saw the girls there. I could see how enticing someone like, um, Katya, could be."

He saw the blood rush to Nekronov's cheeks, making the blackheads stand out.

"Leave her out of it," Nekronov protested.

"So you do know him," Burke said gently.

In the back of his mind, he was surprised at how comfortable he felt skirting close to blackmail. Maybe it was because of all the politicians who had lied to him at one time or another, knowing that Burke knew they were lying, knowing Burke couldn't prove it, knowing that he would have to report their lies as if he believed them. Now, for once, he had the means to force someone to tell him the truth, and he discovered he had no regrets about using them.

Nekronov jumped up from his chair and walked, rubbing his hands together, across the room. Burke was about to jump up and follow him when Nekronov reached into the hall, grabbed the door, and pulled it shut. Then he returned to the desk and sat down. His face was crimped in a way that made his eyes seem closer together.

"What do you want to know, and when will you publish it?" he asked.

Burke took the second question first. He looked at his watch. In New York, it was noon, Wednesday. "It won't be published for another six days," he said.

He could have mentioned that on Friday when he

sent his file via telephone lines to New York, it would be available to whatever security agencies tapped those lines. But he didn't.

"As to what I want to know, there are a lot of questions. Why don't we start with your age and your birthplace."

"I'm thirty-two," Nekronov said. "I was born in Moscow."

Burke reached into his satchel and pulled out his tape recorder. He had to have tape, and Nekronov might as well see it. He turned it on.

"Your parents?"

"My father and mother were both mathematicians." Suddenly and irrationally, Burke thought of a Jewish friend, Barry Stern, who covered the State Department for the *Washington Tribune*. Whenever he had to fill out an application for a visa to an Arab country, Stern wrote "mathematician" in the blank for religion.

"Russian?" he asked.

Nekronov nodded. "The family comes from Saratov originally."

"Where did you go to school?"

"In Moscow. A special school for mathematics."

"Where is it?"

"On Ulitsa Davidova."

"You did well?"

"I was the gold medalist."

"And you went on to..."

"To Em-Geh-Ooh," Nekronov said, using the initials for Moscow State University.

"How long did you stay there?"

"For eight years. Until I got my candidate's degree in physics."

"And then you came here?"

"Yes."

"When did you marry?"

Nekronov looked pained. "Do you have to mention that?"

"I have to know it."

He sighed. "During my *aspirantura*. She was a lab assistant."

Burke thought about the age of the girl he had seen in the hallway, counted backward, and understood why Nekronov had married. He felt a moment's sympathy for the man, for his wife, and for the daughter. He put it out of his mind and concentrated on the task at hand.

"And what's the name of the institute you worked in here?"

"The Third Institute for the Advanced Study of Physics."

"That's it? Not named for anyone? Just 'The Third'?"

Nekronov snorted lightly. "This is not a town with propaganda pretensions."

"So why did you come here?"

Nekronov shrugged slightly. "I wanted to get my doctorate as fast as I could." In Russian academia, a man could wait ten or twenty years after getting his candidate's degree before finally being awarded the doctorate. It was the rough equivalent of a full professorship. "I got it here after four years. And, of course, they offered me this apartment."

"Where did you live in Moscow?"

"With my parents."

"That must have been crowded."

Nekronov just nodded.

Burke tried to slip the next question in casually.

"And you knew you were going to be working on nuclear weapons?"

"Of course," Nekronov replied.

Burke felt a surge of relief. He was halfway home.

"And how did you feel about that?"

Nekronov's voice took on a defensive, slightly surly edge.

"I felt fine about it. I believed then and I believe now that nuclear weapons keep the peace because they assure that governments understand the insanity of war."

Burke almost cut to a question about Syria, but he decided to stay with the chronological line of questioning.

"And what did you work on here?"

Nekronov sighed. "A project called—I suppose I can tell you, because it has been terminated—Rush Hour."

The Russian words were *chas pik*, and Burke repeated them to make sure he had heard correctly.

"*Chas Pik?*"

Nekronov nodded.

"Why that name?"

Nekronov smiled faintly. "It actually comes from your American terminology."

"I don't understand."

"Well, you know that a strategic missile has a final stage that contains the warheads. And the Americans call it the bus."

"Yes."

"We had—have—a missile called the SS-18."

"And?"

"In its deployed variant it carries ten warheads."

Burke caught on.

"And your project was to try to squeeze more warheads onto the bus?"

The Russian nodded, and a small smile momentarily turned the corners of his mouth upward.

"Catchy code name," Burke said.

"Contrary to the conventional wisdom, the Soviet Union did have a sense of humor," Nekronov replied.

"And does the project still exist?"

"No. It ended two years ago."

"And what have you been doing since?"

Nekronov shrugged. "To be honest, nothing. We go into the office. We plan experiments with equipment we don't have, or that we have but can't fix. We imagine programs and calculations for computers we don't have. And at the end of the month, we take the hundred thousand rubles they give us and think about the food our children won't have."

"A hundred thousand rubles is what you get?" It was the equivalent of about fifty dollars.

Nekronov nodded. "We haven't had a raise in two years."

"How do you survive?" he asked, trying to sound as sympathetic as possible.

Nekronov scowled. "My wife gets a salary as a lab assistant. We have a garden plot in the country where we grow vegetables."

"But no dacha?"

"No."

"A car?"

"Of course not. How could I afford a car?"

Burke decided to see how forthcoming Nekronov would be.

"So what will you buy with your first five hundred thousand dollars?"

Nekronov did not blink.

"I am going to buy insulin for my daughter," he said. "She is diabetic."

Burke glanced down at the tape recorder to make sure it was running. The last exchange would be enough to confirm much of what Katya had told him.

"There's no insulin here for her?"

Nekronov laughed harshly. "No. Unless you can bribe someone. They tell us we will have to control it by feeding her the right foods. But of course, we can't afford the right foods."

"How serious is her condition?"

"Juvenile diabetes, Mr. Burke, is always fatal." Burke sighed, thinking briefly of the girl in the hallway, and his own son, and how it might have felt to see him die young because he couldn't put the right food on the table.

"And her name?"

"Tatiana."

A first paragraph started to form in his mind. It would begin with the diabetic girl and the unavailability of insulin. It would end with a powerful kicker sentence: Her father was going to make bombs for Assad in order to save his daughter's life.

He decided to broach the most delicate part of the interview.

"And can you help me understand the work you'll be doing in Syria?"

Nekronov thought for a moment. "I'm not going to say one way or another where I'm going to be working."

Burke tried again.

"But you are going to be working in Syria?"

Nekronov shook his head. "I'm not saying."

That's all right, Burke thought. Katya did say, and you've confirmed enough details to make her story credible.

"Well, let's take a hypothetical country that might be interested in paying you five hundred thousand dollars a year."

Nekronov said nothing.

"Suppose this country had a great desire to do just what your *Chas Pik* project was working on—to miniaturize nuclear weapons."

Nekronov's face remained aloof.

"What would you tell them if they asked your advice?"

"I would tell them to see if they could make peace with their neighbors some other way."

"And if their neighbors refused?"

Nekronov smiled bleakly, as if to say to Burke, All right, we'll play your stupid little game.

"I might help them."

"How would you start?"

"First of all, what kind of nuclear material does this country possess?"

Burke took a guess. "Plutonium."

Nekronov smiled again. "No. Let's say this country has highly enriched uranium."

"How did they get it?" Burke asked, sensing that Nekronov had engaged.

"Let's say, from a gas diffusion cascade process, separating natural uranium from uranium 235."

"How does the country hide this process?"

"It has been working for a long time. Amassing little bits at a time."

"How much enriched uranium does it take?"

"For a simple weapon of, say, ten kilotons?"

"Yeah. Say ten kilotons." The atomic bomb that destroyed Hiroshima, he remembered reading, was about ten kilotons.

"It depends on the designer. The plans your inspectors found in Iraq called for a bomb that would require perhaps 50 kilograms of highly enriched uranium and would weigh, in total, about 500 kilograms. But an experienced and imaginative designer could do much better."

"How much better?"

Nekronov shrugged. "Say, five kilograms of highly enriched uranium. A total weight of 30 kilograms."

Burke's nostrils flared. It was less than airline baggage limits.

"And how big would it be?"

Nekronov shrugged.

"Perhaps a parallelepiped of two cubic meters."

Burke had only a vague notion of what a parallelepiped was, but he figured he could look it up later.

"And how come you can do this and the Iraqis can't?"

Nekronov flickered his eyebrows and shrugged again.

"How much do you know about the construction of atomic bombs?"

Burke decided to be candid. "Not much."

Nekronov pulled a piece of paper from his desk and began drawing something. In a moment, he turned the paper around and showed it to Burke.

He had drawn four concentric circles.

"Any fission device has four elements. There is a

small central core. A second layer of fissile material. Then a third containment element. In the earliest bombs, this was made of heavy metal—iron, I believe. It was very heavy. Then a final, outer layer of high explosives, which are designed to compress the core."

"Causing an explosion."

Nekronov nodded.

"With experience, you can develop ways to lighten the third and fourth layers by several orders of magnitude."

"How?" Burke was way out of his depth scientifically; but as long as the tape recorder worked, he could quote what Nekronov was saying and let some nerd in New York figure out the right spelling.

"Well, for instance, you can use HMX explosive. You can substitute beryllium for the heavy metal."

Burke nodded, trying to look as if he understood. "HMX," he repeated. "Beryllium."

Nekronov snorted. "I'll bet my first year's salary you don't know what beryllium is."

Burke flushed slightly, then shrugged. "I'll take your word for it."

Nekronov nodded.

"And the result is a fission bomb of ten kilotons that could fit in your average shipping trunk?"

Nekronov nodded again.

Burke shook his head.

"Would it get through airport security?"

Nekronov shook his head. "You're really ignorant! Of course it wouldn't."

Burke flushed and refrained from asking why not. "But of course, this is all hypothetical," Nekronov said, in a changed voice that conveyed trepidation, as if

Burke's question about airport security had made him see his bomb from a different perspective. He seemed, for the first time, troubled by what he and Burke had just been discussing.

"Does, uh, does this hypothetical country have, um, plans—"

Nekronov cut him off. "That's enough," he said sharply. "I'm not answering any more questions."

Burke nodded, trying to seem somber and sympathetic. In fact, he had enough for his story already—a story that would sell magazines, be quoted on the TV news, force everyone else in the Moscow press corps to scramble to catch up, and get that bastard Canfield off his case for good.

God only knew whether Nekronov could actually give the Syrians a bomb and what the consequences might be. God only knew how his story might affect the Israelis and the Arabs. Burke told himself that maybe Nekronov was right. Maybe the prospect of a nuclear exchange would bring everyone in the Middle East back to his senses. Maybe it would, in a perverse way, bring peace.

And maybe not. There were occasions when the journalist's job of witnessing events, rather than controlling them, seemed infinitely inadequate. This was one of them.

"There's only one more thing I need," he said.

"What's that?"

"Some pictures."

Nekronov blanched. "No. Absolutely not!"

"Well, um, you know, they wouldn't be published until the story is—" he began.

"Yes, and then every Mossad agent in the world

would start using them for target practice," Nekronov retorted. "I won't allow it. You understand?"

Burke understood.

"Okay," he said. "We'll do without photos."

He studied Nekronov's face, trying to memorize every detail. *America Weekly* had good artists.

CHAPTER TEN

BY FOUR O'CLOCK THE NEXT AFTERNOON, Burke had written the bulk of his file. He had even managed to look up beryllium in the Great Soviet Encyclopedia. It was a hard, rare metal, much lighter than iron. It would make just the kind of convincing detail that his editors loved.

As he stored the file on his hard disk, he changed his name, calling it "COUP.891," and putting it in an old directory with the files of his predecessor. If someone got into his office and searched for the story before he published it, the false name might throw them off, at least for a while. He had no illusions about his ability to foil a determined effort by the Ministry of Security to find whatever it wanted. But if he made things difficult, he might thwart a sloppy effort. The security people, like most other Russian institutions, suffered from sloppy efforts.

With that in mind, he decided not to call New York from his office phone. He knew that all international calls were tapped. But if he called from a public phone, it might take the tappers a day or two longer to figure out who was talking and about what. That would be all the time he needed. He told Olga he was leaving on an errand and walked outside to the car.

Baboye leto, or old woman's summer, had arrived in Moscow. The sky was a clear blue, and the descending sun still warmed the air. The weather further exhilarated Burke; and he punched the gas pedal and got the Volvo up to nearly sixty, slaloming around the lumbering trucks, as he drove around the Ring Road toward the Kiev station and up to the Slavyanskaya Hotel on the banks of the Moscow River. It was one of the post-*perestroika* hotels in Moscow, built for the businessmen who flocked to town thinking of the profits to be made drilling for Russian oil with workers paid the equivalent of a hundred dollars a month.

A Russian boy in a gray suit, his blond hair falling in a cowlick over his pale forehead, opened the front door as Burke walked up.

"Good afternoon, sir," the kid said in English. The Radisson people had hired and trained the staff at the Slavyanskaya for a joint venture. Their first requirement was that no one who had ever worked in a Soviet hotel would be allowed to work there. As a result, the staff was, at least for the moment, courteous and helpful.

Burke nodded and came very close to tipping him.

He walked into the lobby, which was wide and marbled and cold despite the woven rugs on the floors. Near the bar, a string trio had just begun to play something Burke thought was by Vivaldi. A few men in suits were sitting at low tables, their briefcases on their laps, starting the cocktail hour.

Burke walked past the bar to a corner of the lobby where there was an international pay phone. Just ahead of him, a gray-haired man in a crisply cut blue pinstriped suit got to the phone first. He picked it up and pushed a credit card through the phone's pay slot. In a moment he began talking in rapid Italian.

Normally Burke hated waiting in line for anything, but this time he found it tolerable. After a few minutes the Italian looked at him, shrugged helplessly, and conveyed in pantomime that the incompetents in the home office would not be letting him go soon. Burke smiled amiably, went to the bar, and bought a vodka on the rocks. He sat down in one of the overstuffed chairs close to the pay phone, listened to the cello and the violin chase each other over the scales, and swallowed his drink. He relished the burn as it went down.

The Italian gave up the phone, and Burke made his call. He listened to the little beeps of satellite channels making connections and then heard Gen Owen's cheerful hello. It sounded warm and pleasant, and he wondered for a moment if she was married. Maybe he would see her on his next obligatory visit to the home office.

She patched him through to Canfield, and for once he did not have to wait for the foreign editor to pick up the phone. They exchanged the minimal courtesies.

"So what've you got?" Canfield demanded.

"Good stuff, Chris," Burke said. He reminded himself not to oversell it on the phone. Let them read the piece and be favorably surprised.

"Cover stuff?"

"Yeah, I think so."

"You found us a scientist?" Canfield's tone perked up from arrogantly disinterested to arrogantly interested.

"Yeah, I did."

"Good." The voice sounded perilously close to enthusiastic, and Canfield reined it in. "What's his name?"

"I don't want to go into it over the phone, Chris," Burke said. "I'll explain why later on."

"Of course," Canfield replied quickly. Burke had never met a desk editor who didn't love being in on something that smacked of cloaks and daggers. "Let me get Lorraine and Chuck in on this. Hang on."

He heard more pings for a moment, then a couple of new voices that sounded as if they were coming from under water. No doubt they were using a speakerphone. Chuck Wooten was *America Weekly*'s executive editor, a step above Canfield in the magazine's food chain. Lorraine Ginsburg was the art editor. She had once asked Burke to have the Russian Defense Ministry fax her an internal diagram for an old nuclear-powered Soviet espionage satellite that was falling from orbit. For the hell of it, he had called the Ministry of Defense and asked. As he had expected, they'd laughed at him.

"Hello Colin, how's the weather there?" Wooten said. He always asked Moscow correspondents about the weather. He always asked Paris correspondents about the food. He had a fairly primitive understanding of the world.

"Fine, Chuck," Burke said.

Again, he recounted the brief and censored version of what he had turned up.

"We can't talk about the name of the guy over the phones," Canfield explained to Wooten, like an old Moscow hand. "You understand."

"Of course," Wooten agreed. He had the same kind of background as Canfield.

"You took photos, Colin?" Ginsburg's voice.

Burke sighed. He had a fleeting urge to tell her that he had, but his dog ate the film.

"No, I didn't," he said. "He wouldn't let me. He's scared that if his picture comes out, he's gonna be a target. I'll give you a description and we can have a drawing or two done, okay?"

"I don't know, Chuck," Ginsburg said. Her voice sounded whining. "We need to have photos. A story like this doesn't look authentic with drawings."

"Maybe, but the guy just absolutely refused," Burke argued.

"Lots of people refuse the first time you ask them," Ginsburg countered.

"Um," Wooten said. Burke could imagine his calculations. If he backed Burke, he would have to put up with Ginsburg's whining for at least a week. If he backed Ginsburg, Burke would hang up the phone, do his best, and be out of his hair.

Canfield must have been making the same calculations.

"We still have twenty-four hours before photo deadline," he interjected. "Go back to the guy, Colin, and talk him into it. Hang around outside his apartment if you have to. Take him when he goes out for groceries."

"But—" Burke started, intending to explain that the scientist lived in a closed, secret city, where an American journalist hanging around in the street with a camera might attract unwanted attention.

He stopped himself. Talking about the town would add one too many clues to what the eavesdroppers would know. He could make up his own mind whether to go. If he decided not to, how would anyone in New York find out?

Besides, he wouldn't want anyone to think he wasn't ready to fall on his sword for the company.

"I agree with Lorraine and Chris," Wooten said. "Assuming you can get your file done on time."

"Sure. Okay," Burke said.

"Great," Wooten replied. He sounded, through the speakerphone and the satellite, like a diver coming up for air.

When Wooten, Ginsburg, and Canfield had all rung off with the usual feigned bonhomie, Gen Owen got back on the line.

"A message for you from a researcher in the library, dear," she said. "Shall I read it to you or send it to the office?"

"Please, read it," Burke said. Gen Owen was the one person at *America Weekly* with whom he felt like being polite.

"It says: 'Stanford refuses to release student records, citing privacy laws. Yearbooks for middle 70s unshow a Rafit Kassim. Glad to pursue further if you can supply a lead.'"

"Oh," Burke said.

"Well, I hope it's helpful," Gen said, sounding slightly offended.

"I don't know. But thanks. And thank the library," Burke said. "And ask them to look up one more thing?"

"Certainly. What?"

"When did Willie McCovey play for the San Francisco Giants?"

"Pardon me?"

He spelled the name for her, assured her he was not joking, and hung up.

Brooding, Burke went back to his chair and drained the remains of his drink with a long, preoccupied swallow. The flavor of a few moments ago had turned sour on his tongue as he wondered whether he could get out of another trip to Tula. He would have a better chance at getting arrested than getting a picture.

On the other hand, as long as he cashed their paychecks, they had a right to send him wherever they wanted. It was a question of professionalism.

As he contemplated the prospect of another drink, the string trio switched from Vivaldi to something bouncy by Strauss; it grated on his ears.

The next morning he did what he could to make sure no one was following him.

From his office, wearing his pseudo-Russian clothes, he took the Metro to the end of the line, a station called Schelkovskaya. By the time the train arrived there, only four people were left in his car. Two were old women, and one man seemed drunk. He watched the conductor rouse the drunk and throw him, stumbling, off the train and onto the platform. The old women walked slowly to the escalator at the end of the platform. The fourth passenger was gone.

He was, as far as he could tell, alone. But what did he know?

If they were pros, and they wanted to devote enough people to it, they could follow him without letting him be aware of it.

He caught the train heading back to the Kursk station. He got out and joined a stream of people walking through a long plaster tunnel toward the escalator that led up to the out-of-town trains. He passed a couple of tables. At one, a boy with a bright, clean face and long, greasy hair sold religious art and pinup calendars, side by side. For a moment, one of the pinup models reminded Burke of Katya, and he slowed down to look more carefully. No, this model's breasts were definitely bigger. Farther along the wall, a couple of kids, one with a trombone, another with a drum, did a fair rendition of "You Are the Sunshine of My Life."

Burke dropped a few rubles onto the plush green velvet of their instrument case.

As he did, he looked backward. Someone in the crowd, he thought, stopped abruptly to inspect the pinup calendars. He began to wonder whether he was being followed again.

The likelihood, he decided, was that someone would be tailing him, someone good enough to stay behind him, get on his train, and follow him all the way to Nekronov's apartment. Evron's people no doubt had agents all over Tula already. They would not lose him if they knew that was his destination.

Abruptly, he reversed his path and went back to the platform he had just left. A train was just filling up.

"Careful, the doors are closing," a gravelly speaker in the train intoned.

He ran the last three strides, stuck out an arm, and managed to get it between the closing doors. After a second, they popped open again, and he squeezed into the train.

He let the stations roll past as he thought about

how to get to Tula. It was too likely that someone would be watching for him at Kursk station and too easy for someone to follow him on the train. If he tried to drive, the foreign correspondent's license plates on his Volvo would give him away before he got out of Moscow. He wouldn't last five minutes in Nauchny Gorodok.

He would have to find a Russian to drive him. Mentally, he went down the list of friends and acquaintances who had cars. He might be caught. The worst that could happen to him was expulsion. But he wouldn't want any of them blamed as an accessory. They might get jail.

It would have to be someone with something important to gain to make the trip worth the risk.

He got out at the station that he still thought of as Prospekt Marx, though the signs now said Okhotny Ryad, and rode the escalators up to the level just below the street, where there was a bank of pay phones. He fished a coin from his pocket and dialed Pavel Plotnikov's number at *Nyezavisirnaya Gazeta*.

The phone, for once, worked properly. A male voice answered the phone, and typically, said only "Hello."

Burke pressed his free hand up against his ear, trying to block out the droning of the trains in the tunnels below.

"Is this *Nyezavisimaya Gazeta*?'

"Yes."

"Pavel Plotnikov?"

"Just a minute."

Plotnikov got on the line.

"Pavel, it's Colin Burke."

"Hello, Colin!" Plotnikov sounded delighted to hear from him. "When we are going to play poker again?"

That explained his delight. Burke hoped he would not see the night when Plotnikov's carefully hoarded stash of hard currency vanished, bucking a full house with a flush.

"Soon, Pavel," he said. "You interested in chasing a good story?"

"Certainly. What it is?"

"I'll tell you later. You have a car?"

"I can get car."

"Good. How soon?"

"Wait, please. I will ask." Burke heard the phone clunk against a table. A minute went by, and he started to worry that an operator would come on and demand more kopecks. Then he heard Plotnikov pick up the receiver again.

"Colin, good news. One of our cars is available. You need it now?"

"Right away."

"Okay. Where I will meet you?"

Burke figured out the route. "On the out-of-town side of the Yugo-Zapadnaya Metro station in fifteen minutes."

"Okay."

Burke hung up, bought a copy of *Izvestiya* from a vendor, and spent ten minutes reading it. Ukraine and Kazakhstan were balking at giving up the last of their strategic missiles, which probably no longer worked anyway. The Russian cabinet was beginning yet another reorganization. The World Bank had not received enough funds to finance this year's loan programs. There was a wire service account of the aftermath of the Israeli raid. Assad, it said, was demanding reparations from Israel before Syria would return to the talks.

Saddam Hussein and Muammar Qaddafi were calling for an Arab summit, threatening anyone who would dare make peace with the Zionists. Burke felt his stomach twist and tighten.

He got onto the train and started the twenty-minute ride to Yugo-Zapadnaya. He wanted Plotnikov to be waiting when he got off the train. He didn't want to be so late that Plotnikov would give up and leave.

The sun, hidden behind a mass of gray clouds again, had reached its apogee by the time he emerged on the dusty stone steps leading up from the station. He stood on the sidewalk for a minute, trying to spot Plotnikov's gawky neck and stringy hair behind the wheel of one of the cars parked along the curb. Then he saw an old, pale-green Zhiguli, its fenders and windshield caked with brown dirt, start moving slowly toward him. He stepped to the curb and peered inside. Plotnikov opened the door, Burke got in, and they pulled away. The Zhiguli's engine sounded as if a few bolts were loose, and the plastic of the dashboard had a deep crack above the glove compartment. But the car rattled along. Burke peered out the rear window. No one, as far as he could tell, had followed them.

"Thanks for coming," Burke said.

"You are welcome. So where we are going?" Plotnikov responded. He was wearing brown polyester trousers and a blue striped sport shirt, open at the collar. For driving purposes, Burke supposed, he had put on a pair of wire-rimmed eyeglasses.

"Tula," Burke said, feeling guilty at not telling the whole truth.

"Why?"

"I'll tell you when we get there, okay?"

Plotnikov smiled and nodded. The reporting business, Burke assumed, amused him a lot more than solving mathematics problems.

They passed the police checkpoint on the road south out of Moscow. A short time later, they came to a long downhill stretch of road. Plotnikov switched off the engine and let the car coast.

"How much gas have you got, Pavel?"

Plotnikov smiled and said, "Almost ten liters. About enough. No problem."

"We're going to need gas."

"We will find it! No problem!"

"Shit," Burke said. He knew the chances of finding something you had to have in Russia, when you had to have it. About one in ten.

Burke looked back. The road behind them was empty. If they ran out of gas, at least they would do it without being observed.

He peered through the grime on the side window at the muddy brown fields passing by. Once in a while he saw an old man or a couple of women, out gathering some late crops. One of them, a stooped old man in black, carried a long-handled scythe over his shoulder as he trudged toward a cluster of cottages on the barren, wet horizon. A pleasant image, Burke thought.

Plotnikov gently began questioning him again. "Why Tula?"

There was, Burke decided, no further reason to keep quiet.

"I'm not actually going to Tula," he said. "I'm going to a place outside Tula called Nauchny Gorodok."

"I have heard of it," Pavel nodded.

"How?"

The Russian shrugged. "In math department, you heard about that kind of thing. But not details."

"Well, they did nuclear bomb designs there. It's probably still off limits, so if you don't want to go all the way, I can go the last bit in a cab," Burke said.

"This is about that? Nuclear bombs?"

"And bomb designers."

"Anyone particular?"

"Yes. I talked to a guy who's been recruited. He's going to Syria."

Plotnikov whistled. "What you call big exclusive, huh?"

Burke nodded, a trifle pleased by the Russian's reaction.

"Real big exclusive."

Plotnikov mulled this over for a minute, and then turned to Burke again.

"So why you are going back?"

Burke sighed. "Pictures. The guy wouldn't let me photograph him. The New York office says they can't do without photographs. So I've got to go back and get one, somehow. It pisses me off, but..."

"So why you are doing it?"

Burke sighed. "A matter of principle. If you work for somebody, and you're a professional about it, you go where they tell you and try to do the assignment they give you. But it still..."

"Pisses you off?"

"Yeah."

Plotnikov nodded sagely. "Editors," he said, "can be such *duraki.*"

The Russian word meant "fool," but it carried multilayered connotations of innocence and bumbling.

"*Duraki,*" Burke agreed.

"One thing," Burke added. "I told this guy the piece wouldn't be published till next week. You have to protect me on that. You can use it the same day—Monday. There's some risk in it for you, Pavel. I asked you to help me because I think the story will be worth it to you."

Plotnikov nodded in agreement.

He saw a sign with a fuel pump on it, and they slowed down. The station appeared on the right side of the road, with two cars lined up at the pumps. They drove in.

The cars were empty. So was the station.

"I guess those people decided to leave their cars until petrol comes," Plotnikov said. "Better than running out on road."

"Which is what we're going to do," Burke said. "Isn't it?"

Plotnikov smiled and drummed his fingers on the steering wheel. "No problem."

❀ ❀ ❀

The Russian switched off the engine and coasted downhill into a village called Pyanovo, about fifteen kilometers north of Tula. At the bottom of the hill he tried to restart the car. The engine cranked and whined, but refused to start.

"Out of gas?"

Plotnikov nodded grimly.

Burke scowled and struggled to refrain from losing his temper. Instead, he smacked the dashboard.

"Afraid we are stuck," Plotnikov said apologetically.

"Well, there must be someone with gas in this damn place," Burke replied. "Let's fmd him."

Pyanovo consisted of about fifteen cottages, some painted green, some weathered to a dilapidated gray, overshadowed by bare, spiky linden trees, their black bark still damp from a morning rain. The village smelled of manure. Burke saw no cars. Grunting, he pushed the car to the side of the road as Plotnikov steered.

Burke picked the most prosperous-looking place, a cottage with blue paint on the gingerbread trim over the lintels and a couple of fat hens pecking in the grass beside the road. He ducked under the low porch roof at the side of the cottage and banged on the door. He glanced back at Plotnikov, still standing in the road by the car. Plotnikov's body moved into motion one limb at a time, and he shambled up to join Burke on the porch.

No one answered the door. Burke walked around to the back of the house, weaving around mud puddles, Plotnikov behind him.

The back was a fenced acre or two with an outhouse, a small barn, a bathhouse, and a couple of chicken coops. A pigsty, thick with black mud, adjoined the barn, with a couple of piebald sows rooting around for food.

"Hello!" Burke shouted, and in a moment, he heard an "Allo!" in return.

A short, lumpy woman wearing black rubber boots, a blue dress, and a flowered kerchief ambled out from behind the barn with a bucket in her hand. Deftly, she tossed the last grain in the bucket into the pigsty and waved at the same time. Burke waved back.

"Good day," she said, very formally, as she walked up. She smiled and her round face split open to show three gold incisors.

Burke looked at Plotnikov, willing him to speak and handle the negotiations. After a second of awkward silence, the Russian cleared his throat and began.

"We've, uh, run out of gas," he said. "Do you have any?"

The woman snorted. "Huh. No one here has a car."

Plotnikov nodded and turned inquiringly to Burke.

Burke decided he had to speak up himself, even though his accent would stamp him a foreigner if his clothes hadn't already done so.

"Any tractors or trucks?"

The woman's eyes narrowed. "Where are you from?"

"Moscow," Burke said. "I'm a journalist."

The tension he had been feeling intensified. The appearance of a foreign journalist in Pyanovo would be enough to send the woman running to all her neighbors. One of them would have a phone. It might take only a few hours for the local police to learn about his presence.

"Journalist!" The woman seemed impressed. "What paper?"

"*America Weekly*," Burke said. It would be futile to lie.

"America! You sound Swedish!" the woman fairly cackled.

"Thanks," Burke muttered. "Is there a truck?"

"Nikolai Andreevich," the woman said. She pointed down the road toward Tula. "Last house on the left."

Nikolai Andreevich's house proved to be almost identical, save for peeling yellow paint around the windows.

They walked around the house, Burke striding

ahead and Plotnikov tagging along. Parked behind the house, out of sight of the road, was an old, rusty flatbed truck. Its dented cab was a faded blue.

"I am not sure this is good idea, Colin," Ploinikov said with a whining edge in his voice.

Burke began to think he had been mistaken about Plotnikov. He was too much the Russian, too much the scholar to make a good journalist.

They heard a creak from rusty hinges, and Nikolai Andreevich emerged from the outhouse, struggling to pull his zipper up. He arranged his black, muddy trousers satisfactorily and confronted his visitors. He was about sixty, with rheumy eyes and a three-day gray stubble.

Realizing that Plotnikov would not do the talking for him, Burke introduced himself and responded affirmatively to the farmer's query about his being a foreigner.

"I don't know," he said, dubiously, when Burke told him they wanted to go to Tula. "I've got a lot of work."

"I'll pay you for the gas," Burke said. "But I only have dollars. Didn't have a chance to go to the bank to get rubles."

At the mention of dollars, Nikolai Andreevich's doubts changed instantly to enthusiasm.

"Let's go," he said. He grinned, showing four brown tooth shanks and a few large gaps.

Nikolai Andreevich swung a long leg up onto the fender, opened the door, and climbed in. The starter turned over fruitlessly for about a minute, and the battery's strength started to ebb. Then it caught, and he gunned the engine. Crankily, one at a time, all the cylinders joined in and began to roar.

Burke found a foothold near the fender and

climbed in. Plotnikov joined him and they crowded, haunch by haunch, next to Nikolai Andreevich. The truck might have been a relic of the Lend-Lease operation from World War II. At the least, it was a knockoff of a Ford or Chevy sent to help the Russians fight the Nazis. The cab had been stripped bare down to the sheet metal, and the seat had a spring sticking out of it. Burke squirmed to find a position that didn't threaten to impale him.

The entire cabin vibrated and roared with engine noise. Burke's head slammed painfully against the roof of the cab as they hit a series of ruts and bounced toward the pavement. It was going to be a rough ride to Tula. But at least they would get there.

"So you're a foreign correspondent," Nikolai Andreevich shouted over the engine noise.

Burke nodded.

"It must be interesting. I bet you get to meet presidents and movie stars all the time."

The broken spring found Burke's rear and jabbed through his pants.

"You're right," he shouted back to the farmer. "It's glamorous as hell."

The trees along the road were casting long shadows toward the east as they clattered out of Tula toward Nauchny Gorodok. All three had given up trying to converse over the roar of the engine. Burke occasionally glanced backward through the grimy window of the cab. He saw only tractors and trucks. Ahead of them, almost as suddenly as the first time he had seen it, the white

apartment blocks and the massive cubic reactor building sprouted from the fields.

He held his breath as they approached the police
post on the road into the closed city. This time, with no
rain coming down, the *militsioneri* paid more attention to
their duties. One of them, brandishing a black-and-
white baton, stood by the side of the road, checking
vehicles. Burke looked quickly at his lap. His hands and
trousers were smudged with mud from pushing the
Zhiguli. If ever he looked Russian, this was the time.

Nikolai Andreevich blithely rolled down the window, slowed down, and stopped. The cop approached,
gave the perfunctory salute that had been every Russian
citizen's due since 1917, and requested the driver's documents.

Nikolai Andreevich passed them out. The *militsioner*
looked quickly at them.

"Just on our way to buy some feed," Nikolai
Andreevich explained.

The cop took a casual, bored look at Burke and
Photnikov. They nodded amiably. The cop waved them
through.

Burke shook his head. He could not help feeling
something akin to sadness at witnessing a once-efficient
organization's decline and decay. Even the Russian
police.

He asked Nikolai Andreevich to drop them off a
couple of blocks from Nekronov's building. There was
no point in letting the farmer know exactly where they
were going.

The afternoon had grown cold in the hour they had
spent in the truck. He pulled his coat up over his collar
and stuck his hands in his pockets.

Plotnikov touched Burke's arm. "I think I should call office and tell where I left car. If they can find some petrol, they can send someone down for it."

Burke sighed. Time was slipping away. But he understood Plomikov's concern. A working car, even a beat-up old Zhiguli, was nothing to take for granted.

"Okay," he said. "If you can find a phone. But I can't wait for you."

"Understood," Plotnikov grinned. He loped off to the left. Burke turned right.

He walked around the corner onto Kondratieva Street past a children's playground that featured a little wooden village with a couple of varnished cottages, a carved bear, and a carved wolf. A lone *babushka* sat on a bench, watching three or four children play quietly. He caught sight of a little girl flitting into one of the cottages and he stopped short. It looked like Sergei Nekronov's daughter, the diabetic.

Saying nothing, Burke veered off the sidewalk and walked up to the toy cottage. His feet snapped a twig, and the little girl turned and stared at him, motionless for a moment, like a deer caught in somebody's headlights.

He dredged her name up from his notebook.

"Tatiana," he said, gently. "Remember me?"

The sallow-faced little girl nodded slowly.

"I visited your father. I wonder if you'd mind if I took your picture?"

He sounded to himself a bit like Peter Lorre playing the playground pervert. Before the girl could decide what to reply, Burke reached down to open his shoulder bag and extract his camera.

Quickly, he checked the f-stop. He checked the

shutter speed. He glanced over his shoulder to make sure he knew where the sun was. He checked the girl's face for shadows. He squeezed the shutter.

As he did, he felt a sudden movement on his right; and a heavy, thick-fingered hand came down in front of the lens, jamming the camera into Burke's nose. Burke's head jerked backward. He blinked and dropped the camera.

By the time he opened his eyes and snatched the camera from the ground the *babushka* from the park bench was hustling Tatiana away, dragging the little girl by the arm so fast that her legs pawed and stumbled in the dust, trying to keep up with the old woman.

Burke sprinted after them, worried as he did so that he was attracting attention.

The old woman scuttled along faster toward the entrance to the building next to Nekronov's. Burke caught them at the door.

"Sorry," he said, whispering urgently to the old woman. "I didn't mean to frighten you. I just wanted to take Tatiana's picture."

"*Nyet*," the old woman muttered fiercely. She tried to shoulder past Burke and into the building. The hallway, with its light bulb inevitably missing, would be too dark for pictures.

Burke sidestepped, keeping in front of the old woman. He saw no one on the sidewalk. "Not you," he said to her. "Just Tatiana."

"She's not Tatiana!" the old woman nearly screeched. She shoved past Burke and into the building, still dragging the girl. Burke followed a step or two and then, puzzled, halted.

Why were they going into a different building?

Who was the old woman? Why would she deny Tatiana's name?

Older Russians, he thought, carefully guarded their paranoia.

He turned back toward the street and saw Plotnikov coming up the sidewalk toward him. Discreetly, Burke waved and waited.

Burke checked the building number carefully. He had first visited this block in darkness, but he could not have mistaken the placement of the three buildings on Kondratieva Street. Nekronov lived in the middle one.

"It's the next building, I'm almost positive," he said to Plotnikov. Together, they walked down the sidewalk.

Three cars, tires squealing, roared down Kondratieva Street from the opposite direction and skidded to a stop, with a great clashing of rusty brake drums, next to the two reporters.

Now Burke felt like a deer in the headlights. His brain and his reflexes seemed to function a couple of beats slower than everything and everyone in front of him. By the time he realized the cars were after him, the men inside were already jumping out, leaving the doors hanging open. By the time he had noticed that a couple of them wore the black leather jackets common to the old KGB, their footsteps were pounding on the ground by the road, kicking up dust. And by the time it occurred to him to run, they had already surrounded him.

Scowling, he submitted. Next to him, Plotnikov, pale and trembling, did the same.

Burke felt a painful guilt begin to throb in his conscience, not because he had broken any laws worth keeping, but because he had sucked Plotnikov into trouble.

Thick, strong hands grabbed him behind each elbow. A third hand grabbed his camera. One of the black leather jackets flashed a wallet in front of his face, opened it for a millisecond, and said something quick and unintelligible. The wallet snapped shut.

Burke assumed that the man in black leather had identified himself as an arm of the law and notified him of his rights.

"Documents!" the black leather jacket demanded.

Burke pulled his right arm free and silently extracted his press accreditation card from his wallet. He handed it to the man. He felt a sudden wave of nausea and tried to stifle it. He reminded himself that he had been arrested before, back in the bad old days. He had survived. He willed himself to stay detached, to observe, to remember in case he had a chance to write about this experience. The man in black leather, he noticed, had incongruously wide brown eyes.

The brown eyes scanned the accreditation card, checked the photograph against the face in front of them, and stuffed the card into a shirt pocket. The strong hands began to propel Burke from behind, toward the largest of the three waiting cars, a white Volga sedan.

He saw Plotnikov, to his left, being pushed in the same direction, toward one of the smaller cars.

A rear door opened and he was pushed into the middle of the back seat, firmly but not roughly. Two burly men got in on either side of him. The black leather jacket got into the front seat, and a fourth man took the wheel. The car roared off, fishtailing slightly. He got a glimpse of an old man standing toothless and slack-jawed in front of Nekronov's building. Burke glanced at his watch. He couldn't tell with certainty, but he estimated that no more than a minute had elapsed since he saw the cars speeding toward him on Kondratieva Street.

Two or three of the men started shouting questions to him at once. They alternated languages, trying English first, then Russian. Even the driver, pushing the car past sixty miles an hour, turned around to get his face into Burke's and demanded to know what he was doing in a closed area.

Burke sat, his arms folded. He tried to assess the gravity of the situation.

On the one hand, they had caught him in a clear violation of the law. There was no way he could plausibly say he had wandered unwittingly into Nauchny Gorodok.

On the other hand, he remembered, he had no notes or tape recordings with him that would identify Sergei Nekronov. These cops, at least, would have no way of knowing exactly what he had been after. Of course, once they notified their superiors in Moscow, they'd search his office. He wondered how long it would take them to find the computer file with his story.

But that was something to worry about later. Now, he had to concentrate on getting these cops to take him back to Moscow.

The car jerked suddenly to a halt in front of a two-story beige brick building with a pair of blue-and-yellow *militsia* cars out front. The pair in the back seat hustled Burke inside. He got a fleeting look at a desk with a bored potbellied cop sitting behind it before they prodded him down a long corridor lined with dank, dark holding cells. The prisoners inside looked pale and wasted; they peered out at him with wide, desperate eyes. He thought they needed something: a drink maybe.

At the end of the corridor, they entered a stairwell and walked up one flight. He found himself in a long, narrow room filled with the kind of cheap wooden desks that fill college lecture halls. A table and a podium were at the front of the room on a raised platform under a woodcut portrait of Lenin. It was a lecture room of some kind. Burke looked around for Plotnikov. He'd apparently been taken somewhere else.

Inside the room, the tone of his captivity abruptly changed.

"Please, sit down, Mr. Burke," said the black leather jacket in his best English. He pulled a package of Marlboros out of his coat. "Cigarette?"

Burke shook his head.

"You will please empty your pockets." Burke did, putting his wallet and passport and a handful of coins on the table. When he was finished, the black leather jacket motioned for him to stand up, then patted him down.

"Please, it is a necessity that you surrender to us your bag," the jacket said.

Burke handed the bag over. For about twenty minutes, the four plainclothesmen went meticulously over everything in the bag. They examined each blank sheet in the fresh notebook he'd bought. They read all of the receipts stuffed into the back of his wallet. They held his credit cards up to the light, looking for slits where he might have hidden something. Burke had an impression of great curiosity. They wanted to see what an American carried around with him.

For a moment, he felt curiously passive and detached. They had the initiative. He had no choice but to watch and see how they would use it. They had taken the burden of action from him.

They paid special attention to the camera and the rolls of film he'd brought with it. One of the plain-clothesmen laboriously figured out how to rewind the film inside the camera and clumsily extracted it. All of the film went into the side pocket of the black leather coat. He wondered what they would think when they saw the photo of the old *babushka*'s hand coming toward his lens.

That thought blew away his passivity and started his mind darting fearfully from corner to corner of the pictures in his memory. Why had the little girl been with the *babushka* instead of her parents? Why had she gone into a different building? And why had the old woman so desperately stopped him from taking her picture?

And why had the *militsia* appeared so suddenly after Pavel Plotnikov called his office?

CHAPTER ELEVEN

ABRUPTLY, THE FOUR MEN finished their search. The one with the brown eyes handed Burke's wallet back to him.

"Please, wait here," he said. They left, taking the film with them.

After five minutes, Burke got up and tried the door. To his surprise, it was not locked. He opened it and peered down the hallway. It was empty. Downstairs, he could hear the quiet sounds of routine activity—footfalls and murmurs. Briefly, he considered looking for a back door and walking out.

But they were, for some reason, treating him carefully and gently. His chances, he decided, would be better if he waited.

He examined the room more carefully. There was a bookcase against one wall. Over it hung half a dozen faded red satin banners with portraits of Lenin embroidered on them in gold thread, awards won long ago. One shelf held framed photographs of uniformed *milit-sioneri* standing in crisp rows and staring solemnly at the camera. Training classes at their graduations, probably. The books on the shelf also seemed to be relics of another era. He picked out one called *A Leninist Theory of Criminality*. He opened it. The first chapter was called "Property: The Basis for All Crime." He turned to the copyright page: 1986.

It reminded him of how close he was, in time and attitudes, to the era when his being arrested in Nauchny Gorodok would be the beginning of a major international incident. But nowadays they could not, he told himself, prosecute him for espionage. Not now, not with the Cold War over. It was at least a hundred-to-one shot. He told himself.

He heard footsteps coming down the corridor. He put the book back in its place and turned to the door. It opened and a new face entered over a well-cut blue suit. The man was probably in his late thirties. He was good-looking, with a trim waist, wide shoulders, and short, sandy hair.

"I'm Colonel Makarov of the Russian Ministry of Internal Affairs," he said. "You're Mr. Burke?'

Briefly, Burke considered saying no. But, as his father had told him more than once, there was no point in being a wise guy.

"Unfortunately, yes," he said, extending his hand.

"Oh, don't worry, Mr. Burke. We're sure this was just a misunderstanding. I've come to bring you back to Moscow," Makarov said. He was almost unctuously pleasant.

Burke was too surprised to ask why they were letting him off so easily. "Let's go," he nodded.

A guard stepped into the room, carrying some handcuffs. Makarov waved him off, like a rich man dismissing something proffered by a servant.

Makarov led the way down the stairs and past the cells, with Burke following. The inmates who were awake peered at them, and a couple of them started yelling about the food and the lice.

At the entrance, the man in black leather offered his hand. A little reluctantly, Burke shook it. Civil treatment for foreigners was one thing. This was beginning to feel too civil, and it aroused some doubts in his mind. They probably intended in Moscow to slap his wrist and let him go with a warning. That was no reason to treat him like a rich investor checking out sites for a computer factory. Why were they doing it?

The black leather jacket gave a thick brown envelope to Makarov, who put it under his arm. They walked outside to a black Volga sedan. It was dark.

"What time is it?" Burke asked.

"About seven P.M.," Makarov answered.

The Russian opened the back door and gestured for Burke to get in. A driver had the Volga's engine running. Makarov got into the front seat next to him. In seconds, a police car with two blue lights flashing on the roof pulled in front of them, and the small convoy headed north at about a hundred kilometers an hour.

He watched the shadows of trees and occasional low village buildings flit past as the car sped by. The lights on the police car pushed aside the few trucks and cars on the road at that hour. Before nine, they were in Moscow, rolling past the low brick factory buildings and hulking apartment blocks on Varshavskoye Shosse. Along the sidewalks, late-shift workers trudged alone, away from the occasional red neon M's that signified subway stations. The car veered off down the Garden Ring Road at Taganka Square and rolled smoothly to a stop at the Foreign Press Center.

Makarov escorted him into the lobby. A sleepy *militsioner*, standing guard on the night shift, jerked to attention and saluted when he saw Makarov's identity card. Makarov gravely opened the manila envelope and produced Burke's watch, passport, wallet, and the handful of kopecks he had been carrying. Burke stuffed them all into his coat pocket.

"Am I free to go?" he asked.

Makarov smiled slightly. "Technically, yes. But you are requested to have a talk with Mr. Grishin. Upstairs."

They crowded into the little elevator on the mezzanine overlooking the lobby, and Makarov punched five. They emerged into a dark, empty corridor. Toward the end of it, light spilled from a single open doorway.

The first face Burke saw upon going through that door was that of J. Porter McIntire, the press attaché at the American Embassy. McIntire, leaning against a secretarial desk, wore his usual Harris tweed sport coat, gray slacks, and Ben Franklin eyeglasses perched on the end of his nose. He looked tired and annoyed to be working so late. When they shook hands, Burke felt slightly unclean.

"Well, Colin," McIntire greeted him. "What have you gotten yourself into this time?"

"Not sure," Burke said. "I think Grishin is going to tell me. He called you?"

McIntire nodded.

Vasily Grishin stepped into the room from an inner office, wearing a double-breasted blue suit cut identically to the gray one he'd had on at Saturday's briefmg. His face had a look of detached amusement, as if Burke were part of an interesting subspecies that had just exhibited some primitive and unintentionally humorous behavior.

"Ah, Mr. Burke," he said. "How pleasant to see you at such an unexpected time. Mr. McIntire. Nice to see you again as well. Sorry to have called you away from your dinner."

Grishin invited them into his office. He had the standard *apparatchik*'s furnishings: a desk with several phones on it, a conference table adjoining the desk, and an empty hook on the wall that had, presumably, once held a portrait of Lenin. Burke and McIntire sat on opposite sides of the conference table.

"Now," Grishin said politely, addressing Burke. "Please explain to me how you were picked up by the police in a closed city."

Burke wondered how much he would have to tell him. A fair amount of it, he suspected.

"I went down there on an assignment. The police came along and arrested me," he said.

Grishin nodded. "It would appear," he said, "that they confiscated your clothing and gave you some charity donations." His nose wrinkled, almost imperceptibly.

Burke blushed and noticed, for the first time in hours, that he had worn his old, camouflage clothes. They were spattered with mud from the street in Pyanovo.

"And the nature of this assignment?"

He would have to tell him something. "It's about Russian scientists being recruited by, um, other countries."

Grishin nodded. "Why pick Nauchny Gorodok?"

"I came across some information about a scientist there," Burke said.

"You knew it was a closed city?"

Burke hesitated. Though they had led him to believe that the police were through with him, whatever he said to Grishin might be used against him. He looked at McIntire. McIntire was presumably there to protect Burke's interests. But McIntire said nothing.

They would, no doubt, find out from Plotnikov how he had gotten there. They'd know he hadn't taken his own car. That would make it pretty obvious.

"Look, Vasily Ivanovich," he said. "Before I answer, I need to know my situation. Are you investigating this?"

Grishin's face got more serious. "I'm representing the foreign ministry. We value our good relations with your country. I am trying to smooth this whole thing over, Mr. Burke. I think you should give me the information I need."

He weighed whether they would find the cab driver who originally told him Nauchny Gorodok was a closed city. Probably not.

"I didn't ask," he said. "I chose not to find out."

Grishin sighed heavily and nodded.

"Look," Burke added. "If I were trying to find out some technical secret, it would be one thing. But I wasn't. I figured, why ask? It would only have caused you a problem."

"I'm touched by your concern, Mr. Burke."

The Greaseman, Burke thought, employed sarcasm better than any Russian bureaucrat he had ever met.

"But you know you're supposed to get permission for travel like that."

Burke scowled. "Yeah. But you know that rule's observed mostly in the breach these days."

Grishin's eyebrows rose. "Perhaps. But it's still a rule."

"Sorry," Burke said.

It occurred to him that he wanted Grishin and whoever might get a report on this conversation to think that he knew as little as possible of what he really knew and suspected.

"One other thing," he said. "The journalist who was with me—Plotnikov of *Nyezavisimaya Gazeta*?" Grishin nodded.

"He wasn't in on the planning of this. He didn't know where we were going. I just asked him to drive me. He shouldn't be blamed. I hope you'll pass that along to whoever is dealing with him."

Grishin nodded. Burke couldn't tell whether he would or not.

"There remains," Grishin said, after a lengthy pause, "the question of whether national security has been breached."

"You know it hasn't," Burke said.

"I may think it hasn't," Grishin said. "But my colleagues in..." he paused again, "...other branches of the government, shall we say, are going to want some more concrete assurances."

"Like what?"

"They're going to want to know what you were doing down there."

Burke tried not to get exasperated.

"As I said, I was working on an assignment. It shouldn't surprise you after that press conference you gave."

Grishin smiled thinly.

"And did you find such a scientist?"

The likelihood, Burke thought, was that this matter would still be hanging over him when his piece was published. Therefore, it would be foolish to lie about it.

"Yes," he said.

Grishin nodded calmly.

"And may I ask who this alleged scientist was?"

There, Burke had to draw the line. He could not help a Russian government official by giving him information about someone he had interviewed.

"I can't tell you that," he said. "I think you understand why."

"It's a matter of professional ethics in our country," McIntire piped up.

The thin, sarcastic smile appeared again. "I'm aware of your profession and its ethics," Grishin said to Burke. "If you choose not to tell me, that's your business. But let me suggest something as a friend."

Whenever a government flack addressed him as "friend," Burke felt like puffing a protective hand over his groin. He stifled the urge.

Grishin leaned toward him a little. "Don't publish something that will embarrass my government," he said, very earnestly, very quietly. "Not now. Wait till this is cleared up."

Burke bridled a little. It had been a long time since a Russian official had tried to intimidate him. The last time one had, back in the Soviet period, he had done a much more threatening job of it than Grishin had just done. There had been talk of consequences. Was Grishin just being more subtle? Or did he not really care?

Burke looked at Grishin, then at McIntire. McIntire

was intently evaluating the shine on his black wing-tip shoes.

With an effort he forced his voice as close to Grishin's calm and earnest tone as he could.

"Vasily Ivan'ich," he said, formally. "As a friend, you know I appreciate the advice. But you also know that I can't be worried about who's embarrassed by a story."

"A pity," Grishin said. "Well, don't say I didn't warn you."

McIntire cleared his throat.

"Vasily Ivan'ich," he said. "I think I should tell you that the United States feels supportive of the need to maintain secure zones, free of intrusion by foreigners, especially correspondents, and also of the need for duly accredited correspondents to do their jobs, as I'm sure does the Russian government, which has stated its own adherence to the various Helsinki documents on numerous occasions. If an American correspondent ran afoul in some minor way of the travel rules, well, we certainly don't condone that; but we don't think anything should be done that might make an issue that could come between us."

Burke and Grishin both hesitated for a moment, then determined that McIntire, in his State Department way, had come down on the journalist's side. The man had the makings of a department spokesman.

"Your statement is noted, Mr. McIntire," Grishin said drily.

"Thanks, Port," Burke said. "I feel a lot better."

McIntire flushed, but Burke couldn't tell whether it was from anger, embarrassment, or both.

"Well, Mr. Burke," Grishin said. "Do you have anything to add?"

Burke thought about it. "Just to repeat that I was not there to compromise your national security, didn't compromise your national security, and won't intentionally publish anything that will."

Grishin shook his head; and his face showed elaborate sadness, like a kabuki dancer's. "Well, your fate is in your hands," he said.

"That's good to know," Burke said.

Obviously, the interview was over. He and McIntire went downstairs together. It was beginning to drizzle. Burke apologized for causing McIntire to lose his evening. McIntire waved his hand. Came with the territory.

"Can I drop you?" McIntire asked. He had a car and driver waiting on Zubovsky Bulvar.

Burke suddenly felt the full weight of his fatigue, and McIntire's offer tempted him. But he felt the need to be alone and think things through. And he didn't want favors from any government.

"No thanks, Port," he said. "Looks like a good night to walk."

The longer he walked, the more his doubts grew. By the time he passed Moscow's massive outdoor swimming pool, steamy mists obscuring its surface, he had stopped thinking of Grishin, the cell, and the possible consequences that awaited him. He could think of nothing but the little girl, Tatiana, and the old woman who had snatched her away from his camera lens. Why?

By the time he had passed the high brick walls of the Kremlin, he knew he could not print his story without finding out.

By the time he arrived at Sad Sam, his thoughts had come up against a wall. To find out, he would have to talk to Nekronov. To talk to Nekronov, he would have to go back to Nauchny Gorodok. And if he so much as approached the town, he would be lucky to wind up with just an expulsion.

Wearily, he climbed the stairs to his apartment, hung up his coat, and looked at his watch. It was about two o'clock on Friday in New York, and the deadline for copy was about three hours away. He could imagine the acids washing up against Canfield's stomach walls, and the thought gave him a brief moment of pleasure.

He went to the bathroom and splashed some water in his face. Against his better judgment, he looked at the mirror. His eyes had gone completely red. His hair was matted and greasy, and his skin looked sallow and dirty. He looked like a guy who lived on a grate somewhere, a guy whose world had lost its bottom. The thought made him shiver. He stripped off his clothes, balled them up, and tossed them down the trash chute near the toilet.

He walked into the spare bedroom and turned on the computer. He had, it said, electronic mail waiting. There was a series of messages from Canfield, increasingly alarmed and angry. The last one said, "Burke, where the hell are you? Contact me ASAP. Canfield."

Before he could pick up the phone to call New York, it rang.

"Burke," he said.

"Oh, Colin, thank goodness we've found you," Gen Owen said. Her voice was the first soothing sound he had heard since he couldn't remember. Someday, he would have to send her flowers. "Are you all right?"

"Yeah. Got arrested."

"Oh, dear. Well, I'd better put you through to Chris and you can tell me all about it later. He's been having me call you every fifteen minutes for the last three hours."

"Sorry," Burke said, but she was already off the line. He heard a couple of clicks, then Canfield's voice. It had a tense, angry edge to it.

"Colin. Where've you been? Don't you know we're on deadline?"

"In jail," Burke said.

"Jail? What? Are you joking? What the hell happened?"

"I went to take your pictures, and I got arrested."

"Arrested?" Canfield apparently was having difficulty comprehending. He kept repeating Burke's words. "What for?"

"The guy lives in a closed city, Chris. I wasn't supposed to be there. I got caught."

"Jesus. Why didn't you tell us it was a closed city?"

"Because if I explained it over the phone it would only have increased the chance of getting caught."

"I see," Canfield said. Burke hoped he felt a little guilty.

If he did, Canfield covered it up well.

"So, no pictures. We'll put together some art. Where's the damn story?"

That, Burke thought, was an existential question. The story was in his computer, in a file called COUP.891, a few keystrokes and a satellite away from Canfield's computer in New York. He could send it and be done with it. Or the story was somewhere else, somewhere he hadn't been yet. And might never get to.

"Well," he said slowly. "It's not finished."

"Oh, shit," Canfield said, conveying as much disgust and contempt as he could with two words. "But you said it was." Now he was accusing and threatening.

"Well, I thought it was. But it's not. I've got more work to do," Burke said wearily. Like a dog expecting to be struck, he braced himself for Canfield's reply.

'What? How much? A half hour? Fifteen minutes?'

"I don't know. I have to do more reporting," Burke said.

"No," Canfield said firmly. "This piece is scheduled for the cover. Send it, and we'll edit it and fix it up here. If we don't run it, we'd have to run house ads to fill the space."

That, Burke thought, was unlikely. They had enough second-tier foreign stories from the international edition to fill up the section if they had to. Wooten and Schofield would chew Canfield out, but they wouldn't have to run house ads.

"No, Chris," he said. "I can't do that; it needs more reporting."

"Burke, that's not an option!" Canfield's voice had grown shrill. "Send the fucking piece! If it needs work, we'll rewrite it here. We'll write around whatever holes are in it…"

Burke tried to think of a way to explain to Canfield why the story couldn't be sent without tipping off the eavesdroppers on the line about his intentions.

"Chris, I've picked up new information that, um, suggests that what I originally had might be disinformation," Burke said. "I need to do more checking."

"You're not going to send it?"

"I'm sorry, but I really can't."

"You damn well—" Canfield began.

"Sony Chris," Burke said. "I'll send it as soon as I can."

Gently, he pressed the button on the phone and cut the connection. He pulled the jack from the wall.

Burke went to the liquor closet, pulled out the bottle of vodka, opened it, and took a long swallow that burned fiercely on its way down his throat.

He had one other task to handle, and he realized he needed to handle it soon. He pulled out his wallet and checked to see if Plotnikov's calling card was still there. It was, the home address written in pencil.

Burke went to the phone again and dialed Plotnikov's home number.

A woman answered.

"Um, hello, this is Colin Burke of—" Maybe, he thought, now "formerly of," but he didn't know for sure "—*America Weekly*."

"Yes?" the woman said, pleasantly.

"Uh, it's about Pavel."

"Yes?" The woman sounded worried.

"Uh, I wonder if I could come by and tell you personally. It's not something I want to talk about over the phone."

He could hear the woman hesitate. "It's important," he said.

"Has he been hurt?"

"No. But I really want to speak to you face to face."

She hesitated again. Then she said okay.

"Give me your address," Burke said.

She gave him an address on Varshavskoye Shosse. He read the one on the business card as she spoke. They matched.

❀ ❀ ❀

A boy in a U2 tee shirt and a pair of tight jeans answered the door. He appeared to be about sixteen, and he had the same Ichabod Crane neck as Pavel Plothikov. If he was a fake, he was a good fake.

When Burke introduced himself, the boy nodded politely, pulled the door open wide, and said, "Please to come in."

A thick-legged woman wearing a plain cotton housedress walked out of the kitchen and dried her hands on an apron before she offered the right one to Burke. She had gray hair and a jolly little smile.

"Call me Galya," she said. "I know all about it. Pavel called a few moments after you did. He'll be home in the morning."

Before he could say anything, she ushered him into the kitchen. A kettle whistled on the little stove, and some slices of bread topped with sausage sat atop the little family table.

"Please, eat," she said as she put a teacup in front of him. "You must have had a difficult day."

"Pavel said he was all right?"

"Yes," she said. "He said it was all a misunderstanding." She sat at the table across from him and poured herself a cup of tea. She looked like every honest Russian mother he had ever met.

"Eat," she said, as if to emphasize the resemblance. Burke took a slice of bread and a sip of tea. "Well, I'm glad he's out. I'm afraid it was my fault he was down there."

Galya Plotnikova grinned mischievously. "So he said."

Burke sipped his tea again.

"So are you a historian like Pavel?"

"A mathematician," she corrected him.

He tried to look annoyed with himself. "That's right," he said, and tapped his head with his finger. "I must be getting tired."

"No," she said. "I'm an engineer at a watch factory. Would you like to buy it? We're looking for foreign investors."

"I'll keep it in mind," Burke said, standing up. "I may be looking for some new career opportunities."

Back in his apartment, he pondered what he had seen. Galya Plotnikova was either the wife of a mathematician-turned-reporter or a very good actress. Burke shook his head. He wanted to believe her. He wanted to believe that what he saw and what he thought about what he saw were still reliably linked to reality.

And he found himself envying Pavel Plotnikov. He, at least, had someone to come home to when he got back from Tula. Burke had only the knowledge that he had, somehow, to get back to Nauchny Goredok and talk to Sergei Nekronov. And for company, he had only the faithful Ms. Stolichnaya.

CHAPTER TWELVE

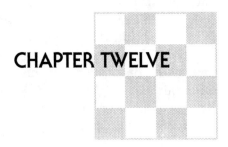

IN HIS DREAM, HE WAS CRAWLING through a desert filled with broken glass. His hands and knees felt slimy; and he was afraid to look at what made them feel that way, afraid that it was his blood. His joints ached. Then the sun seemed to grow an arm and the arm seemed to grow a sledgehammer and the sledgehammer began pounding him in the temples.

He woke up.

The lights in his bedroom room were on. So were the clothes he had been wearing the night before. He turned his face away from the pounding in his temples and saw a blurred glass, one third full of vodka, on the nightstand.

Then he turned the other way and saw Ronit Evron about to poke him once more on the temple.

"Get up," she said.

He squinted at her, turned his head away from the

light coming in the window, and coughed. His mouth tasted bilious, and his tongue felt coated with hot sand. The cough reverberated for a while in the interstices between his brain and his skull.

"I didn't call for telephone repair service," he said. His voice sounded raspy and weak.

She slapped him once, hard, across the mouth, and he tasted a bit of blood on his tongue. It beat bile and sand, but it still did not taste good.

He managed to focus on her. She was back to wearing denim, but her look had changed from perky to implacable. It occurred to him that he was entitled to hit her back, but it seemed like too much trouble to lift his arms.

"Are you still drunk?" she demanded.

"I wish," he replied. He managed to sit up. He saw himself for a moment through her eyes and felt ashamed of his drinking and of being found, stinking and wrinkled, like a derelict in some gutter.

"Good. Then get up."

"How did you get in here?"

"That's not important. Get up," she snapped.

"Why?"

"Because I can't stand the thought of being in a bedroom with a drunk," she spat out. She grabbed him by the shoulders. He pushed her arms away, got up, and walked into the bathroom. He splashed some cold water on his face and went to the living room. She was standing by the bookshelf.

"Let's go for a walk," she said. He realized he had as much reason as she to want to talk outdoors. They left the apartment and crossed under the Ring Road to a little park. The day was gray and chill, with a faint drizzle in the air; but the air was not quite as stale as the air in his apartment, and it revived him a bit. They sat on a white park bench, and he kept a couple of feet of distance from her.

"I didn't know lock picking was one of your skills," he said.

She shrugged. "It's a cheap lock. You should have a deadbolt. There's a lot of crime in Moscow these days." It sounded vaguely threatening. Before he could reply, she began interrogating him again.

"You left the city yesterday. Why?"

"Can't tell you. Maybe you'll read about it."

'That's not good enough anymore," she said, after a moment's silence.

Burke tried to put aside his headache and his anger and his shame and to calculate how much she knew. If she knew about his going out of town, but not where he had gone, it could be that he had eluded whatever tail the Israelis had put on him. He knew that if the Israelis were intent on following him, his little evasive maneuvers of the day before would not stop them. But if they had only enough people to put a single man on him, maybe he had succeeded in giving that man the slip.

"Why isn't it good enough?" he asked her.

"Because," she said, "if you've made contact with a scientist that Kassim is trying to recruit, that scientist is no doubt planning on getting out of Russia before your story comes out. Once he's in an Arab country, our chances of getting to him and persuading him to do the right thing are nonexistent. So we can't wait for you to publish something."

He thought for a moment of telling her exactly what had happened. Then he rejected the idea. He had only a few shreds of self-respect left to cling to. Spilling what he knew to her would add an ethical offense to all the mistakes he had made in the past few days and compound his misery. So he tried to put her on the defensive.

"What happened?" he asked her. "The guy you put on me took a dinner break?"

She flushed, and he suspected he had come fairly close to the mark.

"Don't provoke me," she said quietly. "I'm trying to do you a favor."

"I know, I know," he said. "You could have brought some goons in to stick bamboo shoots under my fingernails until I told you what you want to know." He paused, thinking things through.

"But you can't do that, can you, because you don't know exactly what I have. And if you get rough with me and put me out of commission, you might stop me from finding a scientist. So you have to try to get it out of me gently, don't you?"

She shrugged again. "The important thing is, we'll get it out of you."

"Ronit, look, you know our deal. You find out what I learn when you read it in the magazine."

"There was no such deal."

"Listen," he said. "I've tried to explain to you. I'm a reporter. I don't work for anyone else besides my magazine. I wouldn't help my own government, let alone yours. I'm sorry if you don't like—no, hell, I'm not sorry. That's just the way it is, okay?"

"But you get information from me," she snapped back.

"I get information wherever I can," he said.

"But you don't exchange it," she said.

"Ah, but I do. You can read it."

"And if you had information that might prevent a second Holocaust?"

Burke sighed and scratched his head.

"I'd publish it. Then it would be up to you."

"But we need this information now! We can't afford to wait!" she replied. Her voice remained low, but the intensity in her tone approached desperation. Anger and frustration showed clearly on her face, and he had to remind himself that her face showed only what she wanted it to show.

"I'm sorry." He shook his head. She persisted.

"Burke, I don't understand you," she said, her tone softer. "You stepped in front of a mob and risked a beating to protect a few Jews from being killed and a synagogue from desecration. But you won't answer a few simple questions to save the lives of maybe millions of people?"

He shook his head.

"Why?" she insisted.

He sighed. "Ronit, all I have to work with is my credibility, which comes from people's—only some people's— confidence that I'm not in anyone's pocket. That I don't work for any government. If I lose that, I might as well go ahead and become a press secretary for somebody in Washington."

"But it's so—so trivial. How can you say that?" she exploded.

"And how do you know what's going to happen? If you stop one scientist, maybe that just redoubles Assad's efforts. Maybe a different scientist gets through. Maybe he designs a bomb that does go off in Tel Aviv. Or if you don't stop him, and the Arabs do get a bomb, maybe it sobers everyone up down there, like it sobered up the Americans and the Russians. And you finish your negotiations and live happily ever after. Mutual deterrence, you know? Who the hell can say? You can't. I can't. All I can do is do my job."

"You don't understand—" she began.

"Look, I'll give you an example," he said, not giving her a chance to finish. "In 1961, *The New York Times* found out about the Bay of Pigs plan and was about to publish a story. Kennedy called the publisher and got him to kill it. It turns out Kennedy would have been a lot better off if the story came out and he scrubbed the plan. You see?"

"You just don't understand the Arabs," she said, finishing the thought she had started earlier.

He scowled and scratched his face.

"Look," he said, "I don't think this is getting us anywhere."

"Wait," she said. "Burke, I want you to listen to me," she said. "I like you, strangely enough. You're a good person. You're verging on alcoholism—" He flushed. "—and you're cynical as hell, and you cultivate a certain nastiness—"

"But what are my bad traits?" he interrupted.

"—but you have a certain integrity," she finished.

"And I'm good in bed," he added.

"Be serious!" she snapped, and the force of the words almost snapped his head back.

"You don't understand what you're involved in," she went on, her voice all the more serious because it had suddenly become so flat, quiet, and matter-of-fact. "This is not some story you write one day, and maybe the prime minister likes it and maybe he doesn't, and if he doesn't his press secretary chews you out. This is serious. For God's sake, take it seriously!"

"I do," he said.

"No, you don't! Do you realize that there are people who will kill you if they think it's necessary to get at some information you have? Or to stop you from publishing something they don't want you to publish?"

"Oh, come on," he said.

"I assure you there are."

He paused, looking at her. She seemed very small on the bench beside him, and he forced himself to realize that her appearance had nothing to do with reality.

"Are you one of them?" he asked her.

Her reply was devoid of emotion, a flat statement of reality.

"If it was decided that killing you might help stop Syria from getting the bomb," she said, "yes, I would be. I would be very sorry about it, but I would kill you."

When she had gone, Burke went back to the apartment and into the bathroom for some aspirin. He had none left. So he splashed more water on his face, then forced himself under a cold shower. It seemed to reduce the throbbing in his skull to a dull ache he could live with.

Once he had dressed, he methodically worked through the apartment and collected every bottle that did not contain Diet Coke or seltzer water. He dumped all of them in the trash chute near the kitchen and listened to the sound they made as they clattered toward the basement.

He had, he realized, two tasks left in his life that mattered a great deal. To save his job, he had to find Sergei Nekronov without being caught at it. To save his life, he had to stop drinking.

He went downstairs, got in the car, and headed for the Byelorussky station.

The crowds at the station were thick on Saturday mornings, which made it prime time for Lena Laskova and her friends. Burke walked slowly around the platforms and the row of kiosks outside the pale-green terminal building, waiting for them to show up.

Moscow's railroad stations were great, freewheeling bazaars. Peasant women from the countryside, the mud thick on their black rubber boots, spread little piles of tomatoes, carrots, apples, and onions on sheets of newspaper, waiting stolidly for buyers. City dwellers came with odd bottles of vodka or packs of cigarettes, hoping to sell them for enough to survive another day. In the kiosks, more established vendors hawked warm beer, ice cream, and hot dumplings called *pirogi*.

But neither the beer, nor the *pirogi*, nor the little piles of vegetables were what attracted Lena Laskova and her friends to the station. They came to be among the people, people passing through with money in their pockets.

Burke spotted her just before noon, carrying her little table and stool, wearing the same sunglasses, tight jeans, and ribbed sweater with the scooped neckline she had on when he first saw her operate three weeks ago. He followed her, fifty yards away, until she set up the table and began her game.

She was a good-looking woman, tall and willowy, with long auburn hair and just enough cleavage to make it interesting for men to stand beside her when she opened her little folding chair and sat down behind the table.

Lena's game was simple. She spread out a pile of tiles made of thin pieces of wood, each with four numbers painted on it, ranging from one to thirty-six. A tile cost fifty rubles. When she had sold enough tiles, she invited one of the players to roll six dice. Then she kept fifty rubles and paid the rest to the player with the winning number.

But the game had an important peculiarity. Once in a while, always after a crowd had gathered, it developed that two players had the winning number. Lena would explain that she had never promised that players bought exclusive rights to their numbers.

When two players had the winning number, the tie was resolved by means of a "face-off." The players bet and raised, bet and raised, until the stakes suited them. Then they rolled the dice again, with the high man winning. In this second phase of the game, if a man could not match the bet made by his opponent, he folded and lost.

As Burke sidled up to the table, a face-off had just begun. Lena spotted him immediately, and her blandly impartial face darkened briefly in a scowl. Then she ignored him.

One of her contenders was a broad-faced Byelorussian with wide blue eyes and an old cloth cap. Ostentatiously, he pulled from his pocket a fifty-thousand-ruble note. He looked like a man who had just finished selling a summer's worth of vegetables.

His opponent was a thin, sallow-faced boy who

looked like a student, with long, greasy black hair and a wispy goatee. The boy had on baggy green trousers and a white summer shirt, open at the neck, showing a couple of lonely chest hairs.

Confidently, the Byelorussian laid the fifty thousand rubles down on the table. The boy's eyes widened. He dug into his pocket and pulled out a loose handful of wrinkled old bills.

The girl standing next to him, homely and red-haired, laid a restraining hand on his forearm.

"No, Volodya," she said. "Let it go."

But Volodya shook her off. Laboriously, he counted fifty thousand rubles from the pile in his hand. A thousand rubles remained. He laid the last bill on top of the stack.

"And raise you a thousand," he said, defiantly.

Smirking, the Byelorussian reached into his pocket again. He pulled out a roll of bills about two inches thick, held together by a rubber band. He dropped a thousand onto his pile, then counted out a hundred thousand more rubles.

The spectators, ringing the table in a circle two or three deep, craned their necks to get a look at the Byelorussian's bankroll. An appreciative murmur arose over the background noise of the station.

Grimly, Volodya dug into his pocket again.

"Volodya, we can't. Stop!" the red-haired girl said, more urgently. "We can't afford this!"

Volodya pushed her away.

The girl turned to Lena, who was sitting implacably behind the table, keeping track of the money.

"Can't you stop this?" the girl wailed. "Can't you set a limit?"

Lena shrugged coolly. "Sorry," she said. "Rules are rules."

When Volodya had counted out the bills, he had, improbably, matched the hundred thousand and had a thousand left. He dropped the last thousand-ruble note on the table.

"Raise you," he said again, his face a portrait of wan defiance.

Grimly, the Byelorussian dug into his pocket and pulled out his bankroll. He counted it all out on the table. Three hundred thousand rubles.

Just as grimly, Volodya began pulling more loose bills from his trouser pockets. They were beginning to remind Burke of the little circus car that stops and disgorges an impossible number of clowns.

Now Volodya was pulling wrinkled fifty-thousand-ruble notes from the depths of his pockets, and the Byelorussian farmer was getting pale under his sunburn. Volodya matched the three hundred thousand and put fifty thousand more on the table.

The Byelorussian's face twitched for a moment. Then, quietly, without a word, he walked away. It would be a long ride back to Pinsk.

Volodya scooped up the money quickly, being sure to leave Lena her rubles. He and his red-haired girl walked away in the opposite direction and disappeared into the crowd.

Lena played three more times, with no face-offs. Then, without warning, she stacked her tiles, folded her table, and got ready to move on. The knot of spectators dispersed, as she put the folded table and stool under her left arm. She started walking toward the terminal building.

Burke followed, waiting until they were out of earshot of the spectators and players.

"Lena," he called.

Her spine stiffened, but she did not stop or turn around. He broke into a run and caught up with her, stepping into her path.

"Lena," he said, softly putting a hand on her shoulder.

"What do you want now?" she said. He had the sense she was trying to look angrier than she really felt. "You want to write another story that will cost me a million rubles?"

"I don't get it," Burke said.

" 'I don't get it,' "she said, imitating his accent. "You're too naive to get it. After your story came out, the *militsia* came around," she explained. "Said since we'd become so famous, we'd have to pay more. A million rubles more a month!"

She pushed past him and continued walking toward the terminal building.

"I'm really sorry that happened," Burke said, following. "I thought you'd like the story. I didn't use your real name." He had tried, in the article, to make them seem raffish but sympathetic, which was how he felt about them.

"I should like that description you wrote of me?" she shot back over her shoulder.

He was puzzled. "I said you were pretty."

"And pimples! You said I had pimples!"

He had, in fact, written that she had a faintly freckled face.

"Somebody must have translated it wrong," he said. He explained what freckles were. "In America, they're considered signs of great beauty," he assured her, solemnly.

He saw the sides of her mouth start to curve up. "Like hell," she said, but he could tell that her anger, if it ever really existed, was gone.

"Truly," he said, as solemnly as he could. "I know better than to try to con you."

She smiled for the first time and kept walking. They entered the terminal building. He caught a faint smell of stale urine mixed with mud.

"I want to talk to you about something. It's a chance to make a lot more than a million rubles," he said.

"Follow me," she replied.

They walked up a battered granite staircase at the side of the crowded terminal to a mezzanine on the second floor. There was a door, its glass windows covered by white curtains and a sign that said "Closed."

She pushed it open. It was a small, private dining room, with six or seven tables covered in white linen, obviously once intended for Party dignitaries traveling to Byelorussia and Lithuania. The boy with the goatee and the redheaded girl were already sitting at a corner table, a bottle of Georgian wine open between them.

Lena sat down. Burke said hello to the boy, whose name was Edik, and the girl, Natalia.

"So did you bring extra copies of your article?" Edik asked. "Lena will tell you that she hated it. But really she liked it. You're a good writer."

Lena, for the first time since Burke had known her, blushed.

"Thank you," Burke said. "I'll get some extra copies for the next time I see you," he replied mildly.

"So what's this proposition you have?" Lena asked abruptly.

"I want you to take me to a place called Nauchny Gorodok," Burke said. "And I don't want anyone to know I'm gone."

CHAPTER THIRTEEN

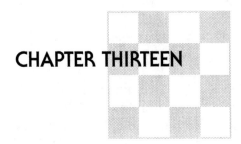

LENA OPENED THE DOOR wearing gray workman's coveralls, stained with what appeared to be axle grease. She had pinned her hair up and covered it with a black cap; and her face had a hint of stubble, applied with some kind of cosmetic. She carried a large plastic shopping bag with "Marlboro" written across it.

The apartment, he could see behind her, was tiny; a wardrobe, a divan, and a Japanese CD player all but filled it. And there was an old woman sitting on the divan. She rose, nodded to him, and didn't speak.

"Hi," he said, uncertain.

"Colin," she said. "You're right on time. I like that."

She had the kind of low voice that sounded sensual and knowing in Russian, but guttural and crude in English. Fortunately, as far as he knew, she spoke only Russian.

She moved toward him and put her arms on his

shoulders, and for a second he thought she was going to kiss his neck. Instead, she whispered in his ear.

"Tell me, 'God, you look gorgeous in that.'"

"God, you look gorgeous in that," he repeated.

She giggled. "Maybe we should put off going to dinner," she said aloud.

Then another whisper. "Say, 'I'm not hungry, anyway.'"

"I'm not hungry, anyway."

She put a finger on his lips, took him by the hand and led him to the divan, her feet clomping on the floor. She nodded at the old woman, and Burke noticed a tape recorder lying on the bed. The old woman pressed the play button.

Lena's voice, pitched a few notes lower, came from the machine. "Oh, God, I love it when you do that," it said. The recording emitted the faint sound of springs squeaking.

"Yes...um...yes," her voice went on, through the machine. Her recorded breathing was getting ragged.

Lena patted the expressionless old woman on the head, then took his hand again and very quietly led him to the door, which she had left open. They stepped out into the hallway, and she silently closed it.

She walked downstairs, and he noticed that she had an ability to move quickly without making any noise. Behind her, he felt elephantine. At the bottom of the stairwell, instead of going out the front door to the street, she turned in the opposite direction, pulled a key from her pocket, and opened a small door. Beyond it, he could see rough stone steps leading downward and the harsh glare of an unshaded light bulb. It seemed to be the entrance to a basement.

She closed the door behind him and led him down seven steps into a low-ceilinged room with stone walls. He could see the pipe intersection where heat and hot water entered the building, and he could smell the garbage in a big bin to his left. Old sinks, tires, pieces of wood, and a big, empty shipping crate littered the floor.

"Put this on," she said, taking a coverall and cap identical to her own from the Marlboro bag. He did.

As he zipped it up, the door to the basement opened, and he froze, certain that it was the police. Two men, wearing the same coveralls, walked in and nodded to Lena. One was tall—Burke recognized Edik from the railroad station. The other man was short and thick with the arms of a much taller man; he looked like a wrestler. The smaller one carried what looked like a toolbox in his right hand, which had the Russian equivalents of the letters "N," "S," "E," and "W" tattooed on the knuckles.

"You know Edik. And this is Boris," she whispered to him. Edik smiled and half bowed, showing bright white teeth.

"All set?" she asked Boris. He nodded.

She turned to him. "The money."

Burke handed her an envelope with five hundred dollars inside. "You get the other half when we get back," he said.

She looked at him reproachfully. "You don't trust us because you think we're thieves," she said. "Maybe we should forget it."

"Oh, I trust you," Burke told her. "In a country where everyone is faking something, you're more up front about it than most. But you get the rest of the money when you get me back. Being from a capitalist country and all, I believe in financial incentives."

She thought about that for a second, then smiled. She stuffed the envelope into a pocket.

"Okay," she said. "Let's go."

Lena took his hand and led him to the crate. She stooped and sidled into it.

"Come on," she said.

Burke blinked. Since he had first heard Susan Blackstone's report on CNN, the rush and logic of events had carried him along, sparing him from troubling thoughts about his legal situation and the risks of being caught. Now, at the point of stepping into a crate and concealing himself, doubt rushed into his mind. He hesitated. It was not too late to strip off the coverall and, with it, his whole involvement with Lena.

"Come on. Hurry," she said.

He took a half step forward and hesitated again. Had he been able to see another choice, he would have turned around. But he saw nothing.

Bending over, he stepped into the crate. She was sitting against the left hand side. He sat on the right, cushioning himself on a wad of packing paper. Their legs touched. A shadow engulfed the interior, and then the light disappeared entirely as Edik and Boris fitted a lid to the outside of the crate and nailed it into place. Then the crate began to move, and he had the sensation of being picked up.

The crate bobbed gently as they went up a couple of steps, and Burke could smell the change in the air as they reached, he assumed, the courtyard behind the building. Then he heard a scraping sound and felt the crate being placed on a flat surface. Twenty seconds later, an engine cranked laboriously to life, and he could feel them begin to move.

"How'd you get all this set up so fast?"

He heard nothing, and decided that she wasn't going to answer the question.

But after a moment, she spoke. "We have friends with a trucking business."

"Private or state?"

"State, of course," she said, and her voice had a hard, sarcastic edge. "How else could they get petrol?"

"Who's the *babushka*?"

"Edik' s grandmother."

"And we're still supposedly making passionate love back in the apartment?"

He heard her clothing rustle, and then a thin beam of light emerged from a penlight she had taken from her pocket. The beam picked out her watch.

"Yes, for about five more minutes."

"Good. If you had me lasting any longer than that, whoever is listening would get suspicious. They know I can't keep a woman panting for more than ten minutes."

"Maybe," she said, "you just haven't found the right woman."

Before he could think of some suitably clever and inviting response, the truck hit one of Moscow's enormous potholes. Burke jounced a foot into the air and then slammed down hard against the wooden walls of the crate. The impact jarred the breath from his lungs and sent pain shooting up his coccyx into his lower back.

"You all right?" he said to her when he had gotten his breath back.

"Okay," she replied. Her voice sounded strained.

The pothole had served to jar his thoughts back to reality.

"So what happens after our ten minutes of passion?'

"We doze, pleasantly satiated, for an hour. Then you make love to me again. Then you fall asleep. *Babushka* has the schedule."

"Well," he said, "the falling asleep part should sound realistic enough."

His thoughts shifted south. "What makes you think that the *militsia* is going to wave us through into Nauchny Gorodok?"

Her voice came out of the darkness, matter-of-factly. "First of all, they're Russian. Second, our documents are genuine."

"And if they open this crate?"

"They won't."

"Won't it be a little unusual for a truck to be making a delivery late in the evening?" He calculated that they would get to Nauchny Gorodok sometime after ten o'clock.

"No." Again the voice sounded confident. "Private truckers often work with trucks that they lease from state enterprises. They use them at night, when the state operation isn't running. In fact, it would be unusual to make a delivery in the daytime."

It sounded sensible, which made him uneasy. All the botched operations ever run had probably sounded just as sensible. Eisenhower had doubtless decided the U-2 flights made eminent sense. Kennedy had thought the Bay of Pigs made sense. Carter thought it made sense to rescue the hostages in Iran, and Reagan thought it made sense to send arms there.

Another pothole popped the crate into the air. It crashed back to the truck bed with a jolt that sent more pain lancing up his spine. One of her legs bounced up and over his, and they ended up intertwined.

"Shit," he cursed, in English.

"Sorry," she said, disentangling herself.

"How many potholes do you think there are between here and Tula?" he asked.

Surprisingly, he got a light, low chuckle in response.

"Should we have a pool?' she replied.

"You mean betting?"

"Sure. Betting is Russia's national sport."

"No," he said. "If you want to bet, you've probably counted them."

There was silence from the darkness again, broken by the rumbling of their truck and those passing in the other direction.

"You think badly of me," she said, in a softer, barely audible voice.

"What?" he shouted, unsure that he had heard correctly. There was movement around his legs, and in a moment he sensed that she was moving, quickly. Then he felt her shoulder pressed against his.

"You think badly of me," she said again, this time against his ear.

He wondered briefly why she might care what he thought of her and why she might want to get close to him to ask the question. Then he tried to decide what she wanted from him. He could think of nothing that she wasn't already getting. Maybe she just wanted to be liked.

He had always been, he cautioned himself, too sentimental about people and their motives.

"No," he said. "I think if I lived here, I might do what you do. Only not so well."

Another pothole jolted them, and she steadied herself by putting a hand on his thigh. It felt hot through the gabardine of the coveralls. He marveled for a moment at the urge to take her in his arms and kiss her, as if this were a drive-in movie somewhere and he were seventeen.

"How did you get into it?" he asked her.

"What?"

"What?"

"Your work. I mean, I assume you didn't learn at school."

She laughed softly. "No. I used to be a singer. I traveled with a show. Some people who worked with the show taught me."

He knew vaguely about the old-fashioned Soviet traveling variety shows, which were akin to vaudeville.

"You sang?'

"Is that surprising?"

"No," he said quickly, anxious not to offend her. "Why did you stop?"

"I couldn't afford it any more. When I started, you know, the Ministry of Culture used to finance touring shows. The tickets were only a ruble or two. Lots of people would come. Then everything fell apart."

"How?"

"Well, the salary stayed the same. It didn't go up with inflation. The Ministry didn't have enough money. And we used to be the only entertainment people had. But then *glasnost* made the television better. Now you can see American or French movies at home for free. Why go out to see a show?

"So, to make ends meet, we started to work the stations a little before we would leave a town for the next show. Little by little, it reached the point where we made nearly all our money in the stations. Then we just stopped doing shows."

"Do you miss singing?"

"I don't miss singing in those shows. They were stupid and horrible. But I miss singing. If I had been born in the West, I think I might have been Billie Holiday. But I was born in Moscow. Do you like Billie Holiday?"

"Yes."

"And is it true that 'strange fruit hanging from the poplar tree' is about hanging Negroes in the South?"

"Yes."

"Someone told me that, but I couldn't believe it could happen in America. I thought that was just Soviet propaganda."

"Sorry to destroy your illusion," he said.

"And it was just about the last one I had," she said. In the darkness, he could her her laugh, briefly and mirthlessly.

After a while he asked where in Moscow she had lived.

"*Internat* No. 34," she said, using the Russian word for an institution that housed orphans, the mentally infirm, or the helplessly aged. "You've probably never been there," she added, a touch of bitterness in her voice.

"No,"he said. "But I've seen the kind of place you're talking about. Not very pleasant. You were an orphan?"

"No, I have a mother," she replied, in a small, hollow voice. "But she put me there. She had no money. She spent it all on vodka."

Burke shook his head. He would have said he was sorry, but it would have sounded inadequate.

After an hour, the truck stopped. Then it rolled on. When it stopped a second time, she nudged him and whispered, "Ready?"

"Ready," Burke said.

In a second they heard the sound of the truck door's rusty hinges squeaking. They sounded frighteningly loud to Burke, like fireworks going off, and he froze, expecting to hear an answering sound, perhaps a siren.

But the next sound was the slight tearing noise as the short nails that held the lid on the crate were pulled up. They crawled out. Burke winced as his joints tried to adapt to movement. His legs felt as if they might never straighten again.

Using a cloth to muffle the hammer blows, Boris and Edik lightly nailed the crate shut again. They retreated to the shadows in the back of the truck, pulling some furniture wrapping cloths over themselves and squatting down. To Burke, it all seemed like a child's game; but he assumed they knew what they were doing. To someone watching from across the street, perhaps the inside of the truck would seem empty once they had gone.

"Make it look like it's heavy," Lena said, squatting down toward the bottom of the crate. "It's a refrigerator. You know."

"You're coming in?"

She rose from her squat and stepped to the side of the crate.

"Yes, of course."

Alarm bells went off in his mind. Why should she go in? Someone, he could see, had to go in with him. He couldn't pretend to carry the crate alone. But why not Edik or Boris?

"Shouldn't one of them go in?" he asked.

"No," she said firmly. "I'm in charge. I take the risk. I need to know what you're doing."

Burke looked at Boris and Edik. They seemed quite accustomed to taking orders from her.

He shrugged. If she was working for the Ministry of Security, it hardly mattered whether she saw what happened inside Nekronov's building. Just the address would tell the ministry all it needed to know about what he was doing. He squatted down with her and lifted the crate.

Slowly, they walked down the ramp Boris and Edik had placed between the truck and the curb.

He glanced around. In the distance, a car's engine whined; but apart from that, the street was silent. A couple of people walked dogs on the opposite sidewalk. About half the windows in Nekronov's building were lit.

Gingerly, they walked the crate into the building and up the stairwell. On the sixth-floor landing, the light bulb was gone.

"This is it, I think," he whispered. They put the box down. She reached into her pocket and pulled out the small flashlight.

The light beam showed the same four apartment doors he remembered, including the black leather door to No. 32. But the white card on the door did not say Nekronov; it said Marinovsky, in neat black letters.

"I'm positive this is it," Burke said. He rapped on the door and pressed the button. Inside, he could hear a buzzer. There was no answer.

"Are you sure this is the right address?" she whispered. Burke felt impatient and annoyed. "Yes. There are only three buildings on the block. This is the middle one."

"Maybe the next floor?"

He shrugged. "We can check. But his apartment was No. 32. His name was on the door. Nekronov."

She went upstairs and he went down. He saw numbers 26, 27, 28, and 29, just as he expected. When he got back to the sixth-floor landing, she was waiting for him.

"Let's check," she said.

Before he could object, she had pulled some kind of key from her pocket and was adding breaking and entering to the list of things he could be charged with.

Silently, she pulled the door open and he followed her inside. She closed it and switched on a light.

It was, he saw, the same apartment, down to the old slippers on the floor of the entrance hall. "The study where I talked to him was right there," he said.

They walked into the narrow, book-lined room, and she flipped on the light. The desk and books were as he remembered them. Then he looked at the diploma on the wall. It was from an institute in Leningrad, for someone named Marinovsky, Sergei Mikhailovich.

He felt like a character trapped inside someone else's movie, no longer in control of what he saw. It made him queasy and anxious.

"I don't get it," he said.

She quickly went through the desk drawers, pulling out papers and examining them.

"Nothing that says Nekronov," she reported, tersely.

He shrugged. "He was here in this room," he said. He pointed to the chair. "He sat there."

She pursed her lips and said nothing. He had the feeling she doubted his sanity.

Without a word, she turned out the lights and led him back into the hallway. She pressed the button on the next-door apartment. No one answered.

She pressed the button at No. 34, and Burke heard feet shuffling in reply. In a moment, the door opened about four inches. He could see the silhouette of a woman's head, framed in a light burning inside the apartment.

"We have a delivery for Apartment 32," Lena said in a voice low enough to be taken for a man's.

'There's no one there," the old woman said. "Marinovsky is teaching this year in St. Petersburg. You must have the wrong address." And she shut the door.

There was nothing to do but walk the crate back out to the truck. Inside, Boris and Edik quickly and silently nailed them back into the box, closed the truck, and started the engine again. The truck rolled away.

This time, the darkness was getting harder to cope with. "I can't understand it," Burke said. "I know Nekronov exists."

Another pothole bounced him into the air and brought his teeth together over his tongue as he hit the floor again, drawing the salty taste of blood into his mouth.

Normally, Burke prided himself on being immune to minor phobias. He went where he needed to go and did what he needed to do. But by the time the truck reached the outskirts of Moscow, claustrophobia and depression overcame him. The depression seeped in first. He envisioned himself acknowledging that he could not locate Nekronov and didn't know why. He envisioned Canfield firing him. He decided he wouldn't care that much. He wanted only to curl up someplace quiet where no one could bother him.

But in a place with sunlight and fresh air. His desire to get out of the crate turned into a desperate urge until his body trembled with it and he felt himself on the verge of tears.

His misery absorbed him to such a degree that when Lena prodded his thigh and repeated her question, it was as if she had awakened him from sleep.

"Sorry. What?" he said, dully.

"So what is this all about?" she said.

"I don't know," he answered.

"How did you find Nekronov originally?"

He thought of Katya and the letter she had shown him along the banks of the river. There was no reason to tell Lena about it.

"I can't tell you," he said bluntly. "All I can tell you is that in that apartment I met a man named Nekronov who said he was a scientist being recruited by Syria." That much, he figured, everyone knew—Mossad, the Ministry of Security, Chris Canfield. It wouldn't hurt if she knew it.

"A nuclear scientist?"

"Yes," he said, wondering if the idea would frighten her.

She gave no indication that it did.

"Maybe Nekronov has been moving around while he works this deal out, using friends' apartments. It reduces his risks," she suggested.

"Maybe," he said. "But I don't think so. It doesn't fit with other information I have."

He forced himself to concentrate and sort out the thoughts that had been tumbling through his mind like clothes in a drier. She had not seen what he saw on his first trip to Nauchny Gorodok, but it had not looked like someone staying temporarily in a friend's apartment. It seemed clear that someone had gone to elaborate lengths to present him with a false picture on one of his trips to Nauchny Gorodok. But which one? He didn't know.

"Do you think—" she began, but he stopped her.

"I really shouldn't discuss it," he said, curtly.

She did not, as far as he could tell in the darkness, take offense.

"We have a saying," she said. "The less you know, the better you sleep."

"A wise saying," he replied.

The truck slowed, made a sharp right turn, and stopped. They heard the door opening, and felt the crate being lifted up. In a moment, they were in the basement again. Burke looked at his watch. It was three o'clock.

She was slipping out of the coveralls. He did the same. "You are going to be a typical man and wake up with an attack of after-sex panic," she instructed him in a controlled, low voice. "Then you're going to leave. Understood?"

He nodded and pulled from his pocket a second envelope containing five hundred dollars. She raised her brows.

"You should be more careful with your money," she said.

"Not when I'm with trustworthy people," he replied, and she smiled.

They went upstairs, and she silently let them into the apartment. He feigned waking up. She feigned trying to persuade him to stay the night. He feigned making up a stupid excuse and pulling his pants on. It was not a role he had difficulty playing.

She walked him to the door; and for a moment he thought she was going to kiss the air next to his cheek, for the benefit of whatever microphones and tape recorders were monitoring them. But her kiss found his mouth and lingered for a moment. Then she broke it off with an audible smack. "Be careful," she said softly.

He let himself out and walked slowly to his car. A full moon, the color of marigolds, was hanging low in the sky, about to disappear.

It struck Burke that he could not remember the last time he had seen a marigold. He had been away from home for a long time.

CHAPTER FOURTEEN

THERE WAS ONLY ONE MESSAGE waiting on the *America Weekly* answering machine when Burke got to the bureau the next morning. It was from Ethan Worthington.

There was also a telex message from the librarian in New York.

TO: Burke, Moscow
FROM: Rock, New York
Source at Stanford called to tell our stringer that Rafit Kassim indeed graduated from the nuclear engineering program in 1977. Didn't pose for yearbook.

Don't know why you're interested, but Baseball Encyclopedia says Willie McCovey played for San Francisco 1959-73, San Diego 1974-76, Oakland 1976, San Francisco 1977-80.

Need batting averages?
Hope this isn't too late to be helpful.
Regards.

It had been sent Saturday night after he'd left the office.

It was indeed too late.

It was conceivable, he thought, that Rafit Kassim could have confused the year he saw Willie McCovey play baseball in San Francisco. But it was not likely, especially given what Burke had seen in Nauchny Gorodok the previous evening. Nothing that he had heard from Kassim checked out. But what was the truth?

He had half-dreaded, half-hoped that there would be a message from Canfield telling him to call. Maybe Canfield would listen with understanding to the reasons why the cover project had fizzled. Maybe he'd tell Burke to pick himself up, dust himself off, and start all over again. Maybe he'd let him know New York still had hopes for him.

The Russians, Burke thought, had an expression for that hope: when pigs whistle.

On the other hand, Canfield could well have sent a message telling him he was fired.

On the whole, he thought, he would have preferred that to seeing nothing on the wire, hearing nothing on the answering machine. Being ignored was the cruelest treatment of all. It was the *America Weekly* equivalent of the death of a thousand cuts.

He looked at his watch; in New York it was 3 A.M. In six or seven hours, the magazine's editors would be striding into their offices on Madison Avenue. If they were particularly favored, they would look from their desks out over the spires of St. Patrick's Cathedral, a view intended to put them in a godlike frame of mind as they contemplated the state of the world this week, the possibilities for *America Weekly's* next cover, and all the lesser stories that would accompany it. They would examine the incoming proposals from correspondents and prepare their recommendations. At about 10:30, they would swing out into the carpeted halls, the men in shirt-sleeves and suspenders and the women looking only slightly more modish in dresses they picked off the rack at Saks, around the corner. They would head for a conference room. There, they would briefly dissect the issue that had appeared on the newsstands that morning and work up a story list for the next one. Then they would take each other to lunch at some of the better restaurants; and just to make sure they could let the company pick up the tab, they would spend some of the time gossiping about whether Burke or Canfield had looked worse last week. He knew which way Canfield would try to tilt the verdict.

It would be nice if they could have read a message telling them to expect something good from Moscow. He looked at his watch. He now had six hours and forty-nine minutes. He could think of no other way to start than by retracing the steps that had brought him to Nauchny Gorodok in the first place.

That would include talking to Worthington, so he dialed the American Embassy and asked for him. A secretary put him through immediately.

"Ah, Colin. How's business?" Worthington said. His voice sounded smooth and reassuring, and Burke realized how much he needed a friend to confide in.

"Peachy," Burke said, inflecting the word so that

Worthington would know that the opposite was true. "Sorry I wasn't here when you called."

"Not to worry," Worthington said. "Elizabeth and I are having some folks in to dinner tonight, very casual; and we'd love it if you'd care to join us."

As a single male, borderline presentable, Burke got invited to two or three dinners a week by diplomats with a single-male slot to fill at their tables. He rarely accepted, since friendship was rarely involved; and he didn't often care to reciprocate.

But he needed and wanted to talk to Worthington anyway. And the thought of scrounging some dinner together tonight and eating it alone was more than he could bear.

"Love to," he said.

"Seven o'clock," Worthington said. "You know the place."

Burke wrote down the names of the people he had to see first. It was a discouragingly short list:

Katya
Kassim
Parents?

He couldn't count on Katya's telling him anything truthful. He had to reckon with the possibility that she had knowingly fed him disinformation about Nekronov. He could count on Kassim's lying to him. And he didn't even know where to start trying to locate Nekronov's parents. They might not even be alive. Even if they were, there were a lot of old math teachers in Moscow to search through.

Olga came in with some coffee and put it on his desk, along with a few articles she had clipped from the morning papers. She normally stayed a step or two removed from things that most engaged his attention. She didn't care whose stories made the cover and whose stock was rising or falling in New York. It didn't affect her salary, nor did it put food on her table.

But she could see that he was upset.

"Problems?" she said softly.

He smiled at her.

"Can I help?"

She knew nothing about reporting, but at the moment he needed all the help he could get.

"Okay," he said. "Go up to Em-Geh-Ooh. See if you can get any documents, class pictures, anything relating to Sergei Nekronov. A physics student. I think he probably got his baccalaureate around ten years ago and his doctorate maybe two or three years ago."

He reached into his pocket and pulled out twenty dollars.

"Here's some money to work the photocopy machines if you need it." It was, they understood, more likely to be used for bribing a clerk. But he didn't want to know about it.

She nodded and left. As she opened the office door, Pavel Plotnikov stuck his long neck inside.

"Anyone is home?" he called out cheerfully.

Burke was patting his pockets to make sure he had his wallet and his keys. He looked up, nodded, and tried to summon a welcoming smile. It was not easy. He looked at Plotnikov's face carefully. It betrayed no sign of guilt or deceit.

Plotnikov walked in and stood before Burke's desk,

wearing a stained brown raincoat with one button missing and a black Greek fisherman's cap over his scraggly gray hair. Solemnly and silently he raised one finger in the air.

"You know what it means?" he said after a moment of posing.

"You're checking the wind to decide whether to hit a six iron or a seven," Burke said.

Plotnikov's eyebrows furrowed.

"No," he said. "What is six iron?"

"Never mind," Burke said. "Jesus is the only way?"

Plotnikov laughed. "No. Give up?"

"Give up," Burke conceded.

"You obviously spent not enough time outside the Russian vodka stores in era of *zastoi*," Photnikov said. "It means I am one person looking for find someone to split cost of the bottle and share with me."

"Oh, yeah," Burke said. *Zastoi* meant stagnation, and it was the political shorthand for the Brezhnev era. Nowadays, he imagined, it would take too many Russian drunks to come up with enough cash for a bottle to make it worth their while to use the sign language. "I remember."

"You are interested?'

Burke realized he was very interested. Somehow, he could not force the word "no" out of his mouth. He had been thirty-six hours without a drink; and it would take very little to have him join Plotnikov in a midday drink, just two journalists sharing one of the small pleasures of their profession. Or one weak American journalist being plied with liquor by a Russian.

"Interested in *zastoi* lore or in sharing a bottle?" he equivocated.

"Either, actually," Plotnikov said, pleasantly. "I am thinking about writing a collection of Brezhnev jokes before they will be all forgotten. They were the best part of that times. Is not same anymore when it is legal to tell them. What good is joke now?"

"I see what you mean," Burke said.

"Would you like to hear one of good ones?"

"Okay." He could use a distraction.

"Brezhnev and Suslov come back from a summit meeting with the Germans. Suslov says, 'Congratulations on taking a principled and Leninist position, Leonid Ilyich. I loved it when you told the German chancellor, "What intermediate-range missiles?"'"

Plotnikov assumed the stiff, hunched posture of Brezhnev's last years and slurred his words, as Brezhnev had.

"'Thank you, Comrade Suslov. But what German chancellor?'

Burke smiled tightly. "Not bad."

"So how about the vodka?"

Burke took a deep breath. "No, thanks. I've given it up."

"So have I," Plotnikov said. "A hundred times."

"And you've always gone back to it?"

Plotnikov shrugged. "Why not? Vodka works. It always eases the pain. And what is there in life that's not painful?"

Burke sighed. "At the moment, not a hell of a lot." His throat, he realized, ached for the smooth, hot feeling of alcohol.

"You have pain, my friend," Plotnikov said, sympathetically. "It is human condition. God put the pain here in world. So he also put vodka."

"Sorry," Burke said with more determination than he felt. "Can't. Got too much work. But before you go, tell me what happened down in Nauchny Gorodok."

Plotnikov shrugged.

"Not much. They took me in. They questioned me. They wanted to know why I had went there. I told them the truth, that you asked me to drive you. I called my editor, and he talked to them, told them everyone already knew about places like Nauchny Gorodok, that any Westerner with business card could see whatever it was they have there, so why could we not? They put me in cell for while. Maybe they talked to you during this time. After while, they drove me back to car. Gave me some gas, told me not to come back there unless I wanted to arrange story beforehand with Ministry of Medium Machine-Building. Was all quite civilized."

"I'm glad," Burke said.

"And what did you find out about, uh, you know…?" Plotnikov said, pointing at the ceiling. It was the universal Russian gesture of caution, used in rooms assumed to be bugged.

"Couldn't find out anything," Burke said. Then for the benefit of anyone Plotnikov might be working for, he added, "I may have to stop working on the story. Too dangerous."

Plotnikov nodded.

"But I've got to go now on another matter," Burke went on, not caring if he ended the encounter rudely.

Together they slogged down the stairs without waiting for the elevator.

"Another big story?' Plotnikov asked.

"Who knows?' Burke grimaced. He walked Plotnikov down to the street and got into his car. "Can I drop you somewhere?" he asked, deciding that it might be useful to pretend that he still trusted the man.

"Uh, no," the Russian said. "I have not a particular place to go. I just wanted to check and make sure you are okay. Call me when you need someone to drink with again." He ambled away.

Burke found a parking spot on the same block as Switsico and didn't bother to call in advance. The same trick would hardly work twice, anyway. Inside the office he found the same secretaries and spoke to the same woman in the same high-necked silk blouse, still buttoned all the way to her chin.

"Hi, remember me?" he said. "I need to see Mr. Kassim." He looked around her shoulder down the short internal hallway. All of the doors were closed, but he remembered the one Kassim had emerged from the last time.

"He's not here."

"Mind if I check?"

"You can't."

"Sorry," Burke said. He took a big first step and was around her before she could get out of her chair. He strode down the hall, hearing her mutter something in Russian, get up, and follow him. He thrust open the door to Kassim's office and stepped inside.

It was empty.

The desk, of Swedish birch, was shining from fresh polish, and there were no papers on it, just a telephone and a pen-and-pencil set. Before he could look further, the secretary stepped in front of him. A flush had spread up from the collar of her blouse into her cheeks.

"We have called the *militsia*," she said. "If you don't leave immediately, you will be arrested."

"Where is he?'

She folded her arms and said nothing.

He decided it was not worth waiting to see if she was bluffing about the police.

"Okay," he said. "Sorry to have to do this, but you already proved yourself a liar once. Remember?" he said. He saw the flush deepen in her face, then strode around her again. In a moment, he was pulling open the two thin drawers on Kassim's desk. They were as empty as the office. He looked at the walls. There were two paintings of what looked like desert scenes. He couldn't tell. Other than that, the walls were bare.

"Bye," he said to the secretary, who was by now turning a bright pink, with purple mottling on the edges. He strode past her a third time and, in a minute, found himself outside on Maly Gneznikovsky Pereulok. He looked around. The *militsia* gave no sign of being on the way to arrest him. He heard no sirens.

He got in his car and pondered.

It was an unlikely prospect, but Kassim might be at his health club. He pulled away from the office building and made a turn at the McDonald's near Pushkin Square. Gray crowd-control fences still divided the sidewalk outside into corridors, but there was no one in them. The days when Russians would line up for hours to buy a Beeg Mek had long since gone. The prices were too high. He made his way onto the boulevard heading northwest out of the city. He still called it Gorky Street, though it was now officially Tversky, as it had been before the Revolution. He cut a jagged path through the scraggly lines of old trucks and buses until he reached the long, dun-colored brick building that housed the health club. He parked in the rear; his was the only foreign car in sight.

The staircase was as dark as he remembered it, with the same stale smell of old cabbage and urine mixed with the fading, acrid odor of fresh paint. He groped his way forward until his eyes adjusted to the dimness. Then he ascended. But there was no welcoming light at the second-floor landing. Someone, in fact, had carefully removed the light bulb that had been burning three days before. He banged on the door, but no one answered. He tried to open it. It was locked and shut tight.

That left Katya. He drove back toward the center of the city and stopped at the Metro station near Dynamo Stadium. The small plaza in front of the station contained a marketplace of sorts. Old women spread whatever they could find to sell on blankets and waited for someone to come along and buy. One had a few packages of Bulgarian cigarettes. Another had a carton of tampons. A third had a few loaves of fresh bread. The fourth had carrots and turnips from her garden, the black Russian dirt still clinging to them. He hurried past them to the bank of pay phones just inside the station doors and dialed Katya's number. There was no answer.

On the chance that her phone might not be working, which was not insubstantial in Moscow, he looked up her address in the map book he carried in his glove compartment. The book contained CIA maps, which the Agency had begun to publish in the old days, when Moscow's street plan was still considered a state secret. The new Russian government no longer considered it classified, but neither had it managed to publish a map as complete or compact as the CIA's.

She lived on a street named for the composer Scriabin, on the southeastern edge of the city in a district of automobile and textile factories. He looked at his watch. It would take him forty-five minutes each way to drive there. It might well be a waste of time. On the other hand, he had nothing more promising to try. Going to her place would at least be doing something. If he returned to the office, he knew, he would brood. The idea of sitting there and contemplating his problems was too painful to consider. He got into the car and pointed it southeast.

She lived, it turned out, in a fifteen-story building shaped like an upright gray brick, surrounded by five-story buildings shaped like squat gray bricks. Sheets of green plastic on the little slivers of balcony gave the building some color. He parked near the front door and walked up the path of packed dirt and broken glass. Three old women sat sunning themselves on a bench near the door. At the sight of his car and his clothing, they fell silent, watching him carefully. Inside, a knot of three or four teenaged boys blocked the staircase, playing dominoes and smoking.

He stepped carefully around them.

"Got any matches?" one of them asked.

"Sorry," Burke said.

Her apartment number was 52. Burke calculated that it was probably on the seventh floor, and inside the elevator he punched that button. Someone had scratched "Motley Crue" into the metal wall of the elevator.

It clanked and rose slowly to the sixth floor. The doors opened and stayed open. He punched all the various buttons, but nothing induced the doors to shut again, so he got out and walked up to seven. He had miscalculated. Seven had apartments 42 to 46. He walked up two more flights to nine. No. 52 was in the middle of the hallway, a black leather doorway with a tattered patch of blue carpet on the floor in front of it. He rang the bell next to the door. Nothing happened.

He took a business card from his wallet and wrote a brief message on the back, asking her to call him, saying he would stop by again soon. He doubted that she would call. Nothing was that easy. He slipped the card under the door anyway.

"What are you drinking?" Ethan Worthington asked Burke.

"Soda water," Burke replied. He had prepared himself for this moment, but he had not realized how taut his voice would feel as he forced the words from his throat.

Worthington looked puzzled for a moment, then decided to smile.

"Occupational hazard for journalists, I guess."

"Yeah," Burke said. "With pitchers, the arm goes. With reporters, it's the liver."

"Soda water it is then."

"Thanks."

Worthington poured Canada Dry into a glass filled

with ice and added a wedge of lime. The embassy store made sure that American diplomats lacked few of the small pleasures of life at home.

Worthington splashed a little Glenfiddich into his own glass, which was already half full. Burke could smell the Scotch from three feet away. They were standing in the front room of Worthington's townhouse, looking out a bay window toward the indoor swimming pool in the center of the embassy complex. A half dozen other guests, all embassy staff, were clustered at the other end of the room, forty feet away.

"So how's your project coming?' Worthington asked, twirling the ice in his glass.

"It's not," Burke replied. "Ran into some problems. Trying to check them out."

Worthington nodded. "Port McIntire tells me you ran into a particular one in Nauchny Gorodok."

"True, I'm afraid," Burke said, shrugging his shoulders. "Ever heard of a guy named Nekronov?"

"Nekronov," Worthington pondered. "How're we talking? Off the record?"

"Okay." It was, Burke thought, a dinner party. He had no right to turn it into an on-the-record interview.

"We know about a guy named Sergei Nekronov. He's one of their best young designers," Worthington said. "This is the one you went down there to see?"

Burke nodded. He felt reluctant to tell Worthington more. Whether his reluctance stemmed more from discretion or embarrassment he could not have said.

"He talking to the Syrians?"

Burke nodded again. "I believe so."

Worthington looked impressed. "So what happened down there?"

Burke shrugged. "I got caught in a restricted zone."

"Before you found what you were looking for?'

"Yeah. I need to get some more information on him. I spent hours this afternoon in the city board of education office, trying to get some data on special math schools and math teachers. I think he went to one, and I think his parents were teachers. All I got was an offer to look more tomorrow. I think the Russians are not so much secretive as disorganized."

Worthington's eyebrows fluttered over his horn-rimmed glasses. 'Well, we have a data bank on those types," he said. "I'll take a look tomorrow morning and let you know what I find out."

"Thanks," Burke said. "I'd appreciate it."

A thirteen-year-old girl with Elizabeth Worthington's ash-blonde hair walked up with a tray full of toast triangles, sour cream, and caviar.

"Have you met Martha?" Worthington asked.

"Your daughter, I presume."

Worthington laughed loudly and took some caviar. "How'd you guess?" he said. The girl's cheeks turned red.

"Martha, this is Mr. Burke," Worthington went on. "He's the one who writes those great articles in *America Weekly*."

The girl almost curtsied.

Worthington nibbled at the edge of his caviar. "Martha's a good writer, too," he said, with evident pride. "You should read some of the essays on Moscow she writes for school. You might want to recruit her. She's thinking of becoming a journalist."

The girl looked like her cheeks might burst out in flames.

"Daddy," she said, reproachfully.

"I'm sure they're very good, Martha," Burke said. "But I think you should look for a more respectable line of work. Savings and loan director. Accident attorney. Something like that."

The girl looked blankly at him, not sure whether he was putting her on or merely being stupidly adult.

Worthington looked hurt.

"Sorry," Burke said, half to him, half to the girl. "Why don't you come down to the bureau sometime and I'll show you around?"

It was an easy offer to make, considering his likely tenure there.

"That'd be real nice," Worthington said, and the girl nodded tentatively, her complexion gradually returning to pale and slightly freckled. The freckles made Burke think involuntarily of Lena Laskova.

"Let's get on over toward the company," Worthington said, taking Burke's arm. As they approached the rest of the guests, Burke saw three couples and a single woman, Alice Simpson, an assistant press attaché who specialized, as far as he was concerned, in creating obstacles between reporters and the people they wanted to talk to. Worse, she seemed to enjoy it. Burke loathed her and, as far as he knew, she loathed him.

He sighed, trying to do it inaudibly. First he had committed himself to offer Worthington's daughter a tour of the bureau. Now this. Free meals were becoming prohibitively expensive.

Just after Martha Worthington served the coffee, Burke made his excuses and left.

Glumly, he sat behind the wheel of the car for a moment, wanting the isolation and quiet. He calculated the hours of legwork he had put in that day—twelve or thirteen. He could feel them in his feet. His mind felt tired. And he had nothing to show for it except an acute craving for a drink.

His body felt old and stifled, so he turned the engine on and drove grimly past the all-night kiosks near the Kropotkinskaya Metro station, where they sold cheap vodka for five thousand rubles a liter. He went home, stripped off his clothes, and got into his running gear. He got back into the car and drove across town to the riverside promenade at the edge of the Lenin Hills. Mechanically, he began to run.

A light mist was rising from the river, and the lights from the center of the city bounced off it, giving it a pale yellow glow. Across the river, he could see a faint glint coming from the gilded domes of Novodevichy, and the hulking mass of Lenin Stadium looked like the entrance to a dark tunnel.

He tried to let his mind relax, to let the fluttering jumble of thoughts sort itself out and become clear. They refused.

No inspiration came out of the mist, and he turned around and started back toward the car. He could think of only one thing to do: to keep pounding on doors until one of them opened.

He completed the last quarter mile with his knees up and his breath coming in long, ragged drafts. By the time he reached the car, he was sweating freely. It was just after eleven o'clock. He would, he decided, try again at the health club and at Katya's.

The Moscow streets were in their usual late-night

torpor. An occasional drunk staggered along the sidewalks; but otherwise the streets were devoid of life, cold and desolate. The people were indoors, drinking or watching television, or, if they were lucky, sleeping.

He found Scriabin Street again and parked in front of the building. The gaggle of old women was gone, but inside the front door the quartet of teenagers had become a septet. Some of them had cigarettes going, and he could see light reflecting off the surface of a bottle. They seemed vaguely menacing in the darkness, and he wondered how they treated Katya when she walked past them.

"Got cigarettes?" one of them asked as he strode past. He didn't answer.

The elevator, he discovered, had given up entirely. He trudged up the stairs. As he walked, the memory of Katya, stepping nude into his shower, leaped to the forefront of his consciousness; and he wondered what she would be wearing if, in fact, he found her in.

Puffing slightly, and reminding himself that he had come only to ask her questions, he reached the ninth floor. He stopped on the landing to catch his breath, a task made more difficult by the odor of garbage and fouled plumbing that became noxious when he inhaled deeply.

The hallway was dark, and the door to No. 52 was edged in yellow light. It was open a crack. He pressed on the button and heard a buzzer inside, but nothing else. He pushed gently at the door and it swung open.

She had a bright red raincoat hanging on a peg inside, plus the usual assortment of shoes, boots, and slippers. The floors were scuffed; and in the corner of the room beyond, a television, new and Japanese, was showing a test pattern.

To his right were a cramped kitchen and a dank little bathroom with a faucet audibly dripping. The far wall held a large calendar with a picture of two golden cocker spaniel puppies. The floors were scuffed and bare.

He took three steps forward and looked left. A single bed stood against the far wall, ten feet away from him. She lay on it, naked and still; and for an instant he thought she was asleep. Then he saw her eyes, wide open; and the way her mouth was frozen in a toothy, silent scream; and the rigid limbs; and the thin, purple gash that stretched from one side of her throat to the other over a pool of glistening blood.

CHAPTER FIFTEEN

FOR TWENTY YEARS, he had been writing about death. He had written about people who died in traffic accidents and people who had been murdered and soldiers who died in war. But he had never actually confronted the violated corpse of another human being, much less the body of someone he knew, someone who had aroused his lust, someone with an oozing carmine gash where she had once had a long white and gently curved neck. He had contemplated kissing that neck.

He took a deep breath and settled his stomach.

Gingerly, as if afraid to waken her, he walked toward the bed and took a closer look. He could see no bruises on her blue-white skin nor any signs of blood elsewhere in the room. The cut was clean and narrow. Whoever killed her had done his work professionally, probably with a razor. He could imagine someone she knew, perhaps someone she was in bed with, producing his blade so deftly and swiftly that she had no time to get off the bed or fight. He picked up first one and then the other limp, cold hand. Neither showed a cut, and he remembered from a trial he had once covered that people stabbed to death generally had cuts on their hands if they had resisted their killers.

But at least the hand was cold. That should put the time of death well before Burke's arrival.

She might have been asleep, he decided, napping in the middle of the day. People who worked at night did that. Maybe she had never opened her eyes. Maybe she felt the blade on her neck, started to open her eyes to see and her mouth to scream, then felt the life gushing out of her artery for an instant before sleep recaptured her.

He shook his head and tried to focus on his options. He could call the *militsia* and tell them the truth. But that would mean entrusting his fate to the Russian justice system.

He could bolt. He could wipe clean everything he had touched, walk as calmly as possible down the stairs, get into his car and go home, and hope that he never heard another word about Katya.

But he knew that he had left his business card there that afternoon, and he had not seen it since pushing the door open two minutes ago. Unless Katya's killer had taken it, it was still around somewhere, and the *militsia* would find it.

He walked, still gingerly, about the room, scanning the top of the table, the single bookshelf, and the chest of drawers.

He felt a drop of sweat bead on his chin and drop

to the floor, where it made a small stain on the wood. Did the Moscow *militsia* have a way of testing sweat for DNA? He doubted it.

He saw nail polish, perfume, a couple of English grammar texts, a small bowl of salt, a handful of coins, and a stack of compact disks. The one on the top was by Cypress Hill. No business card.

He went to the kitchen and found a bottle of Armenian cognac sitting on the little dining table, leering at him. Given the circumstance, he decided, he deserved a drink. With a dish towel in his hand, he picked up the bottle and opened it. He put the bottle to his lips and let a dram slide out onto his tongue. He held it there, savoring it. Then he swallowed it. He could feel it slide all the way down to his stomach. His body enveloped the alcohol like a mother enveloping a baby in her arms.

Stiffly and slowly, he went to the sink and emptied the rest of the bottle down the drain. The police, he realized dimly, might discover what he had done and read something guilty into it. But he had no choice. His hand trembled as he put the empty bottle back on the table.

Still with the towel wrapped around his hand, he began pulling open drawers in the old, scarred, mock-mahogany dresser. The first held lingerie, some black and new and some old, gray, and cottony. He stopped.

Even if he found his card, the *militsia* might identify him by talking to neighbors who had seen him or his car. If the *militsia* learned that he had fled the scene, they would assume he had killed her.

He decided to call them.

Her telephone was on a night table next to the

bed. He turned himself sideways to avoid brushing against the body and sidled into the alcove at the head of the bed.

He did not know what to dial. If there was a Russian equivalent of 911, he did not know it. He had spent most of his time in Moscow trying to avoid the *militsia,* not contact them.

Finally, he got an operator and had her call. He anticipated a quick response. He doubted that the cops got too many calls from American journalists about Russian hookers with their throats slit open.

He wanted desperately to cover the body, to get it out of his sight, to give her some shred of dignity. Her nakedness affected him more than the deep, narrow incision in her neck. But he knew it would be a mistake to touch anything. He had to leave her as he had found her, lest the *militsia* get the idea that he had covered her because he couldn't bear to look at what he had done.

He went into the kitchen, sat down at her table, and wondered who had killed her. His mind kept returning to Rafit Kassim. He could think of no one else with a motive. What would Kassim think she might tell Burke? What would be worth killing her to prevent him hearing?

In a minute, he heard sirens, but they seemed to orbit around him for another five minutes.

He tried to force himself to plan for the interrogation ahead. How much should he tell the *militsia* about her? Should he tell them about Kassim?

Before he could decide, he heard heavy footsteps in the hallway, the sound of several men walking rapidly. Then he heard a loud, persistent banging on the door.

Burke tried to keep one eye on the man asking questions and the other on the men doing the examination of the scene. The one asking questions was short and thick-bodied, with scars around his eyes and a nose that something had flattened and squeezed over to the left side of his face, like Silly Putty. The man's voice seemed to come out of that nose like noise coming through a twisting tunnel. Syllables and words got lost in the bends, and Burke had to strain very hard to understand what he said. His name was Major Something-kov, and he seemed very deferential as he established Burke's identity, just as the *militsioneri* in Nauchny Gorodok had been.

Over his shoulder, Burke watched the other militiamen work. There were three of them. One took pictures with an ancient Soviet camera called a *Zenit*. Another was spreading orange powder around the room and lifting fingerprints. The third was having a closer look at the body. Burke saw him reach under Katya's tawny hair for something. Then the man stepped across the room and wordlessly handed Major Something-kov Burke's business card. One of the corners was stained with blood. Something-kov held the card by the edges as he might have held a photographic negative, examining it. He seemed to Burke to be taking an ungodly long time to read it. Finally, he turned again to Burke, his face solemn.

"Yours?"

Burke nodded.

"You wrote this?"

He nodded again.

"You left it here for her?"

Burke tried not to show any impatience.

"Yes."

"When?"

Burke tried to remember whether anyone had seen him when he walked into Katya's building the first time. There had been some old women. Someone had asked him for matches. He had better tell the truth.

"I think it was about six o'clock."

Something-kov wrote this carefully down in a little notebook.

"You were here at six o'clock?"

"About then."

"And she was not here?"

"I rang the bell. No one opened the door."

"And you left?"

"Obviously. Why else would I leave the card?"

"And then you came back?"

"Uh-huh," Burke nodded. "A few minutes ago."

"And how did you get in?"

"I walked. The door was open."

"How far open?"

"An inch or so."

The detective then spent a long minute reviewing his notes.

"Mr. Burke," he began, raising his head.

"Yes?"

"I'm afraid I am going to have to ask you to come with me to the station. Just routine."

Burke smiled stiffly. "That's what they say in all the bad movies," he said.

Something-kov looked puzzled. Burke sighed. "All

right, let's get it over with," he said. Something-kov beamed. "Thank you," he said, as if surprised and delighted that Burke had agreed.

They rode the elevator down, each staring silently at the chips and scratches in the veneer. Burke's stomach churned slowly.

The handful of kids who had been hanging around the lobby had grown to a crowd of perhaps fifty people, attracted by the ambulance that was sitting in the parking area, an orange light revolving on its roof. They stood silently in the chill air, their breath frosting over their heads and reflecting the lights from the ambulance and three *militsia* sedans.

Burke stopped on the asphalt, uncertain whether Something-kov intended him to drive his car to the station.

The detective looked at the foreign car and understood immediately.

"Your car?" he asked. Burke nodded.

"It can be left here. We will bring you back for it." Burke nodded again and stepped toward the *militsia* cars, but Something-kov continued to look at the Volvo, obviously thinking.

"Would you be so kind," he said, gravely and formally, "as to leave the key with me so we can look inside?"

Burke hesitated. There was nothing more confidential in the car than an overdue American Express bill. He doubted that Something-kov would care about his credit rating. But he hated to let the Moscow *militsia* search anything. On the other hand, if he refused, Something-kov might make him take a Breathalyzer test. He had limited himself to a single glass of wine at the Worthingtons' and

the shot of cognac in Katya's kitchen, but he knew that
Moscow cops could get very strict about drinking and
driving when it suited their purposes.

"It's just routine," Something-kov said, smiling
thinly. "I wish you'd stop saying that," Burke said, and
handed over the keys.

They left him alone for more than an hour in the
empty office of the deputy chief of the Proletarsky
Rayon, which was where Katya had lived. Boredom soon
replaced the nervous twitch in his stomach.

Burke stared for a while at the portrait of Iron Feliks
Dzerzhinsky, the first chief of the KGB, hanging on the
wall opposite the chief's desk. The revolution of August
'91 had toppled the statue of Dzerzhinsky opposite the
Lyubyanka, but evidently there were still places in the
city where he was revered.

Furtively, he scanned the phone directories on the
desk, looking for numbers that might be useful. He saw
one for something called "Moscow Central Command"
and wrote it down. He tried the file cabinets. They were
locked.

He looked at his watch. It was nearly two in the
morning, and he had lots of work to get done the next
day. He decided that if Something-kov didn't show up in
five minutes to finish his questions, he would go look
for him. Maybe he would leave. They had entered the
building via a dark courtyard and a brief, anonymous
corridor, but he thought he could find his way back out.

He was suddenly very tired. Running by the river
had gotten his blood moving. Seeing Katya's body had

started his adrenaline pumping. It almost seemed as if the swallow of cognac he'd had had stimulated him. Now, all these stimuli wore off abruptly, and he could feel his body coming down like a rock tossed off a bridge, headed for the welcoming blackness of sleep.

The door opened, and Burke's head jerked up. He blinked several times to force his eyes to focus on the small, slender man in a baggy gray suit standing in front of him. He carried a red file folder.

The man looked more like a boy waiting impatiently for his secondary sexual characteristics. He stood no more than five-six, weighed about one hundred ten pounds, and had a fine-boned face with wispy white fuzz visible on his pale cheeks. He strode across the room to Burke and shook hands. His grip was weak and, Burke thought, almost feminine. His name was Amulyakhin and he was the procurator assigned to the case of the murder of Yegorova, Yekaterina Jvanovna.

Burke blinked again before he realized the man was talking about Katya. He had never learned her last name.

"So," Amulyakhin said, leaning forward. "Was she a good fuck?"

Burke half shook his head, uncertain he had heard the man correctly, wondering if his Russian vocabulary was adequate to an interrogation.

"Excuse me?"

"Was she a good fuck?"

Amulyakthin's face bore an expression of innocent curiosity that was only belied by the hardness Burke could suddenly see in his eyes.

"I mean," Amulyakhin continued, "did you get your hundred dollars' worth? It's more money than I make in two months, Mr. Burke, and I'm just wondering if she was worth it."

Burke sighed, aware now that he was in trouble.

"I wouldn't know," he said.

"Oh," Amulyakhin nodded, understandingly. "You just had her suck you. Safer that way, I suppose."

Burke said nothing.

"Was she good at it?"

Burke sighed again.

"Look," he said. "I think your questions are—" he tried to think of a polite word—"inappropriate."

Amulyakhin's face twisted and grew red.

"Don't tell me what questions are inappropriate!" he fairly screamed. "If you were a Russian, do you think I'd be treating you so gently? So politely?"

Amulyakhin's ferocity startled Burke. He felt a bead of sweat break out on his forehead and dribble down his temple. He hoped Amulyakhin didn't notice. It was a wan hope.

The procurator seemed to regain control of himself.

"So. You will answer the questions."

Burke nodded.

"So did she suck you?"

"No. There was no sex between us."

Ainulyakhin threw back his head and laughed.

"Mr. Burke," he said, still smiling, appearing to be greatly amused, "Come with me."

He turned abruptly and walked out of the office. Burke followed. They walked down the same dark corridor, Amulyakhin's footfalls echoing and Burke's squeaking, thanks to the running shoes he wore. Briefly, they emerged in the courtyard, where Aniulyakhin turned right and reentered the building through another door. They were in a small entry hall. Burke could see, a few feet ahead of him, a small, heavy steel door with a thick glass window about four inches square. Amulyakhin rang a bell, and in a couple of seconds the door opened.

A guard stepped aside and they entered another corridor, this one lit by a single weak light bulb overhead. The air reeked sourly of urine and disinfectant. Amulykahin paused before a cell door made of riveted steel. It had a heavy rust padlock on the outside next to a revolving tray that apparently allowed the guard to pass food in to the prisoners. The guard opened the lock and pushed at the door.

It was like turning over a rock and watching the maggots squirm. Inside, Burke could dimly see rows of iron bunks devoid of mattresses. Prisoners were groaning and getting up, scratching their heads, and blinking at the unexpected light from the hall. The man closest to the door looked like an overgrown mole. His head was shaved, showing pale white skin underneath, and his shoulders were rounded and powerful. He had tattoos up and down both biceps.

"Have you ever seen an investigative isolator, Mr. Burke?" Amulyakhin inquired casually.

"No," Burke said. "But they say that no reporter's education is complete without the experience."

Amulyakhin smiled again, clearly enjoying this game. "Well then, you know, no doubt, that normally we would let a person caught in your position spend the night in here, then talk to him in the morning."

"I'm sure you do," Burke said.

"So are you prepared to answer our questions? To cooperate?"

Burke sighed. "I have been cooperating."

Amulyakhin smiled again with no teeth showing, as if this was the answer he had been waiting for.

"Very well, Mr. Burke," he said. "I suggest we continue this conversation in the morning. Sleep well."

The guard opened the door wider, pushed Burke gently inside, and closed it. Burke could hear the heavy hasp of the padlock clicking into place. Amulyaklnn said something to the guard that he couldn't quite make out. Then two pairs of footsteps receded down the corridor.

Burke waited for his eyes to adjust to the almost total absence of light in the room. He felt the beads of sweat forming freely on his brow and dripping off his chin. He wondered if the men in the room with him could smell his fear above the rancid mélange of old vomit, urine, and disinfectant that filled the room.

Cautiously, he reached out until he felt the iron rail of a bunk. He kept his hand on it and inched forward into the room. He made his way past two bunks until he saw, dimly, a lower one that appeared to be empty. He ran his hand slowly over its cold iron surface to make sure it was. He felt nothing except the bumps in the metal.

As quietly as he could, he slid down onto the slab, wriggling to find a posture that would allow him to rest.

He closed his eyes and tried to calm down, to still the anxiety bubbling within him. He heard a rustling and a footstep, and then a hand like a meaty pincer closed around his throat, squeezing until the breath was trapped in his lungs.

"You're in my bunk," a guttural voice said.

He clutched at the hand pressing down from the darkness, found the wrist above it, got both hands around it, and pushed. It barely moved—just enough to allow him to inhale.

"I'll move," he muttered,

The hand let up. He still could not see the face it was attached to. Cautiously, he swung his leg over the side of the bunk and stood up. He groped through the room inches at a time, carefully searching until he found another empty bunk. It was an upper, and he swung himself up into it as quietly as he could.

This time, when he heard a rustling, he moved his hand to protect his throat. A fist slammed into his unprotected stomach. Involuntarily, he retched. The bilious remnants of the Worthingtons' dinner erupted onto his shirt.

"You're in my bunk," another low voice said.

He shook his head, trying to clear it, "I'll move," he said again, and slid down from the bunk. The floor seemed to wobble beneath his feet.

"All the bunks are taken?" he said, directing his words in the direction of the last voice. Peering against the faint light of the doorway, he could make out the silhouette of an enormous man—about six feet six inches tall and almost as wide.

"Taken," the man said firmly.

Briefly, Burke considered his options. Fighting with a gargantuan Russian prisoner in a darkened cell was not high on his list of things to accomplish.

He turned away and sought a spot on the floor between the rows of bunks, He sat down, back pressed against the rough stone wall of the cell. The concrete floor was cold and damp and smelled of bile and despair. So, he thought, did he.

For what seemed like an hour, he sat with his eyes

wide open, waiting for someone to rise up from a bunk, tell him that he was occupying reserved floor space, and try to maim him. No one stirred. Apparently, forcing him to sleep on the floor had satisfied his fellow prisoners.

Finally, as he thought he saw light beginning to shine through a dirty little window high on the opposite wall, he closed his eyes.

❊ ❊ ❊

A new procurator replaced Amulyakhin at the morning interrogation.

His name was Viktor Lemeshev; and he had the bland, careful face and western clothes that Burke had come to associate with the kind of man who grew up in a *nomenklatura* family, graduated from one of the better institutes, and survived the fall of the Party by carefully timing his defection into the democratic camp.

But the main thing, as far as Burke was concerned, was that Lemeshev showed only a mild interest in whether and for how much Colin Burke had fornicated with the deceased, Yekaterina Yegorova.

Burke gave him the same answers he had given Amulyakhin. No, he had not had sex with Yekaterina Yegorova, nor had he paid her anything. He had met her at the Olympic Sport and Health Club. He had been invited there as a guest of Rafit Kassim. He had met Kassim while working on a story about Switsico.

Burke did not tell Lemeshev about his second meeting with Katya, or what she had told him, or where that had led him.

Lemeshev made notes, his manner cold and deliberate.

"What were you trying to find out about Switsico?"

There was no point, he thought, in lying about that. The *militsia* and the Ministry of Security would know soon enough if they didn't know already.

"Whether it's a front for recruiting Russian nuclear scientists."

Lemeshev betrayed no surprise.

"And is it?"

"When I find out, you'll be one of the first to know," Burke said.

"And why did you go to her apartment yesterday?"

"I wanted to talk to her about Kassim," Burke said. "Look, it was completely aboveboard. Why do you think I left my card there?"

"Ah yes, your business card," Lemeshev said. "You didn't write on it that you wanted to talk to her about this Mr. Kassim. You just said you wanted to see her."

Burke shrugged. "It's a small card."

A thought occurred to him. "Look, obviously, whoever killed her found the card in the apartment somewhere and slipped it under her head so you'd find it. Why would I have done that? It makes no sense. If I killed her, why would I leave my card there?"

Lemeshev said nothing, confining himself to writing on his notepad. Then he put the pencil down.

"Mr. Burke, you're lying to me."

Burke swallowed.

Lemeshev waited silently. Burke sat, silent and exhausted.

"Let me remind you," Lemeshev finally said, "that the penalty for first degree murder in Russia is death. A bullet behind the ear. And we have enough evidence to charge you already."

The procurator let his words reverberate in a moment of pointed silence.

"Normally," he went on, "we would hold you for ten days while we continued to investigate. You got acquainted with the holding cell last night."

He looked blandly at Burke, who looked blandly back. "One of the great achievements of the Soviet justice system," Burke said of the cell.

Lemeshev's gaze hardened, and Burke thought the man might lose his temper. With a visible effort, Lemeshev remained calm.

"But since you are a United States citizen and an accredited journalist, I am prepared to offer you—" He paused, groping for the right word. "—kinder treatment."

"Specifically?"

"You may go home right now, under the following conditions. First, you leave your passport here. You are not to leave the country until the investigation is over. Second, you must not contact anyone involved with Yekaterina Yegorova or this Switsico story. We cannot allow suspects to contact potential witnesses. It is too easy to coordinate stories. Third, you will report to this office every morning at nine o'clock in case you are needed for further questioning. Do you understand?"

Burke nodded. "And the alternative?"

"The investigative isolation cell. I should add that if you accept these conditions, your activities will be monitored to make sure you are not violating them."

Burke nodded again.

"Not much of a choice, is it?"

CHAPTER SIXTEEN

THE MIDMORNING TRAFFIC on the Garden Ring Road moved first sluggishly, then not at all, thanks to a construction barricade in the middle lane. A crew of women in paint-spattered coveralls was slowly patching an enormous pothole. Burke fumed and drummed his fingers against the steering wheel. He looked in the mirror; but the traffic in the lane to his left was unending, and none of the drivers showed any sign of being ready to yield to someone trying to emerge from the blocked lane.

He did not see the grimy blue dump truck ahead of him start to roll in reverse, its driver intent on gaining enough room to wedge his own way into the left lane. A thud pitched Burke's head forward. He heard the tinkling of glass. Startled, he looked up to see the numerals 84-697, painted across the truck's tailgate, looming ten feet closer than they should have, at an oblique angle.

Burke jerked the parking brake up, threw open his door, and jumped out of the car. It took three seconds to see that the truck had knocked out his right headlight. It took another three seconds for him to bound to the cab, bang on the door, and yell for the driver to come out. Cars swerved to avoid him. In his fury, he did not see them.

When the truck's door opened, Burke lunged upward, grabbed, and closed his fingers around the driver's belt. Convulsively, he yanked the man out of the cab and into the street. He began screaming at him in English.

"Asshole! Stupid motherfucking idiot! Of all the stupid motherfucking moves! Take me three goddamn days to get a new headlight!"

The startled driver, a slender, short Georgian, took a look at the man in front of him, a man wearing filthy foreign sweat clothes, screaming in a foreign language, the skin under his matted hair and stubbly beard turning pink and purple with his rage. Carefully, the driver reached back and got his hand around the tire iron he carried under his seat. He drew it out and let Burke see it.

Burke abruptly stopped yelling. He shook his head, as if to wake himself. His body trembled lightly.

"I'm sorry about your headlight," the truck driver said, calmly.

Burke nodded his head slowly. "And I'm sorry for blowing up like that."

"You should get some rest," the driver said.

"Maybe so," Burke nodded.

He walked to his car and sat down again behind the wheel, still trembling. Eventually, the traffic moved.

He drove to the Lenin Hills, to the paved embankment of the Moscow River, the place where he had

walked with Katya. The day was cloudy and chilly. There
was no sign of *baboye leto* in the air, just the gloomy smell
of approaching winter.

Burke walked slowly along the embankment, his
eyes fixed blankly on the dull golden domes of
Novodevichy across the river. He breathed deeply and
tried to will the faint trembling in his hands to stop.
After a while it seemed to work.

He tried to force his mind to sort out and analyze
what had happened.

First, there was Katya. Someone had killed her and
tried to point suspicion at him. It was, most likely, Rafit
Kassim. But he had no way of proving that, and any
effort to find proof would run afoul of the conditions
laid down by the procurator, Lemeshev.

He looked over his shoulder. An old woman was
walking fifty yards behind him, pushing a baby carriage.
He thought that she quickly averted her eyes toward the
carriage as soon as she realized he was looking back at
her. Maybe she was watching him. Maybe he was just
getting paranoid.

And if she was watching him, there was not a damn
thing he could do about it. He forced his mind back to
his predicament.

Someone, obviously, was trying to foist disinformation on him. But what was real, and what was the
disinformation? Katya, he thought, had most likely been
real. Otherwise, why would they have killed her? Ronit
Evron was real. Why else would someone have tipped
off her mother?

If Katya and Ronit were real, he thought, then so
was the plot to recruit Nekronov. And if that was real, it
meant that everything he had seen on his third trip to

Nauchny Gorodok had to be fake. Someone didn't want the Nekronov story to get out. Someone had taken steps to make sure Burke couldn't get the final piece of the story—the pictures. Then they had taken steps to get Nekronov out of his apartment and make it look as if he had never lived there, down to planting false neighbors. They were counting on the story's falling apart.

But who were they?

It had to be, he thought, old KGB men now in the Ministry of Security. Only they would have the resources. And it was not hard to imagine their motive. Money from the same Arab sources that were ready to pay Sergei Nekronov half a million dollars a year could be used to buy the enthusiastic cooperation of the Ministry of Security. Everything in Russia was for sale. Why not the secret police?

And he had, he thought bitterly, played into their hands by asking Pavel Plotnikov to drive him to Nauchny Gorodok. Only Plotnikov had the opportunily to tip off the boys in the black leather jackets about where Burke was going.

"Idiot," he muttered under his breath, angry with himself. His first instinct had been not to trust Plotnikov, as he had learned in the old days not to trust any Russian who initiated an acquaintance. But he had instead fallen for a sentimental story about a middle-aged man who wanted to become a journalist.

"Idiot," he muttered again.

And now they had him in a box. If he tried to expose them, and they found out, they would toss him into a cell and let their goons beat him.

If he did nothing, the call would inevitably come from Canfield, summoning him home to be fired. Or, worse, stuck on a desk somewhere to become a washed-up reporter waiting for a decent early retirement offer, a reporter eaten up by the shameful memory of being duped.

He sighed and turned back toward his car.

In the apartment, he stood under the shower for a long time until he was sure that all traces of the jail cell and all traces of Katya's corpse had washed down the drain. Two ideas dominated his thoughts. He had to fmd Sergei Nekronov. And he had to do it obliquely.

He had, he realized, only one source who had nothing to do with Switsico and whom he had not questioned a second time: General Vyacheslav Stankevich. He put on a suit, grabbed some coins, and walked outside. A cold rain had begun to fall, and he drove to the Clean Ponds Metro station to find a pay phone under shelter.

He got through to Stankevich's secretary on the second try.

"It's vitally important that I speak to him right away," he told her. She said she would see; and after a couple of minutes, Stankevich came on.

"I need to see you right away," Burke said. "I have something to tell you." It was a long shot, he knew, that Stankevich would even agree to see him, let alone be baited by the prospect of an exchange of information. But he had no other prospects.

Stankevich hesitated, weighing Burke's words. Finally, he spoke.

"You know the Ministry of Defense headquarters

on Novy Arbat? Meet me outside the front entrance at six o'clock."

"Outside the front entrance at six?" Burke replied, surprised, and wishing to make sure he had heard correctly over the rumble of trains in the tunnels below him.

"Don't waste time repeating things," Stankevich said, and hung up.

Six o'clock was six hours away. Burke went home and slept.

Wacheslav Stankevich looked resplendent in his olive uniform with red stripes and piping. There was something new atop his epaulets: a fat, gold marshal's star. He stepped out the door to the ministry, his bearing erect and his face stem, and looked around.

Burke took a couple of paces from underneath the tree where he had taken some shelter from the rain, which had turned into a steady, cold drizzle. He opened an umbrella. Stankevich took a raincoat from an aide, a young captain who walked a pace behind him. He let the younger officer help him slip into the coat, then said something Burke didn't pick up. The aide turned and disappeared back into the building.

Stankevich walked to where Burke was standing. He did not extend his hand or offer a greeting.

"Let's take a walk," he said.

They walked in silence toward the Kremlin, past the Lenin Library and a plaque honoring Ho Chi Minh. Hordes of office workers heading home swirled around them. The marshal waited until they were in the

Aleksandr Gardens, a park at the base of the Krenilin's high brick walls, before he spoke.

"So what is it you want?"

Burke began cautiously. He sidled closer to the man, as if trying to protect him with his umbrella.

"You remember the story I was asking you about?"

Stankevich nodded and grunted.

He outlined, briefly, his pursuit of Sergei Nekronov, being careful not to disclose anything he did not have to disclose. But he told the marshal about Switsico, about Katya's murder, and about the empty apartment he had found in Nauchny Gorodok.

"Anyway," he concluded, "I think that Kassim is working with some elements of the old KGB structure in order to get Nekronov to work for Syria. They're trying to cover their tracks now that I'm close to the story."

Stankevich said nothing for a while. They continued to plod along a wet asphalt walk, past white slatted benches and tall, glistening black trees. Finally, he spoke.

"You remember what I told you the last time we spoke."

"Yes."

"Repeat it to me."

"You said that Russia was quite capable of keeping track of its weapons and components."

Stankevich nodded deliberately. "That is true. And what else?"

"You said it was monitored by a council, by Army officers themselves, and you gave me a wink and a nod about the Ministry of Security's being involved, too."

"A wink and a nod?" Stankevich looked sharply at him.

"It's an American expression. It means you let me know something was true without actually telling me."

For the first time, Stankevich smiled, but thinly. "So now I'm giving winks and nods. All right. What else did I tell you?"

Burke searched his mind, flying to recall. Finally something came to him.

"You said someone else was involved in the monitoring, that I probably knew about it, but you wouldn't tell me who it was."

"Yes," Stankevich said. "Precisely. Have you found out who it is?"

"No," Burke said. "Who is it?"

Stankevich sighed. "I still cannot tell you. But I will tell you this. Little or nothing of what you have discovered so far is as it appears to be. And if you find the answer to your last question, you will know why."

"Is it the Party? Some kind of underground Party organization?" Burke guessed wildly.

Stankevich shook his head. "I can't respond to guesses about it."

"But you want me to find out, don't you? Because you don't like what's going on, do you? That's why you agreed to see me so quickly."

The old soldier turned toward Burke. Slowly and solemnly, he winked. Then he nodded.

A white Volga sedan with two men in the front seat had pulled in behind Burke's car, parked on Khlebny Pereulok a couple of blocks from the Defense Ministry. They waited while he got in and started his engine. Then they started their own engine and turned their high beams on, letting the light hit his rearview mirror and bounce into his eyes.

Burke squinted, turned on his own remaining headlight, checked the traffic behind him, made a slow U-turn, and headed toward the Garden Ring Road. The white Volga made the same U-turn and followed him closely all the way back to Sad Sam, its headlights undimmed. The Volga waited as he parked, then slid into a parking spot behind him.

The message was clear enough, Burke thought. He waved as nonchalantly as he could to the white car, then he walked past the Sad Sam *militsioner*, heading for the imagined sanctuary of his office.

Olga Semyonova, working late, met him at the door. He could tell that she was fairly bursting to tell him something. Her eyes glittered over her high cheekbones and a proud smile was on her lips. She carried a manila folder.

"You've got something," he said.

Her smile broadened and she nodded.

"Well, let's see," he said, walking into his office. She followed. When he was seated, she laid the folder on his desk and opened it.

The photocopier she had used must have been manufactured around 1962 and spent the ensuing years without a change of toner. The copies were made on flimsy coated paper, and blank streaks ran across the pages. But he could see that the first page was a copy of Sergei Nekronov's registration form, dated 1 September 1981. The picture at the top of the page was unmistakable. The next three pages were copies of his transcript. He had indeed gotten his candidate's degree in physics six years later with highest honors. He had been a member in good standing of the Communist Youth League. He had served in the military reserves.

Underneath that, though, were copies of the records of a woman, Larisa Nekronova, admitted to Moscow State in 1980 in the biology department. She listed the same home address as Sergei: No. 47 Dubenko Street, Apartment 72. Her middle name indicated that she and he had the same father. She was, the document made clear, Sergei Nekronov's sister.

Burke looked at the picture at the top of her registration form. A lot of sausage had gone into the woman's cheeks since 1980, and her hair was darker. But he had no trouble recognizing her.

It was the woman who had answered the door when he first called at the apartment in Nauchny Gorodok. It was the woman who had presented herself as Sergei Nekronov's wife.

He looked at Olga, who was standing directly in front of him. As soon as she saw his face, the proud look disappeared, and her eyes became troubled.

"What's the matter?" she said.

"I'm not sure," he told her. "How did you find Larisa's records?'

"They were right next to his in the files. The woman who was helping me asked if I wanted his sister's records as well. So I said yes." Olga paused. "Did I make a mistake?"

He tried to smile reassuringly. "No, you didn't. You did exactly the right thing."

Olga looked mollified.

"I wish I could say the same for myself," he said.

"What's the matter?"

He grimaced. "Nothing. Except that I've seen this woman before, and I didn't realize she was Nekronov's sister."

He put his chin in his left hand and stared dully at the picture of Larisa Nekronova. It explained, he realized, why the old woman on the playground had nearly broken his camera when he tried to take a picture of the little girl he had thought was Nekronov's diabetic daughter. It explained why the old woman had hustled the girl into a different building from Nekronov's.

Nekronov could not have a child with his sister. Someone had quite likely recruited a neighborhood girl to play the role of an ailing child. Someone had been willing to go to great lengths to create a humane pretext for Sergei Nekronov's decision to go to Syria. And that was just one fraudulent detail in a large, fraudulent picture. It had all been disinformation. He had damn near published it. If it hadn't been for the demand for photos, he would have.

His stomach turned over, and he felt faintly nauseated.

Olga was still standing there.

He got up and patted her on the back and started walking her out of the office.

"Olga, if I were half the reporter you are," he said, "I'd open my own damn magazine."

"You made a mistake?"

"Yes."

"A serious one?"

"I don't think so," he said.

"I'm glad."

"Then again," he went on, "Napoleon didn't think

he'd made a serious mistake when he occupied Moscow."

She looked slightly confused.

"Never mind," he said. He reached into his pocket, pulled out his wallet, and extracted fifty dollars.

"Here," he said, proffering it. "A bonus. You did good work."

To his surprise, she refused.

"I'm supposed to do good work," she said. "I'm a professional."

It was only after she had left that he began to wonder what she thought her profession was.

The craving for alcohol poked and pushed at the outer edges of his mind like a cockroach that would not be denied access to a kitchen. It scurried into his thoughts. Maybe, Burke thought, he could pretend to have a drink. He could risk no more. He filled a short glass full of ice cubes, then put it under the tap. He opened the tap slowly, so the water would come out like vodka, and watched the clear liquid burrow around the ice, down to the bottom of the glass. The Russian word for water was *voda*; *vodka* was its diminutive, like "little water." He kept pouring until the water almost brimmed over. He held the glass under his nose for a while and imagined the fumes rising and the liquor chilling. Then he took his first sip. It tasted like water.

He poured the rest out. He had to concentrate on the problem at hand.

Stankevich had been right. Nearly all of what he had seen was not what it appeared. Nekronov seemed to be a scientist, a highly qualified physicist. But was he? And if he was not, who would go to such lengths to fool him? And why?

His mind returned again and again to what Stankevich had said. If he figured out who participated in the Russians' monitoring of their nuclear weapons components, he would know who was behind the disinformation. But that was as far as his thoughts would take him. He considered the GRU, the old Soviet military intelligence service. As far as he knew, it had been reconstituted as the intelligence wing of the Russian army. But its participation was almost a given. They had to be the ones Stankevich was talking about when he said that officers, *poryadochniye* officers, monitored the weapons and components. There was the Ministry of Security, but Stankevich had acknowledged their participation. Who else was there?

The old Soviet army, he knew, had an enormous contingent of political officers. In the early Bolshevik days, they had been Party men, sent out to keep an eye on the professional soldiers who remained from the tsar's army. They had evolved into a permanent propaganda and indoctrination corps called the Main Political Directorate. They were the Party's eyes in the army. Could the political officers have somehow maintained an organization? Could they be the ones Stankevich meant?

Burke doubted it. He had seen nothing in the marshal's eyes to indicate that his guess about the Party had come close to the mark.

But what else could it be?

Loud banging on the door startled him. For an instant, Burke had a vision of jackbooted Bolsheviks in green tunics poised outside, waiting to conduct a search and take him away. How many times in this city had that happened?

Of course, it wouldn't be Bolsheviks now. But it might be the *militsia*. The distinction would be academic.

He froze, afraid to reach out, grab the knob, and open the door. The knocking resumed, but this time Burke heard a voice.

"Burke! You in there?"

The voice, though muffled, sounded American. He opened the door.

Elliott Lantz stood before him, dressed in shirt-sleeves with his tie loosened. He looked as though he had walked downstairs from his bureau, and he looked grim. He had a newspaper in his hand, and he passed it to Burke as he stepped inside.

"First edition of tomorrow's paper. Have a look at page 3," Lantz said.

It was *Nyezavisimaya Gazeta*. Burke turned to page 3. He saw a report on coal production, a commentary on the Russian Supreme Soviet, and a few foreign stories.

"Toward the bottom," Lantz prompted him.

The story occupied two columns in the bottom center of the page.

CORRESPONDENT QUESTIONED IN PROS-TITUTE'S MURDER, the headline said. The story recounted in a dry, factual way the discovery of Yekaterina Yegorova's corpse by C. Burke, Moscow bureau chief for *America Weekly*.

Burke read it and handed the paper back to Lantz.

"Well?" Lantz demanded.

"Well what?"

"Well, is it true?"

Burke's face heated up.

"Yeah, it is."

Lantz couldn't keep his own face from tightening. His eyebrows knit together.

"You knew this hooker?"

"Yeah."

"And you discovered the body?"

"Yeah."

Now Lantz looked at Burke with what he took to be a penetrating stare, one aimed at distinguishing a lie.

"Jesus, Colin. You know what this'll look like? People will think you killed her. Of course, you didn't?" Lantz couldn't help ending the last statement with a question mark.

"No," Burke said, painfully aware that, although he had asked such questions often, he had never in his life had to answer one. It gave him a new appreciation for the way journalism felt to those being written about, rather than those doing the writing.

"Well, everyone you know will believe it," said Lantz. "But you're in deep shit. Were you boinking her?"

Burke shook his head, blushing again. "No. Interviewing her."

"What about?"

"Can't tell you."

"Any idea who killed her?"

"Not really."

"You're in deep shit," Lantz repeated. Burke didn't argue with him. "Every reporter in Moscow's gonna want a piece of you. And the cops. You got a lawyer?"

"No. I haven't done anything."

"I'd get a lawyer," Lantz said.

"I might," Burke said.

But as he spoke, he thought that what he needed was not a lawyer but another chance to talk to Sergei Nekronov to find out who had put him up to his deception. If he found that out, he would not only have his story. He would, he thought, know who killed Katya.

But how could he find Nekronov without running afoul of the procurator's demand that he talk to no one involved with Switsico?

He could think of only one possible avenue. And he would have to call Lena Laskova to pursue it.

"Sorry, Elliott, but I've gotta go out," he said to Lantz abruptly. "Do me a favor, would you? Pass on what I told you to the wire service guys and anyone else who might be doing a story. I'm not going to have time to talk to everyone individually."

"Okay," Lantz said. "But what're you going to be doing?"

"Getting myself in more trouble."

CHAPTER SEVENTEEN

THE NEXT MORNING, TWO MINUTES after Burke returned to the bureau from his obligatory check-in with the procurator's office, Olga poked her head through the doorway into his office.

"That Ronit Evron is calling," she said. "I guess it's about the job. Do you want to talk to her?"

Burke looked up from the Reuters story he had been reading and rereading for twenty minutes. It recounted the *Nyezavisimaya Gazeta* story about Katya's murder and his involvement. He looked at his watch. In seven hours or so, *America Weekly*'s editors would be arriving in their offices. He wondered how Canfield would react when he saw the story.

The word "gleefully" popped into his mind.

"All right," he told Olga. "I'll talk to her."

He picked up the phone and carefully said hello.

"Mr. Burke, good morning," she said. Her voice was low and gave away nothing.

"That's a matter of opinion," he said.

"I can understand why you'd feel that way," she replied, and he sensed a disconcerting smugness in her voice.

"You've read the papers."

"Yes. Of course," she hastened to add, "I know you're innocent. But, still, it's, um, unfortunate."

"Inconvenient," Burke said.

"Inconvenient," she agreed. "But. anyway. there are some things I need to discuss with you. Can you possibly meet me this morning?"

"Well, I'm kind of tied up with all this..."

"I really think it would be a good idea," she said, and he heard the smugness in her voice again.

"All right," he agreed. "Where?"

"At the synagogue. Half an hour."

A chilly, gray sky had settled low over the city.

If it were October instead of September, he would have guessed that the first snow of the season was on its way. Inside the car, he turned up the heater and waited for the warm air to blow into his face. He checked for tailing cars. He thought he saw a white Volga pull in several cars behind him and stay there, but he wasn't sure. It hardly mattered; they knew about his relationship with Evron.

When he pulled up, she was standing on the steps outside the synagogue, wearing a trench coat, black stockings, and high heels. Her tan had faded even more; and she was beginning to have a Muscovite's pallor, set off by her black hair done up in a bun behind her head.

Neither smiled as he walked up the steps. She offered her hand, and he shook it quickly.

"Let's walk toward the river," she said, and he nodded his agreement.

They walked six inches apart, each staring at the sidewalk ahead. For several blocks, she said nothing. They turned left, walking past the enormous façade of the Rossiya Hotel and the little churches that were all that remained of Moscow's ancient "Chinatown," an area of churches and shops a few hundred yards from Red Square. Ahead of them, the river flowed—broad, gray, and sluggish—matching the color of the sky.

She waited until they were on the embankment walk before she spoke.

"You still haven't published your story," she said. "Why not?"

"It still needs work."

"And have you done any work on it in the past few days?"

He had no patience for it. "Jesus, Ronit. Give me a damn break. I told you I couldn't help you. If I get the damn story, you'll read it."

She looked at him dispassionately.

"That's not good enough any more, Colin." Something quietly confident in her tone brought him up short.

"What do you mean, 'not good enough'?"

"I mean you're in trouble now, and you can't afford to get in worse trouble."

"And?"

"And, well, let's just say we don't want you to get in worse trouble."

They passed a man in a tweed cap fishing off the embankment with a long bamboo pole. Burke had always shuddered to think of eating the fish that could survive in those turbid waters; but at the moment, he barely noticed.

"What's that supposed to mean?" he asked, trying to sound tougher than he felt.

"Well, let me put it this way. You're a suspect in a murder. You wouldn't want the *militsia* to find, say, a garrote somewhere in your office or car, would you? Just like the garrote that killed Katya?"

Burke's bowels flipped over, and he stopped. He stared at her for a minute.

"You did it, didn't you?"

She looked at him, implacable. Only someone standing a foot or two away could have seen the faint turn in her lips and the cold blankness in her eyes. The balance of power in their relationship had shifted, her eyes said. and she was enjoying the turnabout.

"Whatever gave you that idea?" she said flatly. Her voice was frighteningly calm.

"You know how she was killed. Shit, I didn't even know that. I thought it was a razor!"

"You're imagining things," she said in the same flat, cold voice.

He looked at her in silence for a moment.

"You're tough," he said.

She returned his stare. "When I have to be."

"You found her, got what you could out of her, killed her, found my business card, and laid it under her head."

She said nothing. She resumed walking.

He grabbed her arm.

"You set me up!"

She shook the arm free and walked slowly along the embankment.

"Colin," she said, and for the first time he heard a softer inflection in her voice. "I warned you once that this was serious business. You chose to be very cavalier. Now you're in it. Don't get in over your head."

"Well, the water does seem to be rising," he said. "What's your point?"

"It's time for you to stop pretending you're some kind of white knight on some kind of sacred quest for pure truth," she said. "This isn't about truth. It's about power and survival. If you keep riding around on your horse with your lance up, you're going to impale yourself on it."

"Or I can survive," he said.

She nodded. "You can start by telling me everything you know. Why you haven't published your story about this scientist, for starters. Where he is now, for seconds. Then maybe you can patch together a story that will suit your editors."

"And if I don't tell you, then this garrote turns up?"

"It might."

"That's, um, I don't know, extortion or blackmail," he said, feeling foolish and weak even as he said it.

"You didn't seem to have a problem with it a week ago. Remember when you told me what you'd do if I didn't pass along information?'

He remembered and flushed.

"Well, there's an American saying I learned at Brandeis: What goes around..."

"Comes around," he finished.

"Let's just leave it that neither of us wants to see you in more trouble than you're already in," she said. She was still walking slowly along the embankment, her eyes focused somewhere on the river, her heels clicking quietly on the pavement.

"I could tell them you did it."

"You wouldn't be able to back it up," she said evenly. "I assure you there's no evidence beyond what points to you."

"Yeah, but I could make it uncomfortable for you."

She shrugged.

"At the worst, I go back to Israel. You do time in a Russian jail."

He took a deep breath and smelled the fumes of a bus that passed them by. The only thought he could muster was delay.

"I don't know where he is," Burke finally said.

"I think you're lying," she replied.

"I'm not," he told her. "But I'm trying to find him. And if you have some goons grab me and beat me now, you'll learn nothing much, and you'll have lost the chance that I could find him." He hoped he didn't sound too desperate.

"Take your time," she said confidently. "We'll give you twenty-four hours."

Lena Laskova made her way to the front of the line in the Estée Lauder store on Tverskaya Street. She had never shopped there. The prices were too high, arid she could get good cosmetics a lot cheaper from travelers who got off trains from Poland or Hungary eager to sell some of the treasure they had accumulated abroad. She had expected to find Estée Lauder's full of prostitutes, figuring that only they could afford it. But the customers she saw in line were the same kind of people she saw in the station: women from the provinces. A trip to Moscow and its little row of glittering foreign stores was as close as they would ever come to a trip abroad.

She bought one of virtually everything she could see: lipsticks, mascara, face creams, soap, perfume, a large hand mirror. Then she bought a black canvas tote bag with the Estée Lauder logo. She paid with a wad of rubles that required two bands to hold.

Outside, she turned toward the Kremlin and into the massive old Moskva Hotel, home of Moscow's Benetton outlet. Piles of bright, gaily colored sweaters lined one wall.

She had been in this store. A friend had advised her to go in just to see the clothing and how it was displayed, and she had found the trip worthwhile. The store would have had an impossibly long line if it took rubles. But it took only hard currency, which kept the riffraff out.

A sales clerk glanced at her as she entered, recognized her for a Russian, and walked quickly up to her.

"May I help you?" she said, formally polite. "We take only hard currency in this store."

Lena glared at her. "I have dollars," she said.

The clerk smiled, trying to hide her embarrassment. "Please, look around. May I show you something in particular?"

"Yes," Lena said. "A blazer."

The clerk nodded and they walked over the soft

plaid carpeting to a nook that contained blazers in black, gray, red, and blue.

"What color would you like?"

Lena hesitated. Gray or black would look best with her auburn hair, but Burke had suggested red. Red, he said, looked more like a uniform.

On the other hand, her Estée Lauder tote bag was black.

"Black," she said. She tried it on. It fit perfectly over the plain gray wool dress she wore. The fabric felt smooth and buttery. The buttons felt heavy and solid.

"I'll take it," Lena said.

"Very good," the clerk said. She folded the blazer over her arm and walked toward the register. "And how will you pay for it?"

"Dollars," Lena said.

The clerk smiled, and Lena sensed that she was being patronized. "No, I meant cash or credit card."

Lena flushed. "Cash," she said.

"Very good." The clerk smiled again. Her eyes said that she thought Lena hadn't come by her dollars honestly. She punched some buttons on a cash register. A computer disk whined.

"Two hundred seventy-five dollars."

Nervously, Lena jabbed a hand into her purse and pulled out three of the hundred-dollar bills Burke had given her. Spending so much hard currency was not easy for her. Even if she had to have a black blazer that looked western, she would never spend three hundred dollars for it. She hoarded every dollar she got her hands on. She would have waited for a shipment of knockoffs from China to come through the station and bought one for rubles. But Burke had insisted. More important, he had told her the money would be expense money on top of what she would earn for staging this little charade and reporting to him what she learned.

For an instant, she considered telling the clerk to cancel the sale. She could take the three hundred dollars and go somewhere where Colin Burke could never find her.

But even as the thought entered her mind, she dismissed it. It was not because Burke was going to pay her an equal amount for finishing the job, although the money was important to her.

It was not that he had charmed her, exactly. He had charmed her, even though in Russian he had an ineradicable edge of awkwardness whenever he opened his mouth.

No. She would work for him because he had somehow convinced her that he trusted, even respected, her. No one else did. Edik and Boris saw her as a piece of meat, albeit an attractive one. She was necessary for the game to work; she was one of the best at it. But even now, when they were drunk, they would talk to her face about finding a younger, prettier girl if she refused to go to bed with them. She always refused and always wondered when they would follow through on their threats.

So, following Burke's directions, she slipped the blazer on, walked out into Revolution Square, and hailed a cab.

A dirty yellow Volga pulled up, and she opened the front door.

"Ulitsa Dubenko," she .told the driver. "It's off Byelomorskaya near the River station."

"How much?" he asked.

"Four times," she said. It meant she would pay four

times the number of rubles on the meter when the trip ended.

The driver shook his head and looked pointedly at the new blazer. "Ten dollars," he said. He was taking her for a foreigner, or at least for someone with hard currency.

"Two," she said, grudgingly.

"Five."

"All right."

It was his money.

Apartment 72 at No. 47 Ulitsa Dubenko was on the fourth floor of one of the five-story walk-ups that Nikita Khrushchev had built by the thousands for the workers of Moscow. In gratitude, Muscovites had nicknamed the buildings Khrushchoby, a pun on the Russian word for slums, *trushchoby*. Five apartments opened on the fourth-floor landing. Lena, following Burke's instructions, called on two of them before she knocked on No. 72. In the process she took orders for five lipsticks and three mascaras. Burke had been right. In a country where Avon and Mary Kay were setting up operations, it was easy to persuade people that Estée Lauder also had door-to-door operations.

She rang the bell beside the padded leather door of No. 72 and listened. Almost immediately, she heard slippers sliding over a wood floor inside. Then came the sound of three bolts being thrown, and the door opened perhaps four inches. Behind it she could see the face of a pudgy man with a graying, slightly ragged goatee and a nose mottled by a few too many bottles of vodka.

"Good morning," she said, smiling and making certain he could see the black tote bag with the logo on it. "I'm your neighborhood representative for Estée Lauder cosmetics. Is Mrs. Nekronova at home?"

"Yes," said the man. He sounded a little uncertain, but he opened the door enough for her to step inside.

The first of Burke's questions was answered. The Nekronovs still lived in the apartment Sergei and Larisa had listed on their university registration forms.

"Just a minute," the old man told her. "She's in the kitchen. I'll get her."

She was in a hallway narrowed by cardboard boxes piled on both sides. Her elbows bumped against them as she took off her raincoat and hung it up. She opened a box and peeked inside. It seemed to be full of books.

A hefty woman in a scoop-necked dress walked out of the kitchen, wiping her hands on an apron. Mrs. Nekronova was about five feet three, in both directions. She had yards and yards of doughy, slightly wrinkled skin above the neckline, which ended in a wrinkled slice of cleavage. She would be, Lena guessed, the type of woman who bought skin cream by the gallon. Her full lips were a bright, purplish red. The scent of cheap Russian perfume preceded her up the hallway. To a door-to-door cosmetics sales rep, she looked the way a drunken sailor with six months' pay in his pocket looks to a hooker. She was a walking demand curve.

"Tamara Nekronova," the woman said, introducing herself with a smile that parted the red lips like a knife slicing a plum.

Lena shook her hand. The old man, she noted, was hanging a few feet back, clearly intent on missing nothing about this strange visit.

Empty bookshelves lined half of the living room. Tamara Nekronova invited Lena to sit on a divan that faced the shelves and a desk littered with papers.

Lena pulled a yellow pad Burke had given her from her tote bag. Then she laid the cosmetics out on the little table next to the divan. Nikolai Nekronov sat at the desk, watching.

For fifteen minutes, Lena opened sample after sample, until Tamara Nekronova had seen the whole Estée Lauder line.

And while she demonstrated, she chatted, recording the answers in her memory to report to Burke.

Yes, the Nekronovs were retired mathematics teachers. Yes, they had two children. No grandchildren. Their children were both scientists. Yes, they both lived in Moscow, but not with their parents.

Lena pulled a pen out of her blazer and prepared to take an order. What would Mrs. Nekronova like to buy at the special introductory prices Estée Lauder was offering for a limited time only?

Nikolai Nekronov spoke up for the first time.

"Tamara, don't buy anything. Soon you'll be able to get all you want," he said. He turned to Lena. "You see, we're emigrating to the West in a few days."

"Kolya, hush!" Tamara Nekronova hissed.

Burke stared silently at the words "to the West." He had scrawled them, by rough count, fifteen times on a sheet of yellow paper after hearing them from Lena. Sometimes he had underlined them, sometimes circled them. Sometimes he had printed in capital letters, sometimes in the careful script he had last employed in the fifth grade.

No matter how he wrote the words or how he stared at them, they made no sense.

What had the old man meant by "the West"? Syria? Someplace else?

Not Syria. Not if he thought of his destination as a place where Estée Lauder lipstick was freely available.

Or maybe Sergei Nekronov intended to use his money to set up his parents in Europe, then join them when his work for Assad was done. Maybe the Syrians were setting up a laboratory outside their country, thinking that it would be easier to order parts and supplies for a physics laboratory in, say, Paris than for one in Damascus. But that would mean the facility would be at the mercy of the French government or some other Western government. Would Assad risk that?

Maybe Lena had misunderstood the old couple.

Or maybe she had deliberately misled him.

Burke stood up and paced back and forth until the office seemed no bigger than a closet. He could do nothing without more information. But his plan to get more seemed hopeless. He sat down and stared at the yellow paper again, covering it with doodles.

He heard footsteps in the front hallway and looked up.

The bony head of Pavel Plotnikov was protruding at an oblique angle through the doorway, connected like an apple on a stick to his pale white neck. He wore the same black Greek fisherman's cap from his last visit. Plotnikov mimed knocking on the door.

"You are in?" he asked, with a tentative smile on his face.

Burke nodded.

The rest of Plotnikov's gangling body joined his head inside the office. He was wearing a ratty brown raincoat, from the pocket of which he produced a half-full bottle of vodka and two small glasses. He sat down at the chair facing Burke's desk and set the glasses near the piece of yellow paper. He filled each one with vodka.

"Let's drink," he said.

Burke blew up.

"Jesus! What the fuck is it with you? You want to get drunk and you have to drag someone down with you? Well, flick off!" He was shouting, and the veins in his forehead were throbbing.

Plotnikov shrank back like a tree bending before a hurricane. With a startled, fearful look, he stowed the glassware and the bottle back in the gray tote bag he carried. Then he leaned forward.

"I am sorry. I came because you are in trouble, my friend," he said.

"Congratulations. You have a nose for news," Burke replied.

If Plotnikov understood the sarcasm, he gave no sign of it.

"I did not write article in paper this morning," Plotnikov continued. "Crime reporter wrote. But I spoke with him. He heard things from procurator he did not put in article."

The Russian stared across the table at Burke. With his jowls drooping and his eyes bloodshot, he looked genuinely sad about Burke's problems.

"Like what?"

"They found your business card with body," Plotnikov said. "They say you were customer."

Burke flushed, then scowled. He wanted to hear whatever message Plotnikov had come to deliver, but hearing it was proving more painful than he had anticipated.

"They're wrong. What else did they say?"

"They say they want to make an example. They are tired of foreign men with dollars being corruption of Russian girls."

"What else?" Burke said, letting the anger he felt show.

"Nothing else."

"Don't you want to tell me that I better not pursue the Switsico story any more?"

Plotnikov frowned, looking genuinely puzzled. The man, Burke thought, was a born con artist.

"No. What is Switsico?" he asked.

Burke sighed, the way he might sigh with a child who persisted in telling an obvious lie.

"Let's cut the *govno*, all right, Pavel?"

The vulgarity so startled Plotnikov that he switched to Russian when he replied.

"Pardon? I don't understand."

Burke stayed with English.

"I said, let's cut the *govno,* okay? I'm tired of it. It insults my intelligence."

"I don't understand," Plotnikov repeated, this time in English.

"Look," Burke said, his voice rising. "You fed me a line about wanting to be a journalist so you could write the truth, and I fell for it. It was clever. Hit my weak spot. So I was sentimental and stupid.

"But I'm not so stupid I'm going to keep falling for it. So why don't you just pass along whatever warning they sent you to pass along and then get the hell out of here, okay?"

"My friend, you misunderstand me!" Plotnikov protested. He put a flat hand against his chest, defending his innocence. "I just wanted to tell you about lawyer who might help you and warn you about what procurator said!"

"Okay," Burke scowled. "You've done it. Look. I can get used to being spied on. I can get used to being passed disinformation. But tell your bosses that when they send you in here to drink with me, that's too goddamn much! Now get the hell out. And take your bottle with you."

For an hour after Plotnikov left, Burke felt himself teetering on the edge. He stared at pieces of paper on his desk, but the words on the paper failed to register. He looked at an old copy of the *International Herald Tribune* and spent some time trying and failing to solve the first word in the Jumble puzzle. He felt that it would take an enormous effort—more than he was capable of—to force himself to focus again on the tasks at hand and find a way to solve them. He could do nothing but let his mind drift.

When the phone rang with the two short, staccato bursts that signaled an international call, he looked at his watch. Only four o'clock. It would normally be too early for anyone in New York to be calling, unless it was bad news. But he was too weak to resist a distraction. He picked it up.

"Burke," he said.

"Colin, it's Chris Canfield."

"Hi, Chris." Hearing Canfield directly, without Gen Owen's soothing mediation, unsettled him further.

"Uh, how are you?" Canfield asked, with a note of awkwardness in his voice. It sounded to Burke as if he had reminded himself to go through the formalities of being pleasant before jumping to the purpose that had brought him to the office early enough to be dialing his own telephone calls.

"I'm fine," Burke replied, equally awkwardly.

"Colin, what's the hell's going on over there? We've got a wire service report says you were arrested and questioned in connection with the murder of a prostitute."

"I was held and questioned. I found the body and called the police. She was connected with this scientist story I'm working on—the recruiter used her to entertain scientists. I went to her place to ask her some questions, and someone had slit her throat."

"This makes twice you've been held and questioned in the last week," Canfield said, tartly. "Have they got any suspects?"

"Not that I know of."

Canfield paused, and his voice got flat and toneless. "Uh, Colin, I need you to level with me. Is there anything here that could come out and embarrass the magazine?"

"You mean like did I kill her? Or was I screwing her?"

"Yeah," Canfield said. His voice sounded accusing. "Exactly."

"No." Burke clipped the end off the word.

"Well, ah, good," Canfield replied, suddenly sounding as if he were imitating a man of hearty bonhomie. "I assumed that was the case, but it's good to hear it from you."

"Glad to be of service," Burke said.

"Yes, well. Anyway, we think here that you need to devote full time to extricating yourself from this."

"I don't really think—" Burke said, leaning forward, as if Canfield might sense his body language from five thousand miles.

"It's for your own good," Canfield interrupted him. "Our law firm here in New York is Coudert Brothers. They have an office in Moscow. They're not experts in criminal law, obviously, but at least they're American lawyers. They're going to get in touch with you and help you through this. Probably hook you up with a good Moscow criminal lawyer, if such a thing exists."

"I really don't think—" Burke repeated.

"And in the meantime," Canfield went on, interrupting again, "we're going to send someone in to relieve you. Tony Webster from London. He'll be going round to the Russian Embassy tomorrow morning and applying for a visa. As soon as he gets it, he's going in on temporary assignment until we can find the right permanent replacement."

"Permanent replacement?" Burke felt numb.

"That's right," Canfield said. "It's unfortunate, but I think it's beyond argument that your effectiveness in Moscow has been compromised. When you get clear of this murder investigation, I want you to come back to New York. Then we'll talk about another assignment."

Burke could imagine what that would be. "Okay," he managed to say. Canfield hung up. Burke leaned back in his chair and closed his eyes, trying to take slow, deep breaths and calm himself down. He had never been replaced before. Then again, he had never been threatened by the Israelis or suspected of a prostitute's murder before.

That was the great thing about a career in journalism. Every day brought new experiences.

CHAPTER EIGHTEEN

BURKE PULLED ON HIS RUNNING SHOES and laced them up. He quickly inspected his reflection in the bedroom mirror. His ratty gray sweatpants and faded blue "CAL" sweatshirt looked just as they always did when he went jogging. The little notebook and the wallet in the pocket of his shorts did not show underneath the sweatpants.

It was almost dark by the time he got to his car and pulled out on the Garden Ring Road heading for the Lenin Hills. He looked in his mirror to see if he could spot a tailing car. But in the gloom all he saw were headlights, and he could not tell if any of them were following him. He checked his watch. He was about three minutes behind schedule. He pressed down on the pedal, swerved into the left lane, and sped through the Gorky Street underpass at fifty miles an hour. A drizzle streaked the windshield, and he turned the wipers on.

When he got to his regular parking spot at the entrance to the riverside park, he was back on schedule. Just as he always did, he spent a few minutes stretching and bending. Then he set off slowly through the mist along the embankment. The black iron railing on his left gleamed moistly. Across the river, the gilded cupolas of Novodevichy shone in the glow of street lights. He strained to listen, but he could hear no footfalls on the pavement behind him. If someone was tailing him, he had stayed by the car.

So far, he knew, his behavior looked no different from hundreds of previous occasions when he had come to the riverside park and jogged a mile or so along the embankment until he was abreast of an ancient ski jump at the top of the ridge above the river. There, he always turned around and jogged back to his car. But this evening he kept going. He picked up the pace until he was doing about seven minutes per mile. All the while he listened for footfalls behind him; he heard only the sound of his own feet striking the black asphalt. After a while, he also heard the rumble of traffic on the Garden Ring Road. On the right, ahead of him, he could make out the silhouette of the Ferris wheel in Gorky Park.

The embankment he was running on snaked through Moscow, describing a large loop that curved by the Garden Ring Road once near Kutuzov Bridge and again at Gorky Park. When he reached the Ring Road, he jogged up a set of stone steps and turned right toward the ticket booths at the gate to the park. There were two cars parked along the curb. One of them, he saw gratefully, was a white Zhiguli, just as Lena had described. He ran toward it.

She was sitting in the driver's seat with the engine going. He opened the door and folded his body into the car. Before he could close it, she was pulling away from the curb and into the Ring Road traffic.

Burke panted for a while, letting the sweat run on his forehead. Then he craned his neck and peered out the rear window.

"Switch lanes," he said.

Wordlessly, she pulled left. He saw no change in the traffic behind them.

"Now please get off at the next right," he said.

She swung the car deftly to the right and got off the Ring Road on the Yauza River embankment, across from an apartment building Burke knew. It was where Andrei Sakharov had lived out his life; and Burke had spent time on the sidewalk there, listening to Sakharov's pronouncements about the course of *perestroika*.

He checked in the rear window again. No one had made the turn with them.

"Well, if someone is following us," he said, "he's damn good at it."

Lena stopped the car and peered back as well. "I think we're clear," she said. "Don't overestimate the *chekisti*. They've got as many dunces as anyone else. The smart ones have all quit and become businessmen."

Their faces were very close, and he found his eyes drawn to the curve of her neck before it disappeared into the collar of the dark turtleneck she was wearing. He could smell her hair.

She turned and caught him looking. She smiled slightly, and he shifted his position back toward his own side of the car.

"Where to now?"

Burke blinked. "Ulitsa Dubenko," he said. "It's the only starting point I know."

Lena nodded, turned around, and soon was heading northwest toward Sheremetyevo Airport. They passed the iron sentinels standing guard at the bridge near the Byelorussian station.

"You think he'll visit his parents?" she asked.

Burke nodded. "Or they'll go see him. Obviously, if they're planning to leave within a few days, they've got things to talk about."

"I had a friend who emigrated," Lena said. "She was frantic for weeks. She couldn't tell what to take and what to leave. Clothes? furniture? books?"

"And they'll be making the same choices, I assume," Burke said.

Lena nodded and continued to drive.

"Where is your friend now?"

"Los Angeles," Lena replied.

"Happy there?"

"So she says in her letters. I guess she is. Sometimes I envy her."

"But not all the time."

She took her eyes off the road for a moment and looked at him.

"I'm a Russian," she said solemnly. "Whatever happens, I belong here."

"Despite everything?"

She nodded. "Despite everything."

"Well," he said, "speaking as a rootless cosmopolitan, I envy you."

She looked curiously at him.

"I didn't know you were Jewish."

He remembered then that the phrase had a history. Stalin had condemned Jews as rootless cosmopolitans.

"I'm not. Misuse of the term."

"Where are- your ancestors from?"

"Ireland, mostly."

"Have you been there?"

"Yes."

"And did you feel at home there?"

"No," he said honestly.

"And what part of America are you from?"

"Originally, California."

"And do you feel roots there?"

"Not really. I haven't been back in years."

"You're an unlucky man," she said.

"I hope not."

❀ ❀ ❀

They parked on the street across from the entrance to No. 47 Ulitsa Dubenko, and she cut the engine. About half the windows in the building were lit, including the one on the fourth floor right front, where the Nekronovs lived. He peered at it, looking for activity and sithouettes. But he saw nothing.

"We're in luck," she said.

"How?"

"The light over their entrance still works. We'll be able to see who goes and comes."

He looked down the building's façade to the other entrance doors. Darkness shrouded all of them.

"You're right," he said. "This must be my lucky day." Silently, they peered through the windshield at the doorway. The rain tailed off and stopped. A couple of elderly women walking dogs came and went. The rain started again, a fine mist.

In the car, it was growing chilly, and Burke wondered whether it would ruin the stakeout if they started the engine and turned on the heater. He decided it would.

At half past eight, a cab drove up to the entrance and disgorged a woman. She was standing under an umbrella as she paid the driver, and he could not get a look at her face. But he could see by the faint light from the entrance that her hair was bleached yellow.

"I think it's Nekronov's sister," he whispered to Lena.

The cab pulled away a few feet and parked. The woman turned and walked into the building. He did not see her face; but the square, dumpy body matched his recollection of the woman who had posed as Sergei Nekronov's wife.

"It's her. It's definitely her," Burke whispered. He felt a surge of energy, a sensual tingle, and realized that his heartbeat had picked up.

"What do we do now?" Lena whispered back.

"Wait till she comes out. See where she's going. Carefully follow her," he said. She nodded.

He stared and saw silhouettes in the window of Apartment 72; after a moment, they disappeared. He could imagine them sitting in the same room Lena had described to him, discussing their plans. He wished he had some way to listen.

"She won't be long," Lena whispered. "She left the cab waiting."

He nodded. He had had the same idea.

But ten minutes went by, and the woman did not

reappear. Burke's energy started to sag as abruptly as her arrival had piqued it.

He looked at Lena, who seemed to him much more composed and at ease with the task of waiting.

"I wonder where she lives," he said.

Lena shrugged.

"If she doesn't live with her parents and she has no children, it probably means she was married, but she threw her husband out."

He looked at her.

"How do you know that?"

She shrugged again. "It's the typical pattern. Probably he drank too much."

She had aroused his curiosity.

"Did that happen to you?"

She hesitated for a moment.

"Yes."

"When?"

She turned to him, a look of annoyance on her face. "Why do you want to know?"

He turned his own face back toward the windshield. "Sorry. Just curious."

After a moment, she replied in a quiet, flat voice. "When I was eighteen I got pregnant, and I married the boy. He drank and he beat me and I left him."

"You have a child?" he asked, then immediately regretted the question.

"No," she replied, voice strained. "I had an abortion." He did her the courtesy of not turning and looking at her as she spoke; and it seemed to him that her toneless phrases, intended to mask her emotions, instead conveyed enormous pain.

"I'm sorry," he said, still looking at the windshield.

She reached over and patted his hand lightly. "Don't be," she said. "It's just life."

Before he could respond, the woman emerged again from the doorway. She was alone but carrying a small parcel wrapped in brown paper and tied with string. She ducked into the cab.

Burke leaned forward in his seat, as if he could hear or see the woman better that way. "Follow the cab, but leave the lights off until we're out in traffic," he said.

Lena immediately turned the key. Nothing happened.

"Oh, shit," Burke said.

She was halfway out of the car before he could move. She threw open the hood and peered inside. He joined her. In the dim light, all he could make out was the manifold cover and a lot of oily dirt.

"I'm afraid I don't know much about—" he began.

"Give me your sweatshirt," she demanded, interrupting him.

He stopped talking and stared at her.

"Your sweatshirt," she hissed, urgently. Mechanically, he pulled the sweatshirt off. She grabbed it, reached into the engine's innards, and wiped down some wires and connections. Then she straightened up, threw the hood down, and ran to her seat.

This time, the engine turned over and caught.

The car was rolling before he had both feet inside. He managed to get in as she swept around a curve, out of the parking lot, and onto Ulitsa Dubenko. Ahead of them the cab was waiting for a light to turn green. It did, and the cab slowly rumbled forward.

"There it is," Lena said. She turned on the lights and followed, a couple of hundred yards behind.

She handed him his sweatshirt. He could smell the oil and engine grime on it, and he let it sit in his lap rather than put it back on.

"Nice job," he said. "I'm impressed."

"These damn cars don't like wet weather," she said. "It throws them off."

"You sing. You run dice games. You start engines. What other talents do you have?"

She glanced his way and smiled.

"Wouldn't you like to find out?" she said.

The cab picked up speed and turned right, heading for the Leningrad Highway. When it reached the highway, the cab turned south, heading back toward the Kremlin. The traffic on the highway at that hour was just right for surveillance: enough cars and trucks to provide cover, but not so many that they risked losing the cab in traffic. The conditions would be favorable for anyone following them, Burke realized. He turned and studied the headlights behind them for a while; but he could not tell if anyone was following them, and there was no time to try switching lanes or making an abrupt turn.

They cruised in pursuit for thirty minutes. The cab swung right, bypassing the center of town, and headed past the Mezhdunarodnaya Hotel toward Kutuzovsky Prospekt, where it turned right again and headed back out of the city to the west.

The buildings along the road changed as they left the city. Close to the center, they were massive, monumental, Stalinesque apartment buildings. Farther out they became row after row of five-story Khrushchoby. And toward the outer ring road that marked the city's boundary, the horizon was full of white fifteen- and twenty-story towers dotted with balconies, built in the

Brezhnev years. Then they were in dacha country, an area of forests and country homes once reserved for the Party elite, now open to the moneyed elite. The road was, not surprisingly, smoothly paved.

The traffic thinned accordingly, and Burke worried that the cab would spot the tail. But a dump truck, its driver off on some moonlight errand, came chugging up behind them. Lena slowed, pulled over, and let the truck pass them. Then she accelerated and tucked the Zhiguli in behind the truck. With its bulk looming in front of them, they lost sight of the cab on the straightaways. But they could still see it ahead of them on curves, its headlights cutting a path through the darkness and illuminating the woods and fields on either side of the road.

"You're very good at this," Burke said.

Intent on the road, she nodded in response.

He almost said that she was too good at it, but he stopped the words behind his teeth. Even if she was not who she said she was, even if she was working for the Ministry of Security, what choice did he have? His only alternative was to surrender to whoever was playing games with him.

For several miles they had woods on the left and a furrowed field on the right. The stalks of recently harvested summer vegetables identified the field as a collective farm. Then they passed two carved wooden animals, a bear and a buck, standing like sentinels on either side of the road; and thick woods replaced the field. Ahead of them he saw the cab slow down and make a left turn into the woods.

"Turn the lights off and see if you can find a spot in the woods to park," he said, but she was already doing it.

She found a notch in the tree line about twenty yards from the road and parked. The dump truck rumbled on ahead of them. There was no moon; but the lights of the city, just over the horizon, bounced off the low clouds and provided them with a dim light. They jogged along the road until they reached the intersection where the cab had turned. They could make out a narrow paved road, barely two lanes wide, cut straight as a bullet's path through a forest of towering pines. High stone walls flanked the road, interrupted every three hundred yards or so by gates. Beyond the walls, they could dimly make out lights shining from the second stories of dachas through the interstices between the trees. The owners of these dachas comprised a very elite colony.

He spotted a gate just ahead on the right, opening on a driveway that led to the first dacha. They sprinted to it and ducked inside. Fifty yards away at the end of a treeshrouded driveway, Larisa Nekronova was paying the driver and apparently arguing about the fare.

Burke crouched low and set off at a jog into the woods, toward the dacha. The ground was covered, he noticed gratefully, with pine needles. They would muffle his footsteps. He could barely hear Lena's, a step or two behind him. He wanted to tell her to go back to the car, but he dared not risk making the noise. He got to within thirty yards of the building and stopped, squatting behind some bushes. Lena crept up quietly beside him.

"Go back and wait at the car," he whispered.

"No," she replied. "It would just make more noise."

She was right. He turned back toward the dacha.

It was an A-frame made of roughly planed boards with carved wood filigree around the eaves. A small covered veranda was enclosed by a log railing. A burly man whom Burke did not recognize was standing silently by the front door.

Larisa Nekronova finished her business with the cabbie and slammed the door. Burke heard the grinding of gears as the driver threw the car into reverse and backed rapidly, angrily out of the gravel driveway, probably miffed, Burke thought, that someone who owned a dacha refused to be gouged for an extra thousand rubles.

Nekronova looked tired. Her shoulders sagged, and she kept her eyes focused on the planks of the two steps that she had to mount to reach the veranda.

She spoke briefly and quietly to the man waiting there.

"I have their passports," Burke thought he heard her say.

The man nodded and walked away, down the driveway, presumably to close the gate. As he did, the front door to the dacha opened. In the doorway, framed by the light from inside, Burke saw Sergei Nekronov. His sister went inside, and the door shut again.

The burly man returned and remained on the veranda. He pulled a pack of cigarettes from his shirt pocket and lit one with a butane lighter.

Briefly, Burke considered simply standing up, walking to the front door of the dacha, and demanding to speak to Nekronov. Now that he knew Nekronov's whereabouts, he had a little leverage. He could always threaten to reveal that knowledge.

But the man at the door complicated things. He wore no uniform, but that did not exclude the possibility that he worked for the *militsia* or the Ministry of

Security. He could work for Rafit Kassim. Whatever the case, his job description was unlikely to include facilitating interviews. He might be under orders to arrest intruders. Or shoot them. Or arrest them and then shoot them.

The problem was how to get out. The gate was now locked, and the guard on the veranda had a clear view of it. Gently, Burke nudged Lena in the arm and pointed back toward the car. She nodded. As quietly as possible, they crept back through the woods to the wall. He picked her up by the waist until she could grab the top. Like a gymnast, she boosted herself up and jackknifed over.

Now, how would he get out? He looked back toward the dacha. He could see the glow from the light on the veranda, but he could not see the guard. In any case, he was out of pistol range. He looked around for a tree near the wall, found one, and managed to climb up three branches until he, too, could get a grip on the top of the wall. He reached out and grabbed it with his hands, getting his elbows over the top.

But as he pushed off, the branch he was standing on broke with an audible crack. Startled, Burke dangled from the wall, waiting for a shout or a shot indicating that he had been detected. The thought made the skin tingle on his neck. But nothing happened. He kicked back and found the trunk of the tree and managed to get enough purchase to help pull himself up and over. He fell in an awkward heap to the grass below, safely outside. His back landed on a rock, and pain shot through his spine. Stunned, he lay there.

In an instant, he opened his eyes. Lena was peering down at him. Slowly he unfurled his arms and used them to get cautiously to his feet, like a boxer rising from the canvas. She reached under his arms and helped him straighten up.

"Nine point nine," she whispered. "I have to deduct a tenth for the sloppy dismount."

Despite himself, he laughed and felt better.

They regained the little paved road through the woods and then the broader road from Moscow. The white Zhiguli was where they had left it.

This time, the engine started immediately.

"Back to Moscow," he said to her. "I can't do anything until I think of a way past that guard."

She nodded, punched the accelerator, and coaxed the little car up to one hundred kilometers an hour. When a mile or so had gone by, he exhaled. They entered the city in silence, Burke pondering the surface of the dashboard and the problem of getting access once again to Sergei Nekronov.

They were under the triumphal arch commemorating Napoleon's defeat in 1812 when she spoke.

"Where to?"

He knew where he wanted to go, but he thought it was inappropriate to ask.

"I can't risk going back to my place," he said. "Drop me at a pay phone. I'll call friends and find a couch to sleep on."

Lena looked levelly at him. "I'm your friend," she said.

She took him to the little apartment with the divan, the wardrobe, and the CD player, but this time there was no old lady sitting there with a tape recorder. Lena punched a button on the CD. Burke heard Vivaldi's *Four Seasons*, with the volume low.

"Wait," she said.

She opened the wardrobe and pulled down some linen and a blanket. Then she unfolded the divan, opening it into a bed. Tidily, she made it up, folding the sheets under.

He watched, waiting for her to finish and touched, in some way, by her display of domesticity.

When the sheets were done, she straightened up in the little space between the bed and the wall. She caught his eye, and he thought for an instant that the look that she gave him revealed her as someone's agent because it seemed to him both knowing and ironic. But that impression was a fleeting one because in the next instant, he decided that it was just a look of honest lust. The ambiguity aroused him.

She stepped back, reached down to the bottom of her black sweater, and lifted it over her head in a slow, graceful motion that revealed her bony hips, then a narrow, pale waist with a deep navel. Her breasts were hidden behind a white bra, and there were freckles in the little hollows around her neck and shoulders. She shook her head so that her hair fell around her shoulders, and she tossed the sweater on the floor behind her.

Burke stepped forward and buried his face in the curve of her neck. He brushed his lips lightly and slowly over her chin and up to her lips. They were soft and open. He kissed her; and as he did, he reached behind her and unhooked the bra. She shrugged, and it fell between them. Her breasts were freckled, with small, boyish nipples. He moved a hand around them and cupped one, running his fingers lightly over the nipple and feeling it harden. Her tongue pushed into his mouth then, probing, and her hands reached smoothly into the waistband of his sweatpants, groped for an instant, then curled around his erection and stroked it. He reached for the button at the top of her jeans.

"Hurry," she said.

That inflamed him, and he pulled roughly on her jeans and panties until both were down around her thighs. He touched her shoulder lightly, and she fell over backward onto the bed. Standing over her, he jerked the pants and shoes off her legs. He tossed them on the floor somewhere. Then he knelt between her legs and tasted her; she was musky and wet and the smell of her intoxicated him. She braced against the bed, arched her back, and pushed herself against his mouth, almost as if she were trying to force herself down his throat. He licked and sucked, matching the thrusts of his tongue to the thrusts of her hips; and in a few minutes she came, moaning and pumping her hips against his lips.

Her hips sagged to the bed and he stood up and began to pull off his own clothes. In an instant she was standing up beside him, pushing his hands away and putting hers in their place. Slowly, she pulled the tee shirt over his head, bending down and gently biting his nipples. Then she pushed his sweatpants and shorts down past his knees, knelt down, and took him in her mouth. Her lips were sweet, hot, and insistent; but after a moment he pushed her gently away. Then he lay on the bed.

"Get on top," he said. "I want to look at you."

Eagerly, she straddled him. She used a hand to guide him to the entrance to her vagina, and then she slowly lowered herself onto him. She closed her eyes, turned her head to one side and moaned softly as he entered her. He watched himself disappear within her; she felt warm and tight. She pressed down until her thighs were sealed to his hips. She shuddered, and he thought that he could feel himself pressing against her cervix. He raised his hands and caressed her breasts; she bent forward to move them closer to him, propping herself on her outstretched arms and lowering her body until he could take her nipples in his mouth. He did, licking gently and sucking until her hips began to move violently again. Shuddering, she climaxed again, dropping her head down to his and kissing him so hard that her teeth ground against his and he tasted blood.

He rolled over on top of her without breaking their connection. He reached the state he was seeking: He could think of nothing but her hips rising up to meet his thrusts, doubling his pace, and the sound of the divan slamming rhythmically against the wall, and the smell of her hair. He groaned, and they finished together.

She lay in his arms until their breathing slowed. Idly, he stroked her hair.

"You're thinking about the guard at that dacha, aren't you?" she whispered against his neck.

"No," he said. "I'm thinking about you."

She reached up and pulled at his chin until his eyes were focused on hers. "Don't lie to me," she said.

"All right," he replied. "I'm thinking about the guard at the dacha."

CHAPTER NINETEEN

THE IDEA CAME TO HIM in the hour before dawn as he lay on the hard, lumpy divan, listened to her breathing, and waited for the blackness outside the window to give way to dawn. He turned it over in his mind, examining it, uncertain.

Lena stirred, opened her eyes, looked at the window, then looked at him.

"Have you slept?" she asked.

"Some," he replied.

She sat up beside him, pulling the sheet and blanket up toward her neck.

"What time is it?" she asked, with most of the sleep gone from her voice.

"I don't know. Before dawn."

"I'll make some coffee."

She got up, and he watched her silhouette move in the darkness to the wardrobe. He could just make out the curve of her hips. She put on a robe and walked over to the tiny kitchen. She turned on a light, struck a match, and lit the stove. He could hear water running as she filled a kettle.

Burke got up, stumbled around, and found his sweat pants in the gap between the bed and the window. He pulled them on. Out of bed, he felt cold; he walked into the kitchen, put his arms around her, and drew her warmth to him. She arched her back and pressed herself against him for a moment, silently.

"So have you thought of a way?" she asked.

"I think so," he said.

She stepped away from him, took cups from a shelf over the stove, and set them next to a chipped sugar bowl and a jar of rank German instant coffee on a small, formica-covered table that hugged the kitchen wall. She sprinkled coffee crystals in the bottom of each cup and sat down. Her hair hung in front of her face, and she pushed it to the side.

"First, tell me why you have to do this," she said.

"I just do."

She wrinkled her nose. "That's not good enough. 'I just do,'" she said, in a decent imitation of Burke's voice.

He smiled.

"It's because someone is jerking me around," he said.

"'Jerking you around'? I don't get it."

"I guess it doesn't translate very well. It means someone is trying to deceive me, to use me to spread disinformation for some reason. They've been playing me for a fool."

"Ohhh." She nodded elaborately, and he couldn't tell if she was being sarcastic

The kettle whistled. Lena got up and pulled it from

the stove, wrapping a towel around the handle. She poured steaming water into his cup. He waited, watching the coffee cool.

"And you don't like being jerked around?"

"No," he said. "I can't stand it."

She nodded and sipped the coffee, holding the cup in both hands.

"And who is doing this?"

"I don't know," he said. He waited a moment. "But I do know that whoever it is is not going to be happy with what I want to do. And since it would involve you and Edik and Boris, you need to know that. And to know that it might involve something slightly illegal."

She picked up a teaspoon and stirred her coffee. Then she grinned, a trifle mischievously

"Illegal! Perish the thought!"

"No, really. Not just a con game at the station."

Her face grew serious.

"Sweetheart, I've seen men murder other men, pay off the *militsia*, and walk away. There isn't a *militsioner* in Moscow who's not for sale. Whatever it is, Boris and Edik will be happy to do it if the money's right."

"And that's another thing," Burke said. He paused to recollect how much money was left in the *America Weekly* account at the Bank for Foreign Trade. "I can pay you a couple of thousand dollars—"

She smiled and interrupted him. "For a couple of thousand dollars, Boris and Edik would take over the Kremlin for a few hours while you rummaged around inside. They spent two years in Afghanistan killing people for fifty rubles a month."

"—but I can't get the money out of the bank until this thing is over. You'll have to trust me."

She frowned. "I trust you. I don't know about Boris and Edik. They tend to prefer cash up front."

"Can you talk them into it?"

She frowned. "I think so. It depends on what you have in mind."

He took a sip of coffee and told her.

By the time darkness fell, Burke had counted the rusty stains from leaks in the ceiling a dozen times, inspected all the dishes and knickknacks in the empty apartment, listened to Vivaldi twice more, and compiled mental lists of all the cover stories he had ever written for *America Weekly*, all the friends he had in the news business who had become editors and might give him jobs, all the women he had ever slept with, and all the ones he had wanted to sleep with but couldn't persuade. He had searched the apartment thoroughly for alcohol and found none. That relieved him of the obligation to restrain himself, and he considered it a blessing. He lay on the divan, staring at the ceiling, and wondered if he could pinpoint a time when his drinking had slipped out of control. He could not. He tried to analyze why it had happened, but only the conventional reasons came to him: he was burned out; he was lonely; he used alcohol as a substitute for love. None of the conventional explanations satisfied him. Drinking was just something he had to stop doing, and he wondered whether he would have the strength. Then he stopped wondering because he realized he was slowly becoming frantic.

Then he wondered if Lemeshev had sent the *milit-*

sia out to find him when he failed to show up at the procurator's office. Or the Ministry of Security.

When the key turned and the door opened, his bowels tightened up and his mouth got dry.

Lena came in, followed by Boris and Edik. She wore a yellow miniskirt that barely covered her rear end, a pair of black tights, and black high-heeled shoes. She had the same ribbed, scoop-necked blouse she wore on the job at the train station, but it was evident to Burke that she had added some padding to the bra. Her lips were painted bright red. She made a convincing hooker.

She carried a wire hanger from which hung one of his sport coats, a shirt, tie, and slacks. In her other hand she had a pair of his shoes.

Edik still had the boyish face and the wispy goatee that he used to portray the starving student in the station con game. But he and Boris were dressed in the remnants of army fatigue clothes, and Edik carried a paper bag containing three pistols.

"We thought you might want to carry this one," Edik said, offering the third pistol to Burke.

The guns looked improbably malevolent against the background of his innocent face. They were nine-millimeter Makarovs, oily and black, with the star of the Soviet Army still embossed on the handle. They were fitted with clips of fifteen rounds and could accommodate exploding bullets that would leave a fifty-millimeter wound upon exiting a victim. They were guaranteed to down a man at distances of up to twenty meters; in the hands of an expert, they could be effective at distances of forty meters.

Burke shied away from the proffered weapon. "God, no. I'd probably blow my own foot off," he said.

Boris, who looked as if he'd been born in fatigues, frowned. "Never in the Army?"

"No."

The Russian scowled and said nothing.

"By the way," Burke said, "what do the letters tattooed on your knuckles mean?"

Boris grinned proudly, showing enough stainless steel to furnish a small restaurant. "North, south, east and west," he said.

"Okay, I give up. Why?"

Boris clenched his fist and pushed it into the air about three inches in front of Burke's nose. It looked the size of a smoked ham.

"Because if you get hit by this fist, you'll feel like you're getting hit from every direction at once," Boris laughed. Edik guffawed in support.

"All right," Lena said. "Is everyone clear about what they're doing?"

Boris and Edik nodded.

"No problem," Edik said.

"What I don't understand," Boris said, "is why we don't just slug the guard, slug this guy, and take him away."

"Because," Burke said, "I don't want to break the law. Especially not assault people and kidnap them. You don't want to, either. Okay?"

"It'd be easy," Boris protested. "Just go in, do it, get out. One minute. No one would know. Quick and clean."

"That's what they said about Afghanistan," Burke said. When he saw Boris began to glower, he hastily added, "Vietnam, too."

Boris's glower subsided to a frown.

"Well, as long as it's working," he said. "But if it's not…"

"If it's not, I'll give you the signal," Lena spoke up. "But wait for me to tell you."

"And if she does," Burke added, "for God's sake don't hit him too hard. Got it?"

"No problem," Edik said. He was obviously the conciliator of the two.

Burke considered going into the kitchen to dress. But modesty, given the circumstances, seemed rather frivolous.

He stripped down to the running shorts.

"Olga give you much trouble about the clothes?"

"No," Lena replied. "She recognized your signature on the note. She handled it very well. She just read it, said nothing, and took me upstairs to your apartment."

"Good." He slipped on the shirt and stepped into the trousers.

Burke knotted his tie. "Okay," he said. "Let's go."

In two cars, one the white Zhiguli and the other an ancient green Moskvich, they drove through the darkness toward Nekronov's dacha. The rain had stopped, but clouds still hid the moon. The night, Burke saw to his relief, was suitably black. Just as it had the night before, the traffic thinned once they were out of the city; and they saw nothing else moving on the road. They came to the carved wooden bear and buck by the side of the road. Edik and Boris, in the first car, drove a half mile farther up the road and pulled over. Burke cut his lights and pulled up behind them.

Edik and Boris hopped out of the Zhiguli. Edik pulled an ice pick out of his pocket, squatted down by the left rear tire, and jabbed at it. The car sagged as the air went out of the tire.

Quickly, Edik and Boris ran to the passenger side of the Moskvich, Lena slipped the door open, and they climbed into the back seat.

"Go," Edik hissed as Lena shut the door.

Burke turned around, drove back a half a mile, and turned up the narrow road that led past the dacha where Nekronov was hiding. He drove past the closed gate until he saw an indentation in the woods on his left. He pulled into it and cut the engine and lights.

All four carefully and slowly extricated themselves from the car. The men in fatigues pulled long hunting knives from sheaths at their belts and began cutting boughs from pine trees. Within a few minutes, Burke and Lena had the little car covered.

"Not professional, but it'll do," Edik whispered.

"Duck! Car coming!" Boris hissed.

An instant later, Burke, too, heard the sound of an engine. He squatted in the foliage behind the camouflaged Moskvich. Headlights probed the darkness as the car rumbled slowly along the narrow dacha road. Had the lights bounced off an uncovered piece of metal on the Moskvich, and would the oncoming driver notice?

But the car, a Chaika limousine, moved sedately past them. They waited several minutes.

"Okay," Burke said. "Let's go."

They scrambled silently out of the woods and down the road to a point thirty yards past the gate to the Nekronov dacha. They halted at a point of pitch darkness under the wall. They checked their watches. It was ten minutes after eight.

"Two minutes," Edik whispered to Lena and Burke. Burke nodded back. His stomach felt tight .and twisted.

Boris gave Edik a boost with his cupped hands, and Edik disappeared over the wall. Burke provided the same service to Boris. He, too, disappeared soundlessly. Burke was impressed. Whatever they had done in Afghanistan, they had been well trained. Burke and Lena retreated to the spot in the woods where the car was hidden.

He looked at his watch until a minute had passed.

"Ready?" he asked Lena. His voice was strained; it came out as a croak rather than a whisper.

She grinned and moved closer to him. "Listen," she said quietly, "if you're going to carry this thing off, you've got to lighten up a little."

She reached around his neck, pulled him to her, and kissed him. He felt her tongue pass through his lips and her fingers massage his crotch. Just as quickly as she had initiated the kiss, she broke it and walked off down the road, no longer quiet, letting her heels click on the pavement and her hips move freely.

Burke watching her, absently wiped the lipstick off his mouth.

She walked up to the gate. It was made of steel plates painted a dark color, with a bit of cheap steel fili-gree at the top. A steel door was mounted into one of the plates so that a person could walk in or out without opening the gates.

Near the door, Lena found a button and pushed it. After thirty more seconds, she began to pound on the gate with her hand, and thirty seconds after that, she picked up a small rock from the side of the road and pounded on the gate with that. The sound of the pounding reverberated in the pine trees like a muffled gong.

Burke heard a key turning and then the door opened. A flashlight beam cut through the darkness illuminating Lena. He could just make out the face of the guard, peering through a foot-wide crack between the door and its frame.

Lena put a hand on her hip and let the beam of light play over her body. Then she took one step toward the door.

"Hi," she said. "I need your help. I was on my way to visit a, um, client, and I had a flat tire. I need someone to help me change it."

The flashlight beam settled somewhere near her crotch.

"Sorry," Burke heard the man reply. "I can't help you."

"Oh, please," Lena said, taking another step toward the man. "It would only take a minute."

She paused. "I'd make it worth your while," she said. "

Sorry," the guard said again, but the flashlight beam was beginning to wobble a little bit.

Burke swallowed. Boris and Edik were waiting in the trees by the gate. Another thirty seconds, he calculated, and they might make their move. That would push this little operation over the line into a felony if they got caught.

Lena stepped toward the guard one more time, until she was close enough for him to smell her perfume.

"Please," Burke heard her say again, and then she leaned over and whispered something in his ear.

"How far away did you say it was?" the guard asked. His voice had suddenly gotten squeaky.

"Just around the corner there," Lena said.

In fact, it was half a mile from the corner. They had picked the farthest point on a direct line from the corner of the Moscow road. Once he and Lena got to the corner, the guard would be able to see the car. But once they got to the car, it would take him at least three minutes to make it back to the dacha on foot—assuming he ran and was in better shape than he looked.

"Okay," the guard said. "Let's go."

He stepped through the door, turned around, and locked it, using a large iron key. Then he and Lena walked down the road together, the flashlight beam pointing the way.

Lena moved close to the guard's side and took his elbow.

"What's your name?" Burke heard her ask him.

"Volodya," the man replied. The flashlight beam wavered again.

Burke watched until they were around the corner and out of sight. Then he tore the branches off the car, started the engine, and drove to the gate. He stepped out and rapped three times, lightly, on its steel surface.

In a second, the gate opened. Boris and Edik pushed both sides out of the driveway. Burke took a deep breath and hopped into the car. He punched the accelerator and drove it as fast as he could to the dacha, fifty yards up the driveway. In the mirror, he could see a plume of gray dust rising in his wake. That was good. He needed as much dirt and confusion as he could muster.

At the dacha, the light on the veranda was lit. He bounded up the steps two at a time.

In front of the door, he paused to go over his story and to get into the role he was going to play. His face grew anguished. He took three deep, raspy breaths. Then he pounded on the door.

"Nekronov!" he yelled. "Open up! You've got to get out of here! They're coming for you!"

There was no answer. He tried the doorknob. It was open. He rushed inside.

The room he entered was paneled with dark, varnished wood; and the floor was covered with a couple of woven carpets from Central Asia. The furniture gave the place away as an old Party dacha. It was heavy and ugly and upholstered in nubby red polyester. There was a fireplace, empty and cold, and a profusion of dirty cups and glasses on the tables. One teacup was overturned, and the liquid was still seeping toward the edge of the table. Nearby, on the floor, a book lay open on its face, its pages crumpled together as if someone had tossed it there.

"Dr. Nekronov!" he called again. "Sergei!"

He saw a door off to one side of the room. He rushed to it and threw it open.

It was a bedroom, and Sergei Nekronov was cowering on the bed, dressed in jeans and a cardigan sweater.

When he saw Burke, his jaw dropped open and he seemed to be making an effort to sink back into the wall.

"Sergei, you're in danger!" Burke shouted. He found it easy to inject the appropriate urgency into his voice. He was feeling about as much urgency as he could tolerate.

"How—How did you find me?" Nekronov's face

was ashen, making the blackheads around his nose stand out.

"No time for that," Burke said. "You've got to get out of here!"

"What do you mean? Where—Where's Volodya?" Nekronov's voice was tremulous.

Burke grabbed and pulled at Nekronov's shoulder. "He's covering the gate! The Israelis know where you are! They're coming after you!"

Hearing the word "Israelis," Nekronov moaned. But he stayed on the bed, heavy and immovable.

"Volodya—he said—"

"Volodya told me to get you out of here and call for help!"

But Nekronov remained on the bed.

Burke grabbed both shoulders and shook them.

"Listen to me! I found out about your sister. Last night, I followed her here. But the Israelis grabbed me today. They made me tell them where you are! They're going to come after you tonight! You've got to get out of here now!"

"But, why...Volodya..." Nekronov seemed dazed.

Burke glanced at his watch. It was time for the next step in the plan, a step he had hoped would be unnecessary.

On schedule, gunshots rang out from the woods in front of the dacha. They sounded like a pair of firecrackers going off.

"Shit, they're here!" Burke yelled. "Volodya won't hold them off for long! Look, it's my fault they're coming for you. I've got to get you out of here! Let's go!"

Thoroughly frightened and confused, Nekronov got to his feet. Burke got him as far as the living room before he stopped and grabbed Burke's arm. Two more shots cracked in the woods. Volodya, Burke knew, would be sprinting back to the dacha now.

"But you—why you?" Nekronov whispered. There were two more shots.

"Stay down!" Burke said, jerking the man's shoulders downward. "Because they knew I was working on your story."

Nekronov gulped.

"I've got a car outside," Burke said. "Stay down, get in the passenger side, and we'll get out of here."

Nekronov hesitated. Two more shots rang out Burke wondered how many seconds he had before a third gun, Volodya's, joined in the firefight. This one would not be shooting into the trees.

"Gotta go!" he yelled in Nekronov's ear. He grabbed the man's hand and pulled. Childlike, Nekronov allowed himself to be led.

Thank God, Burke thought. They scuttled out the door and onto the veranda. Two more shots rang out, and Burke heard a bullet whine toward them and hit the wall of the dacha, twenty feet or so to his left. Nekronov jerked back, startled. In the open air, the shots sounded louder, like explosions.

Careful, Boris, Burke thought.

Still holding Nekronov's hand, he got him to the car, which had its lights on and its engine running. He pushed him into the passenger seat.

"Stay down!" he shouted.

Nekronov performed a contortion Burke would have thought impossible, doubling over until his head was below his knees, wedged under the glove compartment.

Burke slammed the car into gear. He popped the clutch and took off, lurching over the grass and rocks as he left the driveway to make a 180-degree turn and then producing another dust plume in his wake when he regained its surface.

Boris and Edik, hidden in the underbrush on either side of the drive, fired a volley of shots over the roof of the car as he sped down the driveway. They were so close they sounded like bombs going off. He glanced for an instant at Nekronov. He had his hands up and wrapped over his head, like a small boy being beaten. His eyes were fixed on the floor of the car.

He braked lightly at the gate and swung the car into a hard left turn. For an instant he thought he might roll it over. Sluggishly, the old Moskvich regained stability, and the headlight beams turned from the woods back to the narrow paved road.

They illuminated Volodya, sprinting toward the dacha gate, his face suffused with rage. He still had the flashlight, but it was in his left hand. His right hand held a gun.

Burke saw Volodya stop, assume a half crouch, drop the flashlight, and raise the gun, clenched in both hands. He punched the accelerator and ducked his own head until he could not see the road ahead and was steering the car by memory. The car's engine whined in protest. He was still in second gear.

The first crack from the pistol was followed by a crash and a shower of glass over Burke's head as the guard's bullet crashed through the side window where Burke's skull had been a second before.

Ignore it, he told himself feverishly. Just steer.

The second shot sounded like a cannon going off.

He felt a quick, heavy jolt in the left rear of the car near the wheels. But the tires held firm.

He would, he knew, have to risk raising his head if he wanted to find the intersection and make the turn toward Moscow. He raised it quickly and peered over the dashboard. Fifty more feet.

Raising his head fully, he braked and swung the wheel hard right. The tires squealed loudly. He realized he had started the turn a second too late. Then he was skidding off into the soft grass on the far side of the road.

The car bounced and seemed to teeter on two wheels, hanging on the edge of a deep, muddy ditch. Burke leaned right and tried to steer it back up to the road. The tires spun, their noise rising in pitch to a scream, matching the sound coming, he dimly realized, from his own mouth. In the corner of his right eye, he thought he saw the guard, sprinting again, raising the pistol to fire once more.

With a bump, the right-side wheels came back to the ground, increasing his traction. The car gained purchase and climbed back onto the pavement, shooting ahead as it did. He heard the crack of another pistol shot but felt no impact.

Burke worked through the gears until he was going at top speed, a little more than fifty-five miles an hour His hands, he noticed, were trembling. He suspected his whole body would be if he were able to let it.

He glanced down at Nekronov. The scientist was still bent over, hands atop his head. One of his fingers had been sliced open by a shard of glass from the shattered window. A trickle of blood was dripping onto his left ear. He was whimpering softly.

It was just as Chris Canfield had said in his last

memo on writing style, Burke thought. Nothing like a few convincing details to give a story verisimilitude.

He opened the door to Lena's apartment and gently prodded Nekronov inside. The scientist gazed at the room dully, sucking on his cut finger like a child.

"Whose place is this?" he asked.

"It's my girlfriend's," Burke replied. "You should be safe here. Sit down while I get something for that hand."

Nekronov nodded and sat down mechanically on the divan. Burke stepped into the kitchen and came out with a dish towel. Nekronov took it and wrapped it around his hand.

"Thank you," he said. "And thank you for saving me."

"The least I could do," Burke replied. "But I have to tell you, if I had known how closely the Israelis would be on my tail, I don't think I would've done it."

Nekronov smiled weakly and nodded.

Burke strode to the window and looked outside. "Looks clear on the street," he said. "But I want to get you out of here. I don't know how long it'll be safe."

Nekronov nodded.

"Who can help you get out of here?" Burke asked.

Nekronov only stared at him.

"Rafit Kassim?" Burke prodded.

Dumbly, the scientist nodded.

"Well, call him," Burke said. He pointed. 'There's the phone."

Nekronov patted the empty breast pocket of his shirt. "I, uh, I don't have the number," he said.

Burke pulled his wallet out and fished around until he found the Switsico business card Kassim had given him.

"I've got this card," he told Nekronov, flashing it to him. "I'll call him there."

He took the phone and, checking to make sure that Nekronov was not watching, dialed the number for the empty *America Weekly* office. At the other end, the phone rang.

"No answer," Burke said, passing the receiver to Nekronov and letting him listen. "We've got to call someone else. But not your family. I'm sure the Israelis have them under surveillance by now."

Nekronov gulped. He looked so anguished that for a second, Burke felt sorry for him. He pushed the feeling out of his mind.

"Who else, besides Kassim, did you know?" he asked Nekronov gently.

"No one," the scientist said.

Burke tried to keep the scowl of frustration off his face. He needed to look benevolently interested.

"No one?" he repeated.

Nekronov shook his head.

Burke walked to the edge of the window, parted the filmy white curtain that hung there, and peered out. The white Zhiguli was parked where he had hoped it would be, a hundred yards from the entrance to Lena's stairwell. He could see Edik's silhouette inside.

"*Yob tvoyu mat*," he cursed, for Nekronov's benefit.

Nekronov looked up, startled.

"What's wrong?"

"There's a white car parked down the street," Burke said. "It wasn't there ten minutes ago. There's a guy sitting in it who I think is one of the Israelis who interrogated me. Come here and look."

Warily, Nekronov got up and walked slowly to the window.

"Don't get your face where they can see it," Burke commanded. The scientist shrank back against the wall. Then he got to his knees and crept the last two yards, until only his eyes were above the windowsill.

"Down to the left about a hundred meters," Burke directed him. "White Zhiguli. Under a street lamp. Guy inside it. See him?"

Nekronov peered out, then drew in a breath that stopped just short of a gasp. He nodded.

"That guy told me he would kill me if I didn't tell him where you were. And go to California and kill my son, too," Burke whispered.

Nekronov, his face slack with fear, could only nod.

"I'm sorry," Burke said.

"How did he—did he find us?" Nekronov asked.

"Must've managed to get an idea of our direction. Followed at a distance," Burke whispered. "Maybe cruised around and saw it parked." They had parked the old Moskvich two blocks away. "I don't think he knows exactly what building we're in yet."

Nekronov remained on his knees, silent. Beads of sweat dribbled down his forehead.

"We've gotta get some help," Burke said. "Who does Kassim work with?"

"I don't know," Nekronov said in a raspy voice.

"He must've told you something," Burke said. Behind his back, he clenched a fist. He felt a desperate urge to beat the man's secrets out of him. With difficulty, he checked it.

Nekronov simply shook his head; he was a portrait of distress and depression.

"He just told you you'd be going to Syria?" Burke prodded him, still peering through the curtain at the Zhiguli. "Maybe I could find someone at the Syrian embassy."

"No," Nekronov croaked. "Not Syria. What I told you about Syria—that was a lie."

"A lie."

"Yes, I'm sorry. I had to do it," Nekronov mumbled.

"Kassim made you?"

"He said I could go to the West."

"The West," Burke repeated, still whispering. "Where in the West?"

"Anywhere I wanted. They would pay me one hundred thousand dollars a year for five years. They would give me a new identity. They would help me get a job."

"And all you had to do was fool me?"

Nekronov carefully withdrew his head from the window and looked at Burke. He was on the verge of mixing tears with the sweat pouring down his cheeks. He nodded.

"I was going to go to Arizona," he said, almost moaning. "I'm sorry. Please help me. I—I'll pay you," he offered.

Burke knew he could not get angry with the man. He needed him to stay where he was for a while. So he nodded forgivingly.

"It's all right," he told the scientist. "You did what you had to do for your family. So did I. We just have to figure out a way to get out of this."

Nekronov looked grateful.

"You're sure he mentioned no one?"

Nekronov shook his head, still looking miserable. If he was lying, he was lying well.

"We could call the *militsia*..." Burke suggested.

Nekronov recoiled. "No! Then I would never be able to leave the country."

Burke looked out the window a final time.

'Well," he said, trying to sound spontaneous, "We have one advantage. He doesn't know which one of hundreds of apartments you're in. And he's still out there alone. I'll make a break for it, try to get away and find Kassim. You watch. If he follows me, you leave and go like hell in the opposite direction. If he doesn't follow me, I'll bring back Kassim and some help."

Nekronov nodded.

"Whatever you do, don't answer the door or the phone. If they come in this entrance and start knocking down doors, I'd advise you to call the *militsia*. Okay?"

"Okay." Nekronov managed to nod again.

Burke patted him on the back and stepped outside. Slowly, he walked the five flights of stairs down to the ground floor, stifling, as he walked, the urge to put his fist through a wall.

He had, he realized, only one idea left for finding out who was willing to pay a Russian scientist half a million dollars to pretend to be going to Syria to build a bomb.

And it was not, he thought, a very good idea.

Lena was waiting in the shadows of the rear court-yard. Seeing her safe momentarily broke the gnawing anger and frustration he felt. He pulled her into his arms and hugged her tightly.

"I'm glad you made it. Everything worked out back there?"

She pulled her head back and smiled at him. "No problem. Boris and Edik got over the wall while Volodya was still running up the driveway. We drove a kilometer or two on the rim and then stopped to change the tire. No problem."

"Good," he said. "And, uh, did you..."

"Don't worry," she said, smiling again. "He never even got his pants down."

She looked at his face, and her exultation faded. "You didn't find out what you needed to know, did you?"

He shook his head. "I don't think he knows."

"What did he tell you?"

Burke stepped back from her and recounted briefly what Nekronov had said.

"I think he was telling me the truth. He was frightened enough. And I guess it makes sense that he'd have only the one contact."

"What do we do now?"

"Boris and Edik should stay out there until tomorrow morning. It's a slim chance he could tip anyone off, but there's no point in inviting him to walk out and try it. On the other hand, if he leaves, let him go. It's not worth stopping him—then we'd be kidnapping. But I don't think he'll leave. You should get out of sight for a day or so. I'll call you the day after tomorrow—Thursday—okay?"

"Okay," she said. "You're sure you don't need help?"

"It's a one-man job. But I'll need some luck," he said. "Can you arrange it?"

"A person in my business never relies on luck," she answered. "You'd better not, either."

CHAPTER TWENTY

HE COULD NOT, HE REALIZED, expect to go back to his office and stay more than an hour before Lemeshev's people came for him.

So he took the Metro to the Kiev station, got out, and walked over to Kutuzovsky Prospekt to another building in Moscow's foreigners' archipelago, where ABC News had its bureau. The *militsioner* in the little booth guarding the entrance showed no reaction when Burke walked by.

The ABC office was lit up and bustling in preparation for the nightly feed to New York. The hum of electronics filled the bureau's four rooms.

Elliott Lantz, his necktie neatly loosened but otherwise impeccably dressed, was in his editing room, working on a tape of yet another near riot at the Supreme Soviet.

"You look like shit," he said to Burke. "You been out screwing barnyard animals or what?"

"Something like that," Burke said. "Nice to see you, too, Elliott. I've got a couple of favors to ask."

"Okay."

"You got someone doing a courier run to Frankfurt tomorrow?"

"Yeah, Ellen Thomason's going to take some film we've been working on for *20-20*."

The networks found it cheaper to have a producer's flunky fly to Frankfurt and ship their film to New York than to pay the extortionate rates the Russians charged for satellite services. They saved the satellite for deadline news.

"Good," Burke said. "I'm going to have something for her to take."

Lantz nodded. "What else?"

"I need to use an office with a computer for a couple of hours."

"Yours broke down?"

"Not exactly," Burke said. He hated the idea of lying to a colleague, and he hoped he wouldn't have to do it.

Lantz's eyebrows arched upward. "What, you got a woman stashed away over there won't let you work?"

"A gentleman never comments, Elliott," Burke said, forcing a grin.

"Okay, sure. Use my office," Lantz said, smiling broadly. "Always glad to help out a friend in need. You remember where it is?"

Burke did. He walked to the office and shut the door.

First, he took a sheet of stationery and, using an old manual typewriter, typed out a message:

TO: Chris Canfield, *America Weekly*, New York
TELEPHONE: 212-555-1300

FROM: Colin Burke, Moscow

Sorry to pull this on you, Chris, but you must KILL, repeat KILL, the Israeli commandos story transmitted last night. It is deliberately erroneous. Will call as soon as possible to explain why and will attempt to file the real story by the end of the week.

Then he pulled a computer disk from his pocket, slipped it into Lantz's computer, and brought up the file tagged "COUP.891." He added notes on sources and the events of the last few days. He copied it onto a blank disk, then removed the disk and sealed it in an envelope. He folded the message to Canfield, sealed it in another envelope, and pulled twenty dollars out of his wallet. He clipped the money to the second envelope.

Then he slipped a fresh disk into the computer and began to type.

TO: Canfield, New York
FROM: Burke, Moscow
RE: Israeli commandos

In a daring night raid on a dacha in the Moscow suburbs, Israeli commandos kidnapped a Soviet physicist who had been recruited to design nuclear bombs for Syria, according to informed sources.

The commandos were part of a special Mossad unit formed to combat Arab efforts to obtain the bomb using parts and personnel that have gone up for bids since the collapse of the Soviet Union.

In recent weeks, the Mossad agents have been investigating the activities of a purported oil joint venture called Switsico, headed by an Arab businessman, Rafit Kassirn.

Kassim, according to the sources, was actually employed by Syrian intelligence and financed by the oil-producing states of the Persian Gulf.

He recruited one of the most brilliant and accomplished young physicists in the old Soviet nuclear program, Sergei Nekronov. Nekronov specializes in miniaturizing nuclear weapons.

But just before Nekronov and his family were to be spirited out of Russia, the Mossad agents learned of his whereabouts, a dacha in a compound outside Moscow once reserved for members of the Communist Party's *nomenklatura*. On a cloudy, moonless night, the Mossad commandos struck.

After luring away his guards, they spirited Nekronov away to an undisclosed location. The sources refused to say whether Nekronov would be smuggled to Israel or executed.

MORE

Then he wrote a second take, going into detail about the raid. He wrote a third, recapping the information he had gotten from Nekronov in their first interview. Finally, he wrote a fourth, telling of Katya's role in Nekronov's recruitment and her subsequent murder.

When he was done, Burke walked back to Lantz, still hunched over in the editing cubicle. He handed him the envelope with the twenty dollars. "Give Ellen this. Ask her to open it when she gets to Frankfurt, call the guy whose number's on there, and read the message. Okay?"

Lantz nodded. "Got it. Mind if I ask why?"

"Long story," Burke said. "I'll tell you at the next poker game."

Then he handed the envelope with the computer disk to Lantz.

"This is another long story," he said. "Hold onto it for a day or two, okay? I don't want it in my office."

Lantz looked puzzled, but he accepted the envelope.

"Now I'm really curious," he said. "What's going on?"

"I'm not quite sure yet," Burke said. "Bear with me, okay?"

Lantz nodded slowly, folded the envelope, and put it in his shirt pocket.

The *America Weekly* bureau was calm and still, counterpointing the state of his psyche when he walked inside at eleven o'clock. The only sound was the quiet clicking of the Reuters machine in the wire room. Burke sat in the darkness for a minute, trying to force himself to think clearly. Then he slipped the computer disk into his machine and sent the four takes of the phony story humming to New York.

He thought for a moment of the bottle of cognac he kept in a file cabinet, reserved for entertaining guests. He thought about taking a long pull from the bottle and letting the liquor slosh around in his mouth, stinging the insides, before he swallowed it slowly. Then he put the thought out of his mind. It seemed, he thought, to be getting easier to do that. Not easy, but easier.

He wondered how long it would be before he got a reaction from the agencies that eavesdropped on telecommunications to and from Moscow. One of those agencies, he was certain, would have a very particular desire to know how he had come by his story about

Sergei Nekronov's disappearance. Trading for that information was the last card he had to play.

He calculated that the intelligence agencies would act at least a couple of hours faster than the *militsia*. He assumed that the *militsioner* at the entrance to the Sad Sam compound had filed a report on his arrival. But he also assumed that the *militsia* would not move immediately to arrest a foreigner. The Foreign Ministry would have to know about it. So, probably, would the Ministry of Security. At this hour, that would mean finding people at home, rousting them out of bed, and bringing them up to date on what had happened. He estimated that it would take at least three hours. By then, he assumed, he would know what he needed to know.

He switched the computer off and pulled the curtains shut to keep out the glow from the streetlights outside. When the room was completely dark and quiet, he leaned back and gave himself over to his fears, letting them gnaw freely at his stomach and bounce around his mind. Maybe, he thought, if he stopped trying to avoid thinking about the worst things that could happen, he could cope with the fear. And if he could cope with the fear, maybe the worst things would not happen.

And what was the worst that could happen?

He could go to jail, a Russian jail, for killing Katya or for kidnapping Nekronov. He could spend much of the rest of his useful life there.

Somehow, he realized, that did not terrify him even though it should have. He decided that it was because he had, after all, not killed Katya. He had not kidnapped Nekronov, only tricked him. If he had violated any laws, they were stupid laws, lawyers' laws, and breaking them would not bother him. He could, he realized, live with a

Russian prison regime as long as he could believe he was innocent. Or he thought he could.

He could lose his job. He probably would, at least his assignment in Moscow. But that did not terrify him, either. His financial obligations, once his son finished school, were only to himself. He was used to living reasonably well, but he thought he could pare away a lot of the things he had and still get along. In fact, he decided, thinking of the stubby cognac bottle, he would be better off.

What really terrified him, he decided, was the prospect of losing something else, something he could not quite define. It was wrapped up, he knew, in his ability to discover facts and report them. It had to do with integrity. It had to do with the knowledge that other reporters whose judgments he respected recognized those qualities in him. It was a kind of dignity or sense of worth. And if he lost it, he would be left in ruins. He would be an emotionally bankrupt man approaching middle age with nothing but an overwhelming sense of shame. He might as well walk out to the middle of the Kutuzov Bridge and throw himself into the Moscow River.

As he envisioned the way the black, dirty water would look rushing up to meet him, he heard the faint sound of a key scraping in the outer door to the bureau. He took a deep breath and waited. There was a creaking sound as the door slowly opened. He held his breath.

Almost soundlessly, a slender silhouette materialized, moving along the bookshelves on the far wall of the office. Burke switched on the light and blinked in its sudden glare.

When he opened his eyes, Ronit Evron had turned and leveled a small pistol at his head. Her hair was pinned on top of her head, and she wore the same jeans and shirt she wore the night she had seduced him. The gun was greasy and black.

He forced himself to stare calmly at it.

"Ronit, please sit down," he said. "Cognac?"

"You know, you very nearly got yourself killed turning on the light like that," she snapped.

He smiled at her. "But you're a pro," he said. "You don't kill people accidentally."

Her eyebrows moved upward half an inch or so. "You didn't know it was me coming in here."

"I was feeling lucky," he said. "Cognac?"

She ignored the offer and slipped the gun into the pocket of her jeans. She remained standing a few steps from his desk. She folded her arms under her breasts.

"Stop playing games, Colin. It's way too late for that."

He wanted to know how much she knew. Had she read the phony story? He doubted that Mossad could monitor, in real time at least, telecommunications from Moscow. More likely, it relied on the CIA for things like that.

"How did you know where to find me?"

She scowled with impatience. "We've been waiting for you to show up here," she replied.

"What would you like to know?"

"Where's Nekronov?"

"I don't know," he said. "But I'm sure you'll be talking to him soon."

She seemed surprised. "What do you mean?"

"He's your man, isn't he? You set all this up. You gave me the lead on Switsico so I would find Nekronov and interview him. Then you killed Katya because you were afraid she'd tell me the truth. Why, Ronit? I imagine it's because you want an excuse to deploy some of your own bombs. So you get *America Weekly* and CNN to tell the world that Assad has the—"

"You're out of your mind!" she snapped.

Burke looked at her carefully. If she was lying, she was doing it too well for him to detect.

She pulled the gun from her pocket and pulled the visitor's chair away from his desk. She turned it around and then sat down, perhaps five feet from him, with the back of the chair against her chest. She rested her gun hand on the top of the chair back, where he could see it. Only the way her knuckles whitened against the butt of the gun gave away the tension she was feeling. She sighed.

"Colin, I like you," she said, softly. "I really do. So I don't want you to get hurt."

"Thanks," he said drily.

"But if you don't tell me what I want to know, I'll put this gun in your ribs and walk you downstairs to a car that's waiting outside on the Ring Road. Once you're in that car, you'll be out of my hands. You'll be taken to a place where no one can hear you. And there you'll tell us what we have to know."

She delivered the last sentence in a low, implacable tone. Then she paused, and when she spoke again her voice was half an octave higher. It was an encouraging voice, the voice of sweet seduction.

"But I think you'll realize that the right thing for you to do is to tell us. I think you'll realize it's the right thing to do because the lives of so many millions of people depend on it. I think you know that if the Syrians get the bomb, my country will have to take steps to make sure they can never use it against us." She paused.

"Why not just finish the damn peace negotiations?"

Abruptly, she asked, "Have you ever been to Yad Vashem?"

"No," he said, perplexed. He was beginning to believe her.

She nodded. "Maybe that explains why you have such a hard time with this—with understanding this—this request, this necessity. This is what the words 'Never again' mean. Don't you see?"

Burke barely heard her. He was struggling to think through the implications of her presence and her questions. If she knew about the phony story he had just transmitted, why hadn't she mentioned it? And if she had been involved in setting up Nekronov's false tale of recruitment, why would she want so desperately to know where he was now?

That, he realized, assumed she really was an Israeli agent. God only knew how many sleepers the KGB had planted in the waves of Jews who emigrated from Russia in the 1970s. But his instincts told him she was leveling with him. If she were a KGB sleeper, why would her mother show up on the street?

And if she was an Israeli and she didn't know about Nekronov, then she wasn't the one he needed to talk to. He needed, above all, to get her out of his office. Telling her something he hadn't published would violate his principles. But refusing to tell her wouldn't get him any closer to finding out who was behind Rafit Kassim. And it would very likely end up in his body being violated along with his principles.

"All right," he said. "I'll tell you what I know."

She nodded and leaned forward. The chair creaked.

"Where's Nekronov?"

"Nekronov isn't—" he began.

A muffled ping interrupted him. Simultaneously, as far as Burke's senses could distinguish, the left side of Ronit Byron's skull exploded. Her body fell, as if yanked by the hair, to the floor. Blood started to pool on the carpet underneath her head, and the acrid smell of burnt powder filled the room.

Burke's body froze and he cringed involuntarily, waiting for the next shot. There was none. For a long moment he gazed at those portions of the lifeless body that were not shielded from his eyes by his desk—her shattered head and an arm covered in blue denim that was beginning to soak up blood. She had, he noticed, delicate little wrists. Her mouth was open, and a thin stream of blood was beginning to trickle from its lower corner. Her eyes were wide open and blank. She looked as if she had died trying to scream.

Slowly he raised his eyes toward the entrance to his office. Two men were standing in the doorway. The first was Viktor Lemeshev, the procurator in the investigation of Katya's murder. He was holding a pistol fitted with a silencer. It was pointed at Burke.

The second man was Ethan Worthington. He was wearing a buff-brown tweed sport coat and a green wool tie. Except for the pistol in his hand, he looked like a young political scientist who had just made associate professor.

Burke forced himself to speak calmly.

"Hello, Ethan," he said. "Nice company you're keeping."

His voice sounded to him like a croak.

Lemeshev took a step closer, still leveling the pistol at Burke, aimed at a spot between his eyes.

"Where is Sergei Nekronov?" the Russian demanded.

Burke gazed back into the narrow opening of the silencer.

"Ethan, call him off," he said.

"You'd better answer the question, Colin," Worthington said.

"Not while he's got that pointed at me," Burke said. "It makes me too nervous."

"All right, Viktor," Worthington said to the Russian.

Slowly, with evident reluctance, Lemeshev lowered the gun until it pointed at the floor.

"Why'd you have to kill her, Ethan?" Burke asked. He tried not to whine, but his voice still sounded, to himself, weak and wavering.

"I'm sorry," Worthington said. "Truly. But we couldn't take a chance she was wearing a wire."

He bent down and gently poked and prodded at Ronit Evron's body. Then he straightened up. He looked a trifle pale.

"She wasn't?" Burke asked.

Worthington shook his head.

Suddenly, Burke got it.

"Well as long as there're no Israelis listening," Burke said, feeling some anger enter his voice, "Tell me why you set this whole damn thing up."

Whatever discomfort Worthington felt at discovering that Ronit Evron had not been wired evaporated, and he glared at Burke. "You don't know what you're talking about."

"Oh, yes, I do," Burke said.

Lemeshev raised the pistol again. "Where is Nekronov?" he demanded harshly.

"I'll tell you when I'm damned good and ready," Burke snapped. He turned to Worthington.

"You're the ones who've been monitoring nuclear components here, aren't you? And you planted a phony story with CNN in Washington about the Syrians getting them. Then you planted leads to a phony follow-up story about Switsico and Nekronov here in Moscow, both with me and the Israelis, didn't you? You set up that whole Olympic Club thing. You hired Katya."

"You don't know what you're talking about," Worthington repeated, but his voice lacked conviction.

"You did it to scare the Israelis, didn't you?" Burke pressed, his voice a little gentler. "You figured if they were convinced the Syrians had the bomb, they'd go ahead and make the concessions you need to finish the peace negotiations. How much did you have to pay these guys to go along?" He gestured with his eyes toward Lemeshev.

He watched Worthington's face carefully. He saw it twitch around the eyes and mouth. Then he watched as Worthington composed himself.

"Is that..." Worthington began, then paused. "If we had done that, would it be wrong? Would it be wrong to try to bring peace to the Middle East?"

"All I know is that you've gotten two people killed and you damn near got me to print a story that was utter bullshit," Burke snapped. "And what if I had? And what if the Israelis believed it and decided they had to take out Damascus? Another great chapter in the history of covert operations! Tell me you would've had a press conference to take the responsibility."

He stopped, aware that his voice was rising to a pitch that he did not want Worthington to hear, a pitch where anger became tinged with hysteria.

"You're fantasizing," Worthington said.

"Don't bullshit me any more, Ethan," Burke said. "Nekronov told me all about it."

Worthington's face twitched sharply. "He doesn't know!" he hissed.

"No, but now I do," Burke said, quietly. "You just confirmed it."

Worthington's face constricted; but before he could say anything, Lemeshev took another step forward, and the gun came up again.

"Mr. Burke," he said, "let me remind you of a few facts. First, you are under investigation for the murder of Yekaterina Yegorova. Second, you have violated the conditions under which you were allowed to remain at liberty during the investigation. Third, you have apparently participated in the kidnapping of a Russian citizen, Sergei Nekronov. This is another serious crime."

"Yeah; and let me remind you of a few facts," Burke said. "First of all, I didn't kill Katya. She did." He nodded in the direction of Ronit's body.

"And you know it. I don't know how to garrote anybody, I wasn't there when the killing occurred, and I wouldn't leave my card under someone's head if I did it. Second, I didn't kidnap Nekronov. He left the dacha of his own volition. If your guard decided to go get his cock sucked, that's not my concern. And third, you're not going to try me for either one because you know what a stink I'd raise at the trial. This isn't the old days, Viktor. You can't have some troika sentence a guy to the gulag and let him quietly disappear."

Lemeshev smiled thinly. "No, but I can put a bullet between your eyes and leave the gun in her hand."

"You won't do that, either," Burke said. "Because

I've left a computer disk with most of the story on it with a colleague. Kill me and you'll be reading a lot about yourself in the American newspapers. And the Russian newspapers. They'd all be interested in how the KGB has become a subsidiary of the CIA."

"You're lying," Worthington said, but his face said he wasn't certain.

"Don't bet on it," Burke said.

Worthington was silent for a minute, obviously pondering his next move. Then he stepped past the body of Ronit Byron and put his hands on Burke's desk, leaning so that his eyes were level with Burke's.

"Look, Colin," he began, in a tone that radiated sincerity and friendship. "There's no need to get confrontational here. We're not enemies. Why should we get into a pissing contest?"

Burke said nothing.

"Suppose we just clean up here—remove this body and promise that the investigation into that other girl's, er..."

"Katya," Burke prompted.

"Yes, Katya's death, clears you from suspicion. Then you tell us where Nekronov is and we all go about our business and forget about it. I can promise you that we can make you privy to a lot of information. You'll have sources and access in this town that no one will be able to match. You'll be on the cover of that magazine so much you'll think you're Madonna."

Worthington paused again and straightened up so that he could peer down at Burke. Somewhere in his training manual he must have read that this was a position of authority.

"On the other hand," he continued, "if you try to go

with this story you think you have, I can assure you you'll be buying nothing but trouble for yourself. First of all, your magazine won't print it. You don't have enough corroboration, and your reputation hasn't exactly been rising in the last couple of days. This stunt you pulled tonight won't enhance your credibility. And then you'll have all these other problems—this body, Katya, maybe some charges that'll come out of the investigation of what you did to Nekronov."

Burke stared back at him.

"And even if you could print it, would you want to?" Worthington went on. "If the Israelis believed you, the talks would break up. There could be a war in the Middle East. Do you want that on your conscience?"

"Clean up this mess you made," Burke said. "And then call me at my apartment, and I'll let you know what I think."

🏵 🏵 🏵

In the darkened living room of Burke's apartment, the digital clock on the VCR said eighteen minutes after midnight when the phone rang.

Sitting in the darkness, Burke put down the glass of vodka he was nursing and let the phone ring twice more before he picked it up. It was Ethan Worthington.

"Okay, the body is gone and the traces are cleaned up," Worthington said. "Where's Nekronov?"

"He's not under guard, and he's free to leave where he is. In a little while, that'll sink in. He'll run around town, probably to his parents. I expect you'll find him," Burke said.

"I'll take your word as a gentleman on that,"

Worthington said smoothly, "and for your agreement to the rest of our bargain."

"There's no bargain, Ethan," Burke said.

Worthington's voice rose a few notes and cracked ever so slightly. "Excuse me?"

"There's no bargain, Ethan," Burke repeated. "You jerked me around. I'm not happy about it."

Worthington's tone grew threatening and blustery again. "You're making a big mistake. You—"

Burke cut him off. "You're probably right, Ethan," he said, and hung up the phone.

CHAPTER TWENTY-ONE

RABBI YAKOV MIRSHINSKY KNOCKED almost timidly at the door to Burke's office. He peered at Burke through his gold-rimmed glasses, looking for permission to move further.

"Are you busy?" he asked.

Burke turned away from the window through which he had been staring blankly for the past fifteen minutes. When he saw Mirshinsky, his eyes went involuntarily to the faint stains that still remained on the carpet where Ronit Evron had fallen. He forced himself to look at the rabbi instead and to try to act innocent.

"No," Burke said. "Just waiting for a phone call. Come on in."

The rabbi, dressed all in black save for the white tassels of his prayer shawl dangling from beneath his coat, took off his homburg and sat down in the same chair she had sat in.

"And how is it going with your story about our synagogue?"

"It's due to run next week," Burke said. "I'll try to make sure you get copies. How's your head, by the way?"

"It's better, thank you. My mother always said I was thickheaded. Now I know she was right," the rabbi said. But all of the joviality that Burke remembered from the first interview at the synagogue had gone out of the man, and he had the sense that the wisecrack came from habit only.

"I was going to come by to thank you for what you did, but I was laid up for a while, and then I became very busy," the rabbi said.

"Don't mention it," Burke replied. He sensed that the rabbi was about to get to the real reason for his visit.

"There's been a terrible tragedy," Mirshinsky said. "Ronit Evron is dead."

Burke could not bring himself to feign shock. "I'm sorry," he said.

He could see the rabbi's eyes peering intently at him from behind the thick, distorting lenses of his glasses. They made the beard on his pink cheeks seem concave.

"The *militsia* called and said they found her yesterday in Gorky Park. She'd been shot through the head. They think it was a robbery."

Burke rubbed his hand over his eyes, trying to think of something to say. Before he could, the rabbi spoke up.

"We, of course, know that it wasn't."

Burke couldn't tell from the solemn expression on the rabbi's face whether "we" was meant to include him.

"What do you mean?"

Mirshinsky avoided a direct answer.

"She admired you very much, you know," he said.

"I didn't know that," Burke replied, relieved that he could say something honest.

"She thought that you were an excellent journalist. She admired excellence."

Burke waited to see where the rabbi was going. "And I understand that you and she were, um, seeing each other."

"Yeah," Burke said. "In a way, we were."

"I also know that she wanted your help with some things. I told her you would publish whatever you knew, but she was an impatient woman."

"Yes. She was."

"So," the rabbi said, smiling wanly. "I'll be reading *America Weekly* with particular care in the days ahead."

Burke nodded.

"There is one thing, though, one favor that I would like to ask of you," Mirshinsky went on, holding one pale finger up in front of him.

"If I can," Burke said.

"When Israel loses someone, a soldier, or whatever, it is always a great comfort..." the rabbi began. His lips trembled for a moment, and Burke thought the man might lose his composure. With a visible effort, Mirshinsky composed himself.

"It is always a great comfort," the rabbi continued, calmer, "for relatives and friends to know that this person died in the service of our country, that he or she died so that our people could someday live in peace."

"I understand."

The rabbi nodded. "I'm sure you do. So you can tell me if you know something that I can pass on to her loved ones and her friends..."

"You can tell them she died doing her job," Burke said. "In a few days, you should be reading the details."

The rabbi's eyes glistened behind his glasses and he nodded so deeply that he almost bowed.

When the phone finally rang, Burke took a deep breath and looked at it for a moment, as if something in its plastic case and buttons would tell him what this conversation would be like. The phone gave away nothing, and after the third ring he picked it up.

"Colin?" Gen Owen asked. Her voice had never sounded quite as sweet and solicitous, and Burke took it as a bad sign. "Chris Canfield wants to talk to you."

He waited through the ensuing beeps and silences until Canfield came on the line.

"Colin, how are you feeling?"

Even Canfield was managing to sound sympathetic. Burke knew immediately where the conversation was headed.

"I'm fine, Chris," he said.

"Uh, good. I think we need to have you back here in New York. When's the next plane?"

"I don't know offhand. But let's talk about the story. What'd you think of it?"

"That's one of the things we want to talk to you about here."

Burke got to his feet and began pacing around the room with the phone in his hand.

"No, Chris, I'd rather do it now."

Canfield's voice hardened to its usual edge.

"Okay, as you wish," he said.

"What do you think of the story?" Burke repeated. As he moved, the phone wire knocked a pile of papers off the desk, and they fluttered to the floor. He ignored them.

"Well," Canfield said. There was a long pause. "It's a helluva story. But the bottom line is we can't run it."

Burke took another deep breath. "Why not?"

"Well, in the first place we can't corroborate it."

Burke's temper flashed, and he argued even though he knew it would do no good. "What do you mean., 'corroborate it'? I was there, for God's sake. They shot that Israeli right in my office! I can still see the blood-stains on the goddam carpet! I talked to Nekronov! I saw the whole thing! I'm your corroboration!"

Canfield's tone became exaggeratedly gentle. "Calm down, Colin. Please calm down."

"I'm calm, Chris. I'm calm, okay?"

"Okay. We queried the Washington bureau and they checked with State, the NSC, and the intelligence agencies. They all heard the same thing. First of all, the Israeli woman was just a teacher, and she was shot in Gorky Park. The U.S. government says it's never heard of Rafit Kassim or Sergei Nekronov. And they absolutely deny any partnership with the KGB or the Ministry of Security or whatever the Russians are calling themselves these days."

"They're lying," Burke protested.

"They may be," Canfield said. "But we just can't take your word against theirs."

"Why not?"

"Well, Colin, you've been acting a little, um, erratically in the last few weeks?" Canfield ended his sentence with a questioning inflection, inviting Burke to agree with him.

Burke would not.

"Look, Chris, I explained why I sent the false story."

"And I'm telling you it was the most unprofessional thing I've ever seen done at this magazine. And not only that. You've been jailed as a murder suspect. You've missed a deadline for a cover package. And you've been seen swigging straight vodka and getting drunk."

Burke sat down.

"Obviously, the people you've been talking to in Washington have their reasons for saying that," he said. "But I can explain all those things."

"Well," Canfield said, still in his soothing mode, "when you get to New York, we'll be glad to listen to your explanation."

Burke stood up again. "I don't want to come to New York," he said firmly. "I want to publish this story."

"That's not an option," Canfield said.

"Then I quit," Burke said.

With a slightly detached curiosity, he waited to see whether Canfield would try to talk him out of it. He did not want to continue working at the magazine, but he wanted the compliment of being asked to stay.

Canfield said good-bye and hung up.

Lena was sitting on a wooden bench in the waiting hail of the Kiev station. She wore a brown trench coat, and she was surrounded by a mismatched assortment of satchels and suitcases. Two husky women lay stretched out on either side of her, sleeping with their mouths open.

Burke waved to her and almost tripped over a hunchbacked peasant in a grimy blue jacket who was pulling a little wagon behind him. The wagon held bundles wrapped in newspapers.

The old man turned to him,. "Young man," he said, in a tired voice, "watch where you're going."

"Thanks," Burke said. "Good advice."

As he approached, she stood up and stepped into his arms. In her hair he could smell a faint perfume, all but overwhelmed by the odors of old food, alcohol, and engine fumes that encrusted the air in the station. He kissed her, and she squeezed his shoulders.

"Why the bags?" he said when she pulled back from his lips.

"We're leaving Moscow for a while," she said. "Boris and Edik and the rest have already gone."

He felt his psyche go slightly numb. "Why?"

Her brown eyes fell sadly. "We got a warning from a friend in the *militsia*. The Ministry of Security has put out the word that they want us arrested."

"Because of what we did at the dacha."

She smiled bitterly. "That's the real reason. But they can't call that illegal. So they are going to arrest us for illegal gambling the next time they have a chance."

"And you won't be able to make the usual payoff."

She nodded and shrugged her shoulders. He thought he saw her eyes glisten.

He gave her the little canvas satchel into which he had put the cash he owed her.

"So where are you going?"

"Kiev. Boris has a brother there. And the Ukrainian *chekisti* don't cooperate much with the Russians anymore. We'll be okay."

"So if I get there, I'll find you at the station?"

"I guess so."

He picked up her bags and carried them through the station to the platform where the Kiev train was standing, fifteen cars long and murmuring with electricity. All along the platform, clusters of people were saying good-bye to departing passengers, bestowing on them hugs, tears, and hunks of sausage wrapped in newspaper.

Her car was No. 14, a second-class sleeper with white curtains trimmed in red and gold embroidery hanging in the windows. A hefty female conductor stood guard at the steps, and Lena handed over her ticket.

"Have your magazine do a long story about Ukraine," she said. "I'll help you."

He almost told her that he didn't have a magazine any longer, but he decided that she had enough to worry about. So he nodded and smiled.

She stepped into his arms and kissed him, clutching at his shoulders.

"Well," he said, "this is the time when an American is supposed to tell you something like, 'I am also thee now, rabbit.' But I couldn't pull it off."

Her face grew puzzled. "Rabbit?" she asked.

"Never mind," he replied, and patted her cheek. "Bad joke."

He kissed her and helped her up the steps into the train. Then he walked away. As he reached the end of the platform, the train started to move, and he turned to watch it. He stayed until the last car had disappeared into the gray horizon of smokestacks and apartment buildings in western Moscow.

Burke bought a copy of *Nyezavisimaya Gazeta* from a kid in the entrance to the Metro station and looked up the address of the editorial office. It was on a street called Patriarch Nicodemus, which wasn't on his map; but he asked a cab driver outside the station, who told him that it used to be called Proletariat Street. It was not far from the Kremlin and the old Central Committee headquarters.

He found the building and looked for an entrance in the butcher's shop that occupied the entire first floor, but there was none. He walked around to the back of the building, hopping over rutted puddles in the alley. It was starting to rain, and this time it was a cold rain that foretold the end of *baboye leto* and the inevitable advance of winter.

There was a small sign mounted on the wall near a back door that said the offices of *Nyezavisimaya Gazeta* could be found on the fourth floor. Burke walked up the four flights. It was an old apartment building with footprints worn into the stone steps and wrought-iron filigree underneath the curving banisters.

On the fourth floor, the newspaper staff occupied what had once been two communal apartments. There were ancient, rusty coat hooks in the hallway, and some of the internal walls had jagged white edges where someone had knocked partitions away to make larger rooms. He caught the smell of typing paper and cigarette smoke mixed with the older bathroom and kitchen smells left by the previous occupants.

On the wall in front of him someone had hung a painting, a satire on the old group photos of the Politburo that used to appear in *Pravda* on the days following big parades in Red Square. The picture showed a lineup atop the Lenin Mausoleum, just as the old photos had. But instead of dour bureaucrats in heavy coats and homburg hats, it showed a row of cute little pigs, some in Army uniforms and some in overcoats. Some of the pigs had their snouts to the front, and others had turned their curly little tails toward the viewer.

The writers and editors worked in groups at large tables that held two or three computers, a couple of telephones, and the occasional manual typewriter. All of them seemed to wear jeans and to smoke Marlboros and to be younger than Burke; and when they left their tables and moved about the room, they walked with purposeful, absorbed strides.

He located Pavel Plotnikov at a table in a corner underneath a grimy window. He had the only gray hair in the room. Burke walked over and tapped him on the shoulder. The cigarette almost fell out of Plotnikov's mouth when he recognized Burke.

"Look, I wanted to apologize," Burke said. "I misjudged you. I'm sorry."

Plotnikov smiled broadly. "Is okay," he said. "Is old Russian disease. You cannot help catching it if you stay in Moscow so long."

He introduced Burke to the people who shared his table: a man named Lev who had thick, curly hair and little wire-rimmed glasses and looked like Leon Trotsky, and a corpulent woman named Galya.

Burke took a printout of his story from his inside coat pocket. He extended the white sheets toward Plotnikov, then pulled them back. If he handed the story to *Nyezavisimaya Gazeta*, it would not have the immediate impact of a cover article in *America Weekly*. But Mirshinsky and the Israelis would read it. So would every other journalist in Moscow. Within a few days, they would be able to corroborate it. Ethan

Worthington's admonition to his conscience popped into his mind again. Did he really want to risk ruining the peace negotiations?

He had conducted a dozen internal debates on this question in the past twenty-four hours. They had all ended the same way. If the Israelis and the Arabs were ready to make peace, they would make peace. It was not his job to help them; his job was to report what he knew. Better that they made an agreement with their eyes open, knowing as much of reality as they could know.

He doubted that either the Arabs or the Israelis harbored any illusions about the benevolence of the United States and its intelligence agencies. If they did, it might be best that they disabuse themselves of those illusions before they signed a treaty that would rely on the United States as a guarantor. The United States, like all governments, acted as the interplay of national interests and domestic politics impelled it to act.

He handed the sheaf of paper to Plotnikov. Plotnikov read each page and then handed it to Galya, who translated into Russian for Lev. As he read, Plotnikov nodded emphatically and occasionally whistled. Galya and Lev whispered to one another in Russian that Burke could not catch.

"Great story," Plotnikov said when he finished with the final page, speaking Russian for the benefit of his colleagues. "We're working on same story. We have sources in *militsia* who say same thing—that Israelis killed Yegorova. But you have whole story. Congratulations."

Burke thanked him.

"Why show it to us?" Plotnikov said.

"I want you to publish it," Burke said. "I'm freelancing it. I thought you might like to help with the translation."

Plotnikov nodded enthusiastically. Then he sobered. "Why not *America Weekly*?"

"They're a little timid."

Plotnikov shook his head. "I know we'll want it. This is great story."

"Well," said Burke, "let's go talk to your editor. Where's his office?"

Plotnikov laughed. He pointed to Lev. "Here's our editor, and here's his office."

Burke smiled.

"So," he said. "You want the piece?"

The editor nodded. "Of course."

"And you don't want to call the Ministry of Security and see what they have to say about it?"

Lev shrugged. "We'll call them and give them a chance to deny it. If they do, we'll add a sentence saying they denied it. No big problem."

"Okay," Burke said, extending his hand. "It's a deal."

Lev took his hand and started to shake it, then stopped in mid-pump.

"Only one thing," he said. "We can pay you only in rubles. We don't have dollars."

"That's okay," Burke said. "I'm not really in this for the money."